THE ART OF RIVERS | BOOK ONE

The Mystic

DAWN RENO LANGLEY

This is a work of fiction. Names, characters, businesses, places, events, and incidents are either the products of the author's imagination or used in a fictitious manner. Any resemblance to actual persons, living or dead, or actual events is purely coincidental.

ISBN: 978-1-68513-601-7
PUBLISHED BY BLACK ROSE WRITING
www.blackrosewriting.com

Printed in the United States of America
Suggested Retail Price (SRP) $22.95

The Mystic is printed in Garamond Premier Pro

*As a planet-friendly publisher, Black Rose Writing does its best to eliminate unnecessary waste to reduce paper usage and energy costs, while never compromising the reading experience. As a result, the final word count vs. page count may not meet common expectations.

Cover image by David Henry Terry

For my sister
Candace Lee Cioffi

'Forthwith this frame of mine was wrenched
With a woeful agony,
Which forced me to begin my tale;
And then it left me free.
Since then, at an uncertain hour,
That agony returns;
And till my ghastly tale is told,
This heart within me burns.'
from *The Rime of the Ancient Mariner*
— Samuel Coleridge

The Mystic

Hit and Run Truck Found

Everett, Massachusetts:
Everett Police found a 1955 blue Ford F-100 truck abandoned near the Weinberg Junkyard on Everett Avenue today. The blood on its right fender is seven-year-old Cindy Gordon's, the victim of a hit-and-run in the Cherry Street projects late afternoon on November 9.

The truck's owner, John "Jack" Robbins, 26, has not reported to work as a welder at the Charlestown Navy Yard since that morning. Officials are attempting to locate the driver and are making every effort to investigate the matter.

Notify Everett Police immediately if you have information about Robbins' whereabouts or were an eyewitness to the accident.

Everett, Massachusetts

Monday, November 11, 1957

Jack's truck hit a little girl. Tossed her—a perfect arc through the air—one white sneaker flying, landing mere feet from where her body dropped, limp like a rag doll, head against the curb, legs splayed like broken wings into the street, a little girl playing in the street where she shouldn't have been.

Jack's truck put seven-year-old Cindy Gordon in a coma. Barely breathing, she was *mistakenly pronounced dead on arrival at the Whidden Hospital* by the paramedics as the ambulance, red light twirling, roared up to the hospital entrance.

The truck belongs to my husband.

The Red Cadillac

Saturday, November 9, 1957

Moments after the red Cadillac disappears down Broadway hill into the darkness, I remain frozen at the window, unable to compose myself. Though I can't deny what I have seen, I still refuse to believe that Jack climbed into that blonde woman's car only hours after the accident. Why would he leave me? Alone. How am I supposed to manage this without him?

Other cars drive by on the street below. Buicks, Pontiacs, Chevys. The red Cadillac is gone, however. I press my cheek against the cold, wet glass and relive the fight as if it might give me some of the answers I've been searching for during the entire four years of our marriage.

"If you hadn't come after me, Bethie, this wouldn'a happened!" Jack had screamed, his face splotchy-red with anger, his hands supporting himself against the door jambs, successfully blocking any escape from the tiny kitchen where he had me trapped. "You shouldn'a come after me. Shit."

He paced to the living room, stomping so hard that the lamps on the coffee tables rattled. Then, he returned to the kitchen, where I stood against the sink, washing the same dish over and over. He'd already hit me, already bruised my right eye, and I knew I'd have black-and-blues all over my legs from where he'd kicked me, but that's nothing new. I've made him angry before, and I know this is what I get for questioning him. I should know better.

He came back into the kitchen. Slammed his hand against the door. Adrenaline pumped through my veins, tingling like a thousand separate needles. I held my breath for what seemed like years. "Shit, shit, shit," he said. "I can't even take the damn truck with me! Whatever the hell made you leave it in Chelsea? You shouldn'a done that. That's stealing, y'know? I could get you for that. I could get you." He was in front of me, his beer breath hot and nasty. I didn't lift my eyes; I just kept my hands in the sink, my fingers pushing the sponge in circles around the plate, over and over and over.

Finally, he gave up on me, knowing I wouldn't respond, and stomped out of the kitchen into the living room. I heard him dialing the phone and cautiously looked out the kitchen door to see him stretching the black telephone cord as far as it would go, pulling it around the corner into the bedroom, his back to me, trying to hide, whispering into the receiver, pushing his hand through that thick auburn pompadour of hair he'd let grow after he came home from Korea. I'd touched that hair only an hour before when I'd reached up to hug him and begged him to forgive me, even though I knew he would hit me again.

Now I rest my hip gingerly against the window sash and remember the awful words I said as he walked out the apartment door, the words I regretted the instant they came out of my mouth: "You're a drunk, Jack Robbins. A goddamn lush! And now you won't even stick around to deal with this. You're going to leave me here? Alone? How can you do that after you're the one who convinced me to leave after we hit that little girl? You're a coward, and I hate you!"

That was when he'd walked down the stairs and into the car, which took him away.

But I had lied. I don't hate my husband. My heart beats through his. His blood burns through my veins no matter what he does or says to me. I breathe him. If he could see me right now, he would know that.

He had turned his body and mind away when I said I hated him, only listened to my words, didn't see the truth in my eyes. Then he'd left with another woman. *A friend,* he said after he hung up the phone, *someone who would understand, someone who could give him a place to stay until things died down.* I knew better. He had planned this all along. He was waiting for the right time to be with someone else, someone better than me. I have never been good enough for Jack Robbins. I know that. And so does he.

My fingertips tap the windowsill, a tick-tick-tick sound that crawls up the back of my neck. In my mind, the accident replays. The little girl's body flies past the window like a blue blur, blocking out my view of the traffic on

Broadway. I shake my head to dislodge the image and shiver. I can hear that screech of brakes again.

My sketch pad shimmies on my lap, and the charcoal pencil falls to the floor. I reach for it, push the memory from my mind, and sit back on the windowsill. Thankfully, the vision fades to black, like an image in a movie. I sketch the drips of rain that blur the taillights from passing cars on the street below, creating red zigzags like drunken fireflies. It's hard to tell one car from the next. I press my forehead hard against the window and wipe the moisture off the glass with the sleeve of my beige cardigan. The active north end of Broadway comes alive on the sketch pad: shadows of houses set on the sides of Broadway's hill, the distant Glendale Methodist church steeple, and lights from Piarello's Sandwich Shop on the corner of Waverley Street. Broadway at night.

I can't look in the other direction, can't follow the street Jack used to disappear, can't see where he went.

"Bye Bye Love" screamed from the Cadillac's open window when he left, so loud that I could hear it from my second-floor apartment even though the windows were closed. Then the car's lights went south down Broadway, past Harlen's Pharmacy and Kennedy's Meat Market, over the rise in the hill, down toward Everett Square. I couldn't believe the car kept going, that he had finally left, yet somewhere deep down inside, I'd been expecting this since the day Jack asked me to marry him. Why would he stay with someone who looked like me when blonde women with red Cadillacs were ready for the taking? It was just a matter of time. All he needed was a good excuse.

Now, he had one: the perfect reason to leave. Running from the police.

How have things changed so much in such a fleeting period? Jack held my hand when we walked down the street and used to touch me every time he passed by. One rainy spring night before he left for Korea only a few years ago, we stood on the sand at Revere Beach and stared at the Nahant peninsula across the water, then he kissed me and said that I would always be his favorite girl. I looked up at him then, and his eyes were soft, staring straight into mine, and full of love. That full mop of hair he was so proud of swept back from his forehead and shone in the moonlight.

His kiss continued for an hour that night, beginning on that beach and growing in intensity after we returned to the car. It was the first time I'd felt the urge to touch him sexually, but that night, I watched the stars brighten through the car window as we shared each other's bodies. We were in love that night. I will always be sure of that.

What happened, Jack? When did that stop? When did that blond woman take over, the woman in the driver's seat of the red Cadillac with curly blond hair and an open, laughing mouth? Goddamn you, Jack!

You must come home, Jack. I can't face this by myself. You can't leave me here alone. It's not fair.

Though my feet have grown numb, and my cheeks feel chapped and frigid, I still can't stop staring out the window at the cold, wet street below me—even when the anniversary clock on my dining room buffet intones midnight. Flicking the memories away, I shade in a couple of windows. The sketch is spooky. Depressing. I toss it aside.

Jack, come home. I won't say anything. I promise. Come home. Go to work tomorrow morning like nothing happened. They won't find out. I promise. I'll do exactly as you say. I'll tell them it was me. I'll go to jail. I won't say anything about you, about the way your foot slammed down on mine, won't tell them about you.

But he doesn't.

At one o'clock, I pull away from the window and circle the apartment like a caged animal, one end of the apartment to the other. Trying not to think about what it will be like to be in jail, I skirt the maple coffee table filled with <u>Family Circle</u> and <u>Screen Star</u> magazines, then straighten the wedding picture hanging on the wall. To see the stiff, scared expressions on our faces always reminds me of how young we were. Jack in his Navy uniform; me, looking left, away from him, hiding the birthmark on my cheek. The photographer should have switched us. I told him so.

We laughed that day, Jack. That poor photographer barely got two shots of us before he squatted to get a shot and ripped his pants from waistband to inseam. Remember that?

I pause at the kitchen table, clearing off the remains of supper dishes I hadn't yet washed. The macaroni and cheese casserole has hardened into place like a yellow sandcastle, not a forkful missing. Jack's Pabst bottle is in the center of the table. I pick it up and roll it in my palm.

Why, Jack? Why do you have to treat me like I'm the most insignificant thing in your life?

Peeling part of the label off, my nails dig into the rest of it, raking it, ruining it for him. He always prides himself on being able to pull the label off in one piece, always presses the label down on the table afterward, and irons it with his hand. But not this label. This label is ruined.

My hand clenches around the bottle's neck. My throat tightens. *Jack, you goddamn bastard. If you didn't drink...*

If you didn't hit me.

If you didn't leave.

Something in me bursts like a too-tight elastic, and my arm cocks. The bottle flies into the wall, shatters into a million brown pieces, brown streaks on the cabinets, and chunks of broken glass across the white tile floor, and I sink into the chair, staring at the mess but not caring anymore.

None of Your Beeswax

"What was that?" Angela Indelicato rises with a groan from the kitchen chair and shuffles to the wall that separates her apartment from the neighbors, the Robbins. She places her left ear up against the wall, cupping her hand around it. She squints her eyes as if that will help her hear more clearly and bunches her gray cardigan around her with her free hand. At seventy-two, her life is within these walls, and the Robbins' life next door provides plenty of entertainment.

"They're fighting again." Loretta, Angela's sister, still sits at the kitchen table and doesn't raise her head. Eyes downcast, she focuses on the handful of cards she holds in front of her. A Lucky Strike anchored in the corner of her mouth; its lazy smoke lifted in an s-curve above her head. She squints against the smoke. "Listen, you don't come back to the table, I'm going to gin on you. It's late. I want to go to bed."

"I think he threw something against the wall. Sounded like glass crashing."

"So? Is it any of your bee's wax?

"I should call the cops." Angela adjusts the black net over her wispy white hair, knot centered in the middle of her forehead, and lifts her ear away from the wall, nailing her sister with an eyebrow lift and a head nod. She wears a blue-and-white checked housedress with short sleeves, her old gray cardigan over it, and a bright orange and brown Thanksgiving apron over that. On her feet, a pair of pink ostrich feather slippers someone brought home from Las Vegas last year. That's Angela's dream: to go to Vegas, play blackjack with the dealers in their black and white tuxes, and bring home pots of money. Loretta's the better card player, yet Angela always wishes she could go somewhere—anywhere—without her younger sister.

The doctor, though, he says to stick close to home. This diabetes she has, this disease, who knows what's going to happen next with it? Just last week, she heard that *Mrs. Megehan, down the hall—3C—found out she had eye problems all due to the diabetes. That's what it'll do to you, the doctor says.*

So, she needs to stay close to home, and Angela does. Loretta takes care of her, plays cards with her, takes her to the doctor's, does the grocery shopping, and keeps her in line.

"Angela, sit down at this table this minute. I swear." Loretta shakes her head and takes another puff off her Lucky Strike.

Angela mutters as she reaches above the kitchen sink for a glass and shuffles back to the wall, puts the glass up against it, and listens. "He's really going at it this time. Stuff breaking all over the place. Amazing what a little booze will do. Handsome man like that. And that little Beth. She's just like a mouse. Never even says hello when I see her. It's a shame, a crying shame."

"Okay, I'm gonna play your hand for you."

"No, no. I'm coming. Just give me a sec."

"Sec, schmeck. It's after one and time we ended this game. You either sit down, or I'm playing your hand."

Angela adjusts the glass on the wall and shifts her weight to the other foot. All she can hear is that little Beth Robbins is crying.

"Poor dumb kid. He must scare her something terrible." Angela reluctantly moves back to the table and looks at her hand. It hasn't changed: two Jacks, an eight of clubs, and a five of hearts. A bunch of nothing. "Go ahead, 'Retta."

"Gin," her sister says, spreading the cards on the table. Then she yawns and gets up, pushing the kitchen chair back with a screech. "I'm going to bed. Turn the lights out this time, will ya?"

The Police Officer's Duty

Sunday, November 10, 1957

When I wake up on the couch, it's mid-afternoon. I listen for a moment, holding my breath, thinking that Jack might be in the other room, but only my exhale breaks the silence.

He's not here.

A wedge of sunlight throws a weak yellow streak across the polished wood floor, and I stare at it for a little while. My stomach growls loudly. I'll make dinner. No matter what happens, I have to eat. Maybe some meatloaf and mashed potatoes would be good, made the way my mother used to: crush Ritz crackers in the hamburger, mix it with a couple of eggs, some mustard, ketchup, salt, and pepper. Get my hands into it, mash it all together like Mama let me do when I was little, standing on the chair beside her at the kitchen sink. Stir. Mash. Blend. Get those eggs into the meat so the yellow yolk acts as glue.

Mama: her elegant fingers. How vain she was about them, believing them to be the only beautiful part of herself. She used to take off her wedding band to wash the dishes, carefully placing it in a plastic dish beside the sink so she wouldn't lose it down the pipes, talking to me all the while, teaching me songs like "The White Cliffs of Dover." Mama had a lovely soprano voice that skipped over the words, "There'll be love and laughter and peace ever after, tomorrow when the world is free." Mama's breathless singing voice and her delicate hands: a memory strong enough to make me sigh, loud and long, and force myself to a sitting position, stretching a bit to work the kinks out of my neck.

I should not continue this habit of falling asleep on the couch. It's not very comfortable.

For a moment, I don't know what day it is. Then it all comes back with the force of a blood-red volcano, burning its way from my toes up through my belly and into the bowels of my brain.

Jack's truck hit a child.

The memory erases the heaviness. Everything is crystal clear now. I am completely awake. Instantly. I check the clock. Two-thirty-five. Middle of the afternoon. Have I slept that long? Is Jack home? Has he been here? Oh, dear God, let him be sleeping in the bedroom, mouth half open, snoring like someone who hasn't slept in years. PLEASE.

But I know he's not. Silence.

Spinning around, I face the bedroom, but the chenille spread hasn't been rolled down, and the apartment still smells of stale beer. Pieces of brown glass are still on the floor—proof that my nightmare happened.

And it isn't over.

The smell makes me gag, so I turn into the kitchen, grabbing a mop, hot water, and the barrel. It takes almost half an hour, but the room is immaculate when I'm finished. The floor shines, and the acrid smell of Pine Sol fills the apartment. And some of the anger and confusion I felt upon waking up has disappeared. My house is immaculate because I'm always stressed.

Exhausted, I lean against the wall.

It's time to go to the police station. I must tell them what happened. No matter how angry I am at Jack, I'm angrier at myself for allowing all of this to happen. I will take my punishment. *I deserve it.*

A knock at the door. I'm startled into blurting, "Hello?"

"Hello? Can we speak to Mr. Robbins? Mr. John Robbins?" A male voice. Clipped and professional.

I'm at the door in a split second. Hand on the doorknob, I realize I'm wearing only my slip. "Who is it?"

"Oh, I do apologize. It's the Everett Police, Ma'am. Officers Jackson and Cassilli. We'd like to speak with Mr. Robbins for a moment, if we might. Could you please open the door, Ma'am?"

The police. Do they know? Have they talked to Jack? Do they know where he is? Will they let me talk to him before they take him away? God, I'm not ready for this. Think, Beth, think.

My forehead's against the door, and I swallow hard. "I'm...I'm not dressed. Can you...can you wait?"

"Sure, Ma'am." Some rustling. Low male voices. More than one officer out there.

The phone rings. I jump. The only people who call are Jack or salespeople. Turning my back on the door, I whisper "hello" into the receiver.

"Beth, it's me." Jack's voice, familiar and deep and sober, makes my stomach flip, just like it always has.

I reach for the back of the kitchen chair and lean on it, willing my knees to support me. "God, where are you? The cops are outside the door. Jack, I need you here to help me deal with this." I'm angry–furious–yet I miss him, and he terrifies me. "Where the heck are you?"

"At a friend's. I just wanted to check in to see... Are you okay?"

He sounds like he cares. Am I imagining that?

"The police are here." I cup my hand over the receiver because my teeth are chattering and my whole body trembles. *What friend's, Jack? The blonde?* "They're right outside the door, Jack. What am I going to do?"

"Jesus." He exhales slowly, and I can see him in my mind's eye, rubbing his temples and arching his dark eyebrows. It's the look he has when he knows he's done wrong and can't see a way out. "Just tell them you don't know where I am, okay? Don't tell them anything else. Whatever you do, don't tell them I made you leave! Hear me? I'll fucking kill you if you tell them." He breathes hard for a second, as if listening to the cops in the background. "I'll call you later," he says, and I'm left listening to the dial tone, holding an empty line.

You'll call me later, Jack? What am I supposed to do <u>right now</u>? Damn you!

There's another knock at the door. I reach for my housedress and cardigan and think about Jack and what he's said and who he's with and why he can't come back and if he does, he'll kill me, and *I can't go through that again. I can't.* The last time he hit me really hard, and I bled for weeks from my vagina. Unconsciously, I put my hand on my stomach and rub it in a circle, as if it'll make me feel better. *But nothing will fix this.*

"Just a moment. I have to get something on," I yell through the doorjamb, then

I retreat into the bedroom, certain the officers can hear my heart pounding, and pull on the dress. Thank God I cleaned the kitchen. At least there's no telltale beer smell.

Another knock at the door. Stronger this time. "Ma'am, are you all right?"

"Yes. Just...just a moment." Fumbling with the zipper, I turn around with "Will you zip this, Jack?" automatically on my lips. I clamp my mouth hard and twist my arms like a contortionist to bring the zipper all the way up my back. Sliding my feet into pumps, I stumble back into the living room, smoothing my hair, and pulling it forward to cover the birthmark on my cheek. *What am I going to say to these cops?*

I reach for the doorknob once again. *Tell them about the accident. Tell the truth. Explain I don't have a license. Didn't know how to stop.* And take a deep breath. *I'm so horribly sorry for the child. It breaks my heart. I know I should be punished. You have every right to — and is the little girl all right?* I open the door, remembering the phone call and Jack's admonition not to say anything. He's right. *Isn't he?*

Two men in dark blue Everett Police uniforms, hats in their hands, stand in the shadowed hallway. "May we come in, Ma'am?" the taller one asks.

A Negro? He must be the one they wrote about in the newspaper. Only Black policeman on the force.

"We have a warrant for your husband's arrest."

A warrant? My stomach flips.

"My husband's not here." *But that doesn't matter because you don't want him; you want me.* My hands flutter at the collar of the dress, flip it out where it has folded in against my neck, smooth it. Smooth it again. *Keep your head down. Don't let them see the mark, the bruise on your cheek, the ugly birthmark on your chin.*

"Do you know where he is?" The Negro cop is the one speaking. He smells like garlic, and a small spot of tomato sauce below his color tells me they might have just had lunch at the Italian place down the street. *Capone's? Capocollo's? Caprice's?*

"I haven't seen him since last night. No, I'm sorry…the night before. What's today? It was the 8th when he left." I pause. How to say the rest? *Tell the truth, Beth. Take a deep breath. One sentence at a time.*

The shorter cop, with wavy chocolate-brown hair and sharply squinted eyes scanning the room, back and forth, back, and forth, clears his throat. "We really need to see him, Ma'am. Are you sure you don't know where he is?"

I shake my head. *No, he hasn't been here. He's with* — How did he say it on the phone? — *a friend. That woman.*

Still holding the door half open, I hear a creak from down the hall—the Indelicato sisters. Stepping back, I open the door wider to invite the cops in, careful to keep my head down. I turn to the right. "Please come in. My neighbors tend to be a little nosy."

The cops step into the living room, filling it to where I find it difficult to breathe. *We've never had company before.* The apartment suddenly seems small. Stuffy.

"There's been a truck found in Chelsea, Ma'am. It's registered to Mr. John Robbins at this address. That your husband, Ma'am?" The shorter cop again. He looks Italian: a bit chunky through the middle, swarthy skin, thick fingers. The name on his chest: Cassilli.

Nodding again, I wipe my hands against my skirt, grope for the back of the couch, and lean against it, my legs barely keeping me upright. *Let me talk. Let me tell you. I want to tell you about the accident. Want to tell you the truth. Yes, it's Jack's truck, but it wasn't really his fault. It was the booze. He didn't mean it. I was there. I know.*

A shiver zips up my thigh, followed instantly by a physical run snaking its way up my right stocking leg.

"Did you know there's been an accident?" Cassilli speaks again. He doesn't look directly at me, but I'm used to that. No one ever looks directly at me at first. My Africa-shaped purple blood mark on my face turns most people away. Instead, he studies the parlor, seemingly fascinated by the telephone table: the No. 6 pencils standing in a glass cup, the ancient black rotary telephone (maybe the first phone in the neighborhood that has lasted this long), the address book that I love because I can slide the pointer down to a letter and press the button to make it pop open directly to the names I want.

He twirls his hat round and round in his hands. The silver shield on the hat's crown picks up the light from the kitchen. Round and round, the hat goes. Wedding band on his stubby finger. Dirty fingernails. Round and round goes the hat.

"Did you hear me, Ma'am? There's been an accident. Your husband's truck was found in Chelsea. We need to know where he is." The cop's voice is sharper. No patience.

"I don't know where he is." My eyes are still on the hat. "That's the truth."

"Does he have any family? Friends?"

"Yes."

"Who are they? Where do they live? Do you think he might have gone there?"

A pair of dark legs block the twirling hat. I glance up. The other cop—Jackson? — is walking past me as if he knows this place and is heading into the kitchen to make us all a cup of tea. *He is a Negro, isn't he? His skin is creamy, like a cup of coffee with just a dollop of milk in it. Article about him in last week's Everett Chronicle.*

I let him explore, unable to move. *Why can't I breathe? Why can't I speak? Tell them, Beth! But they keep asking stupid questions. I wish they'd shut up. Let me talk!*

I open my mouth, lift my head to speak to him, but he has his back to me and is slowly stepping away from me, further into my tiny kitchen.

"Have you been out, Ma'am?" Cassilli is staring at me, right at my face, peering into my eyes as if he knows when I'm lying by how many times my lashes flicker.

"Excuse me? Out?"

Officer Jackson is in the kitchen now. I can't see him, yet I know he's picking up my coat. The scrape of a chair against linoleum, a chair heavy with the weight of a wet coat.

"Yes, I was…I was out last night…." is all I could get out, even though my brain breathlessly told the rest of the story about how…

I was driving his truck—Jack's truck—without a license. Illegally. He was drunk. I wasn't. The bartender said, "You gotta drive him home, Mrs. Robbins. I ain't got anyone here to cover for me, and I gotta close. It'll be alright. No one else on the road this time of day."

Neither of us saw the little girl until she flew against the windshield. I didn't know what to do afterward at that moment. I struggled to swallow. He forced me to move the truck, pressed his foot against mine on the gas pedal, told me to ditch the truck there in Chelsea, and ran away as soon as we parked. It died, that truck. I couldn't get it started again.

I was out going to come to the police station that day, honestly, but I didn't know how to explain we'd left that little girl on the street, didn't know what to say if someone asked about Jack. Yes, I was driving, but I wanted to stop. He was the one who made me leave, and I know if I tell someone that…if I tell the truth…this time, he won't stop hitting me. This time, he'll kill me. That would be worse than going to jail.

Slowly, I raise my eyes and look past the hat, past each shiny silver button on the cop's shirt, past the silver nameplate that reads Officer Frank Cassilli, to the perfectly knotted Navy blue tie, to the deep cleft on his chin, the small scar off the right corner of his thin mouth, and finally, his eyes: brown and hard and questioning. He's already made his assumption about me.

"There's a little girl in the hospital, Ma'am. She's not doing too well, and her family's real upset. Mrs. Robbins, we have reason to question your husband about the accident, and this warrant gives us the right to take him in. After we found the truck in Chelsea and figured out it was the one that hit that little girl, we impounded it. We'll keep it 'til we have no further need of it. In the meantime, you must cooperate with us, Ma'am."

"If you could just tell us where he is, Mrs. Robbins, we'll be out of your hair." The Negro cop comes in from the kitchen, apparently not thinking the wet coat is important enough to mention.

I watch "Dragnet" on television, and the cops act differently than these two. Joe Friday would keep questioning me, asking about the coat, and pushing about where Jack is, but these two cops don't seem like they're going to push me. Their voices are lazy, like they have already assumed I'm covering for my husband.

What's wrong with you two? Can't you recognize I'm lying? Take me away, then find Jack. Tell him his wife's in jail, that he must come to get her, that he needs to leave the blond bimbo and come rescue me, take me home, take care of me, come get me. Now.

Cassilli shifts his feet, licks the tip of his pencil, and says, "Tell me, Mrs. Robbins, what you know about where your husband was the day of the accident."

"I don't know where he is." I pull my shoulders back and try to stand up, but my knees are literally knocking. *Can they tell? Can't they see me shaking?*

"That's not what I asked, Mrs. Robbins. Tell me what happened on Saturday. Did your husband work that day?"

"He worked the early morning until about lunchtime."

"What time did he get home?"

I stare at the nameplate on the cop's chest, trying to figure out what the G stands for in G. Jackson and swallow hard.

"Ma'am? What time did he get home?"

The Black officer stands behind his partner, yet his eyes still roam the room. He does not look directly at me, though I have a feeling he's not missing the slightest facial movement.

"It was getting dark. Around four. Four-thirty."

We were together. We got home together. I need something to hold on to. I fiddle with the lace doily on the armchair, pretend to straighten it, then pick at the loose edges, unraveling it.

What I don't tell the cops is that the bartender of the Mystic River Café had called around 3 A.M.. "Mrs. Robbins? Your husband is here, and he's pretty drunk," he'd said. "Can't even walk. It's quiet tonight, and I'd bring him home myself, but there's no one else here. You'd better come get him."

It wasn't the first time the bartender had called, but it was the first time he'd asked me to come to get Jack. We had a deal, me and Jack: if he got blotto, I made him promise someone else would bring him home. I didn't trust him to drive, and I didn't have a license. He'd had a nasty accident a few years ago, a close call, so I wanted to make sure he was safe, you know? Until now, the deal had worked well. Jack always came home intact, and I seldom had to go to the bar to get him (though sometimes I did walk by to see whether he was there and who he was with, but I never let him see me).

The bartender watched us get into the truck and saw Jack insisting on me driving, but he didn't see Jack puking as soon as we turned the corner. He didn't see me telling Jack I couldn't drive, didn't hear Jack screaming, "Fuck it, Beth! DRIVE," didn't see the truck jerking down the street as I tried to figure out which pedal to push.

I don't know how to drive, and Jack knew it, but he made me. He shoved his fist into my face and made me drive.

"Did he come home on his own, Mrs. Robbins? Mrs. Robbins?"

How do I answer that? "Yes, he came home." I don't look up at the cops. I can't lie well, and they'll be able to see it.

"Did he seem distracted or anything? Did he tell you anything about an accident?"

He didn't have to tell me. I was there. I shrug my shoulders, still fingering the lacy doily, seeing flashes of a little girl's body flying. That thud, the awful thud of the body falling to the ground.

"How long was he here before he left?" It is the Negro cop—G. Jackson is speaking this time; his voice is lower and calmer than the other.

That voice makes me look up. "He left around...I don't know...eight? Nine? It was dark."

"That blue truck we impounded is his only vehicle, right?"

"Yes, that's Jack's truck."

"Then how did he leave, Ma'am? What was he driving?"

"He wasn't driving." My eyes fill up, and it angers me I have to tell these cops, these strangers, about what happened between my husband and me.

"Who was?" It's the short cop again, his voice impatient.

Damn you, Jack! "A woman. A blonde woman. I don't know who she is." I push off the couch and cross my arms over my chest. Bile rises in my throat, and I want to get to the bathroom to throw up, but the cops are in my way. I can't go anywhere, so I feel my way along the couch until I can sit down. The back of my neck feels clammy despite the chill in the apartment.

"Did you see the vehicle she was driving?"

"Yes."

"What was it?" The cops are speaking in unison now like they rehearsed this.

"A Cadillac. A red Cadillac."

"Did you get the license plate?" It's Cassilli again. He's shifting back and forth on his feet like he's losing his patience. He'd never be Joe Friday.

"No, it was raining, and I couldn't see that far. And it was dark out." *All I saw was her face when she got out to let Jack drive. Her face. Looking up at him and laughing.*

"Is your husband in the habit of leaving with other women?" Jackson asks, and something in his tone is a note of pity.

"In the habit?"

"Does he do this often? Has he ever done it before?"

I can only shake my head, yes. What's the sense of lying about that? Yes, Jack has left before with other women. But he always comes back. He feels guilty, and he always comes back.

"Do you have a phone number for him? Somewhere he can be reached?" Officer Jackson leans down a bit and reaches for my arm but doesn't quite touch me. Everything about his mannerisms makes me feel that he's not someone who will hurt me. He's one of the good guys.

This time, I shake my head no. I wish I had a phone number, but Jack always called me. He never lets *me* call *him.*

"And you're certain your husband never told you about an accident, about hitting a little girl? Because you know, Ma'am, that little girl is fighting for her life right now, and it certainly would help the family if they knew the guy responsible had at least been arrested."

God, she's fighting for her life. My hands tremble. I fold my fingers tightly on my lap, palm against palm, and fight back the bile in my throat.

Jackson reaches forward and touches my arm softly, as if by touching me, he'll find out what I've been hiding. I fight the impulse to pull away. No one ever touches me. "We can see you don't know anything more, Mrs.

Robbins," he says, "but we'd like to come back and ask about anything we've overlooked. Is that okay? Can we come back with more questions tomorrow?"

I nod, and they move toward the door. The cops stand together for a moment, and when I look into their faces, I see—amazingly—sympathy. The Negro: large lion-colored eyes looking at me as if he understands, as though he knows Jack like he's saying: "Don't worry. It'll be all right." Cassilli, the Italian, nodding at me with compassion but disconnected as if he's thinking of something else. He reaches into his pocket, pulls out a stick of chewing gum, wads it into a ball, and pops it into his mouth like a lemon drop, then chews noisily.

I'm used to searching people's faces to see how they feel. I know people look at me and feel sympathy—even a bit of disdain—for the mousy-haired woman with a big wine-colored birthmark on her cheek. I know they're thinking, "She could have been pretty." Both these cops believe I don't know anything, that I'm Jack's victim just as surely as the child he hit. I can see it in their eyes. They feel sorry for me. And nothing makes me angrier.

Yet it's not them with whom I'm angry.

Damn you, Jack!

I close the door behind them, then lean against it, and the sobs come. Big, dry, heaving sobs. And that day replays all over again.

Even though I was not busy and had been relaxing with my feet under me and a half-knitted scarf across my lap, I had argued with the bartender for a moment, telling him I couldn't drive, but he didn't want to listen and repeated, "You've got to come get him," then hung up.

With the dogged resignation of someone who knew there was no choice, I got dressed. I made the long walk down Broadway, through Everett Square, past the factories, and into the Village—a two-mile chilly hike into the triangle of three-story ugly-brown-and-dirty-gray tenement buildings cut off from the rest of the city by railroad tracks and oil tanks. The area spilled over with poor Italian and Irish families who all seemed to have at least a dozen children.

One teenager—dark-skinned and dark-haired, wearing only a short-sleeved shirt though it was below freezing—yelled at me: "Hey, lady! What happened to your face? You in a fire or something?"

I ignored him, ducked my head, and hurried by. Further down the street, I dodged the overhead lights of a basketball court near the train station and finally reached the cafe, a small house-sized building tucked into the corner across the street from the Edison plant. Sure enough, Jack's blue Ford was out front, parked crookedly, as if he couldn't wait to get inside. I exhaled, both relieved and upset. Though I walked all the time and my calves had become as smooth and hard as round stones, I was exhausted and welcomed the thought of riding home in the truck rather than repeating the hike. Yet, I had half-hoped Jack wouldn't be there.

It took a moment for my eyes to adjust to the darkness inside the bar, but it wasn't difficult to spot Jack. He lay, face up, on the floor next to an overturned stool. Snoring loudly, a bottle of beer still clutched in his fist.

Smitty, the bartender, the only other person there, nodded at me and pointed at my husband. "There he is. He's all yours."

I nodded and smiled, then put my pocketbook on one of the stools lined up evenly alongside the bar. The only one out of place was the one from which Jack had fallen. *How could he have gotten this drunk? It was only three-thirty. He must have left work early. Damn him.* I kneeled, shook his shoulder, and said his name. Repeated it louder. He continued to snore.

"Want me to call you a cab, Mrs. Robbins?" The thick-armed bartender leaned over the bar, a white cloth in his hand dangling down toward me like a life rope. Smitty looked as though he'd been a boxer in his younger days, nose squashed to one side, a side tooth missing in his upper plate, but his voice was kind.

"I have to see if he has any money," I answered and searched Jack's pockets. All were empty. I didn't need to check my pockets or pocketbook to know mine were just as empty. How was I going to get a cab? As I sat back on my heels, Jack opened one incredibly sexy (and very drunk) eye. "Hey, baby. You come to see your hubby?"

"I've come to take you home. We're going to have to get a cab."

"Nah... no, we don't need no damn cab. I'll drive." He mumbled something else and turned over, then groaned and gagged.

I hurried out of the way, prepared for the vomit that shot out of his open mouth.

"Shit, Jack!" Smitty slapped his towel on the bar. "Why'd you have to go and do that? I just mopped the damn floor."

"I'll clean it," I said and took the towel off the bar, wiping Jack's mouth first, then the floor.

Jack continued to mumble and laugh at me (and Smitty) as we cleaned around him. Then suddenly, he sat up as if he'd abruptly gotten sober, looked at me, and said, "Keys. I need the keys."

"No, Jack..."

"Aw, honey. Simple as pie. Jackie'll show you." He gave me a drunken grin, reached into his pocket, fumbled around until he found the keys, and then jingled them in my face.

"Please, Jack." I shot a helpless glance at Smitty, who threw his hands up and walked away.

Now, there's a noise in the hallway, a door closing, and I'm back to the apartment. I realize I've been holding my breath. I push away from the door and move to the kitchen, thinking a hot cup of Lipton's tea might warm me up, take away some of the seasick feeling in my stomach, and stop the memories battering my brain. But even as the water boils and the kettle whistles, I can't shut off the flashback and realize I've lost a lot of time.

I know the truck was going faster than the 5-mile-per-hour speed limit.

Jack slumped over toward the passenger window, as drunk as I've ever seen him, but he kept his foot atop mine on the gas pedal. "Just do what I say, Bethie," he mumbled.

Going too fast when the skies split open and gray sheets of November rain fell like knives. I saw the kids on their way home from school, blurry and colorful blobs of yellow and red slickers: kids with thoughts of cold milk and warm chocolate chip cookies and spending the afternoon watching

"Howdy Doody and Buffalo Bob." Kids scattering in all directions. And next to me, Jack was puking. All over the floor, my skirt, and the front seat. I looked down, pulled his head up, and pushed him over to his side, and when I glanced back up at the road in front of us, I caught a glimpse of blue. Too close, too fast, thud against the fender, something flew into the air, legs splayed like a broken bird's wings.

And, again, it was happening. Slowly, so painfully slow.

My hands tighten around the whistling tea kettle's handle. My feet pulse against the kitchen floor like they did against the truck floor. But there is no brake on my kitchen floor.

Where was the brake? Where was the goddamned brake?

Jack, hit the brake! How does the shift work? How do you turn the truck? Turn the truck, Jack!

Oh my God, Jack. That little girl. That little girl, Jack. Oh, my God.

The truck bucked and tossed. My head cracked against the back of the seat. The St. Christopher medal hanging from the rearview mirror snapped the windshield like a gunshot.

"Whutthefuck?" Jack sat up straight, rubbing his cheekbone. "Christ!"

I glanced into the rearview mirror, into the piece of the scene we had left behind: the small core of kids around the blue mound in the middle of the street, and I couldn't breathe. My chest slammed shut with shock and pain and fear, and Jack saw, too.

He screamed: "Damnit! Shit. Shit! Shitshitshit!" He reached across, jerked the wheel, slammed his foot harder atop mine, forced me to speed away though I was yelling, "Stop! Stop!" and the smell of alcohol and vomit gagged me and made me close my eyes, but it didn't matter, because now, he was in control, he had the wheel, he was driving, and I let him.

Jack's truck sped to the end of the street, took a right on Ferry Street, got lost in traffic, and still didn't stop.

"He didn't stop." I've said the words aloud, and for a long second, I have no idea where I am. Then, like a seagull's screech, a child's cry brings me out of my nightmarish memory. *Thank God. I'm here. I'm home.* I'm standing against the kitchen window, and the cold glass against my forehead is good, enough of a chill to shock me back to today, to reality. A group of little girls run by the building, calling to each other, daring each other to run, to fly. Girls that look so much like the one we hit. Little Cindy Gordon.

My sight blurs. I want to flee the apartment and the children and the memory of what we've done. I want to flee the truth I've been trying to deny.

The Kennedy Connection

4 P.M.

After the door to the Robbins' apartment closes, Frankie Cassilli shrugs his shoulders and says, "That broad's got a problem as big as the Park Theater, boyo."

"Yeah, and his name is Jack." Graham Jackson jots a few words in his notes about the coat she'd had lying on the chair next to the kitchen table. *It's still damp*, then squiggles a question mark beside the comment. And *she was nervous. Why?*

"Shit, this ain't gonna be as easy as I thought," Frankie says, and snaps his gum.

"Yeah."

"Whaddya say we try again to find someone who has seen him in the past couple of days?"

Graham glances down at Frankie, knowing he would rather be doing anything but this investigation. Anything that had to do with kids bothered Frank. Graham firmly believes Frankie might be one of the strongest people he knows, but he never would have made it through what Graham saw as a child. There are many differences between them that go far beyond the color of their skin, but one thing they agree on is that crimes involving kids are heartbreaking. "Hate to say it, Frank, but we'll probably have to jog by that barroom and the Naval Yard."

"Yeah, but I think we should start right here with the neighbors: the Indel—what'd she say?" Frankie checks the wrinkled notebook he always uses to track what victims report. He'd pulled the notebook out in the Robbins' quiet, musty apartment and used it for notes he was sure he'd forget. It was too quiet for him in that place. He is used to his four kids and

Sicilian wife, all screaming simultaneously. Things are never quiet in the Cassilli household.

"Indelicato, I think. She pointed next door." Graham lifts his chin, indicating the apartment down the hall.

"That's an Italian name."

Graham laughs. "You'll be right at home, Frankie, me boy."

Frank punches his partner in the right biceps. They've been together for only six months, and it's been a strange partnership. Frank tells everyone that it's difficult to believe he has enjoyed it. *I genuinely like the guy*, he says. *He's quiet and determined, with not one ounce of arrogance in him, and he treats people fair and square.* Frankie admires the courage it took for this intelligent Black man to push for a position on the force. It took a lot of gumption and a boatload of patience to deal with the prejudice. That never did make a bit of sense to him. Either a guy is a good guy, or he's not. Plain and simple. Doesn't matter what the color of his skin is.

Frankie knew Jackson had some powerful pull going for him when a reference letter from Senator Kennedy showed up on Sergeant Flaherty's desk. Still, Jackson's time at the force hasn't been easy. And not everyone in Boston likes the Kennedy family, so it's kind of chancy to have them write reference letters, especially for cops. Especially for Negro cops. Old Joe Kennedy had made himself some enemies during his days of rum-running, but his son Jack was well-liked, and it was Jack who Graham knew well and vouched for him.

They had met when Graham was one of the first Black volunteers for the U.S. Navy right after the government started allowing Negroes to volunteer in 1942. Graham enjoys telling the story of meeting Kennedy on their first assigned ship and matching Bostonian accents with him after dinner in the mess hall. Though he threw every Bostonian slang he had at the Kennedy kid, Jack came back with that roundhouse accent. No denying the man was from Boston. After five minutes of jousting, Graham bowed out, and the men's friendship was sealed.

There aren't too many people who believe the story when it's first told, and it thrills him to no end to see the arched eyebrows turn to shocked and impressed expressions when people realize the stories Graham tells about the Kennedys are true. After all, how could the hoity-toity, American-royalty Kennedy family possibly welcome a Black veteran from the other side of Boston?

Little did Graham know back in the early days of their friendship during the waning days of World War II that Kennedy would become a politician. Then the war ended, and they went their separate ways: Graham went to the inner-city neighborhoods for a couple of years; Jack back to the ocean. Only twenty miles apart, but worlds away.

When they reconnected in Boston while Kennedy was campaigning for the House of Representatives, Graham often moonlighted as a driver for the young politician, and later, when Jack started campaigning for senator, Graham spread the word in his circle of family, friends and church members about Kennedy's views on how Negroes should be treated. Though he doesn't brag about it to anyone on the force, Graham once told Frank he figured he'd gotten Kennedy "more than a few votes from Black folks around the Boston area."

The junior senator was beginning to make a lot of inroads in Massachusetts politics now, and most of the cops liked him—even though he was never one of the working class, as some liked to point out. Graham was proud to have Jack as a friend and more than happy to spread the word about the PT-109 war hero. The support of a quiet but substantial Negro community in Everett had helped solidify Kennedy's popularity within the larger Boston area, and eventually, his popularity spread among the neighboring Boston suburbs. Graham knew all too well that he probably wouldn't have been granted a spot on the police force without Kennedy's influence behind him, though he also realized he'd earned that place, whether someone was going to give it to him.

When Frank was first told he'd have a Black partner (the first Negro cop on the force), he'd gotten ribbed by the other cops, and he'd even had some nasty phone calls, but he didn't put up with it. As far as he was concerned, the city had been built by immigrants like his father and the other guys—like Graham's dad—who leaned their own shoulders into hard labor: hoisting clay pipes, hauling tons of loose stones, carrying slabs of bone-breaking iron, building Boston, its harbors, its brownstone tenement buildings, its austere cathedrals, and dingy barrooms. Despite what everyone else felt, Frank didn't think there was much difference between children of slaves and children of immigrants. Everyone had to work hard to put food on the table. Money—or the lack of it—kind of leveled the playing field, no matter what color you were or where your parents came from. He wasn't about to deprive a good man of a hard day's wage of man, and standing up next to that type of man made him proud to be part of the fabric of Boston.

In the past six months, he and Graham had seen little excitement, but they'd seen each other through shift changes, new captains, and new cruise cars. No gunfights like the guys in Boston saw daily, no murders. Just the boring streets of Everett, Massachusetts. There was an occasional traffic accident, some kids rowdying it up down the Line, and a few scuffles at the annual Everett vs. Chelsea football games, but nothing important. Cases like this kid's hit-and-run were about as newsworthy as Everett gets.

And this one was a tearjerker.

The medical attendants pronounced the kid DOA at Whidden Hospital. Casey and Moranes were there for that one and got the honor of rushing through the hospital doors, yelling for the docs, and getting emergency room personnel to do their duty. Then the kid—a beautiful, blond, seven-year-old, little girl—miraculously came back to life, though she was still in a coma now. The cops on duty rejoiced as though they'd just caught one of Hitler's henchmen.

Frankie and Graham got the after-the-fact work on this case. The drudge work. Beating the streets, looking for the guy who drove the truck that hit the little girl, the guy who disappeared as quickly as snow in May. All they wanted was to catch the bastard who left the little kid for dead. And it was an easy hunt: Jack Robbins owned the truck and was driving it when he left the barroom that afternoon. They've put some of the story together thanks to the wife's part of the story. Now all they have to do is find his rotten ass. Someone in this apartment building had to have some information they could use.

Now Frankie pushes his hat back on his head and tucks a hand down the front of his pants. He checks his watch. "Shit, my old lady probably put the sauce on the back of the stove by now."

"You'll live without your meatballs." Graham slaps his partner's plump stomach and strides ahead. He knocks on the door of 7C, still thinking about Beth Robbins' eyes, the pretty color blue they are, like his grandmother's periwinkles. And sad. Those eyes are too sad for a girl that young. He wonders what Jack Robbins is like and decides he's a bastard. A real son-of-a-bitch.

Something's Going On

6 P.M.

"Well, I told you something's going on, that's for sure." Angela adjusts the apron around her waist and heads for the stove. The beef stew is simmering mildly and smells perfect. She swirls her wooden spoon through it, takes a good whiff, and decides the turnip and potatoes aren't quite soft enough yet. Another twenty minutes. Maybe half an hour. She likes the meat and vegetables soft, almost a mush rather than a stew. "Those cops didn't come over here just for kicks. Know what I mean, 'Retta? Something's going on."

Both Angela and Loretta had answered the cops' questions; Angela even gave them her version of what happened that night, telling them more than they wanted to know ("I think he hit her that night. We heard crashes. *Kaboom*! Then nothing but that poor kid crying.") and making sure that she repeated all the stories about the fights she'd overheard coming from 6C over the past year or so. ("Jack Robbins is handsome, that's for sure, but little Beth Robbins has been struggling with him. He talks with his fists, know what I mean?")

Even though Angela tells them everything she remembers (and some that she invents), she doesn't know where Jack went, and there's one thing she cannot do. She can't lie. She just took it for granted he went back to work that Monday morning, as he always did after one of his drunk weekends.

"One thing you got to say about that Jack Robbins, he always got up every morning—6:10 A.M., on the dot—and went to work," she'd told that nice Italian cop, "I know. I was always up when he went down the hall. But that day...well, I'd retired late the night before—wasn't feeling well. My diabetes, y'know, ate something wrong at suppertime, and it just kicked up a bit—and I overslept for the first time in years. I don't remember the last time I woke up later than six-oh-four right on the button. Right on the button. That's how I know when that Jack Robbins leaves. Have been waking up like that for years, ever since my Harry was killed overseas. He enlisted even though he was too old, y'know. Killed the first minute he stepped foot off the boat over there in France. Foolish man. Knew the minute he died. Woke right up, just like that. Six-oh-four A.M."

She snapped her fingers. "And after he died, I moved in here with my sister—Loretta, c'mere, honey, and meet these two nice policemen—and, well, I still wake up at that time every single day. For the past fifteen years, three months, and five days."

Loretta told Angela to shut up, that the officers didn't want her whole life story, that they had a job to do, and that Angela should let them do it. But Angela hadn't listened. She had a story to tell and was determined that the officers needed to hear it.

"Now, you see why I listen at the wall?" Angela stands at the stove now, the cops long gone, and stirs the stew, inhaling the rich combination of beef, turnip, potatoes, and onions. She thinks about bringing some over to little Beth Robbins later to see if she'll say anything about what happened, maybe even glancing past Beth into the apartment. As often as Angela has knocked on the door, Beth has never done more than crack the door an inch and apologize for Jack being 'indisposed.'

"Someday something big is going to happen," Angela continues, talking into the stew, "and I will be the one to save someone's life. Or at least stop someone from getting hurt, get my drift, 'Retta?"

Loretta sits at the kitchen table, reading the weekly newspaper, pretending not to listen, though Angela knows she's got both ears and eyes open. Sometimes Loretta plays 'possum, but she always listens. Doesn't say much, but she listens.

"You listen at the wall 'cause you're nosy, is all." Loretta shuffles the paper and crosses her legs, swinging her slippered foot back and forth like she always does when thinking.

"You gotta admit you're wondering where that Jack got off to after he hit that poor little girl."

"Hm hmm..."

Angela lifts the soup spoon to her mouth, blows on it, and tastes the hot sample. Nothing like beef stew on a chilly fall day to warm your insides. Yes, she thinks she'll take some over to little Beth Robbins to see how she's doing. No, she's not nosy; she's just bringing over some food to a neighbor. But the stew needs a little more garlic first.

"Milton Berle's on tonight," Loretta said tonelessly. She always tells Angela what's on television—even though they don't own a TV set.

"Maybe someday we'll get to see him, huh?" Angela glances at the clock on the wall, then turns the burner down and shuffles into the parlor to sit at the window and watch the people on Broadway coming and going.

Working Feverishly Against the Whine

November 11, 1957

The Whidden Hospital's Intensive Care Unit hallway hums with people, machines, and accusations. I stand against the wall by the elevator, arms at my sides, head tilted, cuddling my stained cheek against my shoulder, wishing I were invisible, as I have so many times in my life, and I don't know what to do. *This idea was nuts, Beth Robbins. Nuts, nuts, nuts.*

I struggled against the dismal wind only moments ago as I walked up the almost perpendicular hill leading to the Whidden Hospital. I fought hard to keep my mind from racing away, but I knew I had to let the family of the little girl we hit understand what happened, even though I wasn't exactly sure how to do that. But I had to talk to *someone* about it. I had to apologize. Tell someone the truth. I feel like I will burst if I don't tell someone.

The accident plays itself in my head time and time again—when I am in bed, when I am running the water into the teapot for a cup of tea, when the television is on, and when I least expect it. It doesn't matter. That little girl's body flying through the air haunts me constantly.

As I walked up the hill to the hospital, I did multiplication tables in my head, thought about what was on the news that morning, and relived conversations Jack and I had that night—anything to keep my mind busy.

It's a little more than a week before Jack's birthday, November 18th, but the raw chill in the air makes my throat feel like someone scraped it with a dull razor. The wind beat against my cheeks and tightened my skin so much it felt like it would pop if I tried to speak. The solid thud, thud, thud of my heels grasping the pavement echoed the memory of the louder thud of a body against the fender of Jack's truck. Halfway up the hill, I paused, eyed how much further I had to walk, and instead saw the body—the child—

flying past the windshield, picked up and tossed like a piece of paper in the city wind. And it was Jack's truck that did it.

Jack's truck. Not mine.

Every table in my house is littered with charcoal sketches. Studies of the truck, its wheels, the windshield wipers, and the speedometer at 42 mph. Small pen drawings on a yellow-lined tablet. Vignettes of the kitchen counters, the shadow of a bottle to the side, a profile in silhouette. Even I don't know who it is. There are so many sketches that they're overwhelming. I needed to take the walk anyway and soon found myself here.

And I don't know why. Nothing makes sense anymore.

All last night, I'd waited for Jack to call back. I paced by the phone, going from the phone to the window to the television and back again. Every half hour or so, I'd pick up the receiver, listen for the dial tone, and then put it back quickly, thinking that if Jack had called during the seconds I had the phone off the hook, he'd have gotten a busy signal.

But he never called. The only sound in the apartment was the television and the programs I'd come to rely on as if they were my own family: Lassie (the dog I could never have as a child) and Timmy (the dog's ever-faithful sidekick), *Bonanza's* Cartwright family, the group of men who weren't ashamed of being sappy; and the talented part of the family, *Ted Mack's Amateur Hour,* singers, tap dancers and comedians.

When Jack was home, he would watch television with me on a Sunday evening. Sometimes, he even let me cuddle beside him, especially if he already had two or three beers. The smell of Pabst was not so disgusting then; instead, it comforted me. The smell meant Jack was home, not out with someone else, and as I inhaled that smell, I felt his warm body beside me when he fell asleep, his snore often drowning out the sound of the television, and I didn't mind.

During the day, the television became my sole companion, its flickering light filling the empty spaces in our tiny apartment. It was a constant presence long after Jack had left for work, and I had meticulously cleaned the apartment and prepared the ingredients for dinner. I would watch the game shows, the soap operas, and the family shows, sometimes not venturing out of the apartment for more than a week. Lucy and Desi, Ozzie and

Harriet, Dennis and his Mom and Dad (Alice and Henry), the Beaver and Wally, Bud and Princess and Kitten were all my friends, their stories more familiar to me than the people who lived down the hall. Who needed friends when I had the best families right in my living room?

Yet, they didn't replace Jack's phone call, and when I turned off the TV to go to bed, they didn't provide any warmth between the sheets.

Now, the pungent smell of the hospital assaults my senses, making my nose burn and my eyes water, much like the leaky faucet in my bathroom. The smell transports me back to when I was eleven and my beloved Gram was fading away. I spent endless hours in the hospital lobby, flipping through movie magazines and falling in love with the dashing Clark Gable and Douglas Fairbanks. And now, I find myself back in the same hospital, this time with Mama's ambulance. Then with Daddy's...

I pull myself out of the memory with a shake of my head and suddenly realize this visit to the hospital isn't such a great idea, and I don't want to be here anymore. My face feels prickly, hot, and cold simultaneously, so I open the top buttons of my coat and try to take some deep breaths. *Calm down. This is the right thing to do, the only thing to do. Take a step down the hall. Go on. Do it.* Before I know it, I'm in the ICU lobby.

This is where Cindy Gordon is, the newspaper said.

Someone bumps me from behind: a doctor in a blue surgical gown bustles by without apologizing. I realize with a start that he doesn't know me, no one does, and I don't have to hide, but I do have to tell them, *need* to tell them I'm sorry about the accident that almost killed their little girl, that I'm just as much at fault as Jack, probably more, that I shouldn't have let him take over and make us leave the accident.

Then I see them through the glass wall. The woman (*Cindy's mother?*) has her back to the hallway. She's heavier than I imagined: a motherly body, the kind a child can nestle into, sleep against, cuddle. She's sobbing uncontrollably, and her broad shoulders shake under her light blue cardigan as her orange-flowered scarf slides down to reveal the pink sponge curlers in her hair. (*Just like the one home in my bureau drawer.*) The guy beside her must be her husband. He's wearing the same kind of uniform Jack wears— deep blue, a name stitched in white over the breast pocket. A mechanic or a garbage collector. A worker. An honest man. A family man working hard to keep things afloat, to provide something better for his kids. He's probably the kind of dad who goes outside after supper and plays baseball or kickball with his sons and daughters.

Not like Jack. Much more reputable than Jack, who's never had a child and doesn't worry about his responsibilities.

Fascinated by this family, I watch for a few minutes, unable to move.

How must they have felt when they found out about their little girl? *Should I be here? Can I go through with this?* Maybe some other Project kid screamed across the courtyard after the truck took off and banged on the Gordons' door. ("Come quick! Cindy's been hurt.") Then the ambulance's wail brought everyone out of their houses and out to the street where the little girl with the scrape on her cheek lay half on the sidewalk, half off, her pale blue eyes partially open, looking more dead than alive.

Now I have to go up to those people and tell them it was my fault, Jack. Damn you. If you hadn't been drinking, if I didn't have to get you, if you hadn't told me to drive the truck after she went flying, if you hadn't jammed your foot down on mine on the gas pedal and made us drive past, made us leave.

When the mother reached the sidewalk, her knees gave way, and she collapsed beside her barely breathing daughter, sobbing and screaming for someone to help. Before she climbed into the ambulance beside her seven-year-old, she might have yelled to her next-door neighbor: "The kids. What am I going to do about the kids?"

But the neighbor reassured her, "We'll all take shifts. Don't you worry. Go. Go!"

No one hesitated, not even for a second, because they all know how they would have felt if it had been their little girl on that cold sidewalk.

Behind me, the elevator door opens again, and I force myself out of my imagination and move to the side to let a small group of people out. From where I stand, I can see the IV bottles (blood and something else, something clear) hanging above the child's bed, and the tubes running down into the little girl's arm and up her nose, and I hear a wheeze like the last breath of life has left the world, and for a strange moment I think it might be the child dying, but it isn't her. It's me. It's Beth Robbins.

The mother turns to the father now and says something. Her round cheeks are red, but she has no lipstick on. Her face might have been pretty once, but being poor and having kids has drained her dry of what little beauty she'd had. She's worn out and barely hanging on. Some women can get like that, you know. Jack told me I would. He said, "Your birthmark will get bigger." He said, "Your eyes will shrink, your mouth will tighten up like a prune, and your skin'll become almost transparent like the Indelicato sisters."

I used to look in the mirror to see if it was happening, but I'm not even 30. It'll be a long time before what he said comes true. But this woman, Cindy's mother, has had a lifetime of pain in just the past week. Nothing else will ever equal what she's gone through. The father reaches an arm over his wife's shoulders, and they hold each other tight, both of them shaking with sobs I can hear too clearly now.

My chest locks up with their pain, the muscles squeezing my heart, sending spasms down my arms and into my legs. Confident I'm going to die, I grab onto the edge of the nurses' station and pull myself forward, eyes on the parents, determined to get to them, to tell them the truth.

At the door of the room, noises become more distinct. Machines surround the little girl in the bed. *Whoosh and click. Buzz and whir.* Then, a high-pitched whine—a vital sound, it appears. Nurses run from behind the counter, heading into the room, pushing me out of the way, and wheeling in a cart with a massive machine.

The mother screams.

The father yells, "What's going on? What the hell's wrong?"

"Out of the way. Move, move, move!" The nurses take over. One ushers the parents out of the room.

"Get Dr. Marling. Stat!"

Loudspeaker: "Code blue, 121. Dr. Marling. Code blue."

Feet pound. White coats rush by me. Surround the bed. Block my view.

"Give me the—no, no, over here!"

"What's happening? Please, someone tell us what's happening to our daughter!"

I can't see the little girl—*Cindy*—anymore. Nurses and doctors everywhere. Everyone's doing something: operating equipment, inserting tubes, filling needles, checking machines: the *whine, the never-ending whine. Shut off the damn monitor. Shut it off.* Everyone's working feverishly against the whine.

And the parents are outside the room now, crying, yelling, "Don't let her die! Please, God, don't let her die."

My heart beats so hard it feels like my ribs will break. I don't want to see it anymore.

I back away, then turn and press the elevator button and grip the stainless-steel bar on the wall with both hands. When the doors close, my knees buckle, and I thank God I'm alone.

Hold it tight like those subway straps so you won't fall, Beth.

On the elevator, I can't get rid of the image of the child by closing my eyes. She's there on my eyelids, and when I open my eyes, she's there on the wall of the elevator, on the ceiling, on the palms of my red, chapped hands. The hands that held the steering wheel of the truck, those that didn't obey my thoughts, and those that didn't turn the wheel fast enough. The hands Jack covered with his own hands when he turned the wheel, forced my foot down on the gas and took the truck away from the accident scene.

God, is that what happened? It all happened so fast.

This image in front of me, this little girl in the hospital bed, is worse than the one haunting me for the past couple of days because this one has a name: Cindy Gordon.

I burst through the lobby's swinging exit door and cherish the cold slap of winter air. It prickles my skin and clears my lungs as I stand on the hospital steps, simply breathing, concentrating on sucking in that air, then letting it out slowly.

Oh god, oh god, oh god, oh god. We've killed her.

Sicilian Spaghetti

November 12, 1957

Graham sits at Frank Cassilli's kitchen table, drumming his fingers against the red Formica tabletop. Frank and his wife, Sophia, are whispering behind the swinging door that leads to the dining room. Sophia giggles like a teenager, and Frankie chuckles, then says something in Italian that sounds suspiciously like bedroom talk. Shifting uncomfortably in the hard maple kitchen chair, Graham tries to ignore them.

The smells of tomato sauce and meatballs, oregano and olive oil, pasta and coffee still linger in the air like invitations from the isle of Sicily. Graham breathes them in, sighs deeply, and pats his full belly. Every time he comes over to Frankie's house, the first thing Sophia does is cook dinner, and he has never had the heart to say no—nor has he ever been sorry that he's stayed. Now he's satisfied and content but would give anything for a smoke. Sophia doesn't like cigarettes in the house; she says little Alberto hacks and coughs when someone lights up. The poor kid's got asthma and will never be able to play ball. All the kids call him a sissy behind his back. If he hears them, Frankie will ensure they don't make fun of his kid again.

Graham considers the peeling white paint on the ceiling, leaning his head back to stretch his neck muscles. There's a dark mark above the stove, as if Sophia burned something one night, and the house came close to going up in flames. The building is old, the walls thick with generations of brocade wallpaper. Sophia complains that sometimes the windows don't work during the heat of the summer, and Frankie should fix them. "Make them so go up and down," she says in broken English. She's always got a list of things to do for Frank on his day off. Maybe one of them should be repainting the kitchen ceiling.

Graham wonders whether Frank will come back into the kitchen to talk a little about the Robbins guy before it's time to head home. Tomorrow's shift is an early, long day, and they last had an entire weekend off about two months ago. The thought makes him stretch a little further, reaching his legs out in front of him, lifting them off the floor a little, feeling every pull in every sore muscle. He arches his back like his mother's cat, Junior, and the fleeting thought of home and his raucous family reminds him that he needs to call her.

His mother does an excellent job of keeping in touch with her four children, but she's more connected to his siblings and their kids than to him. She's constantly nagging him about getting married and giving her more grandchildren to spoil. She thinks his job is too dangerous and continually wonders why he took it to begin with. Didn't he have enough warfare and fighting in Europe? Didn't he learn his lesson when white people still didn't accept him when he came home–even though he was a hero, even though his country had decorated his chest with medals, even though the white senator from Massachusetts had handpicked him to be in his security patrol?

Stepping out of his "role" as a hardworking Negro was dangerous enough, Mama says. His black face makes a perfect target, Mama says. And his hours are not "regular," Mama says, and he needs to call more, come home for supper, and keep her and his siblings company on Sunday afternoons. The only problem is that he never has weekends off and knows he needs to take all the shifts. If he gives them an excuse to fire him, they will.

Giggles ripple again throughout the hallway, and the familiar pang of jealousy makes Graham lower his gaze from the ceiling to the floor. Sometimes, being without a woman hurts so badly it feels like a living thing has crawled into the very marrow of his bones. But he will not admit it to anyone. Even Frank. This loneliness is Graham's alone. A pain he sometimes actually enjoys feeling—cherishes, as a matter of fact—because it serves as a reminder that there's something good coming, something to look forward to.

He lets his mind wander for a while, trying to think of anything else besides what they're doing on the other side of that door, but it doesn't work, so Graham gives in to his imagination. Maybe Frank's got his hands around Sophia's waist. He's leaning down into her lengthy, black hair, whispering foolish married things in her ear, that he will take her upstairs after Graham leaves so they can do foolish married things in their married bed, things that Graham himself has never enjoyed.

He desperately wants a cigarette now.

Yes, there have been women, but no one's been a wife. And no mother yet for the children he wants to have. There was a woman in France, a light-skinned Ethiopian jazz singer with a honey-warm voice, but he lost her to a sax player with a heroin addiction. It wouldn't have worked anyway, he always tells himself. She would have wanted more excitement than he could have given her. No, he needed a woman who'd be happy at home, in love with him and their children.

Little Alberto calls down from upstairs, interrupting Graham's memory, and there's a rustle at the kitchen door. Sophia yells out, "Go back to bed now, you hear? Don't make me or your papa come up there after you."

Graham chuckles. Some things never change. He'd always thought his mother had invented the phrase, "Don't make me come up there after you." Maybe it was Eve, the original mother, who had first said it because every other mother in the world seems to say precisely the same thing.

The swinging door opens, and Frank bustles back into the kitchen like a satisfied rooster, shirt collar unbuttoned and suspenders off his shoulders, hanging like lariats at his sides. He groans and rakes his fingers through his curly black hair. Graham notices a ridge around the edge of his hairline where Frank's hat sits. It looks like his skull is indented. Must hurt.

"Man, these dogs are beat." Frank slides into a chair and rubs the foot, which is balanced on his knee. "Can't wait to get into a good hot bath."

"I get the hint, buddy. Give me a few minutes, will ya, before you throw me out?"

"You ain't had enough of me all day without wanting to stay half the night? Go home. We fed you. Now go home." Frank chuckles good-naturedly.

"Shut up and listen to me for a second," Graham says, feeling as tired as he knows Frank does. "I have been thinking all day about this Robbins guy. You know, the one whose truck we found?"

"Yeah?"

"I think the wife knows something. She seemed real skittish to me."

Frank, intent on rubbing his feet, only grunts.

"Didn't she seem like she knew something?"

"She seemed pretty mad to me. After all, her husband left her for some other babe, and now she's got the cops knocking at her door." Working his sock off, Frank makes a face at Graham, who's holding his nose in protest. "She wasn't too damn happy about it, but I'm not sure she knows where he is—if that's what you're getting at. Y'know, she wouldn't be half bad looking if she didn't have that huge fuckin' red stain on her face. But she doesn't seem like the type that could keep a guy at home." He longingly gazes at the door, obviously thinking of his wife.

Graham considers that for a moment. He'd thought Beth Robbins had pretty eyes. Funny, Frank didn't notice that, but then again, Frankie always liked those dark-eyed Sicilian girls. Beth's eyes were bright blue—an amazing color.

"That's not the point." Graham leans his elbows on the table and gestures in Frank's direction, trying to get his partner's attention, but it's useless. "Listen, I want to go back and ask a few more questions. See if she wants the truck back. If she doesn't, we know she knows something. Maybe the husband isn't coming back. Catch my drift?"

Frank finally looks up, his forehead wrinkled and a look of exasperation on his face. They've gone through this before. Frank is a good cop, no doubt, but he wants to do his work and get home to his family at the end of the day. On the other hand, Graham doesn't have anyone to go home to, and he often becomes obsessed with the few cases they get, which frustrates Frank to no end. "Hey, pal, you know I'd be the first one to help the kid, but unless the captain tells us to follow up, there are other things we need to do tomorrow. You catch *my* drift?"

"I think the guy hit the little girl." Graham's mouth pulls down at the corners like it always does when angry.

"So do I, but without getting Mr. John Robbins in for questioning, there's not much we can do other than what the boss tells us. And I don't think going back to see his wife will do much right now, either. She didn't seem to know squat other than her husband was gone. Didn't you check out her eyes? Little black and blue around the edges, right? She's fuckin' empty, man. And she knows her husband isn't coming back. He's dumped her for some other bimbo. That girl is going to be alone forever. I think we'd be a helluva lot better off going to the Navy Yard and seeing if we can talk to some guys he worked with. I betcha a million bucks they know ten times more about this guy's life than that mousy wife of his."

"I didn't think she was mousy."

"What'd you say?" Frank's foot plops to the floor, and he rises from the chair, the sign that he's ready to go to bed. It's time for Graham to leave.

"Nothing. I didn't say anything."

"Listen, I can only tell you that you shouldn't go there alone. Know what I mean? Wait until I can come with you. It'll be better that way. Won't look funny."

As Graham gets up to leave, he thinks over what his partner has said, and he resents it just a bit, even though he knows Frank is right. Everett isn't ready for a Negro cop, so he needs to walk a fine line. The racial stuff that happened in Little Rock, Arkansas, just a couple of months ago made everything on the force a bit more tense, especially since there were still federal troops at Central High School to help carry out the desegregation.

Sometimes, the other cops make it crystal clear that Graham's not welcome, even though the Captain warned everyone to keep their comments to themselves. Massachusetts might not be the deep South, but it isn't like Graham's freedom in Europe. Even though there was a war, at least he felt respected for what he was doing. And no one seemed to notice the color of his skin.

He sucks a quick breath in as he hits the cold air, then flexes his fingers into his gloves, slides his hat on, still uncommonly proud of wearing the uniform, still painfully aware it's often the only thing that garners him any respect. As he slips in behind the wheel of his car and the car warms, his thoughts turn once more to Beth Robbins, and something in the back of his mind tells him when there's danger ahead. He's always heeded his instincts but doesn't know what they're telling him now.

Dusting the Truck

Wednesday, 8 A.M., November 13, 1957

"Y'know, I have nothing against doing this—after all, I have kids, too, and I'd wanna know who had hit them if they ever got into an accident—but do we need to be doing this in the middle of a snowstorm?" Frankie grimaces and twirls the brush to dust for fingerprints on the passenger door of the Ford truck John Robbins left in the junkyards, as if that was far enough away to be safe.

Graham is working inside the vehicle, particularly on the steering wheel. Just fifteen minutes earlier, they had visited Beth Robbins and got the key from her to search the truck. Even though it's been sitting in the impound lot since the accident, they didn't have a key since it'd been towed there.

She had seemed distracted, Graham thought, but she smiled at him as he went out the door, touching him on the sleeve and saying, "You look like that baseball player. What's his name? Jackie Robinson?" It struck him as oddly sweet that she would say that—especially since it seemed she knew little about sports.

He smiles now as he sweeps his brush over the top of the steering wheel, highlighting more prints.

"Won't take us but a couple of minutes," he says to Frankie. "Once we get prints, we can be sure it was Jack Robbins who hit the little girl and close this case up."

"You got a thing about wrapping things up. Sheesh. Never seen anyone like you. You ain't happy unless everything's done."

"Nothing wrong with that," Graham sways over his shoulder.

"Nope, but it sure is a pain in the ass when I'm ready to move on to something else."

"Right now, we got nothing else to move on *to*."

Frankie laughs. It's a running joke between them that the city's been abnormally quiet. They bemoaned the lack of exciting gunfights and bank robberies only last week. Frankie said he had expected to have some excitement on the police force when he was a rookie, but now that he had five years under his belt, he knew differently. Someone had once told Graham that being part of the police force was an extension of being in the armed services. Except for an occasional domestic dispute, one supermarket robbery, a couple of break-ins, and the car accidents they might investigate, the most exciting thing that ever happened was when they delivered a baby during a thunderstorm earlier this year. It was far more exciting to be in the service, but all it took was one time, he reminded Frank. Just one shoot-out, a significant investigation success, a big bad guy caught, and they'd be telling that story for the rest of their careers. That's all it took.

"Okay, I think I'm done here. Let's take these prints back to the station and prove that Jack Robbins was driving this truck, not that it'll make any difference. The guy is gone, disappeared, with no intention of coming back, and if that don't make him a prime suspect, I don't know what does." Frank wipes a snowflake from his nose and heads for the patrol car.

"Let me just return this key to Mrs. Robbins," Graham yells after his partner.

"I'll meet you in the car. At least I can turn the heat on!" Frank waves his gloved hand without turning around.

Graham holds the key out to Beth when she opens the door, surprised that she's in a dress with lipstick on her lips. Is she expecting her husband? Does she know something she isn't sharing? He wonders whether his instinct about her is wrong. She doesn't appear able to lie, but maybe she isn't entirely telling the truth.

"Is that all you need?" she asks, hand on the door, chin lowered, foot tapping.

"Yup, we'll take the prints back to the station and see if we can match them up. If we need anything else, you'll be here, right?"

She hesitates, her eyelashes shift to the side. "Yes...sure. Of course."

"And if you see your husband, you'll call us, right?"

"I haven't seen him. He hasn't come home." The answer is short and clipped; this time, she looks directly into Graham's eyes. She's telling the truth. And she feels confused and a bit abandoned. *Why?*

"If he does, you'll call?"

Another hesitation. "What's going to happen to him?" Her voice is tight, as if she wants to say more, but is holding back for some reason.

"If it was vehicular homicide, he could end up in jail," Graham continued, "so he's lucky that the little Gordon girl is still alive. Most likely, he'd have his license taken away. Maybe some penalty, depending on the judge. The family could sue to get the hospital expenses taken care of, but I'm not sure what would happen with that. He has insurance, right?"

"I'm not sure. I don't think so." She shifts from foot to foot as if it scares her that she hasn't a clue about any financial matters.

"That could be a problem, then." It's not the first time that Graham has come across an abandoned wife left penniless and homeless without a choice but to go on the dole.

She grunts and seems deep in thought. A silence falls between them. Graham has asked all the questions he needs to. Now, it's time for the fingerprints to do their work. But he wants to ask more, especially about how this Robbins guy treats his wife, even though that has nothing to do with the hit-and-run. He wants to know about the charcoal drawings of streets and houses scattered across the coffee table behind her. He thinks he should ask if she's heard from her husband, but he's afraid she'll retreat into that shell she seems to have built to protect her from the stares and comments and taunts of schoolkids, past and present. He wants to ask her how she is. That's all.

"Well, I'll be back in touch," he says finally.

"Okay." She backs away from the door, preparing to close it. For one brief second, she glances up; her mouth falls open a little, then she smiles tentatively. "Thanks."

Graham realizes he wants to nail this guy as he takes the stairs two at a time back down to the parking lot. He wants to make sure he pays for whatever he's done—both for hitting the little girl and for what he's done to Beth Robbins. This person wasn't a man, wasn't a human being, but a monster without feeling. A sociopath. The baddest of the bad guys.

A Time for Confession

November 13, 1957, 7:45 A.M.

My father used to say, "Bethie, it takes you a long time to learn your lessons." I call it being cautious because I take my time and think things through, and even though I don't always make the right choices, I do stick to my decisions. And I do learn my lessons. If Daddy were here right now, he'd know I was beginning to understand and accept a tough one about my husband, Mr. John Robbins.

I can finally see that no one's going to arrest Jack (or me, for that matter) for killing Cindy Gordon, and since Jack hasn't called again, it's obvious he's keeping his promise to make me pay for what he's done. He's determined to avoid me and probably realizes he's better off without me.

Well, then, it's time to give myself up.

I, Elizabeth Robbins, must go to the police station and admit that I'm the one responsible for that child's accident. It doesn't matter that Jack was essentially driving the truck; it doesn't matter that he pressed the gas and jerked the wheel out of my hand. I'm the guilty one. I was behind the wheel. It was me and Jack's truck. If I hadn't been there, if I hadn't been driving... no matter that Jack pulled the wheel, pressed the gas, told me to get out of there.

The sky has barely brightened when I head down Broadway, a straight shot to the police station in Everett Square. I've decided not to take the bus. I don't need to waste what little money I have left; besides, it doesn't come until 5. I continue walking down the hill, and several buses have passed by the time I get to the drugstore only two blocks from my apartment on Chestnut and Broadway. Still, the sky has brightened a little, becoming a deep mauve color rather than the navy blue it was when I left the apartment.

Apothecary jars, ancient wooden mortars, and pestles line the front window, but the pharmacy is dark. In another hour or so, Mr. Hayes—the pharmacist who looks like Herbert Hoover, wears gold wire glasses and his hair parted neatly and combed to the right side—will come in, turn on the lights, and prepare himself for the day ahead. He's a dignified man, I think. Serious. Stalwart.

It's early yet. I can hear the delivery trucks behind McKinnon's Grocery next door, the guys yelling at each other, and the clunk of groceries being loaded onto pallets. The air smells like burning wood, and I lift my head to breathe it in. The smell is one of the best in the world; it reminds me of home and Daddy. Somewhere on these side streets, families are stoking their kitchen stoves, getting the fires burning, and it's easy to imagine what they're saying to each other: who's cooking breakfast, how many kids are getting up for school. I wish we had a fireplace in the apartment, but Mr. Fits burns coal. The grime coats the windows and the knick-knacks on the parlor table with a gray film that doesn't disappear until after spring cleaning.

Passing the imposing white house on the corner of High Street, where Dr. Stoller lives, I mutter rhymes, desperately trying to distract from the looming uncertainty. I replay the jokes Milton Berle shared on his television show last night, which failed to elicit a laugh yet remain etched in my memory. I replay whole TV shows in my head so that I won't have to remember what happened to Cindy, and I won't have to think about Jack not being home or calling. So that I won't have to imagine what it would be like in jail.

The high school, now shrouded in darkness, triggers a flood of silent witnesses to my memories. I can vividly recall the classrooms, can almost smell the dampness of the gym on rainy days, and I can almost hear the cacophony of our joyous voices on the last day of school before the much-anticipated summer break. However, the absence of students lined up and the classrooms devoid of light are stark reminders of the present. But the school is empty, bereft of the life it once held. It's not until I reach the St. Anthony's Catholic church near Everett Square that I encounter signs of life: a few women, their heads covered in black wool scarves, entering the front door for their morning prayers.

In Everett Square, businesses are rousing. Most stores are still dark, but the Dubbl-Dipt Donut Shop is alive with a flurry of brightly lit activity. I lick my lips, thinking about a warm honey-dipped cruller and a steaming cup of coffee. But I'm on a mission. Police station first.

I'm tired and numb when I arrive at the police station only a few blocks away. I stand on the sidewalk and watch the blue-suited officers striding in and out of the door, stopping on the stairs to talk for a few minutes, patting each other on the back, and laughing. Blue uniforms creased and polished, silver badges catching the early glints of the sun. The mean sun. The sun that rose to remind me that another day has gone by, and I still haven't told the truth. My charade had already gone on too long. Jack isn't around to help, and I must do this alone.

This is the most daunting part, but I no longer refuse to be paralyzed by fear. Once I step through that door, I know everything will be set in motion and taken care of. Whatever the outcome, I am ready to face it.

I tuck my cheek into the high coat collar. *Here I go, here I go, here I go.* Concentrate on putting one foot in front of the other and start up the stairs to the station. Ignore the polished black shoes coming toward me, moving off to the side as I maneuver past. Listen to the broken pieces of conversation that float past with the shoes, but no questions ("Can I help you, Ma'am? Ma'am?"). When I slide through the door into the tiny lobby, raise my head to see the partition window where I step forward, and tell the man behind it I need to see the sergeant in charge, I feel a hand on my elbow, and I'm ready to scream, *Please take me,* and prepared to plead for them to leave Jack alone, to take me instead. There's something—someone—to my right.

"Mrs. Robbins?"

The badge and nameplate align with my line of vision: Officer Graham Jackson. I lift my eyes, and for an instant, I'm shocked to see his dark face so close to mine. His deep amber eyes are as intense as his hand on my arm, and I realize he knows. His eyes mirror my face, the pain of my guilt making me sure I can tell him the truth. He'll take care of everything. For some reason, he makes me feel safe.

"Can I help you, Mrs. Robbins? You know, it's funny that you're here because we were going to see you today. Has your husband come home? Has he been in touch with you? We need to talk to him." He slides his hand down to my elbow and guides me to one of the wooden chairs lining the hallway.

I shake my head. "No... I mean, yes, you can help me. But he's not home. Jack hasn't come home yet."

"Listen, you're trembling like a leaf. Let me get you some coffee, and we can talk."

Yes, anything would be better than this hallway filled with blue uniforms and gruff voices. Everyone's too tall, and I can't see faces. Please. Some quiet place where I can...let me tell you. Let me tell you what happened.

The room he ushers me into is no bigger than a closet, but then he leaves me alone, says he'll be right back, and I'm left to stare at the gray walls, no pictures, not even a calendar.

Fingerprints: Fingerprints, dust, and dark and dirty marks are on the wall and along the baseboards. I want to grab some Spic N Span and my sponge and wipe down the walls to eliminate the smell. I can still hear the bustle of cops changing shifts in the hallway, then everything quiets down, and finally, Officer Jackson returns and hands me a steaming cup of coffee with a smile.

"I made it regular. Hope you like it that way."

Looking at him over the coffee cup, I can see he's got lovely eyes. Calm and wide, with long, curly lashes, like a girl. And his fingers are long, too. They are graceful, and when they brush against me, they're soft. It's the second time today he's surprised me.

I take another grateful sip and almost choke on the scalding, burned taste of the station's coffee, then swallow, keeping my head cocked to the side, always mindful of the mark on my face. My eyes are downcast, fingernails biting into my left palm, and my hand fisted on my lap under the table where he wouldn't see it. My tongue is blistering, but I swallow again, then smile tentatively at him.

"So, tell me, Mrs. Robbins," he says, taking his hat off and smoothing the ripples of black hair on his perfectly round head. "When do you think your husband will come home?"

"I don't know. He hasn't...hasn't been home since he left..." *Why is this so hard? Why can't it be easier? Why are the words...why are the words not coming?* "I know that...I know the child is dead."

The table wobbles as Officer Jackson leans forward. "No, no, no, she's not dead. Officer Cassilli and I just went to the hospital last night. She's still in the ICU, and they're going to operate on her today, but she's not dead. How did you...why did you think she was?"

Inhaling, I tighten my lips, put down the coffee cup, and raise my eyes. "I was there. I saw."

"At the hospital?"

I nod.

"When?"

"Monday night. Around eight o'clock. I wanted to...wanted to talk to them—the parents. Apologize. But I couldn't get in the room. The machine. It went—you know—that—that sound. It started beeping. Everyone came in...all the noise...her parents. I couldn't stay when I knew she'd died. I couldn't." Now they come: the tears dammed up inside me like fizz in an unopened Coca-Cola. The guilty tears spill from beneath my lids, silently, soundlessly, down my stained left cheek, and I swipe at them furtively.

Don't you cry, Beth Robbins, don't you dare. This is your fault. You have no right to feel sorry for yourself. Buck up. Get on with it. Don't be the namby-pamby Jack knows you are. Prove to him that you have some guts.

The officer hands me a handkerchief, and I pause before accepting it, but I use it, breathing in the surprisingly sharp and clean laundry scent. Then I take another deep breath and try to continue. *The girl's not dead. She's going in for an operation. We didn't kill her.*

"You were there trying to apologize? For your husband?" The look on his face is sympathetic.

God, he's making this more difficult than I thought. Why can't he just be mean to me? He's not supposed to be this nice. Can't he see I'm guilty? What kind of cop is he? He can't even figure out who the criminal here is.

"Mr. and Mrs. Gordon, the parents, they just want to make sure their little girl's going to be okay, just like any other parents. And we just want to find your husband. So, tell me, Mrs. Robbins—may I call you Elizabeth?"

"Beth." I knot the handkerchief around my index finger, swallow hard, and struggle to get the saliva to pass through my closed throat.

"Tell me, Beth, does your husband have any family nearby? Anyone he'd call? Go to? Stay with? I know I asked you this before, but I must ask again. Is there anything you aren't telling me that would help us find him?"

Plenty. I haven't told you the most essential part that would help you most, but you don't need to know about Jack. You need to know about me.

He takes a small pad of paper out of his breast pocket and a pencil much smaller than the ones I usually throw away. "Why don't you give me his family and friends' names and phone numbers? Then we can do our job."

"There isn't anyone. I mean, it's just me and him." *And the woman in the red Cadillac.*

"No sisters? Brothers? Friends?"

"Just the people at the Yard. He only knows the guys at the Navy Yard. And that woman, that blond woman. If you find her, you'll find Jack." *Why did I say that? You won't want to find her once you hear me. You're not asking the right questions.* I press my fingers to my temples, close my eyes, and rub hard.

"We'll talk to the guys at the Yard today, Beth. We already know their names. As for the woman...without a license plate, I doubt we'll be able to find the red Cadillac. But tell me, why do *you* need to apologize to the family?"

There is a knock at the window that diverts Officer Jackson's attention. It's his partner, pointing at his watch. Officer Cassilli mouths, "We have to go. Come on."

Pushing his chair back, Jackson stuffs the notebook and pencil back in his breast pocket, buttons and smoothes it with the palm of his hand, then slides his hat back on his head. He adjusts it just a little and taps the brim to straighten it. "Don't worry," he says. We'll find your husband. Now, we've got duty. Do you need a ride home?"

I angle forward, my hands tight around the chair's arms. "Wait, I need to—"

The partner, Officer Cassilli, opens the door. "Hey, Jackson, man, come on. We're gassed up and ready to go. Sorry, Ma'am." He drums the fingers of his other hand against the wall. These partners have more important cases than trying to find a hit-and-run driver.

"We've got to take Mrs. Robbins home." Jackson looks Cassilli in the eye and reaches over to pull the chair out for me, ushering me out of my seat, out of the room, and back into the cold hallway.

The words are still trapped within my brain; the confession is unsaid. And I hate myself.

All the way back to the apartment, I sit silently in the back seat of the cruiser, hands folded over the pocketbook in my lap, listening to them reviewing their plans for the shift and wondering how much longer I will be forced to keep my secret.

Amazingly, they left me on the sidewalk outside the Parlin Arms Apartments without asking me any more questions. "If your husband comes home or calls, Ma'am, make sure you let us know immediately," Officer Graham Jackson says before they drive away.

I pause in front of the sand-colored stone building for a moment, looking up at the sky where the weak November sun is fighting valiantly to warm the day. A red car flashes by, startling me. Its brake lights blink as it slows for a woman wheeling a carriage across the street. I watch the carriage and then the car moving down the street. It's not a Cadillac.

I check my mailbox in the lobby—more proof that Jack's not home. I never check the mailbox. He's always had the key and is the one who picks up the mail, but the box is full. It's my turn to see the letters and bills first. He has deserted me, left me for the other woman, left me to deal with this nightmare alone. With a certainty that weighs more than the apartment building itself, I know that he has used this horrible accident as his excuse to get rid of me, and for that—and for many other reasons—I finally hate him.

I gather the envelopes in the mailbox without checking who they're from, drag my weary body up the marble stairs, fumble with my keys to open the inner door, and head down the dark hallway to my apartment.

Meeting in the Hallway

9:15 A.M.

"Cheese 'n crackers! There's a cop car pulling up outside. Oh, my soul, they're letting out little Beth Robbins! They must've found that Jack. Loretta, come see! Come see!"

"By the time I get there, she'll be in her apartment and taking a bath. You watch. I'm busy."

Angela glances behind her and sees Loretta's shadow pass down the hallway, headed for the bathroom. If she's not reading at the table, she's reading in the bathroom. That woman is always reading when there's so much life to see right outside their windows. Angela sighs, then turns back to the window and watches Beth disappear inside the front entrance.

"She's coming, she's coming! I bet they found out where that Jack is and know what happened with that little girl. Let me bring Beth some spaghetti. Poor thing, she probably hasn't eaten in days."

Angela opens the refrigerator, takes out one of the many bowls of leftovers she keeps. She cooks enough for an army, Loretta always says, but there's always someone to share it, always someone who likes Angela's gingerbread or her meatloaf, her Irish stew, or her walnut chocolate-chocolate cookies. She slides a piece of wax paper over the bowl, wipes her hands on her apron, and yells down the hall to Loretta, "If I'm not back in an hour or so, I'll be over at little Beth Robbins' place. Going to bring her some spaghetti."

There's a grunt from the direction of the bathroom as Angela slips out the door. She's just in time to catch Beth before she fits her key into the lock.

"So glad I saw you coming in." Angela thrusts the bowl forward. "I made some spaghetti last night, and I know you must be so hungry with all that's going on lately. Here. Take it." She presses the bowl into Beth's hands and clucks maternally. "You need to eat, honey. Keep up your strength."

Beth accepts the bowl, her key already in the door. It edges open, and Angela peers into the apartment, her curiosity piqued more than usual. "Jack home yet?"

The poor girl looks as frightened as a baby sparrow that has just fallen out of its nest. Her hands flutter, the keys drop, and a small moan issues from her pursed lips.

"I'm sorry, dear. Didn't mean to scare you. Here, I'll get the keys." Angela huffs a little as she reaches to the floor for Beth's keys, then straightens up with a wheeze. It's getting harder and harder to bend down these days, but she forces a smile and keeps her voice cheerful. "So, tell me. Did they find your Jack? Is he okay? What happened with the police? I hope they didn't ask you lots of nosy questions. You know how they can be. You must be so tired. Let me help you get you a cup of tea and get you settled. You must need someone to talk to, huh?"

Beth shakes her head so hard that her Veronica Lake hairstyle swings back, revealing the birthmark. She grabs her keys and bowl and mumbles, "Thanks for the spaghetti, but I don't need any help." Then she squeezes through the door and closes it before Angela sneaks in behind her.

For a moment, Angela stands in the hallway, the door mere inches from her nose. "Well," she says. "Well. How rude. How very rude."

Licking My Fingers

The smell of the spaghetti is too much for me. It rouses memories of eating supper with Mama and Daddy around the maple kitchen table in front of the double window that looked out onto the driveway side of the house. Outside the window, Mama had hung a bird feeder, and Daddy would name the small fluttery things that came calling every morning when I, aged six or seven, sat there eating Shredded Wheat.

"The mousy brown one's a sparrow," he'd say, pointing his thick finger, his spoon dangling with a drop of milk ready to fall back into the bowl. "See the little black mask? Chickadee. The big noisy blue one: Blue Jay. The ones that pull worms early in springtime: Robin. And the tiny ones—just like you—are Finches."

Later, I would draw the birds, choosing Crayola's 'Wild Strawberry' for a cardinal or 'Blue Violet' for the splendid wings of the occasional Bluebird that would show up at our window. As I drew, Daddy would explain why the females were duller than the males. "Just like my little Bethie: to blend in with the scenery and be safe."

I often wish I could thoroughly blend in, as Daddy suggested, but somehow Jack would always rout me out, and then he'd pluck my feathers one by one. It's hard to hide when you're naked and bleeding.

Without taking my coat off, I drop onto the parlor couch, cradling the bowl in my lap, long tears wetting my cheeks. Before I know it, my hands are immersed in the spaghetti. I'm eating the long, skinny strands like I did as a kid: one by one, letting each strand trail down my chin, not caring how messy I'm getting or whether the blood-red sauce is staining my coat, shoving the meatballs in my mouth whole, groaning with the pleasure of tasting some real food for the first time in three days.

Not thinking. Just eating.

When the bowl is empty, and there is no more sauce to scoop up with my fingers, when all my fingers are licked dry, and I've stopped chewing, I take a deep breath and look around the apartment, noticing for the first time since I walked in the door how quiet it is. Dead quiet. No television. No snoring. No newspaper rustling. No Jack. And once again, the sobs swell my throat, make me gasp, make me want to lose myself in the pain. Wrap myself in it. Luxuriate in it. Forever. Pain is the only thing I want to feel.

Then, a knock on the door brings me to my senses. *If that's you, Angela Indelicato, I've finished your spaghetti, and it was lovely, but I don't want any more. Go away. Please leave me alone.*

"Mrs. Robbins?" A man's voice. *The cops again. Maybe they found Jack.*

I unwrap my legs from beneath me, rub my knuckles against my face, and use the sleeve of my coat to dry my tears. I plunk the glass bowl on the cocktail table, then walk to the door, expecting to see Officer Jackson, but it's not the cops. It's my landlord.

"Rent's due," Harry Fits says. He's 60ish, a widower who never quite got the hang of housekeeping or laundry after his wife passed. Long black hairs curl from his cavernous nostrils, and his thin brown lips twist in a sneer as he shuffles the black leather slippers he wears twenty-four hours a day. Yellow stains ring the underarms of his white t-shirt. He holds out a well-lined palm as if I have the money to slide into it. A green ledger book is wedged into his armpit, as always.

"Rent?" *How much? How often? You never told me how much the bills were, Jack.* "My husband's not here right now—."

"I heard the cops are looking for him." Harry Fits looks me up and down like he's wondering why I'm wearing my coat. I'm glad I'm still wearing it. Maybe it'll give him a hint that the apartment is never warm enough. "But rent's still due if you wanna keep living here."

"Oh."

"Listen, Mrs. Robbins, I'll give you 'til tomorrow, but no longer. Don't want no excuses when I come for it neither, hear? If your old man ain't here, I can rent this place to someone else quicker than you can snap your fingers." He snaps in front of my face to illustrate how serious he is.

I watch him shuffle down the hall, whistling. Then, a grip of panic grabs my chest as I realize I have nowhere else to go, and when Jack comes back, he will need to find me. I need this apartment. I need to stay. "Wait!"

Fits stops and slowly swivels around, pushing whatever he's chewing to the other side of his mouth. "Yeah?"

I duck my head to the side. "How much is it?"

He snorts. "How much is the rent?"

"Yes, please."

"Twelve bucks a week. Don't your husband tell you nothin'?"

"Thank you." I close the door, anxiously wishing Fits' hand had been on the doorjamb so I could slam it on his fingers. The jerk.

Twelve dollars. Where am I going to get twelve dollars?

The Pawnbroker's Monocle

November 14, 1957

Less than three hours after Fits leaves, I'm on the bus to Chelsea. I don't like Chelsea and never have, but Everett doesn't have any pawn shops, and that's what I need right now. The bus drops me off in Chelsea Square, right at Woolworth's. My left hand is in my coat pocket, clasping Mama's gold locket and wedding ring, and I seriously consider turning right around and taking the next bus home. When I get there, I'll lock the apartment door and ignore anyone who knocks. Can Harry Fits kick me out if he can't talk to me?

No, that won't work. He has a key, so he can come in and fix the toilets and stuff. God, just do it, Beth. Sell the ring and get it over with.

But it's not that easy. It hurts, and I struggle to stop the tears from running down my cheeks.

Before I left the house, I'd gone through every coat pocket, every pants pocket, every pocketbook, and every wallet I could find. It meant releasing Jack's stored-up scent from his shirts and rustling through his bureau drawers, but I forced myself to stay calm as I slid my hand into satiny coat pockets, pulling out a dime here, a nickel there. I turned cottony pockets inside out, sorting through nails and screws to find an occasional quarter, and rejoiced when one of my old pocketbooks turned up a whole dollar. But when I'd gone through everything and piled the change and bills on my kitchen table, the grand total was only $3.43: two dollars, three quarters, three dimes, five nickels, and thirteen pennies. It looked like a lot, but it didn't come anywhere near what I needed for the rent, and now I was another dime short since I'd paid for a round trip on the bus.

With a pencil and sketch pad, I sat at the table and doodled for a while, drawing the change on the table, the kitchen window where the sun streamed in, and the teapot on the stove. I thought about where to get the money and tried to quell my rage. Now that Jack was gone, no matter what I tried to do to keep my mind occupied, I spent most of the day angry. I had to think, concentrate, and figure out how to get what I needed for the rent. The other bills had to be paid as well. *Electricity, water, food. Damn you, Jack. Damn you.* I drew a pigeon at the window while I thought about how to stretch the meager bits of food left in the fridge and the cupboard. He'd screwed me up this time.

What am I going to do? This will not work. There isn't any more money.

A fat, black-eyed bird emerged on my pad, sketched in #2 charcoal, wings spread in raggedy flight, beak pointed like an arthritic finger. Whenever I see something I've drawn, I wonder how it happened and how someone like me can pick up a pencil and draw a face, animal, or tree that looks so alive. And that bird, that gawky crow with threadbare wings and an all-too-crafty look on its face, made me envious. I want to fly like that bird, look down upon the earth and all its problems and leave them all in my wake, and flying from the heartbreak and the troubles that follow every human being. I'm jealous of that crow's dark freedom.

I rose from the kitchen table three times and went to the telephone desk, where I habitually place the mail for Jack. I picked up the black phone receiver and listened to the dial tone each time. (During the past couple of days, I'd gotten into the habit of doing that every time I passed the telephone table, disappointed when I realized the phone still worked, but Jack hadn't called.) I poked through the pile of bills and stacked them neatly on the table. Jack always paid the bills. I did not know where he kept the checkbook until today, when I'd unearthed it from the telephone table drawer. He'd never shared the account with me and always told me to "just stay the hell out of it." There was only $132.20 in the account, which required Jack's signature. If I wanted to stay in the apartment, I had to pay Mr. Fits, and to pay Mr. Fits, I needed cash because no matter what was in the checking account, it was no good to me since I didn't have Jack to sign the checks.

After the third trip by the table, I finally held the telephone bill in one hand and the electric bill in the other, weighing them as though their physical weight would signal their importance. If one is heavier than the other, I should open it and pay attention to the contents. If it's not heavy, it's not essential. *If Jack's not coming home, I need to pay for these: electricity and a phone to live, an apartment, a roof over my head, and hot water and food.*

Opening the telephone bill first, I studied it, my heart sinking—$12.15. Then, the electric bill: $7.22. A quick addition of the rent, phone, and electric bills proved that even if I could use the money in the checking account, I wouldn't be able to hold my head above water for long.

I returned to the kitchen table, picked up the brown bag again, and drew a sparrow—this one nesting, pensive.

I need Jack to come back. Either that or I need an excellent job where I can earn a man's pay.

Flipping through the bills one more time—as if the amounts might have changed—I finally decided I had no choice. I need to figure out how to get the money out of the bank, no matter how mad that would make Jack. He asked for this, anyway. *He shouldn't have left with that blond.*

I knew then that the only way to raise money was by selling some of what I owned.

As I exit the bus, the noises and smells of Chelsea surround me like a dirty blanket. It's louder here than in Everett, and it's grimier. Everything smells like pickles and ham hocks for some strange reason. I glance left, then right, holding my purse against my belly as I orient myself. The street is busy, with cars challenging each other for space and locals yelling at each other as trucks unload vegetables and boxes full of apples to the grocery store on the corner. The ripped and dingy storefront awnings block my view of the street numbers etched on each door.

Finally, I stand in front of "Isaacson's Pawn Shop." In the window: saxophones, trumpets, guitars, and flutes hang from a string at the ceiling, and all the instruments shine like gold even though the window itself is dark and hasn't been washed in at least a decade. At eye level, on red velvet cloth, sits what seems like hundreds of diamond rings, gold wedding bands, men's pocket watches, pearl necklaces, and antique ruby earrings. Abandoned. Sad, as if their owners have given up on them like unwanted children.

My grip on Mama's jewelry tightens. *Mama, you understand, don't you? Please don't be angry with me. You'll always be in my heart, and that's what truly matters. If Jack hadn't left...if he hadn't gone with—if I hadn't hit—I have no choice, Mama. I have no choice.*

The locket feels warm, and the wedding band is worn, dented and soft, as if they've accepted their fate, resigned to living in this smudged shop window.

The pawn shop doorbell clunks when I close it. Not a musical clink, but an irritable, off-tune *thunk.* I step in, breathing the age-old air. Shelves full of leather-bound books, Army-gray trunks, antique jewelry boxes, instruments of all kinds, tabletop radios, Motorola televisions, mismatched silver service sets, flower-covered porcelain teapots, and glass cases full of jewelry. Every square inch of the shop overflows with someone's discarded treasures. I wonder how many previous owners felt as desperate and close to tears as I am now.

The odor in here mingles with another scent, a deeper, more distinct one, yet I can't recognize it until I spot a short, slight man coming from the back room, pipe clenched in his mouth, puffing like an old locomotive as he makes his way to the front of the store.

"Hello, hello, hello, pretty lady. And what can I do for you today? Perhaps you will come to buy something nice? Or do you have a treasure for me?" The man's high-pitched and shaky voice matches his bony body. He wears a wrinkled white shirt, a red bow tie, and black pants held up over his shoulders by a set of suspenders that have seen better days. He hitches them up now as he slides behind the nearest glass case and eyes me as if appraising what I haven't yet taken out of my pocket.

Under his scrutiny, my free hand automatically rises to my face and pulls my hair down over my cheek, hiding my birthmark while awkwardly trying to balance the pocketbook slung over my other arm.

"Do you buy jewelry?" I ask, though it's clear from the signs on the walls and the items in the case that he buys just about everything.

"Well, that depends on what you have, my dear girl. Depends on what you have." The man produces a jeweler's glass from a chain around his neck, widens his eye, and then fits the glass into his eye socket like a monocle. He holds out his small, bony-knuckled hand for whatever I have.

For a moment, I can't move. This is not something I want to do. It's not something I ever thought I'd *have* to do. Slowly, I bring my fist out of my pocket, unable to open my hand to let the little man see what I'm holding, all the while seeing memory snippets of my mother: the locket glittering around her neck as she threw her head back to laugh; a close-up shot of Mama's hand, the wedding ring she never took off until the day she took her own life. She had placed all her jewelry in a neat little pile next to the bed, then went into the bathroom and let the water run over the slices she'd made on her wrists. Until her last breath, she kept everything neat, with no mess and no telltale signs. Ever.

"It's never easy to give up something special to you," the pawnshop owner says. "I have people coming in here in tears. In tears! And I've never been able to take their things without feeling some of their sadness. Never have. Every piece in this shop has a history." He waves one slim hand in front of his face and flutters his fingers like a ballerina's legs. "All have histories. Just like the people themselves. Like the people. Yes, yes, yes." He sighs heavily, as if affected by every person who's ever walked through his door.

His compassionate monologue makes me feel more comfortable, and I unfold my fingers one by one. He smiles a crooked tooth grin and winks, and I allow him to remove the ring and the locket. I try not to feel as though they are connected to the very veins that run through my body, try not to think that those veins in my wrists are opening, just like my mother's did, spilling my family's blood as I stand there giving up the only precious bits Mama left me: an only daughter's legacy.

"Nice piece," the man says, eyeing the gold locket through the monocle that makes his pearl-gray eye appear twice its standard size. "Fine etch work on the casing. Whoever made it was a master. And the ring? Hmmm...worn with love, I can see. But simple. Yes, simple. Not something I can use. Keep it, my dear. I couldn't give you anything for it. It's more important that you keep it." He places the wedding band back into my still-open palm and presses my fingers closed around it. "Worth more in sentimental value. You know? Sentimental value?"

I nod, afraid to ask what he'll give me for the locket. I don't know how such a transaction should go, what to do, what a fair price would be. But nothing would be fair. Nothing could replace the memories.

"How much do you need?" the man asks, eyes on the locket, examining and opening it. He doesn't look at me but purses his lips and shakes his head as if no matter what I say, he won't be able to meet my price.

"I'm not sure. It was my mother's..."

His monocle drops out of his eye, and his chin quivers as he jerks his head up to stare at me. "I'm afraid I couldn't give you much. Five dollars, maybe?"

I hesitate. *Five dollars? Is that all my life was worth?* But I know Mr. Fits will be back tomorrow. I reach out to touch the locket again, and the pawnbroker draws back.

"Maybe I could give you seven-fifty."

I take a deep breath. "How about ten?" My voice sounds like it did when I was five. High. Querulous. But a bit audacious. What does it hurt to ask?

"It's a delightful piece, Miss—a really nice piece. But ten dollars is a bit steep. Things are pretty tight right now. Yes, yes, yes. Can't do that. Nope. Can't do that." He lays the locket on the counter and removes the monocle from his eye. Final.

I panic, heart pounding, sweat popping out around my temples. "What about both the locket and the wedding band?"

"Already told you. Don't need the wedding band. I have too many already. People seem to have suspicions about wearing them. Let an old Jewish man give you a piece of advice, my dear. Go home and make up with that man of yours. Tell him everything is fine, that he doesn't have to worry anymore."

I shake my head violently, not because I don't want Jack home but because this man has no idea about my life. But neither do I, for that matter.

"I need the money," I say. "The rent..."

Shaking my head has moved my hair and his eyes flicker to the birthmark. He stares for longer than he should. I see the question in his eyes, the instant pity, just like I see in every salesperson's eyes, on my neighbors' faces, in the pity I heard in the face of every teacher I ever had: *Poor thing.*

What happened to her? The tiny piece of anger that invariably ignites whenever I see that look on someone's face flares into a fire that burns my cheeks. I take a breath and look him in the eye.

"Yes, yes, yes. Always the rent. The baby needs milk. The husband has disappeared, lost his job, or drinks too much. I hear these stories all the time. Hear them all the time." He sighs. A theatrical sigh, and he's a horrible actor. "Nine dollars is the best I can do, my dear. And I'd advise you to take it since I can't offer any more. If anyone finds out how much I've given you, they'll break down my door—yes, breaking down my doors. I can't have that. No. I'm just a sympathetic old man. Take the money, dear. Take it and go home."

I leave with the five and four ones tucked neatly inside my purse and take the bus back home, my mother's wedding band safe inside the change purse in my wallet. At the last moment, the pawnbroker shoved it into my hand as he pushed me out the door. "I don't need another wedding band. No, no, no. Go home now before I change my mind."

Police Work To Do

4:25 P.M.

"What do you mean the captain says 'no'?" As Graham twists in his seat to face Frank, he presses his foot on the brake and brings the patrol car to the curb. They're on Parlin Street, a quieter part of the city. The trees feel bigger here than in other parts of Everett. Strange for a town that's only two square miles.

"What are you doing? Come on, we don't have time for this." Frank's chewing on a Tootsie Roll, his cheek swollen like a squirrel storing nuts for the winter.

"Tell me why the captain says we can't still cover the Robbins case."

"Christ on a short rail! Ain't never seen you like this, pal. Didn't you hear me? I said there's been a goddamn bank robbery." He enunciates each word slowly. "We got to cover that! Not an accident. Not a guy who's left his homely wife. Shit. Get goin'. We got work to do." Frank settles his ample body back in the seat, eyes forward. "C'mon, these folks don't want a cop car sitting on their street."

Graham pauses for a moment. He knows he can't change the captain's orders but hates leaving things undone. Shifting gears in the middle of a case makes him nuts. "We can still go question the guy's co-workers, right?"

Frank burps loudly and rubs his stomach. "Man, you give me *agita*. Just go, will ya? Don't ask any more questions. Just do what you're told."

"I'll do it myself then. On my own time." Graham pulls away with a screech and slips into the oncoming traffic on Broadway. "We need to find a witness."

"You're nuts, Jackson. Why take on more work than you need? Besides, why are you the one who always wants the exciting cases? Ain't a bank robbery more exciting than a car accident?"

"Not sure about that." Graham dangles his hand over the steering wheel, slumps into the seat, and tries to figure out why he's so upset. Frankie's right. He's always right in an off-handed, rougher-around-the-edges kind of way. He knew the tough guy's language. But he also listened to his wife, and she wanted him alive.

Because of very different reasons, he and Frankie have been trying to break out of the patrol car and into detectives' suits for as long as they've been partners. Graham doesn't need to be reminded that it's ten times harder for him because of the color of his skin. Even if Frank doesn't say it, he knows as well as Graham that there will never be an easy road to a promotion for either of them. His reasons for wanting more from the Force differ from Frank's. Frank needs more money to support his growing family; Graham just wants to continue up the ladder to be the first Negro detective in Massachusetts. Why not? Though it will be ten times as hard as being the first Black officer on the police force, it's something he's always wanted and willing to sacrifice for it.

"Hey, pal, lighten up." Frank reaches over and punches Graham in the arm. "You need a woman. That'd fix you."

"What I need is to finish what we started. And it would be ten times easier if we had a witness. There had to have been someone at the playground that day."

"I give up on you."

For the rest of the day, they speak in monosyllables and go through the motions of doing their job. But they don't find out anything about the bank robbers, and by the time their shift is over, Graham is so tired from questioning bank tellers and customers that he's almost forgotten Mrs. Beth Robbins.

Until he crests Broadway at Chestnut Street, and his attention is drawn to a shadowy figure sitting on the windowsill in what he figures was the Robbins apartment. He slows a little over a block away, and her profile appears in that second-floor window. She stares into the distance, over the tops of the cars, past the buildings. Up into the sky as if she can see Jupiter.

He imagines a little line between her eyebrows and then sees the sketch pad on her lap, the pencil moving quickly, her attention on the horizon, and she never sees him driving below her window.

His heart doesn't stop pounding until he drops the car off at the station and doesn't know why.

The Snow Globe

Friday, November 15, 1957

Before leaving for the hospital to see Cindy Gordon again, I pause to stare at Jack's photo beside our bed. In the past twenty-four hours, I've begun looking at him differently. I'm not even sure I know him anymore. I'd fallen asleep last night looking at the picture and thinking, *there are so many things I didn't tell you, Jack. I forgot to tell you I love you like I always do when you leave, and this bed is so cold, Jack. I don't know why you'd leave me handling something as awful as this. It's not fair. It's just not fair.*

Sometimes, all the anger I feel during the day disappears late at night, and between the cold sheets, I find a spot on the bed where he used to be. I remember how he'd snore just a little when he first fell asleep; then he'd cuddle up behind me, cradling me against his belly and wrapping his arms around me. It didn't matter then if he'd yelled at me earlier in the day. It only mattered that I was the one in his arms. I lie awake in the middle of the night now and wonder what I'll do if he never comes home. Last night, that thought twisted my chest with worry, and I knew as soon as I woke up I had to give in and phone the Charlestown Navy Yard to see if he'd come back to work.

When I asked for Mr. Irwin, I gripped the receiver tightly, even though I knew how the conversation would go. When he came on the phone, he was nice as pie, almost as though he felt sorry for me. I questioned whether he'd seen Jack for the past couple of days without explaining why I was asking, then got off the phone quickly when the answer was no. Mr. Irwin said he'd seen the newspaper and asked if I was okay.

"Fine," I lied to him, as well as myself. "I'm fine."

Now, I put the call out of my mind as I close the apartment building door and head up the Chestnut Street hill.

The trek to the Whidden Hospital goes quickly. I sprint through the Projects, trying not to stare at the spot where the accident happened, fighting against looking at the street for telltale signs of blood. I ignore the children in the playground—little ones, kids who are not in school yet. Mothers sit huddled on the benches, their brightly colored, home-knitted scarves snapping in the wind. Snow is in the air. Clean, brilliant-white snow covers the ground, making the world pretty again.

A couple of weeks ago, I would have stopped and watched the kids, imagining—as I always did—having one of my own. But today, I keep my gaze focused straight ahead, one hand holding the collar of my coat up around my neck when people pass. I don't raise my eyes.

In my pocketbook is a snow globe I've had since I was eleven, the year after my mother died. A Christmas present from my father was the only thing I could find in the apartment that might appeal to a child. I'll leave it with Cindy: a gift to say I'm sorry. *Please forgive me.* The globe's weight makes me feel rich somehow. It bounces against my leg like something important, something worthwhile, that fills my pocketbook like nothing else ever has.

Strangely, it makes me happy.

When I'm in the hospital again, it's all painfully real: the reason for being there, the hallway leading to Cindy's room, the words I'll say.

The mother and father are there, sitting on the edge of the bed, but the child is sleeping. A small lump in a big bed. All the machines beep incessantly like geese that refuse to leave the lake when the season ends. The nurses swoop and flutter, dipping and touching down momentarily, leaving a box of tissues or checking the intravenous bottle, whispering, touching the mother and father with efficient fingers, murmuring, then silently flowing out back to their station. They don't pay any attention to me—small consolation.

I stand at the doorway to the room for several minutes before realizing I need to speak or clear my throat, shuffle my feet, or unbutton my coat. Get someone's attention. It's stifling hot, but my fingers are still cold. The pocketbook is getting heavier.

"Hello?" My voice is tentative and cracks like a teenage boy's.

The mother turns around. Pale, round face, questioning hazel eyes. She looks like she hasn't slept for days.

"I'm Elizabeth Robbins."

Silence.

"Jack Robbins's wife."

The father turns now. Slowly.

"I'd like to talk to you. Just for a minute. If I could." The words make my throat tight.

Their stares are so empty, so completely sad, that I feel they know what I've done. Somehow. And for some crazy reason, they've forgiven me and taken pity on me.

"My husband…" I hold my pocketbook with both hands in front of me. "…my husband's truck was in the newspaper. They said it was the one that, you know… I've been praying for her, and I've been trying…I've been trying…." I swallow hard. *Say it, Beth, just say it. I was responsible for the accident that almost killed your little girl, not my husband, not Jack. He was drunk. Yes. But I shouldn't have let him drive. Say it, Beth, for god's sake, say it.*

The mother's eyes grow a transparent, sharp green, voluminous with pain. She points a heavy, square finger. "Don't tell me you're going to pray for my Cindy! How. Dare. You. Come. Here!" She speaks like she's forcing the words to the back of her throat, clucks out the short vowels, and snaps the sharp consonants against her teeth.

Her husband puts a grease-stained hand on her shoulder, then reaches the other to cup her chin and forces her to look at him. "*She* didn't do it, honey. Look, she's just trying to say she's sorry." He glances at me with eyes as red-rimmed as a long-distance truck driver who's been on the road for three days straight. "Aren't you?"

I stumble through more empty words, telling them the cops came to my house, that my husband is gone, and I don't know where he is. *Why am I saying all this? Why not just tell them? They don't need to know everything. But look at her: that little white lump in the bed. Why doesn't someone put a Band-Aid on her forehead? Why can't I take it all back? Yesterday and the day before, and the day before that. And my marriage to Jack and watching him go away and my guilt and this horrible way I feel. Just tell them, Beth. Open your stupid mouth and say it!*

"He's gone," I say again. "I don't know where he is."

"Good." The mother raises her fist and holds it before her pained face. "I hope to hell he drinks too much in some skunky barroom and kills himself by smashing into a tree. That's what I hope. Kills himself! Get it? Dead!"

The image of Jack's truck smashing into a tree makes my heart lurch because another image immediately follows it. Blond hair. A small body. Flying above the windshield. Falling limply to the street. No cries. No noise except for the dull thud. The small dent. The blood.

I cry then. I can't help it. *God, I'm so tired of this. I can't take this anymore.* Then the mother wails. The father sniffles. And we all turn away from each other. The mother treads to her child's bed and sinks against it as if the child in it will provide the comfort the mother so desperately needs. The father paces the hall, obviously unable to deal with the emotions. I take the snow globe out of my bag, nervously take a few steps to the other side of the bed, put the globe on the bedside table, and sneak away.

Elephants in the Mystic

My legs are so frozen I can barely move them. I'm standing in the marshes of the Mystic River, the Tobin Bridge looming above me, my breath coming in short pants.

How did I get here?

This is one of my favorite places, and I used to always come here to draw, especially when my father was in the Naval Hospital atop the hill behind me. I have dozens of drawings and paintings of this part of the Mystic River. Drawings of the bridge, the rough and gray waters, the ice in the wintertime, and one moment during my early childhood when I watched elephants from a traveling circus bathing in the river beneath the elevated bridge.

I catch my breath and find a rock to sit on, open my pocketbook, and take out the small drawing pad I always keep. Even though my fingers are stiff for the next fifteen minutes, I slow down my heartbeat by sketching the marsh grasses and the boats further upriver. Tiny snowflakes still fall lazily from the sky, though they aren't accumulating, just dropping enough moisture to wet the black grass, sea lavender, and marsh elder that grow along the riverbanks. I shield the paper from the snow for a few moments, but then my sketch is finished, and I realize that there's no reason for me to sit out in the snow when I have a warm apartment to go to.

The walk from the river through Everett and up the hill to my apartment feels like it takes me a lot longer than the frantic dash from the hospital earlier. I briefly wonder whether I should have returned, but quickly relinquish that thought. I'm not sure I want to face Cindy's mother again.

I see the Indelicato sisters' curtains close when whoever's at the window sees me glance up, and it makes me smile that they're watching me so closely. If only they knew everything that was going on. They haven't a clue.

My apartment is dark and quiet and chilly. For a moment, I stand in the living room, still wearing my heavy winter coat, and feel overwhelmed by loneliness. It's a foreign feeling: being lonely. It's different from simply being alone. I'm used to being alone. It's not scary for me. Sometimes, Jack came home for dinner, didn't say more than a few words to me, and then fell into bed. I became comfortable with brief questions and answers and kept out of his way, especially when he was drinking. Being completely alone every day was different, though, and I'm not sure I like feeling lonely.

The phone rings, startling me into dropping my pocketbook. I didn't even realize I still had it in my hand.

It's Jack. He doesn't even ask me how I am, simply launches into, "I heard the cops are looking for me, and if you tell them anything—anything at all—I'll kill you. Do you get that? I'll come over there and pulverize you, Beth. You understand what I'm saying?"

Could this day get any worse?

I nod but realize he can't see me and follow up with, "I understand, Jack, but..."

"No buts, you little bitch. Shut your trap, that's all."

"What about the truck?"

"What about it?"

"The police have it. In the impound yard or something like that. They asked if I wanted it back, but I have to pay money...well, you'd have to pay it because I don't have any."

Ironically, the truck is technically mine. I gave Jack the money to buy it after Daddy died, and I received his life insurance. The title is in my name, though Jack holds the registration. It dawns on me that Jack realized that when he deserted the car—and me. If the truck is mine, can I sell it now? Maybe that would be a way to make the money I need to keep my head above water.

I wonder if he's thought of that.

Long silence, like he's put his hand over the phone. I hold the receiver with both hands, trying to get it to stop shaking. I have no idea why I told him about the truck, except that maybe he would come and get it, and I could see him then. But do I even want to see him? Do I want to chance that he'll hit me again? It might be best that the truck stays in impound and Jack stays away.

"Find out how much they want to release it. I might be able to get it out."

"And the rent, Jack? The electric bill and food…" I'm pushing it, I know, but if he has the money for the truck, surely he can give me some to live on.

"Beth, I'm gone. I'm not taking care of you anymore. Find a way to feed yourself. And don't say a fucking word to the cops. Hear me?"

He didn't wait for me to answer before hanging up.

Sisters, Sisters

Saturday, November 16, 1957

"So, what do you think we should do for Thanksgiving? It's the week after next, y'know." Angela is vacuuming the threadbare parlor rug and yelling above the roar of the machine, though she already knows the answer to her question. The sisters haven't done anything different on Thanksgiving for the past ten years: they spend it with each other, eating a small turkey breast, walnut and liver stuffing, mashed potatoes, and boiled pearl onions—the fancy kind they sell in a glass jar. And maybe if Angela wants to get fancy, some boiled turnip. A baked apple pie for dessert. That's it. No company since they don't have any living relatives or friends they'd care to ask over—just the two of them. But Angela always needs to ask, anyway. Every single year.

Loretta sits on the couch, feet tucked underneath her, eyes on the latest issue of *TV Guide. The cover features singer Patti Page, who graces the cover with red, smiling lips.*

"Hey, you listening to me? I asked you about Thanksgiving." Angela turns off the vacuum cleaner and stands over her sister with her hose in the air like a baton. "Why do you read that damn thing, anyway? We don't even own a television set. You'd think you could find something else to do. Like help me clean, maybe?"

With a slow and lazy movement, Loretta stretches, licks her index fingers, and smoothes her eyebrows. "This place is so immaculate you could eat off the toilet seat. What do I need to do that you already haven't?"

"Well...well..." Angela glances around the parlor at the three Currier and Ives prints on the walls, the gleaming mahogany end tables, the polished brass floor lamp, and the brown leather armchair opposite the couch where Loretta's sitting. Nothing is out of place. Nothing is dusty. Nothing needs cleaning. Just as Loretta has said. But Angela has to say something. She can't let this opportunity pass. Loretta's looking at her and paying attention. "You might help me decide what we will have for Thanksgiving."

Eyebrows up, Loretta laughs out of the side of her mouth. "We going to have something different this year? Pheasant under glass, maybe? Chinese food we can eat with those funny sticks?"

"Well, maybe I should get out the cookbook and find an unusual dressing, or maybe I'll make broccoli instead of turnip..."

"Unusual, huh? You do that and let me know when you find something un-use-you-all." She goes back to reading her magazine.

"Maybe I should ask that little Beth Robbins to come eat with us," Angela says quickly, then holds her breath.

This gets Loretta's complete attention. She drops the magazine to the floor as she rises and moves toward the kitchen. "Beth Robbins? What makes you think she wants to have dinner with two old ladies? You're just nosy, huh? You want to know what's going on over there. Well, if that's it, you can have dinner with her alone. However, if, on the other hand, you want to become friends, well, I'll think about it..."

"She doesn't have anyone else now that Jack is gone."

Loretta stares her sister down. "And what makes you think he won't be back tonight? Or tomorrow? Or Thanksgiving day itself? And what if she has someone else she'd rather be with? People have families, you know. Other people do more than stare out the window and watch the world go by." She has stopped now and is leaning up against the doorjamb, thin arms folded across her chest, an insolent expression on her face like she's right and knows it.

"You should talk, Loretta Indelicato! You should talk! At least I do something around here. All you do is smoke them damn cigarettes and criticize me. At least I take an interest in what's going on. Can you tell me what happened in anyone's life but your own for the past few weeks?"

"Sure can. Beth Robbins left the house every day at about the same time. The cops were here. Mr. Fits came by and collected the rent. The Herlihy family went out for a ride in their new Buick last Sunday, and the Simones had a boiled dinner last night."

Angela's mouth clapped shut. Obviously, Loretta had heard everything she said during the past week, even though it always seemed like she was in another world. "Only reason you know that stuff is because I told you."

"That's my point! You watch everyone else's life but don't have one of your own."

"Neither do you!"

"I would if I wasn't living here, taking care of you!"

"Taking care of me, huh? We both need to bring in money to pay the rent and buy the food. And it seems to me that you are the one who cheerfully said, 'Let me do the cooking, Loretta. 'I like to.' And it seems to me that you're the one who was so broken-hearted when your dear old hubby died, you had to move in on me..."

"That's a low blow, Loretta." Angela plops down in the leather chair, an instant image of Irwin coming home from work, a toothy grin on his face, his thin gray hair swept back off his forehead. A sharp pain collapses her shoulders and makes her grasp her chest.

Immediately, Loretta scoots to Angela's side. "You okay? Listen, I didn't mean anything. You get me so mad sometimes that I wanna spit."

"I know. I know." Angela pats Loretta's arm and takes a deep breath as the pain subsides. "But you didn't have to say that about Irwin. I miss him, you know."

"Yeah, I know." For a moment, they sit side by side, patting each other's shoulders and sighing, then Loretta gets up, brushes imaginary dirt off her slacks, heads for the kitchen, and says (without turning around), "If you want to ask that Beth over for dinner, go ahead. But don't expect anything special from me."

From her perch on the couch, Angela smiles, gets up, and puts the vacuum cleaner away in its rightful spot in the hall closet. She is already thinking about what to do for next week's dinner.

Playing Checkers with the Gordons

Monday, November 18, 1957

Boots creating little puddles of melted snow, I stand in the Intensive Care Unit hallway, watching the Gordon family for a moment before the father spots me. He's got a blue crew-neck sweater on this time and dark circles under his eyes, but his hair and hands are clean. He nudges his wife, who turns and looks over her shoulder and shakes her head as if she can't believe I had the gall to come back again, but she says nothing. She simply turns back to her husband. Two little kids sit on the floor beside the bed, playing checkers. One looks about five, and the other is just a toddler. Both towheads. I would love to have both kids on my own. The older boy looks up, scrambles to his feet, and enters the hall.

"My mama says your daddy hit my sister." He stands in front of Beth, finger in his ear.

"Not my daddy, honey. My daddy's dead."

"Who then?"

Glancing up, I shift my stance and feel the urge to tell the parents the truth. *What's stopping you, you stupid woman?*

"Lady, what happened to you? You got a boo-boo?" The child lifts his hand to point at my cheek and throat, and my own flies up to cover the birthmark. An innocent question. One I've been asked many times.

"C'mere, lady. I'll kiss it and make it better."

My heart melts.

The parents are watching now. The mother rises, her face hard, and she quickly moves close. I freeze for a moment, but when the child reaches up with two pudgy hands, grinning and expectant, I can't resist. As I bend down toward him, I'm still aware of the mother watching me.

The little boy plants a wet kiss on my cheek. It feels like the blessing of an angel. "All better now," he says. "How'd it happen? Does it hurt?"

"I was born with it, sweetie. It's called a birthmark." Amazingly, I don't hesitate, even though I have not talked about it with anyone but Jack throughout my whole life. The boy looks at me earnestly, his hand still on mine, trusting and endearing. His eyelashes are white, his eyes are clear blue, and he is intelligent. I close my fingers around his little hand. "I've had it all my life, and my mama used to tell me it made me one of God's chosen."

He stares at the birthmark and seems to consider my comment. Then, from behind him, his mother's voice. "Scottie, come here. Don't bother the lady."

My heart sinks. *Don't tell him to go away. Don't make him think I'm no good.* I reach out, but the child goes as quickly as air. *Whoosh.* — and so goes my confidence. As I watch the mother settle the child back into his game of checkers, my heart bounces against my ribs, scaring me with its ferocity.

She rises and looks at me, then heads in my direction. The woman sighs and pauses a few feet away, heavy hands folded over her stomach. Her hair is down today, with no pink rollers, and her shoulder-length chestnut curls soften the square lines of her face. "Didn't expect to see you again," she tells me. "Bill says I should apologize for what I said to you the other day, but...." She looks behind her, expecting the child in the bed to move or her husband to say something. "I was upset. I'm sure you can understand."

I nod and swallow hard.

"Appreciate the snow globe. It's pretty."

Nodding again, I feel as mute as the snow globe itself.

"Wanna sit down? I could use a couple of minutes' break. Can't go too far, though."

"Sure." We walk down the hall and find a small waiting room filled with overstuffed chairs. Smells of smoke. And worry.

"I'm Theresa," the mother says. "Theresa Gordon. My daughter's name is Cindy, but you already knew that."

"Yes." I cough to clear the lump in my throat. "I read that in the paper." I look down at my hands, twisted in my lap, think about the cops, and wonder if they're here.

"I gotta ask this. Has he been home? Your husband?"

Here's my chance. Tell her, Beth.

No, I can't. If I do, she'll be angry and upset.

"No, he hasn't come home yet," I answer, trying desperately to keep my confusion in check. If I lower my eyes, maybe she won't see my guilt. At least it's true that he hasn't come home. At least that part's not a lie.

"I gotta wonder what kind of man would hit a child and take off." Theresa's eyes are piercing, and for a moment, it's as if she knows. "After you left that day, I talked to Bill, and we realized how bad you felt, you know, with a husband like that. Especially since he doesn't have the guts to come home and at least deal with this. You must be a little upset about this yourself, Bill says. And he's right, huh?"

The words are there, right in the back of my throat, and I push my chest forward a little, ready to choke them out. No matter what the cost. It's a struggle to stop my eyes from tearing up, almost impossible to keep from begging Theresa to pause for just a second, just long enough so I can finally say what's been causing those nightmares that jerk me awake, bring me straight out of bed, make me pace uneasily in the empty apartment that still feels like Jack. But there is no pause, and the words slide back down my throat to settle in the pit of my stomach, burning and rolling with their horror, keeping me in pain.

"I know this must be hard on you. Being alone and all." She finishes her opinion of my situation with an eye roll.

The tears I've been forcing back finally burn my eyelids. *You have no idea.*

"My husband—Bill—" Theresa jerks her chin toward the room. "He hasn't been to work in a couple of days." She takes a wrinkled handkerchief from her pocket and wipes at her own red eyes. She's been crying more than I have. That much is obvious. "The doctors, they say she doesn't need any medication 'cause she's in such a deep coma. They want to operate. Say something's up against her spleen." Again, she sighs heavily. "You got kids?"

I freeze. *If you only knew how badly I want one.* The memory of a time about two years ago brutally inserts itself into my thoughts. *I think I'm pregnant, Jack. Jack, why are you looking at me like that?* Then, the feeling of hot blood running down my legs. The wrenching cramps. The toilet bowl was full of red clots, and Jack was crying. His apologies. His hugs. If he hugged me like that whenever I had problems, I would have invented them to get his sympathy.

But later, his accusation that I couldn't even hold on to the child cut me to the quick. He swore I would never get pregnant again, that having a child was a gift I would never have. And I knew he was right.

I shake the memory, as I have so many times before. *Put it behind you, Beth. There'll be other chances. Jack was lying.*

"No, I don't have any kids, but I want some. I want at least four or five," I finally answer.

Theresa's eyes flicker, and she clucks her tongue. "No matter how many you have, each is different. Each of my kids is so special—each is a part of me, Bill…both of us. Cindy's got his eyes, y'know, and the little ones got his hands. Funny, you notice stuff like that right away when they're born. It's almost like looking in a mirror sometimes, y'know? And when they hurt, you do. Never understood that before I had kids. Never knew why my ma was the only one who made me feel better when I scraped my knee, y'know?"

I started to reach out. I wanted to touch Theresa's hand and tell her what I'd been hiding. But the possibility of being able to talk to this woman again, to see that little boy, to get another kiss, and most of all, to find out what will happen to Cindy is all too tempting. I don't want to give that up. Anger wells up at Jack. At myself. The rain that fell relentlessly that day came down straight and hard and fast, like bones, dead bones falling from the sky, making it difficult to see.

No, I can't tell her. It would hurt her too much. I'm not going to tell anyone. If I do, these people won't talk to me again. I won't be able to see the kids, and I want to. I want to know this family, learn about them, and help them through their anguish. Yes, I want that, but eventually, they'll find out. Maybe by the time they do, Jack will confess his part in the accident. If there is a chance he'll stand by my side and we can apologize together, I'll take that chance.

In the past week, I've felt more aware of the world than ever. I've interacted with more people and been part of more lives than since Mama died. It's scary. Terrifying. Wonderful. *How can that be?*

"I'd like to come back tomorrow," I tell Theresa. "Sit with you, maybe?"

"Sure." Theresa smiles: a slow smile, uneven, filled with expectations and surprise. "I could use someone else to talk to. The nurses here, they're great. The Irish, they make great nurses. But I could use someone else to talk to. The people in the projects all have kids and can't come up with much. But they send food. We got more food than we can eat."

With my heart beating fast, I realize Theresa needs a friend as badly as I do. It's the first time someone has asked for my friendship in years. A ghastly accident brought this about, yet caused me to feel good. How ironic.

"My mother was Irish," I say. "Black Irish, they called her. She always sent food when there was some tragedy, too. I remember her cooking big pots of corned beef and cabbage. She'd stink up the kitchen for days."

"Mine was German. It's where the kids get their blond hair. Ma would make cakes. She made the best chocolate cake."

"They're beautiful kids."

"Yeah, I know. Cindy's an A student." Then the tears flow again, and Theresa's broad shoulders shake, so I move closer, encircle her with tentative arms, comforting her, and at that moment, I feel comforted myself.

Spying from the Hallway

Graham ducks into the stairwell as Beth Robbins leaves the Gordon girl's hospital room and feels instantly guilty for doing so. Still, something about the interchange between Beth and the girl's mother brought unexpected tears to his eyes. And Graham Jackson never cries.

He waits a few seconds before hearing the elevator door close, then slides back into the hallway. Though she is physically gone, her scent remains, and he inhales it as if it would tell him her life story. But it doesn't, of course.

The nurse at the desk raises her head, catches his eye, and pauses. He straightens his hat, making sure she sees the shield. Confused, she nods, then returns to her paperwork. Graham grits his teeth, unable to squelch the discomfort he works hard to control when the people who have never seen a Black cop before stare at him as if he's an alien. He forces a smile on his face, approaches the desk, and asks where Cindy Gordon's room is, though he already knows.

Adjusting her glasses, the nurse points across the hall without a word.

"Thanks so much for your help." He injects an abnormal amount of cheer into his voice, taps his hat visor, and turns on his heel, heading toward the room where he can see Theresa Gordon sitting at her daughter's side.

"Excuse me? Mrs. Gordon? I'm Officer Jackson. I was here the other day."

"Oh, yes." Her voice shakes as though she's been crying. She holds a tissue to her eyes, swipes at them, then stands up. "Did you find him? Did you find the guy who was driving the truck?"

"No, no, I'm sorry. I am not here on official business. I happened to be in the hospital and thought I'd check to see how your little girl is doing."

"See for yourself." Theresa slumps back into her chair. "She's ...she's strong, the doctors say, but I think...I think she's struggling. I can see it in her jaw. She's barely...holding on." She dabs her eyes again and blows her nose. "What are you—the police department—what are you doing? How difficult is it to find this guy?"

"We're doing everything we can, ma'am, but he has disappeared. He's not at work, hasn't returned to his home—"

"I know. His wife, Beth, she comes here to see about Cindy, and she hasn't seen her husband since the accident."

"Can you share anything with me about what she's said?"

"Not much. Really. She's been trying to figure him out, I think. But he's not home with her; I know that much. He's a real ass, you know? Not only does he run from an accident, but he left Beth with nothing. Won't be long before she's out on the street."

Graham wants to agree with Theresa but knows that'd be unprofessional. Besides, he needs to put the pieces together to find Jack Robbins. No one can disappear altogether, and most people check back in at home eventually, no matter how badly they want to hide.

"Does she say anything about friends or family? Anyone who might know where he is or what he's doing?"

Theresa shakes her head. "That's the sad part. She doesn't have anyone. No friends. No family. I think her husband was it. She's alone now."

Typical abuse situation, Graham thinks. Keep the abused under control by limiting their connection to the outside world.

The little girl shifts in her bed, a tiny bump under the white sheets. She groans, and Theresa's attention instantly shifts away from Graham. "Cindy, sweetie, I'm here. It's okay, baby. I'm here."

A rustle at the door announces the nurse, who bustles in, stethoscope in hand, and immediately takes Cindy's vitals. "I'm sorry, Officer," she tells

Graham as she pulls white curtains around the bed. "Mom, you can stay, but he needs to leave."

Both women ignore him as he moves to the door, but he looks over his shoulder one last time, longing to ask Theresa one last question: Did she think Beth was covering for her husband?

He has a feeling he already knows the answer.

Shopping at the A & P

5:10 P.M.

On the way home, I stride down the dusky and deserted streets, my boots relentlessly pushing clouds of light snow out of the way. Fearless. That's a strange feeling for me. I think about Jack because his birthday is tomorrow, and I hope he will come home, but if he does, he will be hungry. I don't have any food in the house, nothing to make a cake, so I take Hall Avenue and cut down to Broadway, crossing the street after looking both ways—only the bravest come out during the first snowstorm, *so I must be brave*—and head for the A&P.

The store is nearly empty except for a cashier cleaning out the coffee machine at the end of her counter. I inhale the wonderfully rich Eight O'Clock coffee smell and the store's warmth as I shuffle through the sawdust covering the entire floor. Undoing the first button of my coat, I head down the vegetable aisle. In a couple of weeks, the shelf above the potatoes, carrots, and onions will be filled with toys for Christmas: trucks for the boys and dolls for the girls. Now, it's decorated with pumpkins and gourds for Thanksgiving.

Next week. Thanksgiving. Jack loves my turkey. Where will he get a meal like mine again? Will the blonde cook it for him? I don't want to think about that. My stomach constricts. I don't want to think about him with that woman.

A family bustles up behind me—two kids and parents—laughing and talking about supper. I duck my head, pretending to be looking at the bottled beets on the shelf on my left. They pass.

Meatloaf for Jack's birthday. I already have crackers at home to crush and mix with the hamburgers, mustard, eggs, ketchup, and some salt and pepper.

I've got flour, sugar, and chocolate to make the cake. So, hamburger, bread, milk. And eggs: all I need for now.

I pause before the meat counter, knowing that Butch Crocker, the meat cutter, will call out in his booming voice, "And what can I do you for today, Mrs. Robbins?" and I won't have to answer any questions more complicated than that. Opening my pocketbook, I count the money I've counted more than ten times since paying Mr. Fits his rent yesterday. It hasn't changed: $5.72—two quarters, two dimes, two pennies.

At the register, the clerk packages up two pounds of Hamburg, a loaf of day-old bread, a half-dozen white eggs, a stick of margarine, a quart of milk—and a quarter bagful of coffee because I can't resist the luxurious smell. Outside in the wind, I clutch the brown bag to my chest and lean, walking the short distance home, congratulating myself that I still have almost three dollars left in my pocket.

Won't Jack be proud of me?

Happy Birthday, Jack

Tuesday, November 19, 1957

I twirl in the living room and bedroom doorway, loving the feel of the starchy petticoat against my silk-stockinged legs, remembering how I used to twirl round and round and round when I was a kid on my new pair of black patent leather shoes. I must have been about five when I first learned the magic of new shoes. Their soles slick with virginity, their toes stiff and unyielding, their heels even—no wear on the right edge as there would be after I'd worn them a week or two. I always have been hard on shoes—and new dresses. There haven't been many with skirts as wide or swingy as I'm wearing now—bright red with black polka dots. The petticoat, crimson with black trim, looks like a negligee. It feels risqué wearing it. Sex like Rhonda Fleming, the redheaded actress Jack loves.

Sexy. It even sounds dirty. I'll show him exactly what he's been missing while out carousing with that blonde.

The television's on. I love the noise of it and like hearing my TV friends like Lucy and Ethel. The Nelsons and the Cleavers never fight and never talk about money except in calm, reasonable tones. I want to be like them. And I love it when Milton Berle puts on women's clothes and makes me laugh. I hate to admit it, but I talk back to the programs when I'm alone, something I'd never do when Jack was home, and now I leave the television on all day. I set my day by it now. It's lunchtime when the soap operas come on, and I go to bed to the scratchy nightly warble of "The Star-Spangled Banner."

For the first time since Jack left, the house smells like supper: real food: meatloaf and onions, and a leftover coffee smell from this morning when I sat at the kitchen table, nursing a good hot cup, eagerly expecting Jack to walk in at any minute.

He's got to come home. It's his birthday.

I spent the day preparing for a beautiful birthday supper and made a small cake this afternoon. While it was baking, I washed my hair with Ivory soap, rinsing it over and over in cold water to make it shine. I'd splurged on a bottle of lemon juice at the grocery stores, thinking it might give my mousy brown hair a few highlights. When I came out of the bathroom, head in a towel only a few hours ago, the citrusy smell filled the apartment with warmth, promising a memorable evening.

For some strange reason, I haven't been hungry at regular times since the accident and haven't even bothered to turn on the stove to make toast in the morning. But tonight—tonight—he's going to be home, and we'll act just like he never left, like nothing's wrong. I won't mention the accident at all.

Trying to ignore the warning voice, I twirl again, a little slower now. A little disheartened. I stop on my tiptoes—*swish, swish, swish*—in front of the parlor window. A light snow is falling, reflected in the streetlamp to the right. It's almost 5:30 p.m., nearly two hours after Jack usually gets home, almost half an hour since I've turned off the stove. I glimpse myself in the window, the brightness of the crimson, the darkness of my hair, and I almost look pretty.

I'm about to go back into the bathroom and touch up my lipstick when someone knocks at the door, and my heart about pops out of my chest, my knees buckle, and ten thousand prickles like witches' fingernails rake their way up the back of my scalp.

It's him. It's Jack. Thank God. Oh, God—I'm terrified. What am I going to say? What will he do? Please, God, don't let him get mad.

As I walk toward the door, I feel like it is moving farther and farther away with each step. A tendril of fear wraps around my throat, making the smile on my lips even more forced, but I push the snaking tendril back. *Why is he knocking? He has a key.* In the few seconds it takes to reach for the doorknob, I've convinced myself I'm excited to see him again. Truly.

But it's not Jack's familiar face when I open the door.

It's Angela Indelicato's.

"Oh, I'm so glad you're home," Angela trills. "Loretta was telling me she'd heard some noises in here when she passed by to get the mail earlier, then I heard the shower running a few hours ago, but I ain't heard anything since, so I didn't know if you were home. Don't you look pretty in that red dress? I don't think I ever saw you look so wonderful. Turn around and let me see you, honey. My, my, my. You're a sight." Her round face plumps up as she smiles, and her eyes almost disappear. She lifts a hand to her own gray hair, caught up in its usual black net, as if remembering a time when she, too, dressed up for her husband.

"Listen, honey..." She bustles her way in the door, closes it behind her, quickly scans the room, and lifts her nose to the air as if figuring out precisely what I'm making for supper. "Loretta and me, we've been talking, and we know the Mister ain't home, right?" Her eyes dart as if ready to seek Jack out beneath a couch or behind a closet door.

I shake my head, adrenaline still rushing through my body. I don't quite understand why Angela is in my apartment.

"Since he ain't home and since we kind of get sick of each other sometimes." She cackles with delight. "Well, we thought it might be nice if we three girls share dinner next week." Pauses, hands in her apron pockets, smiling expectantly at me.

"Next week?"

"Thanksgiving, Honey. It's next Thursday, and we'd be pleased as punch if you'd come over and spend it with us."

"Oh, no...I couldn't...really...Jack..."

"But of course, you could, and you will! You'll come right next door next Thursday around noon, and we'll have a little glass of Manischewitz and visit for a while." She winks and elbows me. "And around two, we'll have the bird and all the fixings. It's going to be fun. Lots of fun. And good for you. You need to get out more." Patting me on the arm, Angela does a last scan of the apartment and moves toward the door—almost reluctantly.

By now, I've recovered enough to usher the old lady out while thinking: *If Jack comes home, no, he'll think I'm telling the neighbors all our business, and I don't want him to think that. No, no, no.*

As the door shuts behind Angela's flurry of activity, I retreat into the apartment, which has suddenly grown colder. With a jolt that makes me place my hand on my fluttering chest, I realize I never want to grow old alone.

Angela is the only person who comes into my apartment for the rest of the evening.

Jack must be celebrating with that blonde woman; I think as I pull the red dress over my head and hang it back up in the closet. He must be having a cake she made, letting her sing Happy Birthday to him, I think as I peel the nylon stockings from my legs. He must have meant it when he said he was gone for good, I think as I pull on my old flannel nightgown and burrow beneath the covers with my hot water bottle.

I think maybe I'm officially alone as I watch the traffic lights at the top of my window until the darkness takes over.

When the television woke me up blaring "The Star Spangled Banner," I gathered the crocheted throw around my waist and padded from light to light, extinguishing them all and finally acknowledging defeat.

The Silent Wall

5:30 P.M.

"Well, what'd she say?" Loretta comes out of the bathroom, drying her hands on a towel. She has just taken a bath and wears her terrycloth robe tied in the back like a geisha. Her hair is wrapped up in a towel and the effect tightens her skin, making her look much younger than her fifty-six years.

"Not much. She was all dressed up like a French whore, though. Some red and black thing. Like she was expecting him to come home." Angela returns to the stove and checks the cornbread in the oven. The toothpick comes out clean, so she takes the pan out and sets it on the hotplate. "Poor kid really seems to think he's coming back. I wanted to tell her real bad, but I could smell supper, and there were candles and two plates on the table in the kitchen."

Their kitchen table is awash in newspapers. It's Thursday—supermarket day in the newspaper—Angela has been clipping coupons, and Loretta's been doing the crossword puzzle. She moves the stack now, sits down, pulls the puzzle in front of her, and fills in a couple of blanks. The house is silent for a moment, and then she looks up at her sister. "Are you sure you want to have this girl over for Thanksgiving?"

Angela pauses. "I'm surprised you don't want to have the poor thing over for a meal. Wouldn't you want to be with someone on the holidays?"

"I think we're asking for problems."

Now they're staring at each other, and it's unnecessary to put what they're thinking into words, but Angela doesn't like blank spaces. "What kind of problems?"

Loretta raises thick eyebrows and looks at the wall separating the two apartments—the wall against which Jack Robbins threw plenty of dishes, bottles, and occasionally his wife—the one that has been silent since he left.

"What kind of problems?" Angela asks again, her patience with her sister fading as quickly as the light outside the windows. The snowflakes enlarge and begin accumulating against the window frames.

"You know."

"No, I don't, my dear. Why don't you tell me?" Can't keep the sarcastic tone out of her voice.

"Men like that..."

"And how would you know about men like that? You haven't been physically near a man since—"

Loretta puts up a warning hand. For a few moments, they stare each other down: Loretta's hand still up, Angela's eyes clouded with anger, but then they both back off, retreating from each other, not wanting to talk about what brought them together—and has also forced them apart.

All-Points Bulletin

Wednesday, November 20, 1957

Graham shrugs into his jacket, zips it up, then settles his hat on his head. As always, he checks the mirror, touches the brim of the hat, and feels the indescribable pride that he does every time he sees his reflection, the badge on the hat shining with his number: 851. Frankie's mumbling something into his locker. He probably busted another button off his shirt. It's only a matter of time before the man realizes he needs to get a larger uniform, but Frank has insisted that his wife has been shrinking his clothes for the past couple of months.

They worked late a week ago, running the fingerprints from Jack Robbins' truck. As they had expected, Robbins' fingerprints were all over the truck's cab, and another set—smaller and female—was everywhere, including several sets on the steering wheel. Between the fingerprints and the blood spatters on the front bumper that matched Cindy Gurdon's, there wasn't much question that Robbins was the hit-and-run driver, not that Graham and Frank had any doubts about it.

When he came in for his shift, Graham talked to the sergeant, and they put out the arrest warrant for Robbins. Maybe once he's brought in, the pressure will be off both the Gordon family and Beth Robbins. Though he hasn't told anyone, Graham has spent some of his off hours looking for Robbins, has interviewed a couple of guys at the Navy Yard, and has been searching for the red Cadillac Beth Robbins referred to, but so far, no luck. The guy has done an excellent job of disappearing.

Good thing he didn't kill that little girl.

The Hope Chest

Thursday, November 21, 1957

I've turned the heat down, hoping to make the oil last. Thankfully, we'd filled the tank shortly before the accident, so I should have enough to keep the place heated for a little longer. But the apartment has become bitterly cold, forcing me to dig deep in the hope chest at the foot of my bed, searching for the wool blankets I know are under the paper-wrapped packages on the top. My bed quilts just aren't doing the trick anymore. I need as many layers of blankets as I can pile on the bed to stay warm.

When I find a thick, Army-green one, I wrap it around my shoulders and will myself to stop shivering. While I'm into the hope chest, this is as good a time as any to look for more things to pawn. Though I have very few items of value (my wedding ring is the only thing I own that is of any worth at all, and, knowing Jack, he got it at a bargain price, then spent the rest on beer), I have saved some of Mama's family heirlooms. It's the only way to remember my mother's family: grandmother and grandfather, one aunt. On my father's side, no one was alive when I was growing up except a few distant cousins who lived on a farm in western Massachusetts. I've lost track of them; I was never close to them.

Against my chin, the blanket smells musty but familiar, bringing back unbidden memories.

Jack's laughter that day we went to New Hampshire for a picnic. We rode through the White Mountains until we found the perfect place. Tall emerald green pines, a river rushing over bronze boulders softened by time, the light coming through the trees like heaven. Spread out the blanket and sat down, but no picnic basket. He'd been in such a rush to leave—come on, Beth, hurry up, Beth. Are you ever going to get out of that bathroom, dammit?—we'd left the picnic basket on the kitchen table. Didn't we laugh. And the love afterward.

One of the few times he whispered how much he loved me. Now, those words fall as cold and bristle as this November afternoon.

I sift through the paper-wrapped items, unable to remember what they are. Then, reverently, I unwrap each and, with my fingertip, trace the medals Jack won for his service in Korea: the crossed swords, the Purple Heart, his stripes and stars, the bronze star, and his uniform, still creased and ready for war. I bury my face in the shirt, hoping for a trace of his smell, but the fabric smells of mothballs and other old things.

In a box near the bottom of the chest, I know there is a stack of letters: mine, sent to Jack while he was in Korea. He came home with them in the bottom of his duffle bag. All neatly folded. Some pages were worn through as if they'd gone into battle with him. Others crinkled with what he called "soldiers' tears." He said he had read the letters so much that they had become invisible. How appropriate. The way he made me feel. When I had originally unpacked them from his duffle bag over four years ago, my words on those thin pages brought tears to my eyes, and I realized then how much he'd loved me. Or so it seemed. Maybe it was just the memory of me that he liked, because when he came home, he seemed disappointed with the reality of being with me daily. Sometimes, he looked at me as if he'd made some horrible mistake he couldn't fix.

I sit back on my heels and think about how he'd pushed past me when he left home the night after the accident. The Jack I knew before he left for Korea has disappeared completely, and I often wonder whether it's the war that took him from me or whether he would have been like this, anyway. I open the first envelope. The smell of old roses mixed with dust wafts into the air.

June 11, 1952

Dear Jack,

I've never thought I'd miss anyone as much as I miss you. Today, I saw Susan at the park, and she told me that Bill was coming home in a week. Forgive me for saying this. I wish it were you, Jack. Even though Bill is coming home because he was shot, I wish it was you instead of him.

I can't continue reading the words I wrote. It's wise not to touch the rest of the letters now. I know them all by heart, anyway. What's the use of digging them out and making myself feel worse than I already do? It's excruciating to be reminded of this stuff when Jack didn't show up last night…I didn't sleep well, and I woke up feeling pretty drained. I'm not sure how to think about him anymore.

Shifting, I wrap the blanket tighter around me and dig into the other side of the hope chest instead, where I keep my childhood treasures. There's a doll in here some place: a small Japanese doll Jack sent to me for Christmas the year before he came home. It's not something I can pawn, but I can bring it to the hospital this afternoon and give it to Cindy.

The tips of my fingers hit the wax paper that had covered the doll, and I moved it aside. Mama's English teapot and her sterling silver sugar and creamer set are there. Maybe the old pawnbroker might give me something for them. But I'm not ready to sell them. I take the doll out and place it on the floor beside me, rearranging my mother's items and Jack's Army mementos, then squeeze everything back into the hope chest and close it, relegating the memories to stay in that mothball and cedar haven.

When I get to the hospital about an hour later, I place the doll on Cindy's hospital bed, smooth its skirt, and quietly say, "This doll comes all the way from Japan, Cindy. Her dress is called a kimono, and her shoes are sandals. The Japanese people take their shoes off when entering someone's house. And all their windows are made of something called rice paper."

I'm not thinking clearly, just randomly repeating the bits of information Jack gave me about the doll so that I'll have something to say. It's painfully clear that Cindy doesn't hear a word, but Theresa Gordon is sitting in the chair in the corner, and the woman has listened to every word.

"Your husband gave you that doll, didn't you?" Theresa says.

"Yes, he did…"

"I don't want Cindy to have it if it came from him."

Reaching out, I touch the doll and remember the moment he gave it to me. I asked him why a doll. Why not a jewelry box or a kimono? He'd said that's what most of the other guys brought home for their girls.

I honestly can't blame Theresa for not wanting this. At this point, I don't either. "It's not from Jack. It's from me. I wanted to bring something up, and that's all I had."

Theresa is silent. Her husband is not there. She already told me he had to go back to work because everyone else needed to eat, and he's enjoying his new role in the kitchen, cooking all kinds of omelets, spaghetti and tuna casseroles, and fancy hot dogs.

"I guess it's okay then," Theresa shifts in the chair. She wears pink slippers, and her stockings rolled below the knee as if she were home in her own kitchen. The oversized gray wool sweater slung over her blue plaid housedress used to be her husband's. "Just don't tell Bill, okay? He wants to kill that husband of yours."

Uncomfortable, I stand beside the bed. *Do I sit down? Should I ask?* Without thinking, I brush back a strand of hair on Cindy's forehead. There's a scratch beneath her hair on the left side of her forehead, the only visible sign of the accident that has damaged so much inside her body. It's not much of a scratch. It's a jagged line down her forehead hairline, not the gash you would expect her to have, considering she's in a coma. Yet that tiny scratch hides the reality that the child's internal organs are so traumatized that some of them have been stunned into silence. "Like when little birds slam into windows they don't see," Theresa says. "They flop down on the ground and look dead but give them a moment or two to catch their breath, and they're up and flying away."

"It's really hard to sit here day in and day out and not know whether my little girl will wake up. Sometimes, I'd like to kill that husband of yours with my bare hands." Theresa's comments are sharp, but her voice is tired. She's making statements, not launching a war.

I don't reply and hate myself for it, but *what's the sense of saying something now? Will it miraculously fix everything so that life goes back to normal? Will saying something now make matters worse?*

"Why'd you come up here, anyway?" Theresa asks, her voice gruff and curt, almost suspicious.

"I just want to make sure she's okay."

"She's not. She never will be. Even if she opens her eyes, even if she learns how to talk again, how to walk, she'll never be the same."

"I know that." *God, do I know that.*

"Your husband's going to pay for this someday. The cops'll find him, and they'll arrest him. Then he's going to jail. He'll pay for it."

I study my fingernails, bitten to the quick and red around the edges. She's right. Jack should pay, but so should I. I should have stopped him. Maybe I should have left him in that barroom. Let someone else take care of him. *That's mean, Beth.*

Theresa turns her gaze to the nurses' station. All three floor nurses are there doing their reports. Behind the glass window, their white caps bob up and down like sailboats on a choppy sea.

"The nurses here, they're great. I couldn't ask for any better," Theresa says, though I haven't asked. She's repeating herself, but that doesn't matter.

"Yes, I know," I say. "They took care of my gram, then they tried to save my mom and my dad."

"What happened to them?"

The directness of the question stuns me for a moment. I've never had to repeat the stories about how the three most influential people in my life died, and I don't know how to put that pain into words, but Theresa is watching me expectantly.

"Gram died from a stroke. Mama..." I take a deep breath and avert my eyes. "She took her own life. Slit her wrists. They couldn't do much for her. And Dad, he had a heart attack. The nurses were great with him. They made sure he was comfortable, but then he had a second one, and he was gone..."

"Sheesh. That's awful. I haven't lost anyone. I can't imagine what it would feel like..." Theresa looks at the bed and her silent, fair-haired daughter.

"I miss them. Mama and Dad."

"I can imagine. Any sisters or brothers?"

"No, I'm the only one."

For the next fifteen minutes, Theresa asks questions, and I go through the motions of answering her. She asks about my family. What were they like? What did my father do? She asks me to describe my mother and my grandmother. She coaxes me into sharing memories I haven't told anyone, and soon, I'm laughing, telling stories about Dad's funny voices and Mama's beautiful hands, how she used to make the most intricately embroidered pillowcases. An hour goes by, and I relax in the chair.

Then, the conversation switches to husbands.

"I don't know how you can deal with a guy who hits a kid and leaves, you know?" Theresa wrinkles back her lip and brings her eyebrows together. "I can tell you're pretty upset about it, and now that I think about it, I'm glad you're here. You seem like a nice enough sort. But I'd be a raving lunatic by now if I were you. I'd be ready to kill the guy."

"He left with another woman," I yell and instantly regret saying it when I realize what kind of light this casts on Jack. *But why should I worry about him? He's the one who left. He's the drunk who cheated on me. He beat me. He threatened to kill me. I can't believe I'm defending him.*

"That bastard!"

"I think he might have been seeing her before. For a while now. I think he started seeing her a year ago…" It's the first time I've admitted this. Saying it aloud makes me unexpectedly angry. And embarrassed.

"And he hasn't been back to work either, has he? The cops told me they can't find him."

I shake my head. "The women next door, my neighbors, the Indelicato sisters, they've invited me over for Thanksgiving because they know Jack's not around, but I'm not sure I should go. I thought he'd be home for his birthday, but he wasn't, so maybe he'll come home for Thanksgiving…"

"Why would you want him to? I'd tell the bastard to go to hell." Theresa slaps her hand on her knee. Her mouth twists with words she chooses not to voice. She stops for a moment and fixes me in her gaze. "If he does come back, would you tell me?" Leaning forward, walnut brown eyes anxious and pleading, she takes my hands.

I want to say yes, but that would be telling another lie, and there have been enough lies. This has to stop. I pull back.

"I understand…" Theresa drops my hands. "You'd be torn between what's right and your husband. But look at it this way, Beth, you'd be helping him. Better that he comes forward and confesses. The longer he waits, the more the courts will throw at him."

We stay silent momentarily while the nurses check Cindy's vital signs. I think about leaving the room, about how wrong this is, about how I'm only making things worse by letting this friendship charade continue. *When the hell are you going to level with these people? When are you going to own up to what you've done? When Cindy gets better? When she's out of danger? I'll do it then.*

"I grew up in a big family. Thanksgiving was always my favorite holiday." Theresa settles back in the chair and wipes her hand over her weary eyes. "Turkey, ham, roast beef. Piles of pies. My mom always cooks my favorite buttered turnip. Not this year, though. This year, we'll be eating hospital food."

"Maybe there'll be some leftovers, and I can bring you some...."

"Oh, no, don't you worry about that. There'll be plenty of food here from my family. They live a ways away, out past Peabody, but they'll come down for the holidays. My sisters will take care of me. All of us."

"I always wished I had a sister."

"Don't know what I'd do without mine. They're saints. All of them have been calling and asking if I need anything. When they get here, they'll be cooking up a storm. Those girls make the best food you've had east of the Rocky Mountains."

We talk about the difference between having holidays with family or with friends. I share my reluctance to go to the Indelicato's. An excellent listener, Theresa nods in all the right places and shares her own stories about growing up, stories about her kids, especially Cindy.

Then, and I can't figure out how, I'm suddenly telling Theresa that I don't know how I will pay the bills without Jack's paycheck coming in, and Theresa, like a good friend, offers her condolences.

"You should probably go to the bank and see if they'll let you get the money out of the checking account. It's your money as much as it is his, and if he wants to leave you holding the bag—the rat—then you have a right to at least be able to pay the bills. That's his job, y'know—to take care of you. You are his wife. No matter what else he does, you're his wife," Theresa says as she nods to the nurse headed down the corridor past them. "That's what I'd do. For sure. I wouldn't let any guy get away with what that husband of yours has done to you."

Theresa and I are now pacing the hall outside Cindy's room. The afternoon sunlight has faded, and shadows in the far corners of the hall have deepened. Theresa doesn't seem in any way eager for me to go home. She's already said the kids are with her sister, and there's no way she can stay at the house alone. "I'm going stir crazy." She can't leave her baby alone, especially since Cindy has yet to wake up. "They say she's healing, and she could wake up, say something, be looking for me. Anytime."

Walking along the hallway arm-in-arm like friends, I realize I'm the only thing keeping Theresa awake. My mission now becomes: keep Theresa talking and moving, no matter what.

"I didn't think I'd ever be in a position like this," I say, meaning the accident and how damn guilty I feel, but I know she won't understand.

Theresa nods. "One of my sisters married a no-good manager at Filene's, and he took off in the middle of the night after wiping their bank account out earlier that day. Left her with nothing but three kids in diapers. My Bill says that's the worst kind of man, the kind that deserts his family and leaves them with shit." She laughs shortly and harshly, then casts a guilty glance back at her daughter as if finding something funny is sacrilegious.

We pass a room where a large oxygen tank makes rhythmical breathing noises for its patient, a skeleton of a man who calls out to us incoherently. The nurse in the station rises and calls out, "I'm on my way, Mr. Duffy."

"I've got enough stuff to sell, I think," I tell Theresa. "Maybe I can make enough money for the bills. Maybe I can be okay until he gets back." I fiddle with the buttons on my sweater and fight the hot flush creeping up my neck.

"You need to check with the bank and see what money he left in the checkbook." Theresa spins on her heel and heads in the other direction.

"I did, but I can't go to the bank and ask for the money," I answer as I shuffle to catch up with her. "Jack wouldn't be happy if he came home and found out I went through his checkbook. He doesn't like that." Yesterday, they shut off the phone, and Mr. Fits told me when he saw me in the hall not to forget that the rent would be due again in a couple of days. All of it makes me petrified, paying bills with no money coming, and somehow, during the conversation with Theresa, I find the strength to share that fear. It's a minor miracle to have a friend to talk to and one I embrace, like a sailor hanging onto a worn-out life preserver in a raging sea. *(Given the circumstances, I don't think that's too dramatic.)*

"Who cares whether he'd like it? He lost that right when he left, didn't he?" Theresa's strident voice echoes through the hallway.

The red-haired Irish nurse at the desk turns to stare, finger to her lips. Theresa waves her away, grabs my arm, and pulls me close.

"He's the one who left, remember?" she whispers. "You have every right to be able to buy some food or pay the bills. If he'd wanted that money, don't you think he'd have taken it when he ran out on you?"

We walk a few more steps, still arm in arm, yet silent. I like to believe that Jack didn't plan on leaving. He was just scared, and that's probably why he didn't take anything. He didn't go for the same reason Theresa thinks he did. He didn't leave because of the accident. That's on me. He left for the blonde woman in the Cadillac. The accident just provided him a convenient excuse.

But that's something I'm not ready to share. Not yet.

It feels good having someone to talk to, someone who needs me as much as I need her. I wonder what everyone thinks as they walk by. Two women, heads close together, talking earnestly about essential things, sharing their lives. Are they seeing us as friends? Is Theresa?

"Seriously, Beth," Theresa keeps her voice low, but her eyes slide to the side as they pass by Cindy's room. No change. The room is dimly lit. Low-hanging bottles of blood and other life-preserving liquids all connect to the little bump in the middle of the bed. Theresa sighs, and we keep moving. "You need to go to that bank tomorrow. Get your money to pay for the phone and the heat. No matter how low you keep the thermostat, it's nothing compared to how cold you'll be once it gets shut off. Believe me, I know. I remember one winter when we had that big storm—Remember that? Couple years ago? Plows out for four days straight, and no one had power. No way we could stay warm, no matter what we did. I remember Bill got the worst cold and Cindy, well, we thought we might have to rush her to the hospital. She had such a bad asthma attack." She "tsk, tsks," and shakes her head. Her eyes fill up.

Don't cry. Don't cry about Cindy. Not now. Please. What can I do to make it better? How can I turn back the clock?

I hold tighter to Theresa's arm. She turns and smiles wanly, probably thinking she's being comforted. But it's my fear that makes me grasp her.

I've had nightmares of going to jail, being locked up in a tiny cell, thousands of voices taunting me, calling me dirty names, telling me I killed Cindy, left her to bleed in the middle of the road, lied to the police, sent my husband away, that I'm no good, worthless, and should be sent to the electric chair. The nightmare's effect lasts well into the next day, and I have flashbacks of the accident. Of the cell I'd have to stay in, a box of a place, smelling of urine and pain, and a ball of panic rises in my chest, chokes off my air supply, makes me break out in a cold sweat even though it's below freezing outside, and I realize I can't go to jail, can't face being in court, can't face the cops again.

I concentrate on what I *can* do. I can talk to Theresa, bring gifts for Cindy, and try to act like life will go on without Jack.

It will.

It will, soon.

It has to.

An Independent Woman

Friday, November 22, 1957

Heart pounding, I stride into the Everett Independent Savings Bank, plunk my purse on the nearest mahogany desk, and approach the clerk—a skinny, gray-haired woman wearing rhinestone-studded gray eyeglasses that match the severe gray suit she wears.

"My husband has an account here. We want to get some money out of it. I don't have the checkbook with me. Can you help?" I hold my breath after blurting out the words, thinking that if I don't breathe, no one will guess that I haven't asked Jack for permission to take out some money. And that he'll be furious when he finds out what I've done. *Tough. He should have thought about it before he left.*

But a little voice in the back of my mind keeps saying that I have every right to this money, every right to keep food in my belly and a roof over my head when my husband isn't doing it for me, and that little voice belongs to my new friend, Theresa. The fact that I can call Theresa a friend thrills me to no end and gives me the strength to pull back my shoulders and release the breath I've been holding.

The clerk glances up at me and curls her lips up, imitating a smile, an obviously painful gesture. "And your name is?"

"Robbins. Elizabeth Robbins. The account is in my husband's name. Jack. John Robbins. That's his given name, you know. John Edward Robbins. But he always likes being called Jack." I shift from one foot to the other and force a smile. A wave of heat rises from within my clothing. I'm wearing enough wool to keep me warm for the brisk walk down Broadway, but far too much for the bank's heated lobby. The hair on the nape of my neck is soaking wet.

The clerk nods as if she couldn't care less what Jack calls himself and turns away to shuffle through some account cards in one of the desk drawers. Her gray herringbone dress clutches her shoulders and stretches one way, then another, as she flips her fingers through the account cards before finally pulling one out. "Account opened three years ago?"

I nod, though I have no idea when Jack opened this account. People around me are waiting in lines that crisscross the white marble floor. Customers sit in front of large mahogany desks, talking to clerks who look much like the one I'm talking to: gray suits, glasses, chignons at the back of their necks. Oddly, this formal, library-like place is where Jack keeps his money. I can't see him here interacting with the bank personnel or standing in line patiently to cash his weekly paycheck.

"Can you give me your current address, please?" The clerk doesn't lift her gaze from the card before her.

"Chestnut Hill Apartments, Broadway. Here in Everett. You know that building at the top of the hill by the pharmacy? Near the A&P?" I point north, but it doesn't matter. The clerk has already walked away. She comes back seconds later, a yellow slip in her hand.

"I've filled in the account number for you, Mrs. Robbins. All you have to do is fill in the amount you want to withdraw and your husband's social security number, sign your name over your husband's name, and then go to that window." She points to a black wrought-iron cage against the far wall. "And make your withdrawal. Good day." Without losing a beat, she returns to her black Remington typewriter and begins pounding the keys.

This is too easy. Theresa must have been right when she told me that everything a husband has belongs to his wife and vice versa.

Seconds pass into moments as I'm whisked through the withdrawal process by another bored clerk and thanked for my business. After she hands me the money, I walk numbly through the bank's cavernous and somber lobby into the chilling slap of the November afternoon wind.

Stunned.

Breathless.

Amazed I had the guts to pull that off.

And I'm now $131.82 richer, enough to pay the rent for two more weeks and have enough left over for food, electricity, and phone—though I might not turn it back on. I don't want to give Jack a way to contact me.

I walk up Broadway's long, sloping hill against the wind, keeping my mouth closed and my head down. The last of the season's leaves whirl around my feet, chilling my legs. I should find Jack's old Navy pants and tailor them so I can wear them. Winter hasn't kicked in, and I'm already tired of being cold.

When I return to the apartment, I slip off my shoes, turn on the TV, and flex my toes to warm them. As I reach next to the door for my slippers and slide them on my feet, Burns and Allen are joking about what they will have for dinner. Sighing, I lean against the kitchen doorjamb, close my eyes briefly, and smile when Gracie says, "Well, George, I simply don't know."

"You tell him, Gracie," I say as I unpack the bag of groceries I picked up on the way home—feeling rich—and slide the small bag of rice onto the top shelf in the corner cupboard and take a good strong inhale of the fresh butter-and-egg bread before placing it in the green breadbox on the counter.

I hum the show's theme song, shrug out of my coat, lay it over the back of the kitchen chair to dry a bit, and then push up my sweater sleeves.

Who was that person in the bank? Was that me? Did I really do that?

The apartment is still cold, but I feel surprisingly warm. Probably the exertion of almost running all the way home. I'm also still relishing the satisfaction I got from stopping Mr. Fits in the hallway and pressing the rent money into his fat little fist, seeing the surprised look on his face when I triumphantly stated that was the money for next week. A week ahead! I'm paying the bills!

As I laugh out loud about that now, my chest expands, and I'm sure everything will turn out all right. It feels so good that I dance right out of the apartment and am in front of the Indelicato sisters' door, rapping smartly on it, before I realize what I've done. But I recover nicely, if I say so myself, when the other sister—*Loretta*—answers the door.

"I just came to see what I could bring over for Thanksgiving dinner," I say.

Where did I get the guts to do this?

Loretta appears as unsure as I am and holds the door with both hands curved around the jamb, her nose against the wood. She looks odd, like a picture of Kilroy. "I don't have any idea. Let me get my sister. She's the cook." Disappears. "ANGELA! The girl from next door is here!"

In the damp hallway, I pull my sweater sleeves down to my wrists again, arrange my hair over my cheek, and listen to Angela Indelicato's solid steps as she comes to the door, thrusts it wide open, and stands there with a silly grin on her face.

"Well, if it isn't little Beth Robbins! Come in! Come in!" She ushers me inside, where it's warm and smells like corned beef and cabbage. Her hair clings to her forehead in damp crinkles, sneaking out from beneath the net she always wears. Her cheeks are pink and shiny, like the nesting dolls Nana used to put out at Christmastime.

"Loretta, pour a cup of tea for all of us, would ya?"

She turns to me. "Sit! Sit! Sit! It's so good to see you at home. You'd been gone so much lately that I wondered whether you might have disappeared like your hubby did!" She cackles as if she's made a joke fit for "I Love Lucy."

Loretta slides a steaming cup of tea in front of me, though I have no intention of even coming to the ladies' apartment, never mind sitting down to visit. A plate of shortbread cookies appears out of nowhere.

Angela doesn't quit talking, even after she's asked me three questions requiring answers I haven't given. She keeps going on and on about how long Jack has been gone, what the weather's been like since then, and how she saw an accident down the hill towards Glendale Square when she was looking out the window the other day, the same day she saw me head off up the hill towards Chestnut Street, and what it's been like to walk past my apartment door and want to knock on the door to see how I am. "How have you been, anyway?" She hopes I've been well because a horrid influenza is going around. Mrs. Lord had it last week and sent her husband to the pharmacy twice for medicine.

Finally, she stops chitchatting long enough for me to insert, "I came over to ask what I can bring for Thanksgiving."

"Oh, just yourself, honey." Angela pats me on the hand as if she's the old lady in the woods and I'm Gretel. "Just bring your little old self."

"Wouldn't hurt if she could bring a pie or something. Kinda chip in," Loretta pipes up from behind her sister. She stares at Angela's back boldly—a challenge.

"You don't ask guests to bring something to Thanksgiving dinner," Angela retorts, a smile on her lips, but her brows knit together as she avoids her sister's gaze. "That kind of ruins the invitation. After all, it's the day we share with others. That's tradition."

"She offered."

"You just bring yourself, dear," Angela says to me and again pats my hand. This time, she's the grandmother who smells like bread and Ivory Soap.

"If you want to bring a pie, it's okay. I like apple myself." Loretta clunks her teacup back into its saucer.

Silence.

Angela slowly turns to give Loretta a menacing, straight-lipped warning. The air in the kitchen stops moving. I swear some of the dust particles are frozen in time. Nothing is said for an endless moment; no one moves, not one eye blinks. Then Angela gathers the cups and saucers on the table and, without losing eye contact with her sister, says, "Well, you bring whatever makes you happy, Beth, and we'll be quite pleased with your generosity. Won't we, Loretta?"

Loretta's response is a cryptic grunt, and she abruptly pushes her chair back with both feet, leaving me to ponder the hidden meaning behind her actions.

Angela's swift intervention is a welcome relief, guiding me out the same way I had entered. With a warm smile and a reassuring "We'll see you Thursday," the door closes, and I find myself back in the hallway, my mind swirling with unanswered questions.

Speaking a Language You Don't Understand

Saturday, November 23, 1957

A cold drizzle falls softly like the murmur of a bird's wings against the windows. Moments of quiet void of family arguments, the clatter of pots and pans, and the pounding of children's feet against the bare wood floors— are rare in the household, and Graham relishes being able to hear the shushing cars as they pass by below the window of his mother's house.

Everyone has eaten and gone home or disappeared to other parts of the house, leaving him to solitude and his book, John F. Kennedy's *Profiles in Courage*. It's Graham's second time reading the text, and he's reminded that Jack—Senator Jack—is determined to share his pride for his country and his admiration for those who came before him. There are moments in everyone's life when you become determined to make a change, Kennedy says, and if you can rise to the occasion, you can divert the course of a war or display incredible acts of courage. Graham knows that one person can indeed make a difference. One person can change the lives of others.

He holds his finger in the section on Daniel Webster (one of his favorites) and folds the book over his hand as he thinks about how far his family has come since the days of slavery—and of how much more is yet to come.

Dad bragged constantly about being part of the 369th Infantry during the First World War, though everyone in the family knew he saw little action beyond playing his trombone in the Infantry's band. He told everyone that music ran in the family since all the boys played an instrument of some kind, and all the women had voices that soared above everyone else's in church choirs.

Graham chuckles with the memory of his father's voice, drumming his fingers against the book. He's the only one with no musical talents. The best he can do is drum his fingers or nod his head to keep beat with the gospel songs his family fills this house with whenever more than two of them are in the same room together. In a way, what Dad did by breaking the color barrier and getting into the war through music paved the way for Graham's military service and his membership in the same infantry unit. This service prepared him for a different kind of war: the one held in the police station daily.

Though Graham tries not to spend a lot of time thinking about how he has been treated by the people he grew up with in Everett and focuses more on what could be ahead, he wishes others could see him for who he is, that human being, that person who loves books and can't sing; the man who can remember all the details about a historical event; that person who admires Lincoln and Kennedy and Roosevelt and George Washington Carver; and the man who knows what it means to be surrounded by people who speak a language he doesn't understand. He's the person who longs for justice and for the freedom to defend that justice. He's also the person who'd love to share himself with a woman who loves him. He thinks about that more often than he'd admit, even to those family members and friends who know him best.

"What are you doing, son? You look like you're out there by the moon someplace." His mother's soft laugh precedes her scent—a mixture of the coconut oil she uses on her skin and the spicy chicken she cooks for the extended family that fills her tiny house every weekend. She plumps the pillows in the chair beside him and gestures toward the window. "Good day for a book and a hot cuppa tea, I always say. November rain. Nothin' colder or more miserable. *Brr.* Glad I don't have to go out in it."

He smiles at her, thinking she's a marvel: short, bristly, stocky and square like a bulldog, and just as challenging. All her children know her to be strong, yet when she's with her grandchildren, she giggles as much as they do. Wiping her hands on her worn cotton apron, she shakes her head at him.

"When you gonna find yourself a nice woman so you don't have to hang out with your old mother on rainy weekends like this?"

"No one as good as you, Momma. Why should I even bother looking?"

"Man needs a woman. You need to have yourself some little ones. They'll take care of you when you're old and gray." She slaps his knee playfully.

"I don't see anyone taking care of you...when will you let someone do that for you?"

"I ain't old! When I'm old, then we'll worry 'bout it!" Reaching across him, she wipes a speck of dust off the windowsill. "I need to get some Spic 'n Span in here. Those windows need cleanin'."

"Relax, Momma! C'mon, sit down and talk to me a bit." He pats the couch next to him, though she never sits there. Her perch has always been the worn rocking chair in the corner. Everyone teases her it's because she can pop right out of it if she sees something boiling on the stove, and there's seldom a time that the stove burners are off. When they are, the rocker becomes her napping spot.

Arching an eyebrow, she pauses a minute and settles on the edge of the rocker opposite him like a nervous cat. "What do you want to talk about? You got somethin' to tell me?"

"Not really. I just wanted to spend a couple of minutes with my mother. Nothing wrong with that, right?"

"Guess not." Taps her foot. "What's that you're reading?"

"Jack Kennedy's book. *Profiles in Courage.* Just won a Pulitzer."

"He's a nice boy. Doing good things, I hear."

Graham smiles. His mother doesn't read newspapers. Instead, she gets most of her information through her friends at church. "He's going to run for president, I think."

"President? Ain't he kinda young for that? He's your age!"

"He'd be good for us, Momma. We need someone like him. He knows what's right and has no fear. He'll fight for us."

"Guess so. But no politician's gonna change things for you. You got to do that for yourself. I remember your grandma and grandpa always told us kids that there's 'no hill to climb for a stepper.' You have to just put one foot in front of t'other and keep goin' forward. Don't look back. Just focus on what's ahead of you. No one's gonna do that but yourself." Her face is resolute, her lips pressed firmly together, as she nods like she's just made a statement that she's been determined to live by throughout her whole life and has to remind herself to follow every day.

Graham thinks about that and about the struggles she's had, about the many children—her own, her grandchildren, other families' kids — she's raised through the years, and he rises, overcome with love for her, and gives her a quick hug, as he fights back tears. They don't hug often. They're not that kind of family. But when they do, the hugs are strong, the love is real, and the emotion is right below the surface. "Love you, Momma."

"Now, where did that come from? You're gettin' soft on me, boy. Can't go doin' that when you're out there policing the streets. Now, get goin'. Don't you have work to do?" She pushes him away, rises from the rocker, and snaps the dish towel at him.

"I'm off today. No work."

"Go back to your book, then. I got work to do." Stomping out of the room, she disappears into the hallway, humming a little under her breath and leaving him alone again.

Still a little surprised by the emotions brought up by their brief conversation, he settles back into the chair and picks up the book, but his thoughts are diverted. As he gazes out the window, he remembers his last discussion with Frank about the Robbins case, and the nagging need to solve the case comes back to haunt him.

"There were two sets of fingerprints on that steering wheel," Frank had said. "We know one set was Jack Robbins', but the other was smaller. His wife's, maybe? Can't be sure who was actually driving, you know."

Beth Robbins was in the truck that day. They know that. But was she driving her drunk husband home when they hit that child? Or was she trying to pull the wheel away from him?

Family Pictures

Sunday, November 24, 1957

"You can always tell members of my family in pictures. They all smile with their mouths closed, their thin lips pressed tightly together, and their cheeks puffy as if they're holding back a huge chuckle, trying to hold in their giggles because they have bad teeth. But not that they had bad teeth. Just the opposite. All of us Gordons have great teeth, huh, Bill?"

Theresa is half asleep in the green Naugahyde chair in the hospital waiting room, with Bill leaning his head on her shoulder. The kids left only moments before with Theresa's mother, a squat, square, and serious woman—the epitome of a mother with thirteen children.

I hate to see them go. It makes me feel like a mother when I hold the littlest one, two-year-old Elaine, on my lap. Nestling my face against the girl's hair, I take a good strong whiff of the child's scent, sitting there in the hospital chair with my eyes half closed, pretending Jack's sitting directly behind me, that Elaine is ours and that he's chuckling at our child in my lap. I soak in the comfort the child always gives; she makes me feel confident. Having a child on my lap, a living child, a child whose cheeks are rosy, whose hands are warm, helps to stop the corrosion of my soul.

At least temporarily, but you know, Beth, it's just a daydream. If you had your own children, Jack would yell at them and you, never acting warm and cuddly like you imagine he would.

At any other time, I'm sure that I am the most heinous form of human being, and that realization creates a physically unbearable weight on my chest. I don't want that feeling anymore. I would rather cherish this warmth, this feeling of family and love.

Cindy's been in surgery for more than three hours, and I have spent every moment with Theresa and Bill, listening to Theresa as she talks and paces, paces and talks. And I'm nodding now as Theresa tells me her family's history. She has already shown me every photo in her wallet when this conversation originated. One photo was Cindy's last school picture: apple cheeks, bright and beaming for the camera, lips curved upward but closed, as Theresa points out. And then, pointing to each photo as she flips through the glassine inserts: "See? Closed mouth on Bill. Closed-mouth smile on all three of my kids. Closed mouth on me. All of us. Family trait."

A few moments later, Bill is pacing the hallway, smoking a cigarette, and the conversation between Theresa and me in the waiting room has turned to Marilyn Monroe's recent movie, "The Prince and the Showgirl."

"I think she's prettier in this one than in any of the others, don't you?" Theresa holds the magazine she's been reading up for me to see: a two-page spread of photos from the movie; one a luminous portrait of the actress's face, wide-eyed and questioning, a halo around her white-blonde head.

"She's gorgeous," I agree. "I'd give anything to look like her."

Theresa glances into the hallway as Bill goes by; her eyes follow him as he passes, deep in thought, almost as if she's reaching out to touch him with her heart, almost as though she knows exactly what's going through his mind at this very moment, almost as though she, too, is deep in thought. In that second of studying them, I know they are sharing one of those husband-and-wife moments that I never could experience with Jack. I feel a flash of jealousy, but I admonish myself instantly, and it's gone as quickly as it flared. There's no sense in being jealous of someone else's relationship.

"You're plenty pretty," Theresa finally says to me, but it's as if she thought about it too late, and the comment falls flat and hard on the floor between us. That's okay. I know she's just being nice, and I appreciate that, even if she doesn't mean it.

Out in the hallway, a gurney rattles by, a patient connected to life by an intravenous cord flowing with yellow liquid. The nurse's uniform rustles almost as loudly as the wheels.

Then, the hallway is quiet again, except for the steady rhythm of Bill's pacing footsteps.

"It's nine-forty-five." Theresa cracks her knuckles and glances at the clock. "They've been in there a long time. Seems like we would have heard something by now. Don't you think, Honey?" She glances up at her husband and twists her fingers, cracking each finger in succession. Then she turns to me. "I wish they'd let us know what's going on. I just hate waiting. I'm not good at waiting at all."

"No one is," I say. "I'm sure everything's okay. And they'll be out soon." I am not so sure myself, yet I'm accustomed to trying to please Jack, and the reassuring phrases come quickly for me.

Bill walks by again, and Theresa glances at his bent shoulders, saying she's worried about him being worried. Both have a life at stake here: their daughter's. And no one in the world can feel their pain more acutely than the two of them do.

I've got to do something for them to help ease their agony.

"When Cindy's better, let's take everyone to the movies." I keep my voice perky and act cheerfully without seeming obnoxious. It's a feat for me to act, but I do my best. It's my fault they're here in this hospital, to begin with, and my voice rises in tone and pitch as I try to reassure the couple that everything is going to be all right.

It will be, right?

It doesn't work, though. Theresa's lack of response suggests that she's unwilling to make any plans until she finds out what will happen in the next moment, for that moment might permanently change her life.

For two more hours, we share insignificant, inane conversations about movie stars, decorating the house, and stories about the kids and their funniest moments—anything to keep our minds off what the doctors might be doing with Cindy.

At one point, Theresa leans over, voice lowered in confidence, and says, "Y'know, sometimes on a hot summer night, we all just pile in the car and go to the Melrose drive-in for an ice cream cone. The kids like to take a drive in the country. And Bill and I need to cool off. We roll down all the windows, find the shadiest roads, ride for hours, and then finish at the ice cream stand. Cindy always gets chocolate chips with jimmies. I love pistachio. Bill gets raspberry, and the little ones take licks of everyone's. I love those nights. I want more of those nights." Theresa's fist tightens on my knee until I almost cry out in pain.

"You'll get more of those nights," I assure her. *The way it's supposed to be. The way I wanted it with Jack. Rides to the country. Sunday dinners in a big house with a mahogany table set with white napkins. Tucking the kids into bed with stories and singing songs about leaving some cookies for Santa. A family.*

When Cindy has been in the operating room for five hours and twenty minutes, I tell Theresa I'll be right back, and I visit the ladies' room, where I sit on the cool white-and-black tiled floor and hang my head into the toilet, throwing up for ten solid minutes. I don't know whether it's nerves, worry, or the lack of food, but my upset stomach won't settle. After deep breathing and cold, wet pieces of toilet paper across my forehead, I finally feel well enough to return to the waiting room. We've been there for hours, and the room is littered with paper coffee cups and borrowed magazines and newspapers that I'm sifting through, looking for one I haven't read when the doctor walks in the door. He still wears his scrubs, and he's got a little spot of blood on the toe of his white shoe. I can't take my eyes off it.

"Mr. and Mrs. Gordon, may I see you in the hallway?" he asks.

Theresa clutches Bill's arm and moves stiffly toward the door, her frightened eyes on the doctor's somber face. I rise. I want to go with them, but I shouldn't. It's not my place, and they're not my family. I sit back in the chair, sliding my hands under my hips and folding my shoulders like wings.

The doctor closes the door to the waiting room, but his deep, comforting voice reverberates like the rumble of a tympani drum. Through the window, Theresa crumples into Bill's arms, and he stares blankly at the doctor, almost as though the doctor has suddenly become invisible, and Bill can't believe his eyes.

Oh God, don't let Cindy be dead.

For a few seconds, all I can hear is Theresa's anguished wail, which quiets down to a fervent murmur. The Gordons huddle with the doctor in the hallway for another fifteen minutes, and then the doctor pats both on the shoulder, spins on his heel, and disappears.

My stomach cramps as Theresa and Bill, arms around each other's waist, come back through the door into the waiting room.

"We can't see her for a while," Theresa tells me. "They have to bring her out of recovery first. I want to see my baby…" Then she breaks down, sobs into the handkerchief she holds, and, loose-limbed, sinks into the chair next to me and holds on for dear life. Sobbing. Shaking. Mumbling something about taking out Cindy's stomach, putting it on the table, no medication, the primary artery down the spinal column crimped in two places, had to be repaired. None of it makes any sense except the word "coma."

"They don't know whether…if…she's… she will be okay. Whether she's going to make it." Bill stares at the wall, dark circles under his eyes and deep creases around the edges of his mouth, making him appear ten years older than he was a week ago. "Doctor says she's still in a coma, and the first twelve hours are critical. And…." He swallows hard, as if he can't bear rolling the words through his throat. "And even if she does live, he doesn't know whether she'll be…normal."

My heart stops. The blood in my veins has stopped pulsing, and I don't want to breathe.

I am responsible for this. I want to die.

Somehow, I force myself up and out of the chair and do the only thing I can: I hug Theresa and rock her like a baby as she cries. She sobs. Wails for her daughter. And I cry with her. Not for myself—I hate myself right now—but for Cindy. And for the Gordon family. And for their pain.

I could have—I should have — done something about it a long time ago. The only thing I can do now is hug Theresa.

The only thing I can do is to be here for her now.

I'll tell her when Cindy wakes up. I will. I have to.

Apple Pie and Tears

Monday, November 25, 1957

"We did have some cinnamon in here. I know we did." Loretta's voice is muffled, her head in the cupboard below the sink. Her job every Thanksgiving is to make the pies, specifically the apple pie, even if that means delegating the task to someone else. Even though there are only two of them to feed these days, they still cook as though their parents, aunts and uncles, cousins, and Angela's husband are sitting at their usual spots at the dining room table in the Hosmer Street family home. It makes them both feel better about continuing the tradition, even though what's left of the family hasn't gathered in at least five years. In Loretta's heart of hearts, she is secretly pleased that Angela has invited Beth to share dinner with them. At least there'll be some conversation at the dinner table. Angela's meaningless chit-chat is irritating, at best.

"It's there. I swear." Angela continues bustling above Loretta, paying very little attention because she's concentrating on gathering the ingredients for her specialty: a frozen cookie roll that she'll cut up and cook on Thanksgiving morning. She's thinking today that if she mixes up enough, she might have an extra roll to put away for the holiday season. It's nice to have something she can pop into the oven for a quick gift for the postman or even for Mr. Fits, though she can't stand him. If she gives him some sweets during the holiday season, maybe he'll repair the plumbing quickly when it leaks—which is often.

"Found it." Loretta pushes one hand on the floor and huffs hard as she raises herself off her knees. "Why do we put the spices in the lowest cupboard in this kitchen? Would make a helluva lot more sense to have them right next to the stove where we could reach them easily."

Angela doesn't answer. No need to. They've had this conversation many times, and since Angela is the person who usually cooks, she's told Loretta more times than she can count that she wants the spices in the bottom cupboard. "And that," Angela says, "is that. Period. End of story."

Throughout the next hour, the two sisters work silently for the most part, other than the occasional grunt or a request for something to be handed from one side of the kitchen to the other. There's no necessity for discussion. They're at their most relaxed when cooking, and they share an unspoken agreement to skirt around each other rather than say, "Excuse me." It's a dance of sorts. One that family members choreograph without conversation.

When Angela's chocolate chip cookie mix is ready to roll into wax paper casings, she stops and runs the water to take a long drink. She eyes Loretta, who's cutting the Macintosh apples they picked up at the A&P and mixing them with sugar, butter, cinnamon, and maple syrup for the big apple pie she makes every year. "I hope the weather is better for the football game than it has been the past couple of years."

Loretta doesn't miss a beat: "What do you care? When was the last time you went to a football game?"

"That doesn't matter, does it? I'm just hoping it's nice..."

A thump next door interrupts them.

"What was that?" Angela says, reaching for her glass and moving to the wall. She positions herself near the refrigerator where she's always said she gets the best 'reception,' puts the glass on the wall, and cups her hand around the glass and her ear.

"Jack isn't even there, or is he?" Loretta stops what she's doing. Usually, she doesn't care what's going on next door, but with the cops prowling around regularly and knowing that Jack hasn't been there for almost a month, her curiosity is piqued.

"Not that I know of..." Angela whispers, as if the people next door can hear her. "It's Beth. Sounds like she's sobbing."

"Huh. Why would she be crying—unless he's back?"

"I don't hear his voice. It's only her."

Suddenly, Loretta feels as though they're intruding on Beth's privacy, and she's as guilty as Angela for being curious (beyond curious) about what's going on with this girl.

"Get away from the wall, Angela."

"She's throwing stuff," Angela whispers again.

"Get away from the wall."

"Shhhh…"

Loretta washes her hands, grabs the dish towel, and crosses the room to where Angela is still positioned at the wall, with the glass in her hand and her ear against the glass. Loretta grabs Angela's shoulder and pulls her away. "Enough! You need to quit this."

"What's wrong with you? Get your hands off me!"

"This is a sickness. Your obsession to know what's happening with everyone else is driving me crazy. You have to stop."

"You're just as nosy as I am. It makes you feel better if I'm listening and I tell you about it. That way, you're not guilty."

"Not true. Now. Get. Away. From. The. Wall."

Angela squints her eyes and puts her hand up as if threatening Loretta with physical harm if she speaks again. The camaraderie they experienced less than five minutes ago has completely dissipated. Slowly, Angela leans back into the wall, the glass up against it.

For a few moments, there is silence. Then she pulls away. "It's over. Everything's quiet over there. Satisfied?"

Steaming, Loretta goes back to her pie without a word. There are days she gets so angry with Angela that she daydreams about what it would be like to live some place else.

Alone.

Fleeting Images

Tuesday, November 26, 1957

The mailman brings a bill from the Mystic Electric Company and an official-looking envelope from the Charlestown Navy Yard. I open the electric bill and meander down the hallway to my apartment. *Yes, it's my apartment now. I've been here—alone—for three weeks.* I've moved things around and brought out the few pretty things I own. I guess you could say I've done a little redecorating.

The bill is $5.65. I have $107.38 left from what I withdrew from the bank. *Enough to pay this bill and buy more food.* Though I've been managing my own money for only a few weeks, I feel like I'm getting the hang of it. Or at least I'm convincing myself I am. I'm not looking more than a day or so into the future. Any further than that scares me.

It's been two days since Cindy's operation, and the doctors say she's still in a coma while she's healing. I hover at the hospital a couple of times a day—visiting hours are 8-11 a.m., 2-4 p.m., and 5-7 p.m.—and sometimes I don't know how I got there, and I wait for the moment when I'm able to release the horrible fear I keep guarded inside my chest. I feel like I weigh a million pounds as I pull myself through the hallways, standing at the edge of Cindy's room while Theresa cries quietly inside.

Sometimes, all I do is stand in the hall, determined to stay away when Theresa's family or friends are there. They need their time together. I shouldn't even be there. I have no right. Other people, including their families and nurses, ask me too many questions, and I don't want to answer any more about who I am or how I know the family. I want to talk to Theresa and Bill, then walk back home to the apartment and spend the evening there, television on, sketch pad in my lap, drawing portraits from memory, or waiting for the hour when I can return to the hospital again.

An apartment door opens down the hall, and footsteps sound, walking away from my apartment. I don't raise my eyes, still staring at the letter from the Navy Yard, turning it over and over in my hands. *What if it's something important? Something Jack should know about? How will I get hold of him to tell him? But why should I worry? He hasn't bothered to call. Even if he does, I shouldn't tell him anything. He doesn't deserve to know what's going on. Besides, if he cared, he'd still be here.*

I stop, shocked to have thought about Jack in that way. Uncaringly. Harshly. I glance over my shoulder, suddenly afraid I'll find him there, staring at me, reading my thoughts, his anger exploding in the silent hallway.

But he isn't here, of course, and in the next second, I feel a strange mixture of relief and disappointment. If he'd been here, I might have had the courage to ask him what he thought he was doing.

What about our marriage, Jack? What about all the promises? The death do us part, the I love you always and happily ever after. Do I get that? How much more are you going to make me suffer?

My head pounds as I slip into the apartment and quietly close the door, knowing that Angela Indelicato will poke her head out if she knows I'm in the hallway. Though I promised to be there on Thanksgiving, I'm having second thoughts about connecting with those sisters—especially after the other day. I swear I heard them fighting after I left their apartment, and I don't want to be caught in the middle.

Captain Kangaroo's talking to Mr. Green Jeans on the television, so I plop onto the couch and watch the program for a moment, giggling a little at Mr. Green Jeans' unkempt hair and his sidekick, the Dancing Bear, until the weight of the envelope in my hand gets to be too much. A few days ago, I watched "I Love Lucy," and Lucy steamed open a piece of mail for Desi. *Will it work? Will I be able to re-seal the envelope so Jack won't notice?*

The tea kettle takes five minutes to boil and start giving off steam. Trying not to burn my fingers, I hold the envelope's lip down over the white steam, tugging at the corners until they moisten enough to slide my fingernail under and coax the envelope open. The act makes me feel as guilty as a bank robber, and my heart skips a beat when there's a loud noise in the other room—the *television*. I walk back into the living room, sit under the lamplight, and slide the slim letter out of the envelope.

The single page is an official dismissal from his boss, stating that since Jack hasn't shown up for the past couple of weeks, he's fired. It says something about the union. It's nice and neat. Three paragraphs.

Obviously, Jack hasn't called anyone, and he has no intention of coming back. I'm not surprised, and that brings up a wave of disgust that starts in my stomach and rolls up toward my mouth, leaving a sour taste. It's obvious that he's done, and at that moment, I realize I am, too.

The Maxwell House "good to the last drop" commercial comes on the television, reminding me there's still some coffee left in the pot. Maybe it'll take the foul taste out of my mouth. Leaving the letter on the coffee table, I head back into the kitchen, my mind whirling with curiosity and questions that have been unanswered since that first night.

Where did he go? Was that woman in the red Caddy someone he'd been seeing for a while? And why didn't I know about her? Why didn't I figure that out sooner? Am I as stupid as he always said? Yes, I am. I'm silly and guilty as hell. And is she rich enough to support him since he's not working anymore?

Emotions clog my throat and burn my eyes for the millionth time in the past couple of days. Standing in front of the stove, unable to see the pot, I blindly pour the steaming hot coffee into a cup. And I don't care whether I burn myself.

I wrap my fingers around the cup, inhaling the bitter aroma and blowing on it to cool the coffee enough to drink. Another noise—this time, a knock at the door—makes me jump, and the coffee spills down the front of my white sweater, burning my chest. I yelp, peel the sweater off, and the cup clatters on the floor.

"Beth? Open the door. Why the hell doesn't my key work?"

It's Jack. *It's Jack!*

Holding the sweater to my chest, I run to the door without another thought and fling it open. There's my husband in the hall, key in hand, and a surprised expression on his face.

"What the hell are you doing, Beth? God, you're half-dressed. Get in the damn apartment." He pushes past me, grabbing my arm and pulling me with him.

"You're hurting me," I say, shrugging back into the stained sweater.

"Well, think before you answer the door next time," Jack says. He's wearing a new white shirt, crisp and creased, and his black leather shoes are polished as if he's ready to go out dancing.

We stand in the middle of the tiny living room for a moment, close enough to feel the heat from each other's breath, but neither of us moves. Without turning his head, Jack scans the apartment and, finally, stares directly into my eyes. He huffs and turns away as if he can't stand to look at me.

"I need some stuff." He heads into the bedroom, and I follow on his heels. "Clothes, socks, shoes. I'll be out of your hair in a minute." He opens a drawer, turns around, and slams into me as if he's playing football, and I'm the opposing linebacker. I stumble and fall against the cherry bedpost, hitting my tailbone and crying aloud.

"Well, get out of the fucking way, and you won't get hurt." Jack throws an armful of t-shirts and boxers onto the bed, yanks me by my arm, and sends me flying against the wall. This time, he doesn't react when I cry out in pain.

I gather myself from the floor and back out the door into the living room, staying as far away from his reach as possible, retreating behind the couch. "Are you coming back? Or are you gone for good?" I'm not sure how I want him to answer, and to be honest, I'm surprised I even have the strength to ask.

He doesn't answer, fills a duffle bag he must have brought, slings it over his shoulder, and heads for the front door. "If you know what's good for you, you won't tell anyone I was here. You hear me?" He shows me his meaty fist as if reminding me he's not afraid to use it, and then he opens the door and leaves.

The apartment is as cold as if I'd opened all the windows to let the winter air inside.

I sink into the couch, happy that he'd forgotten to ask for a new key. I don't want him to come back. Ever.

Sleeping Beauty

Wednesday, November 27, 1957

Cindy's hospital room is full. Theresa's family is there: her square-faced mother, overweight and very loud father, a couple of bland and blonde sisters, and a brother-in-law (equally nondescript), Theresa's kids, and Bill's parents, quiet and pale, sitting off by themselves as if afraid of the other side of the family. I'm standing near the nurse's station and have been at the hospital with Theresa for hours before anyone else showed up. The doctor called Theresa late last night. "Almost gave me a heart attack to hear the phone ring. Thought Cindy had died. But, no. He'd seen some eye movement and even hoped Cindy would wake up soon, so he wants me and Bill there immediately. Thought you might like to know."

She was still shaking when I walked in at eight-fifteen in the morning. "The first night I went home to see the other kids, the first time I'd been in my own bed for more than a week, and I had to rush right back. Boom! We were at the hospital in less than five minutes. Bill drove like he was shot out of a cannon."

As the day wore on and Cindy remained unconscious, Theresa made some phone calls. One by one, the families came, sure that this was a moment they could all celebrate together. They were sure they'd have something to be thankful for on Thanksgiving. But nothing happened.

As each one arrived, Theresa introduced me. "This is Beth, Jack Robbins' wife." Then quickly added, "She's just as angry about all this as we are. She's been here almost daily with us and hasn't seen her husband. Isn't he rotten to take off on her like that? He's scum! They should string him up and leave him for the vultures!"

I can tell by their eyes that Theresa and Bill's families don't feel the same pity for me that Theresa does. I've been studying people's eyes lately. (*Have you noticed that one eye is always larger than the other? And how people's eyes shift to one side or the other depending on whether they're trying to hide what they're thinking?*). Mama used to say something about the eyes being the windows of the soul, and it has dawned on me that I never looked directly into anyone's eyes. I have always been afraid to see what they're feeling about me, what they think about the ugly way I look. But now, I *want* to see it. I *want* to know. I don't want to be caught unaware again like I was with Jack. Never again. And I firmly believe that if I scrutinize people's eyes, I will see the truth they might not speak aloud.

One of the Intensive Care Unit nurses hurries by, her arms filled with folded white towels. She briefly pauses at the door to Cindy's room and glances in at the crowd around the bed, thinking she should kick them all out and that there are far too many visitors in there, but she shakes her head and keeps going.

It's almost like Theresa and her family believe that if they touch Cindy and let her know they're there, she'll wake up, look around, and instantly return to normal, like Sleeping Beauty. They hover around her bed like hummingbirds pollinating morning glories. I can identify the backs of their heads from where I stand: Theresa's straight and slightly unwashed chestnut brown head huddles with her mother's gray one near the foot of the bed. The two towheaded kids are up in Bill's arms. Theresa's bald father stands against the side wall, feet apart and arms crossed. Her two kerchiefed sisters fuss around and flit from one person to the other while the brother-in-law makes jokes that are a tad inappropriate, and Bill's folks stand to the side, arms linked as if supporting each other, whispering.

I'm not even considering the possibility of being out of place. I'm just there. I am ignored, as I have been by most people in my life. It feels perfectly normal to stand out in the hallway: an observer, not a participant, not a member of the family or someone's wife, no one's mother or sister. Just Beth Robbins. Alone. And quite comfortable with that.

Two hours later, when they all drift away back to their own families, their lives, and their homes, I sit in the quiet waiting room with a sketch pad in my lap filled with portraits of everyone in the room. The drawing of Theresa's mom: her stubby fingers pushing back her glasses, her other hand resting on her stomach. Another of Cindy: A small face amid the folds and curves of the hospital bed sheets. Several kids huddled like little turtles over their coloring books on the floor.

The family has left Bill and Theresa alone with their oldest daughter, peaceful and beautiful in the nest of white sheets, beeping equipment, and snaking vines of intravenous lines. The doctor has come and gone several times. Nurses drift in to administer medication, check vital signs, and see whether the IV is dripping properly.

Still, Cindy hasn't woken up.

I'm about to leave when I hear footsteps behind me and a slight cough. I fold the top of the sketch pad over, always reluctant to share my drawings with someone else, but a dark finger stops the cover.

"You're talented," Officer Jackson says. "Can I see?"

Lowering my eyelids, I breathe in deeply, inhaling both the chilly dampness he brings from outside, and the scent of his starched uniform, and something else: the warm smell of his skin. He's leaning against the chair. I imagine his weight against my back and am surprised by the heat that crawls up my cheeks. Reluctantly, I hand him the sketch pad, and he moves into the seat opposite mine, and I'm now forced to look at him. Focusing on the shiny buttons on his jacket, I ignore his face for a couple of seconds, but when he flips the pages, grunting a little as if surprised by what he sees, I can't help but look up. He's intent on my drawings, his dark brown eyes pausing on each one, studying the lines—I can tell by the way his eyes move that he's taking in all the details, not just glancing at them and moving on or giving them a cursory look that says he doesn't care like someone forced to pay attention when they really would rather be elsewhere. No. He's studying. Analyzing.

His eyelashes make a perfect oval curve against his high cheekbones, his lips are slightly parted, and he's so close that I can see the shades of color between the bottom curve of his lip and the mauve fleshiness of the interior of his mouth. His skin is the color of dark caramel, and it strikes me—once again—that he looks like Jackie Robinson, the baseball player. He's handsome, especially when he smiles.

I'm uncomfortable. But it's a good feeling, not like when Jack is nearby. There was no fear with Graham Jackson, just curiosity.

"These are really good," he says, folding the sketchbook up, then giving it a pat and handing it to me. "Did you go to school for art?"

Shaking my head, I smile a little. "No. I never went past high school."

"You should. This guy does drawings for us occasionally–like when a witness comes in and describes someone we want to identify—he went to a university for art, and now he has a good job. You could probably do something like that."

I nod again. I'd love to go to one of those big fancy European museums and see the great works of art. That's what I'd really love. I want to share that with Graham Jackson, but he'd probably laugh at me. Most people do.

We sit quietly for a moment, and I study my fingers and re-cross my ankles. He coughs.

"I came to see the little girl," he says. "Has she come out of the coma yet?"

Glancing up, I see Theresa and Bill quizzically looking in our direction. "No, she hasn't, but the doctors think she will be okay. Her parents are here..." I gesture toward them.

He rises and goes to greet them. I can't hear them through the glass window, but I imagine from the soft smile on Theresa's face that they're thanking him for coming. I should leave. I really need to get something to eat. But for some reason, I can't move and don't really want to.

The officer stays in the hospital room, nervously turning his hat in his hands for about five minutes. Before he bows out, he places the hat back on his head and returns to the waiting room. I've got my coat on, and I stand. It's time for me to leave. I've been here all day.

"Cold out," he says. "You want a ride home?"

Everything I know tells me to say no. He's a cop. He's investigating my husband. He's a Negro. I'm married. But my head is nodding yes, and soon, I'm following him through the parking lot to the Everett Police sedan parked in the far corner.

It's a brief ride, but in the five minutes, we talk about Cindy, about Thanksgiving (*he's spending it with his family—more than twenty of them—*

and his mother who fries a turkey in oil. Never heard of that), about how much colder it is this year than it was last. Though we don't talk about him, I'm sure we're both thinking about Jack. Throughout the conversation, my mouth might move, and it may seem like I'm talking, but what I'm doing is thinking about Graham Jackson, the man. And about how hard my heart is pounding and how difficult it is to keep from smiling like the Cheshire cat in Alice in Wonderland.

What the heck is happening to me?

Give Thanks, Damnit

Thursday, November 28, 1957

On Thanksgiving morning, I change the sheets on the bed, and I can't resist burying my face in them as I ball them up and shove them inside a pillowcase. I can't stop trying to smell Jack on my bed, even though he hasn't been here for weeks.

For some reason, no matter how dirty or drunk Jack was, he never smelled. Never had that sour, unwashed stench of the men I've known, but there's no scent left, nothing that marks the bedroom as once his, and why should there be? I've changed the sheets three times since he left, and now I'm looking for something that no longer exists, and I'm trying to compare it to the scent of other men who are now in my life: Bill, Graham, the guys at the supermarket, the man at the pawnshop. I can't bury my head in Jack's clothes anymore because he removed them all.

Memories of my father, grandfather, and uncle mingle with thoughts of everyone in my life who's new. My grandfather had his own chair, covered in a nubby brown fabric, stern and unyielding, just like him. A permanent stain lingered where he laid back his head, and a cloud of his cheap peppermint hair tonic hung around the chair itself. My father brought the stench of his cigars into every room he entered—whether he had one lit. And my uncle reeked of pungent whiskey. No matter what time of night or day I saw Uncle Stanley, he always had dragon breath.

But not Jack. He smells like Ivory Soap, even though he usually has a Pabst in his hands.

I have seen women on television who've lost their husbands or boyfriends and know how they cry into their pillows because the pillow always smells like the man they love. That's romantic. I've inhaled Jack's scent from the clothes he left in the hamper, his pillowcase, and the last towel he used. But his trademark aroma dissipated after he left. The smell I loved was gone as quickly as the man himself.

I bring the clean sheets into the bedroom, inhaling their odor, the smell of Ivory Snow, a fresh smell that indicates new beginnings to me. Changing the sheets feels like recovering my virginity. The sharp, clean sound of snapping linen and the fresh scent of outdoors spreads through the room. The dust from Jack's side of the bedroom puffs up from the bureau and the bedside tables. I sneeze a second time, then again. My stomach turns a little, and I rub the bruise on my arm that blossomed overnight from where he grabbed me. The memory of that moment brings up a sour taste, and I swallow hard.

Maybe I can use my indigestion as an excuse for not going to the Indelicato sisters' apartment this afternoon, but the notion vanishes along with the nausea. I'm fine. I'm going to be all right.

Besides, I promised Loretta. Now, there's a pumpkin pie in the oven and the scent of cinnamon creeping into the bedroom. I inhale the holiday aroma as I create sharp corners in the sheets, tucking them in neatly. I'm proud of my housekeeping skills. I learned them all from my mother, who kept reminding me that I needed to be clean and neat and that no man would ever want me unless I could keep an immaculate house. "That's all most women are worth," Mama had said. "The only ones who can get away without knowing how to cook, clean, or sew are the pretty ones, the women with slim bodies and full chests, creamy skin, perfect nails, and beauty-styled hair."

But I'm not one of those women. Am I, Mama?

"You have to take what you're born with, right, Cap'n?" On the television blaring in the living room, Captain Kangaroo talks about the importance of learning all about Thanksgiving. He hasn't heard what I've said.

Once the bed is made and the laundry is piled by the door, I look around the apartment. There's nothing left to clean. With only one person around, the house is simple to keep. *Neat as a pin. Are you watching me, Mama? You'd be so proud of me. I can keep the cleanest house in the world, but do you see a man here to enjoy it? What did I do wrong, Mama? I did everything you told me, and the bastard still left. When I needed him most...*

A knock at the door and Angela's voice: "Whoo-hoo, Beth! Come get some eggnog."

With a sinking feeling, I straighten up from making the bed and wearily cross the room into the parlor to open the door. Angela stands outside, a poinsettia-decorated cup clenched in each fist. An apron stenciled with a fruit-filled cornucopia encircles her dumpy body. "Look at you! Are you still cleaning the house? You silly girl. Come, come, come. The bird's in the oven, and most of the vegetables are scraped, cut, and ready to go. Come over and have a cup of eggnog with us. Get the season started. Maybe Loretta can even talk you into playing a game of Scrabble."

"No, no... I really couldn't. I have a few things to do, and the pumpkin pie..." *Not Scrabble. No word games. Please don't make me show you how stupid I am.*

"Certainly, you can! And you will! Wash that pretty face of yours and come over wearing your best Thanksgiving grin. We've got a big day ahead of us." Angela's now-familiar cackle echoes down the hall. "And the best part is we don't have to go to the damn Everett-Chelsea football game."

My hands on my hips, I watch her push the cup in my direction. I don't want to drink eggnog. I don't want to celebrate Thanksgiving—too many memories. Jack always made it a point to attend the traditional game every year. As students of Everett High, we spent all our teenage years at the games, even after I quit school.

Will he be there at the game today? Will he be sitting near the end zone like he always does? Will he have the blonde woman with him? Will she hold his hand like I used to?

A brief memory of us cuddling, his quick kiss on my cheek, the way he would take my hands and rub them as hard as he could between his own to warm them. I protested, saying he was rubbing too hard, and he laughed.

Will she jump up from the bleachers and scream when Everett makes a touchdown like I used to do? Will she stay with him even if it's cold, wet, or snowing? Will they go to The Rainlight for hot chocolate afterward?

I shake my head, kicking myself for treasuring those moments with Jack when he was all man and swaggering, saying hello to the guys he knew from work or his old school buddies. Smiling that sideways smirk of his and making comments about how short the cheerleaders' skirts were getting and how cute their ponytails were when they bounced. He loved football, and for that reason, loved Thanksgiving. To him, the two of them were synonymous. He'd be astounded to know I was spending his favorite holiday with the old ladies next door. I'm also surprised but don't want to be alone, especially after his unexpected visit.

Angela steps closer, presses the eggnog into my hand, then raises her own cup to make a toast. Pushing Jack to the back of my mind, I dutifully follow suit and force a smile to my lips. Angela toasts Thanksgiving and friends and family and congratulates Senator John Fitzgerald Kennedy and his wife on the birth of his first child. A daughter, I believe. Carol or Caroline, something like that. And when we clink cups, she laughs again, and I find myself laughing with her.

"We always put up the Christmas tree on Thanksgiving." An hour later, Angela grunts and dumps another cardboard box of ornaments on the parlor coffee table. She's wearing a turkey-emblazoned apron now. Its shoulder ruffles make her look somewhat like a bird herself: she's orange and brown, fat around the middle like a turkey, but her frazzled head and red-as-apple cheeks resemble one of those crazy birds like Dave Galloway had on the 'Today' show the other morning.

"My mother used to decorate the tree with us when we were kids. Remember, Loretta? She was so thrilled when she opened each box of ornaments. I can see her now, taking out the silver glass eggs from Germany and those funny-looking feathered things she brought from the old country. What were they called, 'Retta? Do you remember?"

Nursing her fifth cup of eggnog (*I have a habit of counting drinks, got into it after the first year of being married to Jack*), Loretta nods absent-mindedly. We are sitting at the kitchen table, watching Angela through the doorway, while we play a game of Scrabble. Yes, I'm losing badly, but so far, I've been able to create simple words, though I'm embarrassed to say I don't know half the ones Loretta spells. Thankfully, Angela feels the need to comment on each word as she places the tiles on the board, so I've gotten clues and haven't had to ask any ignorant questions.

And the turkey will be ready in an hour, Angela predicted five minutes ago.

"Loretta used to make the popcorn balls every year, but she don't do it no more. Turned into an old Scrooge a couple of years ago, and now I have to do it all by myself." Angela reaches into a box and comes out with a purplish-blue glass ball that sparkles as it catches the late afternoon sunlight coming through the window behind her. "I don't mind, though. Isn't this pretty? My great aunt brought it home when she went to visit her husband's family in Greece one year." She sighs and makes the ornament dance in the light, swaying back and forth as she does. I imagine large brown feathers sprouting from her behind, which makes me stifle a giggle. "Always thought I'd like to take me a trip someday."

Loretta harrumphs. "Why don't you just have one of the neighbors take one for you? Then they can come back and tell you all about it, and you can see it through their pictures and stories. Travel vicariously. That's the way you do everything else."

"Vicariously? What the hell does that mean?" Angela's fists are on her hips, and her voice raises a notch.

About to add "alive" to the Scrabble board, I pause, hand in mid-air over the tiles. *Not again. Do they always argue like this? How come I never heard them before? Why did I come?*

"Vicarious means you live your life through other people. You don't have a life of your own." Loretta's patient explanation seems forced as if she has to explain things to her sister regularly and has grown tired of it.

It's Angela's turn to harrumph. "I have a life, and I'm quite happy with it. Just because you're not happy with yours doesn't mean you need to start picking on me."

Loretta shoots me a look under her lashes, a 'how-can-I-put-up-with-someone-like-this' look. I recognize it because it's something Jack does all the time. I ignore what's happening between the sisters and insert the letters "a-l-i-e" around the "v" in Loretta's last word: evolve. Alive.

"Y'know, you're embarrassing me in front of our guest." Angela taps one foot, hands still on her hips, voice raised to a squeaky pitch.

"You're embarrassing yourself," Loretta intones, building "keyhole" of the "l" in my "alive."

"Excuse me?"

"Stop acting like an idiot, Angela. You remind me of Auntie Nina when you do this."

"All right. That's it. I've had it!" Angela punches both fists into the air, then stomps away into what I suppose is her bedroom.

"I've got the last two tiles," Loretta tells me, ignoring her sister.

From the bedroom comes muffled grumbling and thumps, as though Angela is rearranging boxes deep inside the closet.

"The tree will be decorated before the bird comes out of the oven if Angela enters her Speedy Gonzales mode." Loretta shuffles her tiles and snickers. "She always gets more cleaning done when she's mad. Goes like a buzzing hornet."

"Loretta!" An ominous crash follows Angela's screech. Then, silence.

For a moment, our eyes meet above the Scrabble board. Without a word, Loretta knocks over her chair in her scramble to get up. She flies into the bedroom with me close behind.

Angela's lying on the floor, her head in a crushed box of Christmas decorations, splinters of red and green glass surrounding her like a holiday halo. One leg is twisted under her; her right hand is clutching her left breast. Her eyes are wide open. And vacant.

"Sweet Jesus! Angela? Angela! Are you okay? What happened? Did you fall?" Loretta leans down, lifts her sister by the shoulders, and tries to brush away some of the glass surrounding her. "Angela! God, Angela, when will you ever learn? Angela...."

Angela's eyes stare past Loretta to the ceiling. *They're not blinking.* Lifeless.

I clutch the doorjamb. Paralyzed.

"Call an ambulance! Get some help. A doctor. Something." Loretta's face is purple, her eyes frantic, her arms wrapped around her sister.

Still, I can't move.

"Beth! Go call someone! NOW."

Hesitantly, I step backward, hands out in front of me, groping. *I've got to get out of here. Find a phone. Where? How?* Out of the corner of my eye, I can see Loretta's mouth moving. I know she's screaming, but I don't hear her.

I don't see Angela's body lying there in front of me. I see Cindy in the street. Mama in the red bathtub water. Daddy in his casket.

And it's all my fault. All those people. All that death.

A dagger in my gut doubles me over. Sharp, searing pain. Bile in my throat. I groan, and this time I hear Loretta scream: "Call for help, goddamnit. You stupid fool, call for help!"

My limbs feel like lead, but I pull myself off the floor, and in a fog, grab the black phone on the table with shaking hands, frantically pressing the receiver button up and down, get a dial tone, and do not know what to say to the operator. I must repeat the address and the apartment number repeatedly, at least five times, before the voice on the other end says, "Hold on, someone will be right there. Leave the apartment door open and stay with your friend until the ambulance arrives."

I get to my knees beside Loretta, who is now sobbing and stroking Angela's cheek, and it seems forever before the siren announces the ambulance's arrival. The white-suited attendants pry Loretta away from her sister, then talk in hushed tones to me as if I'm capable of taking control, but I don't want to. I wasn't even supposed to be here.

"You gotta help us with her," the attendant tells me. "Keep her out of our way for a few minutes. Just wait right over there in the kitchen. We've got everything under control. Everything's going to be all right."

But I can tell by how they're moving more slowly and putting away their stethoscopes that Angela is gone; there is no saving her. I've seen this happen too many times—Nana, Mama, Daddy. When the ambulance attendants shake their heads and whisper to each other, I'm sure. Awkwardly, I put an arm around Loretta's shaking shoulders, thinking the woman feels smaller than she seemed an hour ago—smaller and older.

Long moments later, the ambulance leaves with Angela and Loretta inside. No siren, no lights, quietly easing into traffic. Gone. Quickly. No fuss.

I am left standing in the apartment building doorway when the police car pulls up. Its lights *are* on; its siren *is* blaring.

The cops jump out. Two of them. Heads up, eyes concerned, alert. Graham and his partner. For a split second, I think they're there to arrest me or to tell me Jack has turned up and they've arrested him, but Graham says, "Did the ambulance get here for Miss Indelicato?"

I nod mutely and point down Broadway, where I can still see the ambulance's roof above the cars behind it.

"You're shaking," Officer Jackson says, his voice low and rumbling. He takes my arm, murmuring something about it being cold, and we'd best go inside. The other cop swoops in on my right, asking questions, following me upstairs where the Indelicato's door is still open, the smell of turkey and stuffing filling the hallway. Mr. Fits shuffles towards us, an ever-present cigar puffing from where it sits in the corner of his mouth.

"What's going on? Hey, someone tell me what's going on. I saw the ambulance. Was it one of the old ladies?" He addresses his questions to the cops, but his eyes keep sliding toward me.

"She's dead," I tell him, feeling like I need to put the blame somewhere; as much as I need to say it, I need to face the truth. It's always easier if you get the words out right away. I practiced saying it—"She's dead. She's passed away. She's gone on."—for days after Mama died, and it came more easily with Dad. Yet that grip of pain still circles my heart. Squeezes. Hard.

Other apartment doors open. The murmur of curious people makes me duck into the Indelicato's kitchen. I fiddle with stove knobs, not knowing whether to shut everything off since the turkey isn't done yet. Officer Jackson is right behind me; his words are irrelevant, but his voice is kind and soothing. Together, we pull the turkey from the oven and turn the jets off under the boiling potatoes, turnip, pearl onions, and green beans while Officer Cassilli deals with the neighbors.

"Were you here when it happened?" Jackson drains the potatoes, then slides some waxed paper over the top of the turkey. I wonder if he does the same at his house. I sneak a look at his long, dark fingers. His hands are pretty, like a woman's.

I nod, trying in vain to pour the onions into a small bowl. *Who's he saving the turkey for? What if it just sits here and spoils? Angela's perfect bird.* A lump hurts the middle of my throat. The sauce splatters and burns me. He takes the bowl away, grabs me by the shoulders, shuffles me to the sink, and runs cold water over my hands. He's close enough for his shirt buttons to scratch my forearms, close enough for me to smell the cigarette he just had, close enough to notice how his black eyelashes curl upwards. Close enough to make me realize this is the closest I've ever been to a Negro man. Close enough that my stomach flips.

I pull away and open a few drawers, looking for a dishcloth I can dampen to cover the freshly baked bread. "How could it have happened so quickly? She was bringing out the Christmas decorations. They'd just argued. Then we heard a thud, and she was on the floor. I knew. I just knew she was gone."

"It was good you were here," he says from behind her. "You helped. It's almost impossible for most people to leave a loved one to make that phone call for the ambulance. And, if it makes you feel any better," he reaches out and touches my arm, "I think she was gone immediately. It's a blessing that way...when it happens like that."

I concentrate on the spoons I'm holding in my hands. *Why did I take these out? I don't know what I'm doing here. Got to get home. Put this stuff away.* And lord knows, I understand nothing, see nothing. My hands shake so badly I can't spoon the green beans into a casserole dish. *How can I act like a family member in this stranger's home?* I can't believe that Angela is no longer a stranger, that she has died, and that I am now taking care of the dinner she had planned for the last two weeks. I can't believe that Angela won't be poking her head out the door anymore when she hears a noise. Or that these police think I am friends with the Indelicatos.

Nothing is real anymore.

"I didn't know them," I say. "They just asked me to dinner. I've never been over here for dinner before."

"It's okay." He moves towards me slowly, as if afraid he'll frighten me. "No one's blaming you."

They should. They should blame me. Why can't you see that? Why can't you see what's right under your nose? If I were your boss, I'd fire you. I'd put you right out in the street without a job. What kind of cop are you if you can't spot a guilty person? A dirty, lying snake of a guilty person standing right in front of you, lying through her teeth—why can't you see?

His dark chocolate brown eyes flicker, then the corners tighten. A sense of confusion creeps over his face, and I am afforded a momentary glimpse of his thoughts. I know he can't figure me out. He thinks he knows me and might even question me a little, but he's still in the dark, fooled by my shyness and pitiable face. I want to scream and rail at him. I want to beat my fists against the badge on his chest until the clasp opens, and the sharp edge pierces him until it awakens his third eye so he can see me the way I really am. A liar. A bitch. A sick, sick, sick person.

Instead, I sob, leaning against the kitchen counter, letting a howl loose from the deepest part of the dark place where I hide my anguish and when he comes towards me, he tries to comfort her, but I don't want to be comforted. *Shouldn't be comforted. Don't deserve it.* I strike out, slap him with full hands, and tell him, "No, no, no!" And he backs away, doesn't say another word, closes the apartment door against the murmuring neighbors, and sits at the kitchen table until I'm done.

When my sobs have become hiccoughs, and my shaking has calmed a little, he says, "Come, sit." He pulls out a chair and leans back on his own.

Drained, I sit, breathing deeply, incapable of speaking. I lean my forehead against my folded arms on the table. Sipping ragged gasps of air, I raise my head and look at him. He returns my look. Gently. Waiting for me to gain control.

"I'm sorry."

"Don't be. I think you have plenty to cry about." He nods a little, reaches out, and touches my hand. "Wish I could do that sometimes. We guys don't let it out enough. Holding things back hurts more than what you just did."

My shoulders are so heavy I don't know if I can move. I might sit here in Angela Indelicato's chair and never worry about the rest of the world again.

A knock and Officer Cassilli pokes his head in. "Everyone's gone back to their apartments. You okay, Ma'am?" He tilts his hat back and raises his thick eyebrows at me, then at his partner.

"I'll be fine." I push the chair back, lift my incredibly cumbersome body out of the chair, and drag myself through the doorway without saying goodbye and without worrying about what the cops will do in the Indelicato sisters' apartment. I'm sure they'll do the right thing. Officer Jackson seems trustworthy.

I can tell by his eyes.

She Lived a Good Life

Friday, November 29, 1957

Graham has the day after Thanksgiving off and traditionally uses it to do his Christmas shopping—a habit his mother got him into—but today, he has carefully shaved, applied some Old Spice, paid attention to how neatly his shirt is ironed, and now heads up Broadway to Beth Robbins' apartment. She will need someone to talk to this morning, and he's decided to be her shoulder to cry on.

One of the hardest things he'd ever done was to leave her last night, but he knew she needed privacy to retreat to her silent apartment to grieve. He sensed she was fragile, though he couldn't figure out why. Or maybe he could; after all, her husband has disappeared, she's in the middle of a police investigation, and now her next-door neighbor and friend is dead. Who wouldn't be a bit off-kilter?

When he and Frank left the Indelicato's apartment, he stood outside Beth's door listening to her sob, which broke his heart.

"Graham, you can't stand here all night, buddy." Frank pulled him away and didn't say another word. Sometimes Frank Cassilli displays more empathy than the nuns whose soothing words echoed in Graham's ear long after his grandmother's funeral.

Though it's part of his job to comfort someone he barely knows, it's tough to do so when the sun shines like it is now. It feels more appropriate to offer solace during funerals when it's raining. Today, it's a hard sun, a reminder that spring is not right around the corner and that winter will be in the air for a while to come. He squints against the sunlight flickering off his windshield as he slides into a parking space in front of Chestnut Hill. At the last moment before he left home, he had tucked his harmonica into his coat pocket, and it's now digging into his hip. He always plays it when he's upset or depressed, so he thought that he'd play it for Beth. Since it helps him, perhaps the music will do the same for her. He adjusts the harmonica as he slides out of the car, then shakes his head and chuckles at his naivete. He's thought about the many other things he can do to make Beth Robbins feel better, like reminding her that there are people born for every person who dies. Just yesterday, Senator Kennedy's wife had a little girl. Caroline, they named her. Maybe he'll share that with Beth Robbins. Maybe that will help her realize that life continues.

The hallway of the apartment building is eerily quiet, and he can't help but wonder if Beth will be home. Yet, a part of him, a nagging intuition, assures him she will be. He notices the puddles on the floor, evidence that someone has been there before him. The familiar scent of cabbage and potatoes wafts through the air as he passes the Flanagan apartment. He recalls the name from the list posted near the front door. Before he even reaches Beth's door, the sound of the television, tuned to the Channel 5 afternoon news, reaches his ears, its volume enough to fill the entire floor.

When he knocks, there's a thud and a rustle from within the apartment. The television is turned down, and her soft voice asks, "Who's there?"

"Graham Jackson," he says, twisting the harmonica in his pocket and glancing down the hallway, though no one's there. "Uh...Officer Jackson. You know, from yesterday?"

The lock snaps, the door opens, and she stands there staring at him, holding the door so that only half of her face is visible. Her blue eyes are wide, her mouth partially open. She looks scared.

"Hi." He nods, shifts his feet, and wonders why the hell he came. "I just thought I'd check to see if you were okay. Y'know, with all that's happened lately."

Over her shoulder, he sees the apartment as if he's never been there before. The room has her imprint on it now: the open *Ladies Home Journal* magazine on the coffee table instead of *Popular Mechanics*, the pink cardigan tossed on the back of the sofa, and the soft light from the pole lamp beside the couch. Wedding pictures on the table against the wall. *Hers? No, they're older. Her parents, maybe.* The air smells like snow, and it feels like the windows have been opened.

His gaze turns back to her, and he grins idiotically, then self-consciously wipes it from his face. It's not the right time to smile. It's inappropriate. As before, he feels penetrated by her cornflower blue eyes. Studied. And questioned. It's as if she's not about to let down the guard she's had around her all her life. She's not about to open the door either. Her foot is squarely against it like someone used to keeping salespeople out.

"I'm okay," she says. "Everything here is fine." She nods her head up and down, up and down, as if trying to convince herself as well as him.

"It was really horrible, what happened to Mrs.—" Why can't he remember the old lady's name? Usually, he's excellent at details, but he's afraid if someone asks him his own name right now, he won't be able to spit it out. Why does this woman make him so nervous?

"I always call them the Indelicato sisters, but I think her married name was Weldon or Whelan or something like that." Beth moves her foot and swings the door open a little. She's wearing a somber gray dress, long and full with a high collar and button-down sleeves. "I haven't seen Loretta today at all..." Her eyes fill with glassy tears, and she glances away.

He pauses at his opening and steps into the doorway. "If you want to go over and say hello, I'll come with you. I'm kinda used to this kind of thing. Y'know, offering condolences to the bereaved and so forth."

She swallows so hard he can see her throat constrict. "Do you think I should?"

"Most people do. Some people bake something for some strange reason. My mother's always running a casserole over to people when they have a death in the family. I think it's so that grieving people don't forget to eat." He thinks of his mother, squat and dark, spritzing a little cologne on herself before stepping out the kitchen door with her world-famous cornbread and catfish. Unlike Beth, who appears tentative at best, Mama has a confident and breezy way about her while Beth is almost scared of her own shadow. Totally unlike his mother. "But maybe you'd rather not?"

"I don't have...I have cooked nothing...." Beth flutters her fingers. They're long and pretty, adorned by a simple wedding band. Hands that look like they should be held. "I'm sorry. I'm being rude. Would you like to come in?"

Closing the door behind him, he realizes how cold it is in the apartment and involuntarily shivers.

"I'm keeping the heat down." She slips on the sweater laying on the couch. "The landlord just told us we all have to pay our own heating bills, so I'm trying to save...."

They're standing less than two feet away from each other. She fidgets and turns toward the kitchen. "I'll make some tea. My cup has gone cold, anyway. Would you like some?"

He nods.

While she's in the kitchen, Graham scans the room, automatically in police mode, and looks for signs of her husband, yet he is reluctant to find them. Surprised at himself, he realizes he doesn't want to be reminded that Beth Robbins shares her life with another man, but all the clues are there. He notices the *Popular Mechanics* magazines he saw the first time he and Frank came to the apartment are now tucked on the bottom shelf of the coffee table, out of sight. The pictures on the side table are not of Beth, but the woman in the wedding dress resembles her, only daintier and more fragile, yet with the same open and frightened eyes. The man next to her has Beth's smile. *They have to be her parents.*

He hears the water running, so he takes a few steps to the telephone table and flips through the envelopes stacked beside the phone. Bills. No letters. All addressed to John Robbins. Nothing for Beth, though all have been neatly opened and filed by date. A vase full of plastic flowers sits on the corner of the table, a pink ribbon tied jauntily around them. Graham wipes a lazy finger on the table and comes up clean. It's seldom that a house is this free of dust. He moves toward the paintings hanging on the parlor walls: each one is a river scene, and some are familiar, though he can't place them. The signature. Is that her name? He needs to ask her. The door to the bedroom is closed. Maybe that's just as well.

It could be anyone's apartment except for the stack of mail. He finds the blandness of it all sad and instinctively knows Beth doesn't want her life this way, so empty and vague. Something under this woman's exterior has yet to come out, to be alive. She seems unfinished, incomplete. And his sixth sense is telling him it's not because her husband is gone. It's something else. Something she hasn't expressed yet, but he can't put his finger on it.

As she walks back into the room with a small tray, a commercial for Jell-O comes on the television, and he surprises himself by saying, "Boy, that stuff kills you if you eat too much of it—especially that lime green kind. My mom always makes it for Thanksgiving, and I feel like she's punishing all of us, forcing it down our throats."

Beth laughs, a timid, tinkling, and slight sound, and hands him his tea. He wants to ask her to laugh again and searches for something funny to say, but he's not a funny man. Never has been. The moment is lost, and they awkwardly find places to sit, juggling the cups and saucers on their knees, glancing away from each other.

"My mother used to make wonderful ambrosia for Thanksgiving," she finally says quietly. "No one in the world could ever make it better than she did."

"Did? She doesn't make it anymore?"

"No. She died a long time ago." Bending her head, Beth sips her tea. And he can't see her eyes, but her voice says volumes. There's a catch in it, like she's holding back tears.

"You must miss her."

This time, she looks up, surprised. "Yes, I do. I miss her every single day."

"Your neighbor is going to miss her sister, too." Graham wants Beth to keep staring into his eyes like she is now. The thought surprises and terrifies him.

"I know." She studies her cuticles for a second, then glances up. "Maybe I should go over, huh?"

"I'll go with you, if you want. I really wanted to see how she was doing, anyway."

For the first time, she stares at him directly, seems to notice his chinos and open-collared white shirt, and recognizes he's not in uniform. It's not uncommon that once people see him as a cop, they don't see him as a human being afterward. It usually bothers him, but it's nice that she's looking at him like that.

"You came over here just to check up on us?" she asks.

He nods his head, takes another sip of tea.

"That's nice." She smiles a little, rises from the chair, then she sits back down, pulls her hair over her cheek, and looks at him sideways, suddenly shy. "I think Loretta will like it you've come. But I... I don't know her so well. That was the first time I was over there...yesterday. They invited me for Thanksgiving dinner. I think Angela felt bad for me because Jack—my husband—hasn't... hasn't been around, but I don't think Loretta wanted me there." Her cup rattles against the saucer a little, so she puts it on the coffee table. "They argued, you know. Right before, Angela—"

"I know. You told me last night." He puts his cup next to hers, reaches out a hand, and touches her briefly on the arm. She looks soft, but there's a hard muscle underneath, almost like her personality: she has a protective wall around her heart. He knows a strength in her he didn't sense before. "Don't blame yourself for her heart attack. It had nothing to do with you."

Her eyelids snap up. "How did you—"

"Comes from being in the police business, I guess. People often blame themselves for things they can't control. I suspect we all do, but I just see it on a regular basis, y'know?"

"Thanks. I've been feeling kind of..."

"Responsible?"

She nods and wipes her eyes with the corner of her sweater.

"Well, you're not." He stifles an urge to put his arms around her, knows it's inappropriate, and reminds himself she's married and that he's a cop. Even though her deadbeat of a husband isn't around and probably won't be back, Graham Jackson has scruples. Besides, he'd be in hot water if anyone knew he was over here on a social visit. On top of everything else, he's Black, and she's white. No one needs to remind him what happened to that poor kid, Emmett Till. "Listen, let's go over there and make her feel a little better. There's nothing worse than losing the only person in your life."

She turns and quickly disappears with a swish of silk stockings into the bedroom, and he feels he's hit a really touchy nerve with that last comment. He spends a couple of moments waiting for her to return, berating himself for saying too much, scaring her off.

When she comes out of the bedroom, face scrubbed, hair brushed, she gives him a straight-lipped smile and says, "I feel funny going over there empty-handed. Wait a minute. Let me see if I have anything in the kitchen." A couple of cabinet doors slam, dishes rattle, and then she returns, holding a small plate covered with a blue and white dishcloth. "It's not much, just a little leftover cornbread, but at least I feel better being able to offer you… something. I bet both of our mothers would agree you don't go to visit without bringing something, huh?"

Opening the door for her, Graham nods, stands back, enjoys watching her smile again, and follows her into the much warmer hallway.

No Longer Razor-Straight and Defiant

3:15 P.M.

My fingers are frosty, and their tips are numb from staying in the cold apartment for so long. In the toasty warmth of the Indelicato sisters' kitchen, I inhale deeply and stretch my hands. I long to go into the living room, lie on the couch, curl up like a kitten, and take a nap, but Loretta sticks her pale face in front of me and silently questions me. Searches my eyes.

How can she know me so well that it feels like she's crawling through my brain?

From behind me, Officer Jackson says, "How're you doing, Ma'am? Is there anything you need? Anything I can do for you?" He sweeps a kitchen chair out for her and motions her into it with a gentlemanly sweep.

Woodenly, Loretta slides into the seat, her solemn face turning from me to Officer Jackson and back again as though suspicious of our ulterior motives. Still, she settles into the chair, moving more slowly than a few days before, like she's aged a decade. Her hair is askew, the tail of her shirt hanging out of her manlike trousers. She pulls a cigarette out and lights the wrong end. The officer talks about the weather, the holiday traffic, and how the heat clanks when it has to work hard to push warm air through the radiators.

His kindness and natural solicitations remind me I'm not here to relax, but to offer support and help. I'm not used to it—not that I don't want to help people, but Jack didn't like me visiting the neighbors or talking to strangers. Besides, I have no idea what to say...or do.

Do I hug her? The only people I've ever hugged are my parents and Jack. I've wondered lately whether I'm going to hug anyone ever again.

What would a Graham Jackson hug feel like? Where did that thought come from?

Seeing Loretta now, broken and weak, her eyes blood-red and ugly, her nose dripping with crying snot, forces me to look at myself and realize that's what Jack saw in me: grief and sadness. For a moment, I'm taken aback, and then I realize with a jolt that Jack was disgusted with me. Somewhere deep inside, anger arises. For the first time, I don't want to ignore that feeling. Loretta's grief-stricken face is akin to looking into a mirror. I know her pain, and I understand it. Jack never could.

What do you do when you go to someone's house after a sister dies? How do you console someone you really don't know when you don't really want to stay very long, but you have to because someone else made you? What do you do?

Following Graham's lead, I pull out a chair at the kitchen table, sit quietly, and listen to him talk to Loretta about last night. She cries, and my instinct is to pull away, hide, and ignore my part in this melodrama.

Loretta's voice breaks. Her shoulders slump, no longer held razor-straight and defiant. Her eyes appear unfocused, as if she's no longer sure what she's seeing or how. It's as though she's had an all-necessary crutch snatched away, and she's just realizing that she *did* need it even though she's tried to ignore it for years.

"What can we do to help you, Miss Indelicato? Can we make some phone calls for you? Go to the funeral home?" Graham leans forward, his eyes on Loretta, his hand over hers.

Now, I can't help but pull away. The pain in my chest feels as piercing as when Mama died. Disbelief sits on the sternum. Fear twists the lower abdomen. *No. I don't want to go to the funeral home with this woman. I don't even know her, for god's sake. Please don't bring me into this! Leave me out of this. She's not my family, no relation to me whatsoever.*

It's been eight years since Mama died, yet it still feels like yesterday. I pull away again, trying to reason with myself.

Loretta's just a neighbor whose sister invited me over for a Thanksgiving dinner. She made me come even though I didn't want to, and now she's trying to make me part of this. But I'm not part of this. I don't want to be part of this. We have nothing in common—nothing, nothing, nothing.

I rock back and forth.

This isn't right. He shouldn't be doing this all himself. Lend a shoulder, Mama always said. Lend a shoulder. Come on, Beth, get yourself together. Lend a shoulder.

Graham and Loretta's voices fade into the background. The dishes are piled up on the counter—the pans crusty with brown leftovers: the uneaten turkey dinner. Automatically, I rise from the table and go to the sink, run the water, and begin washing the dishes and pans while humming under my breath as if the sound will transport me elsewhere. I think about going to the hospital to visit Theresa, find out what she did over Thanksgiving, and see how Cindy is.

I'm deep into an imagined discussion with Theresa about what happened with Lucy and Desi on today's show when a hand clasps my arm above the elbow. It's an intrusion, a step into my privacy, and I look at the hand, unsure for a moment to whom it belongs. Then I return to the present, raise my eyes to Graham's face, and focus on what he's saying.

"...don't you think that'd be a good idea?"

"What? I'm sorry. I wasn't listening."

"Hard to hear over running water," he says, reaching across me to shut it off.

Involuntarily, I inhale his scent, sense the radiant heat from his skin, note the way his eyebrows are jet black with a few silvery gray hairs etching the arch, and I'm overwhelmed by the prickly feeling that begins behind my knees and works its way up in a rush to the place beneath my breastbone. My hands fly out of the water, ready to push him away. (*I love Jack still, no matter what he's done. He's my husband. I must.*) But Graham moves. And he hasn't noticed my reaction to him at all. He's leaning against the counter now, less than a foot away, one leg casually crossed over the other, crossed one on his hands behind him against the counter, his eyes on Loretta, a slightly benevolent smile on his face. I battle my reaction to him, hope he can't see how hard my heart is beating, and I feel horribly unfaithful.

"I was telling Miss Indelicato that I didn't think it'd be a problem at all for me to take you two ladies to the funeral home," he looks straight at me, flashing a white-toothed smile. "She needs to go down there to sign the papers and make the arrangements, and I'm sure she'd feel better having a female friend along. We can go anytime she wants, right, Mrs. Robbins?"

Now he stops and stares at me, questioning, expecting an answer, and I don't have one. I duck my head, study the water swirling down the drain, and curse myself for coming over here to begin with.

"I can't tell you what that'd mean to me," Loretta's voice sounds nothing like the Loretta of yesterday, the Loretta who didn't want me in the house at all, the Loretta who argued with her sister, made Angela upset enough that she keeled over with a heart attack.

This quick change scares me. How can people swallow their personalities and act like someone I don't know? Jack did that, and it confused me. I don't know what to make of it and certainly don't want to figure it out.

"You don't know how much I appreciate what you've done, Beth." Loretta threads the end of a napkin back and forth through her fingers like she's weaving a basket. "If you weren't here, I couldn't have made the phone call to get the ambulance...." That's as far as she can go before the tears flow again.

Graham crosses the small kitchen to comfort her, but I am frozen against the sink. For a moment, Loretta sobs, then gains control of herself again, telling Graham, "I'm all right. I'm all right. You know, my sister had a lot of bad habits, and she did a lot of things I wouldn't, but she was a good person. She lived a good life, my sister. She had her faults, but she lived a good life." Loretta's voice rises higher, and she's staring at me now, trying to convince me.

I nod, wondering why I have to be persuaded. *You have no argument from me, lady. I know how nosy your sister was. I know how she watched Jack and me and wanted me over here so she could find out about everything, but I'm not going to tell you anything. There's nothing about me you want to know. Please don't ask.*

"She seemed concerned about you, Beth. When she heard the noises coming from your apartment, she said she always wanted to protect you. Even though we both thought Jack was a fine-looking young man, we knew what you went through. We knew he was beating the crap out of you, and it was all I could do to keep Angela from charging over there and knocking his lights out with a baseball bat. But you have to forgive, I guess. We all need to forgive." She shifts in the chair and pulls another cigarette out of the pack. This time, she lights the right end and puffs a moment. "You never met him, did you, Officer Jackson?"

Graham straightens, his attention heightened, and he appears to want to hear more. *Why are they talking about Jack as though he's dead?*

"Many men these days don't make it to work as faithfully as Jack did. Every day, he'd go down the hallway at the same time, no matter what he did the night before," Loretta continues. "Always on time for work, he was. And every night, he'd come home at the same time. Could set your watch by him. That's reliability for you. A good trait to have, Angela always says. Sorry. Said. Angela always *said*."

Loretta sniffs and wipes at her red nose with the handkerchief balled up in her hands. She rises, stretches her back, reaches out, and touches my shoulder. "When you have someone like that, someone you trust to do the same thing all the time, every day, like clockwork, you have to keep him. Sometimes, you have to learn to forgive the other stuff. Do you know what I mean, honey?"

Loretta's in front of me now, so close that I can count the wrinkles that stretch out from both sides of her mouth, making her look like a ventriloquist's puppet.

There's no place to go, and without warning, my chest constricts, the room spins, the breath I've been holding leaves my body, and as hard as I try, I can't suck in enough air. Everything starts losing its color, fading to black faster than a finger snaps, and the animal urge to flee grabs me by the throat. I push Loretta aside, mumbling something like, "I'd love to help you, honest, but I really have to go. There's something I forgot..."

And then I'm in the hallway. The cold draft of unheated air snaps me rudely back to the here and now, and I race to my apartment, grab my coat and boots, run back out into the hallway, and flee the building. I am ignoring Graham Jackson calling my name.

The snow that's fallen chokes the streets. There isn't enough room for two cars to pass, so I hurry to the side and wait. The plows have pushed the snow into big piles that the kids use to build igloos. A few of the children slide down the six-foot-high mounds, then crawl inside the holes they've made, screaming, laughing, and pretending to be Eskimos.

The calm feeling I usually get from watching children play doesn't happen this time. Instead, I stare at Broadway and see it as a stranger would. The shape of the street is like the shape of a life: straight and dull, with one chief point and no curves, a life that goes nowhere and does nothing. A stopping place between two other destinations. It makes me feel empty, like I've never quite lived my life, and maybe I never will. I'm suddenly overwhelmed with sadness...and so sick of being unhappy.

For a long moment, I stand in the snow, the yelling kids behind me, the sounds of the city muffled by the piles, and I think about my own existence. It's something I've never considered before. At least not consciously. But now, in my mind's eye, I see myself and haven't even tried speaking to another human being for many days. I mourn all the friendships I've missed. All the laughter I could have shared. All the tears. And I wonder what it would be like to do something with my art, to study the masters and to work with different paints, maybe even to attempt a sculpture.

A car crunches by in the snow, and I visualize my apartment and realize it doesn't represent a home. It's just a place where I go to sleep. It was not distinguishable, not a place that would tell a stranger something about me, Beth Robbins, but simply a couple of rooms that could belong to anyone. It was a living space with no personality—like me—a blank slate upon which nothing has been written.

The snowflakes melt on my cheeks, creating tears down my now-frozen cheeks, and I realize I don't want to live an empty life anymore. I don't want to come to the end of my existence and find that no one will remember me. I don't want someone else to feel the same way about me that I just felt about Angela Indelicato.

I want happiness.

I have a chance now. I can make a new start. There are people in my life now. People I wouldn't have known if not for the accident. There are possibilities. There are feelings I never thought I'd have before.

I stand on the sidewalk, holding my belly with both hands, and I feel a surge of determination. My feet feel as though they're made of iron, but my spirit is unyielding. When the kid playing in the snow stops to nudge his friend and then points at the 'crazy lady' crying in the middle of the street, I continue to let the tears fall. But amidst the tears, I swear a silent oath that no matter what happens, no matter what God throws my way, I will repair the hurt I've caused. This determination, this resolve — it's a new feeling for me, and it's empowering.

Somehow.

Changes

Saturday, November 30, 1957

"King me!" Scottie triumphantly grins up into my face. We're both lying on our stomachs on the waiting room floor down the hall from Cindy's room. He's been chattering away, answering all my questions, playing games with me, climbing into my lap occasionally, and I'm loving every minute. His blue eyes squint with laughter as he plays, helping me see the world from a child's vantage point, and it's easier down here. Less is expected of an adult who keeps busy and quiet on the floor. With Scottie, I can giggle, but no one even notices. One of the best things that's come out of these horrible weeks is that I've been able to get close to Theresa's kids. It's almost like being an aunt. And with Scottie, it's more than that. It's like having a piece of my heart outside my body, running around, laughing, and playing. It's a connection that fills me with a deep sense of empathy and understanding.

Scottie's a rambunctious kindergartner, can be both angel and devil in a split second. His honesty reminds me that children are the only human beings who, without fail, say everything that comes to mind, then forget what they've said two seconds later. They can be angry enough to scream and kick, but when they're finished, it's done. There are no memories of the anger, no repercussions days later, no guilt thrown in your face for something you've already suffered through.

Elaine is now sleeping under the chair in the corner ("snug as a bug," one nurse noted when she passed by a few moments ago), and Theresa and Bill are in with Cindy. Without words, they've left me in charge of the other children. I hand Scottie a checker and watch him place it carefully atop the other black one he's just moved to the king square. Leaning close to help him, I inhale the sweet smell of his hair, hear the little puffs and grunts he makes whenever he moves his pieces, note the way he gnaws on his thumb—

almost sucking it like a baby, but aware he can't go all the way, can't slurp like a toddler, because he's a big boy now.

I wish these moments could last forever, but I can't daydream about what if these kids were my own? That is too dangerous a fantasy. That imagination got me into this trouble, to begin with.

"Where's your mommy and daddy?" Scottie asks, not looking up, still concentrating on piling the checkers atop each other like King Midas with his precious gold.

"They died a long time ago, sweetie."

"Oh."

"You're lucky to have your mommy and daddy with you now. Do you know that?"

"Uh-huh. And Cindy, too. And sometimes Elaine." He looks at his little sister and sticks out his tongue. She chuckles at him lovingly, her chubby fingers trying to hold the crayon she's been pushing against the page, making circles and scribbles but unable to stay within the lines.

"You're fortunate, Scottie. I never had any brothers or sisters."

He sits back on his heels and cocks his head. "Never?"

"Nope. Never."

"I have to share my bedroom with them." His bright blue eyes shift to his sister, then back to me, then to the side as if looking toward Cindy's room. "I want bunk beds, but Mommy says we're too little. I don't like 'em, anyway."

I duck my head and move a checker; I don't want him to see me smile. "You'll like them better when you get older."

"No, I won't."

"Don't say that now, honey. Look at how sick Cindy is. You don't mean that, do you?"

He screws up his mouth, rolls his eyes. "She's fakin'. She's always fakin'."

The innocent comment surprises Beth so much that she catches her breath. "Scottie, she's not faking. Cindy is very, very sick. She almost died."

"So? She always closes her eyes and pretends to be dead. She's the BEST when we play Cops and Robbers. I shoot her and shoot her, and she always falls down and dies and stays there for the longest time. Mommy says

Cindy's a little actress like Shirley Temple." He moves a checker into a space where I could easily make several jumps and capture three of his pieces.

"I don't think she's acting." I jump one of his pieces and push it to the side.

"If she'd cut it out, we could go home. I'm tired of Auntie Gail's cooking. She doesn't make a beef stew like Mommy's. She puts 'matoes in it. YUCK!" He sticks out his tongue and crosses his eyes, wraps his hands around his throat, and makes a choking sound.

A bubble of laughter comes from a place so foreign I'd forgotten existed and forces its way into my throat, surprising me with its strength. I'm still laughing when Theresa pokes her head around the corner.

"Well, it looks like you three are having a great time." Theresa smiles and looks younger, with less pronounced lines on her face.

I stop giggling. "Everything okay?"

"Everything's absolutely wonderful." Though she's smiling, Theresa has a hand to her lips, and her eyes are full of tears. If not for the smile, I'd bet Theresa had just gotten bad news.

Then Theresa starts laughing: A high ripple of a titter that goes on and on, then deepens and becomes more of a moaning sound. Behind her, Bill grabs her shoulders and squeezes. Hard. They mumble something, then the phrase becomes more succinct, and as they repeat it over and over, they both reach out their arms to the kids, who scramble off the floor and join them in a circular group hug.

"Cindy has woken up. She's out of the coma. She's going to be okay!"

And now the laughter comes from all of them, echoes down the hall, and up to the heavens, where I lift my head, mind, and heart and send my gratitude.

Oh God, thank you!

Did You Really Do This?

Tuesday, December 3, 1957

When I get off the bus in Chelsea Square the following day, the first thing I notice is that the street is full—packed. People scurry in and out of the Five and Dime, packages in their hands, excitement on their faces. With a slight start, I remember it's officially Christmas season, and people are taking advantage of the sales, *just like Mama used to.*

Always uncomfortable in crowds, I shrink into my wide wool coat collar (wishing it was fur) and hug the bag of China plates, teacups, and framed paintings I've brought to sell to the pawnbroker, shouldering my way past a heavyset Italian woman dressed totally in black and trying to keep her three dark-eyed kids in tow. Her voice rings out in the street as though she is calling someone five blocks away, but she's simply speaking to the children whose eyes and attention are on the Santas and reindeer in the shop windows they're passing. *And what child wouldn't be fascinated by those Christmas decorations?*

Following their longing gazes, I pause for a moment to watch an animated version of Santa's Village set up in the front window of Woolworth's. All of my senses are alive. Music fills the street, and the people bustle by, the snow crunching beneath their feet. The smell of pine trees being sold on the corner draws me in and makes me want to bring one home and set it up in the corner of my living room. I promised myself this morning that after visiting the pawnbroker, I'd go shopping to find something to take to Theresa's for supper and pick up some food for myself. Last night, when I finally got home from the hospital, I reached into the canister by the sink for a tea bag, and it was empty. My kitchen cupboards now hold a little sugar, some salt, and a can of peas (Jack's favorite vegetable—and the only one I despise). I had made a cup of hot water and sugar, telling myself it was enough. I folded my hands around the cup and pretended it was tea. But it wasn't enough, and I spent the rest of the evening trying to figure out where I could get a job. How much longer could I hold on by selling my few possessions?

My anger at Jack grew with each passing thought.

Theresa and Bill were understanding when I explained my absence at supper, attributing it to Loretta's need for my company. What I didn't reveal was my own desperate need for her presence. Talking about my parents, though initially painful, somehow eased a deep-seated ache in my gut that I had endured for the past fourteen years. If only I could find a way to ease the pain Jack has inflicted, perhaps I could finally *breathe again*.

At the first feeble light of morning, I was up, my breath making clouds in the frigid apartment. The cold made me hunch over the ironing board as I pressed my best dress, a brown and red plaid light wool shirtwaist. Then I hunted through the apartment for items I'd take to the pawnshop and made a last-minute decision to take not only the paintings from the wall and the few pieces of China but two drawings I'd done in charcoal back in high school, back in the days before Jack made me put all of my artwork away because it was a "time waster." I suppose the pawnbroker will laugh at me, but I have nothing else I'm willing to part with—and I'm hungry. Loretta's offer of sharing food has become mouth-watering.

Theresa rescheduled dinner for tonight, and I'm both excited and terrified about going. My stomach growls at the thought.

Charcoals are the Rage

1:50 P.M.

The pawn shop is as dim as it was the first time I saw it, but Mr. Isaacson, the little man with the monocle, greets me with the warmth and enthusiasm of an old friend, though I am not alone with him this time. Seven other people are in line before me. It's the Christmas season, and people need money, so they've brought things in to sell: a rosewood banjo, two brooches in the shape of a heart and a flamingo, a hand-painted lamp the hawk-nosed man holding it identifies as "done by Handel." *Whoever that is.* A young couple—a pimply-faced boy in a Navy uniform and a red-headed girl with a high-pitched giggle—take an agonizingly long time to buy wedding bands for themselves.

I try to wait patiently to the side until the pawnbroker and I are alone, but a small trickle of moisture runs down my back. He gives me two dollars and a sad smile when I offer him the box of things I've brought (everything but my drawings—I think he probably won't want them).

My stomach drops as I hold the two bills in my hand.

As I sit here, I can't help but feel the weight of my dwindling funds. The numbers I calculated before I arrived here are haunting me. The rent is due again soon, the heat and electricity will be another bill to pay in a week, and the groceries I need will cost at least $3. Even the bus ride home will set me back another ten cents. Desperate, I offer him my artwork, hoping it might be my saving grace. *What's the worst that can happen? He'll say no.*

"I have one more thing," I say as he shuffles toward the back room. I slip the ribbon off the roll of drawings I'd dug out of the bottom of my hope chest and carefully spread the three sketches on top of the glass case.

The first, a study of my mother's hands, is something I'd done when I was fifteen, and Mr. Nash, my art teacher, had given me an A+ on my ability to draw the human body. That encouragement was all I needed. I filled page after page with sketches of feet and legs, hands and fingers, and faces. So many faces. Now that the sketch is out on the counter, I think that if I close my eyes and touch the sketches I made of Mama's regal fingers, maybe, just maybe, all the wrongs in my life will magically disappear, and I'll be back in the kitchen chair again, leaning back on its legs, sketch pad in my lap, Mama at the counter chopping up celery and onions for that evening's soup, the smell of the simmering vegetables filling the air, and Mama telling me that I had finally done something to be proud of, that I can indeed be an artist if I keep on practicing, that I'm as good as *Van Gogh or that guy who did the church in Rome—what was his name? Michael something—Michael Angelo, that's it. You're so talented, Bethie.*

Mr. Isaacson's palsied fingers reach for the drawings, interrupting my reverie. "Let's see the others," he says, his tone bored. I know I won't get any more money from him today, but I comply, as always. It's how my parents raised me: keep going and trying, no matter the odds.

The other two drawings are charcoal sketches of the statue in front of the Parlin Library in Everett Square, the one that was erected after the servicemen came home from World War I. I've always liked the statue's shape: the way the man stands, looking skyward, his wide-brimmed doughboy hat so soft and slouched that you'd think it was actually made of felt. The man's forearms are bare, capable, and strong, holding a rifle, bayonet attached and ready. One leg is in front of the other as if he's striding into battle, fearless, meeting the enemy with pride and honor, somehow etched into his chiseled bronze face.

On the day I sketched the statue, two children were playing with marbles in the shadows beneath it, so I included them, never realizing how the drawing symbolized the lives the soldiers had fought to protect. Mr. Nash had seen this drawing, too, and praised me for it, calling me a "natural artist." I will never forget that.

The third charcoal sketch, a closeup of those children, was one of the hardest I've ever done. It was complicated to portray the soft lines of their faces and the innocence in their eyes on paper, especially since they didn't sit still. But I drew them, sketching them quickly, my heart beating in excitement as if I had found something precious and stolen it, and that was the moment I knew I wanted to have children just like those two. Lots of them. Giving away this artwork pains me as much as forgetting Mama's hands. But I know I can sketch others and duplicate these from memory. I have plenty of paper and pencils. Besides, it'll give me something to do.

There are other drawings, too. At the bottom of the hope chest, there are twenty more, some still in sketchbooks, and others rolled and beribboned like these three. And I create more every day. There is never a moment when I sit at a table or beneath a lamp without a sketch pad and pencil. Drawing helps me find a way through the pain and heartbreak.

"Who's the artist?" Mr. Isaacson asks after a long silence.

I don't know how to answer—I never considered myself a professional artist. Sometimes, I dream of becoming one, but it's just a dream. I enjoy drawing because I enjoy it and because Mr. Nash always gave me the highest grades in the class. Even Dad liked my drawings. But an artist? Not me, not Beth Robbins.

"Ah, I see the signature in the corner. Elizabeth Ahlberg, is that it? I haven't heard of her, but then again, I'm no art expert, you know what I mean?" He laughs and coughs a little. "Maybe you should bring them down the street to that there guy who's selling the paintings. What's his name?"

He's not asking me but looking toward the ceiling as if the name is written in the heavens. "What's his name? What's his name? It's right on the tip of my tongue. Skinner? Stinner? Steiner? Shingler! That's it. Shingler. Nice Jewish man from Germany. He hasn't been open long, so I don't know anything about him, but he'd probably be able to help you. I'm sorry, dahlink, I can't take something like this. Pretty, though. Very nicely done. Go see Shingler. Maybe he can help, okay? All right then. You take care of that ice out there—lots of people slipping and sliding today. Just a few minutes before you came in, this big lady went down—whoosh—right in front of the door. I had to go out and help her up; it almost broke my back." He laughs and comes around the end of the counter, holding the door open for me, nodding. "Good luck there, dahlink. You come back and see me again sometime, okay?"

On the street, I stand outside the door, blankly staring at the cars going by. *An art gallery. He wants me to go to an art gallery.* A large gentleman in a beaver hat and fur-trimmed coat pushes past without an apology. I slip and almost go to my knees, but someone else raises a steadying hand. "Thank you," I murmur, but the person has already blended into the holiday crowd.

Down the street on my right, I can see the sign: Shingler Art Gallery. It is trimmed in gold with black letters, all fancy and scrolled like something from Europe. Rich. I feel like racing back to the bus stop like a coward, but my stomach rumbles, and I long for a cup of coffee and a piece of toast. The hunger walks with me down the street and brings me into the small shop, into the warmth and the light of Shingler's Art Gallery, where I might get some money to buy some food.

On the shop's walls hang paintings I haven't seen since Mr. Nash showed me books filled with the treasures held by museums worldwide. I shake my head skeptically—*Shingler will laugh me out of the shop. I'll go home hungry, forced to beg Loretta for something to eat, then next week Mr. Fits will come by for the rent, and I'll have to pay him so he won't throw me out on the street where I'll freeze and die, and Jack will never know the difference.*

"Hulloooooo!" A jolly, high-pitched voice calls out from the back room. A tall, gaunt man with large hands and a comically wide smile emerges from behind a solid white partition. He adjusts the red scarf at his neck, then sweeps his hand to one side as if welcoming the queen. "Are you an art lover? You must be if you've come to Shingler's Gallery. Ha! See what you've made me do: I've created a line of poetry. Come in, come in. Please put down your packages and stay awhile. I've just hung some of my most recent acquisitions, and I'd love to tell you all about them."

Though I have no idea what 'acquisitions' are, I nod enthusiastically, then burst out, "Mr. Isaacson down the street sent me. He thought you might be interested in these." I shove the rolled drawings in the tall man's direction and hold my breath. *Why would he want my amateurish drawings when he has genuine works of art hanging on the wall?* No matter how great my grades were in high school, I am not an artist.

"Ah, you've brought some artwork. Yours?" He takes them, his huge hands making the drawings appear suddenly miniscule.

I nod, swallow, and glance at the impressive landscape on the wall to my right. Canary yellow, raspberry red, violet, and sapphire blue flowers fill a jade-colored meadow. The details are exquisite, and I am transported to this other land. I step closer, ignoring the man who has now spread my drawings on the desk near the door. Slowly, I walk down the middle of the store, soaking in the effects of the other paintings lining the gallery's left and right sides. Spotlights shine down from the ceiling like stars.

Here's a view of the ocean, a tall sailboat tossed by steel-gray waves. There, a study of three tall white birds against the backdrop of a blooming magnolia tree. Then, a portrait of an ancient fisherman, his face scarred by years of weather, his eyes telling of the days he's spent aboard ships, the years he's been away from his wife and children, the whipping storms at sea, the harsh sunlight of the tropics, the heartache of a fishing expedition which brought him home empty-handed.

"Where did you go to school?" Mr. Shingler asks from the other end of the store.

Startled that I've wandered throughout the whole gallery, I turn and answer, "Everett High School, but I didn't graduate."

He arches an eyebrow and loses his broad smile. "No, my dear, tell me the truth. Where did you go to *school*?"

I shouldn't have come. Why did I listen to that old man at the pawnshop? Now, this one's making fun of me.

Embarrassed, I cross the store and try to take the drawings from the desk, but he places his large hand atop mine.

"What are you doing? I want to know where you went to school, that's all. When I represent someone, I need to know all the details. You know school, who you studied with, what your best mediums are, how much you expect to get for your work."

When does he represent someone? What's he talking about?

"This one will look stunning in a gold-toned frame." He holds up the study of Mama's hands, cocking his head and squinting his suddenly sharp hazel eyes.

"I don't want to buy a frame," I utter hopelessly. *He wants me to buy something. I should have known better.*

He laughs, the sound full and snorting like a happy horse. "Dear child, have you never sold any of these wonderful drawings?"

I shake my head.

"Well, aren't I the lucky one? We'll have to frame these up and light them right, but I think they'll fetch a decent amount. Do you have more? But, of course, you have more. What artist doesn't? And you'll be continuing. Creating some more sketches of other subjects?" He nods at me, eyebrows still arched, and I nod right back.

"Is this the only medium in which you work?" His attention is back to the drawings. "I bet you'd be wonderful in watercolors. How about some more children? People love paintings of little tykes, especially at this time of year. Why, the other day, Mrs. Shaw was in—you know her, don't you? The Shaws of Beacon Hill?—and she bought several of my Martin Bells. She's simply wild for children. Loves them frolicking in a meadow or at the seashore. I'm sure if I had some Chagalls, she'd snatch them up like that." He snaps his fingers. "But...I deal mostly with local artists. Nothing like finding new talent."

He goes behind the desk and pulls out a drawer. "Let me write you a check to hold these, but as soon as they sell, I'll give you your forty percent. That's enough, isn't it? Of course, it is. That's the standard, as I'm sure you know. So, when will you bring me some more?" He stands before me now, close enough to see the small tomato sauce stain on his tie. Holds the check out to me.

I peer up into his face, stunned.

"Isn't that enough? I wrote it for twenty-five. Maybe I should give you thirty?" He pauses, but only for a heartbeat, then strides back to the desk, sits down, and writes another.

When he rises again and thrusts the check at me, I laugh.

Surely, he's joking. Did Mr. Isaacson call and tell this guy to be kind to me?

"That's not nice," I say. "Please don't tease me like this."

All the old mocking voices come back in a thudding rush that almost knocks the breath out of my chest: the kids who taunted me in the playgrounds, the boys who forced me to cross the street when they called me 'blood face,' the husband who convinced me no one would ever want me but him. But instead of letting the voices take control, anger rushes in, and I fight a compulsion to knock this tall Ichabod Crane right on his skinny ass. That compulsion shocks me even more than the check he waves in my face.

"Of course, I'm not joking, dear one. You'll probably get at least seventy-five to a hundred for each. Charcoals are the rage these days, you know." His smile is sincere. He honestly doesn't believe my ignorance. I can tell by the "I know more about this than you do," look in his eyes.

Abruptly, I know this is real. He's giving me a check for my drawings and wants me to create more. This check will enable me to turn the heat on a little higher, and maybe I'll even buy Theresa and Bill a fancy cake for dinner tonight. *Could I even buy some canvases and paints?*

With tentative fingers, I reach for it. His questions about when I'll be able to deliver more and about what I will work on next seem far away as my heart beats again and fills my ears with a steady thump.

Celebration Dinner

6:45 PM

The kids are in bed, and Theresa's apartment is quiet. We sit at opposite ends of the kitchen table, silently looking out the window between us. The winter wind gently sways the frozen clotheslines. There's no other movement outside, no people, no kids calling to each other across the courtyard. In the sky above, the crescent moon is etched like a piece of white satin in a black velvet quilt.

It's been a good night, full of celebration for both of us. Theresa couldn't be happier about Cindy's progress, though she's itching to return to the hospital. But she has promised Bill she'll spend an evening with their other two babies ("Let them know their mother still loves them as much as she loves Cindy, he said.") while he works late. Since coming back to consciousness, Cindy has amazed the nurses, even telling them she wants to walk. It'll be a long time until she's the child she used to be, but she's getting there.

"She'll be fine," Theresa says again, pulling on her sweater sleeves. Her smooth, round face is relaxed for the first time in days, and her hair is soft around her cheeks, out of the curlers she usually wears.

"Yes, she will," I answer, and I truly believe my words. I silently thank God that I can say that.

The Gordon household is as welcoming as I knew it would be. The small kitchen is still warm from the evening's meal: a baked chicken stuffed with breadcrumbs and nuts, roasted potatoes, and creamed corn. I am full of good food and companionship and don't want to move. Through the kitchen archway is an equally small living room filled with turquoise blue leather furniture ("easier to clean," Theresa said earlier), piles of colorful kids' toys, and a television that looks much like mine. I went upstairs earlier to use the bathroom and peeked into the two bedrooms: the kids sleep in small bunk beds Bill made, and Little Elaine still insists on staying in an ornate Victorian crib made of tiger oak rather than joining her older siblings in 'big kids' beds.' (When Theresa made that comment earlier, I caught the kids sticking out their tongues at each other and laughing so hard they collapsed into giggles, too.)

Theresa and Bill's room is decorated with thought and a tight budget, in blue, gaily striped curtains and a turquoise and green floral bedspread, matching toss pillows at the head of the maple bed. The whole house is cozy and colored with the comfortable messiness of having far more critical things to do than chase dust bunnies. Every inch of every room speaks of family, love, and pride. The Gordons might be poor, but they're happy with what they have. Thankful.

"Tell me again about the guy at the gallery," Theresa says now, her hands deep in sudsy dishwater. "I couldn't hear you before with Elaine crying and the TV going."

"Well, he really looked like Ichabod Crane," I begin. Theresa giggles and leans forward against the sink, paying attention like a girlfriend, and I'm encouraged to launch into the story, remembering every detail for her. I delight in having someone to share the tale with, laugh with, and love every moment.

The Fallen

Wednesday, December 4, 1957

I am entranced. The charcoal sketching tablet in my lap grows from a blank page to a memory of my mother's quilts flapping in the wind on a sunny spring day. It will be fun to paint the image with my new watercolors, but for now, it's unfinished. A knock at the door brings me off the couch with a start, and my tablet and pencil scatter to the floor. I hesitate to open the door, instantly wondering if Jack is back, though he's taken all his things. There's nothing left in the house that he might want. Not even me.

It's Graham Jackson. I almost don't recognize him in his civilian clothes: a gray wool coat and plaid muffler, his eyes bright as black diamonds from the cold. For a moment, neither of us speaks.

"Um, I was just over at Miss Indelicato's, and we kind of...I just..." He fumbles like a teenager and cracks his knuckles. "I asked her if she wanted to, you know, get out of the house, maybe see a movie, and she said yes. Then I thought you might like to, you know, you might like to go, too?" He ends his words on an upward, questioning note, as if he's not sure he's doing the right thing and hopes I'll approve.

"A movie?" The back of my head prickles, and I reach to rub it.

"There's a Cary Grant movie showing at the Park Theater. I thought maybe..."

"Yes." My heels lift off the floor as I answer with a vehemence that surprises the stuffing out of me. "Yes! I love Cary Grant."

"Good." Graham smiles widely. His eyes crinkle when he does, and a dimple appears on his chin. "Good. I can pick you up around 5ish, and we could all get something to eat first if you'd like. The show starts at 7."

Mentally calculating how much that would cost, my hopes sink. *Why did I agree? I didn't budget for movies.*

Somehow, Graham realizes what's going on and reaches for my arm. "My treat," he says simply.

His genuinely reassuring smile stays on his face, and I find myself returning it. Openly. Then I feel something new, a flip in my stomach, and I must turn away. *This isn't right.*

"I'll be ready, then," I say, and there's an awkward moment while we both pull away from the door, saying our goodbyes and repeating the time we're going to meet several times before I finally close the door and lean against it, listening to his clipped footsteps echo down the hallway. Then something strange bubbles up inside me, like the nervous laughter I'd felt when my parents scolded me after misbehaving, even though I knew I'd make it worse if I let it out, but I couldn't help it.

I lean against the door, giggling for no apparent reason.

How Easy Would It Be

3:35 P.M.
Graham gets into the car and realizes his hands are shaking. And he's smiling, grinning like a damn fool. *What the hell is going on? This woman is married. Married! God, I love her eyes.*

He has never admitted to Beth that he'd tried to call her before he visited the Indelicato woman on the pretense of asking more questions and that he'd discovered her phone had been shut off. Or the thought of her trying to support herself bothered him. He knows she doesn't have a job, and now that her rat bastard of a husband seems to be gone for good, she has no income. There is no way on God's green earth that Graham can understand men who leave their women on a whim. The least a man—a real man—should do is explain to his wife why he feels the need to leave, and once he's gone, he should take care of her. No matter how many lies his father and uncles have told in their lifetimes, no matter how many women they've cheated on, they always made sure the ones left at home had food and that the bills were paid.

Jack Robbins does neither. Thus, Jack Robbins is shit in Graham Jackson's book. He's known guys like Jack. In the service, there were plenty of them: guys who enjoyed killing, the ones who polished their guns with smoky violence in their dark eyes, the guys who never entered a village without taking advantage of the women. He knew men who raped. He had seen unnecessary cruelty. His stomach roiled with the memories of soldiers incensed by war and consumed by bitter hatred. With a sense of guilt, he had often stayed quiet simply because when those men were raiding villages and abusing the people, that meant that they—the soldiers who he had fought alongside—were not paying attention to him, not barraging him with racist remarks. He welcomed the respite, but that didn't mean he condoned or understood their actions. Nobody deserved the abuse those soldiers dished out.

A woman like Beth Robbins deserves much better.

He turns the key in the ignition and drives away from the apartment house, feeling satisfied. Miss Indelicato had looked so excited when he'd suggested the movie, trying to hide her grin as if she felt guilty. And Beth had just about popped out of her skin. It felt good to think he'd done the right thing by asking them both to go out, even though he'd never tell his partner because Frankie would never understand why, and Graham wasn't sure he wanted to try to explain.

A couple of days ago, they'd finally had a moment to investigate the accident more. Since the hit-and-run, they'd had to pick up the slack for a couple of other cops who'd been out with injuries after a high-speed chase down Broadway. Ironically, it was more important to find out who had driven the truck that injured a couple of cops than the one that had almost killed a little girl. That was one thing that always made Graham wonder what he was doing with his life. When did men become more important than a child who got in the way of a drunk driver?

Apparently, Jack Robbins has a history of always being drunk. Smitty, the bartender, reported Jack was there every night after work, and on the day of the accident, he called Beth to come pick up her husband. Smitty said it wasn't the first time he had to call her. Because of the bartender's comments, Graham has done some snooping on his own, though he hasn't said anything to Frank. He even visited the truck in the impound lot and found Beth's handkerchief on the front seat, though he has told no one about that, especially since he now keeps it in his pocket. He's never done this before. He's always prided himself on being the most honest cop on the force, and here he is, hiding investigative details.

Together, Graham and Frank interviewed the group of guys Smitty told them about, the ones that Robbins drank with regularly. None of them liked him. They all reported he was a nasty soul, someone they couldn't talk to, a man with much more on his mind than the wife who patiently waited for him at home. He never spoke kindly about her, they said. He never wanted to go home and always made passes at the waitresses and the other men's girlfriends or wives. That caused more than one fight.

Maybe that's why Graham secretly keeps Beth's handkerchief. His sympathy for her has skyrocketed.

"This guy had to leave some tracks somewhere," Frank noted as he lowered himself into the driver's seat of the patrol car. "Someone's got to know more than they're telling."

They drove to the Navy Yard, brainstorming and putting their questions together. Graham suggested they should question Robbins' supervisor and then talk to Robbins' friends and anyone else who worked on the same shift. It was a piece of cake. Someone was bound to talk.

Two hours and four people later, Frankie sighed as he looked over his notes. "The guy's an asshole," he said in his typically blunt way. "He doesn't show up for work half the time, takes off for three-hour lunches, keeps a bottle of whiskey in his locker, and the guys he works with couldn't care less whether he comes back. Yet these are his buddies. And why haven't they fired him by now?"

"There's something more." Graham negotiated the tight turns where the snowplows hadn't entirely cleaned the streets. The patrol car's chains crunched loudly but pulled them through. His mind worked in almost the same way, grasping at facts and grinding into them until he could gain some purchase on what made sense and what didn't. "That woman the guys kept mentioning has something to do with it."

"Yeah, and why didn't his wife say anything about that? Think she doesn't know? Man, I can see why he cheated on her with some blonde bimbo. His wife's like a little brown sparrow without the tweet, know what I mean? She would drive me nuts. Too quiet."

Graham shot Frank a dirty look, but his partner wasn't paying attention. "She's just shy. And she's hurting. Shit, her husband left her, and now she's got to deal with a bunch of cops coming around. Isn't bad enough she's been dumped, but she's got to be treated like a criminal herself? Give her a break, man."

"The point is, we got to get to the blonde somehow." Frank kept his head down, not bothering to address Graham's indignation. "I have a feeling she's not only the key to this whole deal, but she probably has Robbins cuddled up right next to her every night." He snickered.

They were quiet as Graham negotiated a skinny street where many kids slid down snowbanks on their Flexible Flyers. The kids came from nowhere, yelling as they crashed into each other. Some sat on their sleds, their feet anchored against the steering bar in front, but the older boys flopped on their bellies, sleds sliding under passing cars, taking chances with their lives that would give their poor mothers heart attacks. The street was a mess of blue and red snowsuits.

"Beep the damn horn, or they'll never get out of the way," Frank suggested irritably.

"For someone with kids, you don't have much patience."

"It's not patience you need. You have to show them who's boss. C'mon, beep the damn horn. I want to get out of here sometime today."

Graham beeped the horn, wondering if Jack Robbins had done the same thing or if little Cindy Gordon had come running from behind a car without looking before she'd crossed the street to go home. *How easy it would be to hit a kid*, he thought. *Too damn easy.*

When they returned to the station, Graham realized they still did not know where to look for Robbins. Beth was the only person who could give them more, but he didn't have the heart to push her, even though Frank argued they should visit her again.

"She doesn't know anything," Graham said. "Believe me."

"Well, we'll just make our report and let the Captain decide where to go from here. The kid's all right, isn't she? What's her name? Cindy?"

"As good as she's gonna be. I heard she came out of the coma, and it's gonna be a long haul, but she'll probably be all right." What Graham didn't tell Frank was that he knew Beth had been going to visit the Gordons in the hospital, and that he'd also visited them.

He especially won't tell Frank how he feels about Beth Robbins or that he's visiting her during his off-hours.

Now, he thinks about washing his car, so it'll be perfect for Beth and Miss Indelicato, but the cop part of him continues to work. He should keep his eyes and ears open, never know when someone like Jack Robbins will show up again, and because Graham's a good cop, he will keep his ear to the ground. But he's also a man, and the part of him that feels some affection toward Beth is getting harder to control, especially since it's interfering with his work.

He shrugs his shoulders to release the tension in his shoulders—too many secrets.

In Love with Cary Grant

9:15 P.M.

The movie is "An Affair to Remember," and Cary Grant is more appealing than any man has a right to be. He's serious in this movie. Suave, yet reachable. Sympathetic. The kind of man any woman would love.

Immediately drawn into the story, I forget I'm with two people I didn't know a month ago and allow myself to be transported. I'm in love with Grant, always have been, and understand entirely why Deborah Kerr is, too. I'm sobbing openly when the stars finally come into each other's arms, and the theater lights brighten with the movie's closing credits. I'm embarrassed.

Slinking down in the theater seat, I listen to the sniffles of others around me and am brought back to reality. My elbow is touching Graham Jackson's. My knee leans against his. Pulling away, I tuck my chin in and dab the tissue one last time at the tears still running down my face. Within my chest, a hundred butterflies have been released.

"Nothing like seeing a real tearjerker on the big screen, huh?" Loretta thunders, then honks her nose into a large handkerchief.

Everyone rises and begins filing out through the exits. Graham patiently and slowly meanders down the aisle before me, and his aftershave leaves a rather pleasant trail behind him. His broad shoulders tower above me, and I bend my head to look up at him.

His jet-black hair is parted neatly, and a few tight curls caress his ears. The smooth skin on the back of his neck is a coffee color, a little lighter than his face. As he walks, his shirt tightens and pulls against the waistband of his pants. I can imagine the muscles in his back, and the thought makes my cheeks hot. He's nothing like Cary Grant, with no English accent or perfectly tailored suits, but there's something about Graham Jackson that's attractive and, surprisingly, makes my stomach do flips.

Stop it, Beth.

I dressed carefully this evening, partially because Mama always said it was important to be neat and well-groomed, but also because I felt a heady euphoria accompanied by an overwhelming weight of guilt. Two strange and compromising emotions. The red wool dress I initially pulled out of the closet earlier this evening would have been too flashy and out of place, so I chose a dark blue shirtwaist with pretty, heart-shaped, mother-of-pearl buttons. After a long look in the mirror, I figured a blue ribbon in my hair would be a nice touch, but I pulled a curl loose to cover the birthmark. Then I swept the rest of my clean, Breck-shampoo-shining hair back, tied it with the ribbon, added a pair of pearl earrings, and swiped my lips with a touch of red lipstick. I finger them nervously now.

It feels odd being out socially. I've never gone to the movies with anyone but Jack. When I wasn't with Mama or Nana, I was with Dad, and as soon as he died, it was Jack and has been ever since. I always thought that no one else would want to listen to what I said or spend any time with me. And, sad as it seems to me now, it never really bothered me. I've been quite happy with my family or Jack or alone with my sketch pad—I can honestly say I've spent some of my happiest moments with a charcoal pencil. It surprises me that I've been enjoying other people lately, especially since they have all somehow wormed their way into my heart.

Loretta is behind me now, a running commentary on the movie streaming from her lips as smoothly as the smoke floating skyward from the tip of her Lucky Strike.

We stride quickly to Graham's car: something big and rounded, red and white. I'm never quite sure of the difference between a BelAir and a Buick, but I guess it's one of the two. Maybe I'd know for sure if I sat up front and could look at the dashboard, but I tell Loretta she should, and she does without hesitation. As our doors close and Graham flicks on his headlights, Loretta continues her rant.

"I just can't believe she would have waited that long for him, y'know? I mean, here he is engaged to someone else, and she's engaged to someone else, but they fall in love, and because they can't take the time to talk to each other, and before you know it, they both think the other one is...well, y'know what? It happens all the time. Happened to me when the guy I was going with went overseas. He thought I said something to someone, and I thought he said something and come to find out we were both wrong. It wasn't until about ten years later when Angela told me she'd seen him on the street, that I found out what he thought I said. It took that many years, and some people never find out, y'know what I mean? They go through their whole lives like those two lovebirds in the movie. Hollywood, ha! Those stories are a dime a dozen. A dime a dozen." Loretta pauses and inhales a massive swallow of smoke, then lets loose with some killer smoke rings. She laughs and pokes her cigarette through one, coming close to putting a burn hole in the car's immaculate white leather ceiling.

From the back seat, I watch Graham cock his head and give Loretta a sidelong glance. I can tell he's wondering whether this crazy old lady will be okay in his car, but the look is fleeting. Have I imagined it? *Beth, you can't tell what's going through that man's mind. He's a stranger concerned for his car. Nice enough to take out two sad ladies who happen to live next door to each other. He probably earns extra points from the Policeman's Benevolent Association every time he does a kind deed, like helping an old lady cross the street—like a Boy Scout.* The last thought makes me grin, and I'm glad no one can see me.

In the shadows, the oncoming traffic lights outline Graham's profile. Pieces of him in the flickering lights. An eyelash. The flash of a toothy smile. The flicker of the whites of his eyes as he checks for other cars in an intersection.

I feel protected around him. He's a good cop, I can tell. A good man.

"You know what I think Cary Grant's best movie was? That one he did with Audrey Hepburn. Something about an archeologist." Loretta lights another cigarette off the half-smoked one she still holds between her teeth.

"*Katherine* Hepburn."

"'Scuse me, Beth?"

"I said it was Katherine, not Audrey."

"Oh, yeah. That's right. What was the name of that one?"

"*Bringing Up Baby.*" Graham and I say the title simultaneously.

"Cut me some slack, razorback," Graham laughs and reaches over the seat, his right pinkie held in the air, cocked. "Well?"

We're stopped at a light, and he looks at me and grins, his pinkie still ready.

"I'm sorry…I don't understand."

"We both said the same thing at the same time, so we're supposed to grab pinkies. Didn't you ever do that when you were a kid?"

"No, I didn't. I don't remember anyway," I respond.

The traffic starts again. He withdraws his hand and returns his attention to driving, but he catches my eye in the rear-view mirror. We lurch forward.

"We had all kinds of crazy sayings like that. You know, step on a crack, break your mother's back."

"That's an old one," Loretta pipes up. "We said that when I was a kid, and I'm a helluva lot older than you two."

The conversation ambles along, Graham and Loretta comparing notes while I listen, nodding and laughing as they try to outdo each other. The ride home is far too short, and we yell our goodbyes to Graham, who can't find a parking space in front of the apartment building, as Loretta and I climb out and hurry into the lobby. It's cold enough to take away our breath, and we both wordlessly stomp the snow off our feet, then head into the dull brown hallway and up the stairs to our apartments.

By the time I put my key into my door, the glow of the evening has started to fade a little and when Loretta's goodnights recede down the hallway, it's all too clear how empty my apartment is.

Conversations Behind a Lace Curtain

Thursday, December 5, 1957

"I thought if I brought something from home, it would make her feel a little more cheery, so I packed up some of her dolls and stuffed animals, but she just wants that one you brought up that first week she was here. Do you remember that, Beth?" Theresa is knitting, her needles clacking furiously.

The kids are home with their father tonight, and she is taking what she calls "the night watch." And here I am beside her. It's the first time in several days that we have been alone together, and only a few moments ago, the doctor came in to visit, telling Theresa how lucky she is to still have her little girl. He's amazed that the tiny blonde child not only survived such a historic operation but is well on the way to recovery.

I overheard the entire conversation, even though the doctor took Theresa into the hallway to talk. They stood behind a lace curtain, dark silhouetted heads bobbing, hands gesturing. Sometimes, he patted Theresa on the shoulder. The doctor is tall and skeleton-thin, with bulbous eyes that roll forward as his chin recedes. The dark circles under his eyes must result from worrying about all the children under his care.

Now I tell Theresa that, yes, I remember the doll. And I also remember the first moment I saw Cindy in the hospital bed. The first moment I saw Theresa and Bill comforting each other. The moment they almost lost Cindy, when the monitors went haywire, beeping and blinking. Someday, I'll tell Theresa why, in that very moment when Cindy almost died, I came alive. But for now, I can only promise myself that I'll spend at least part of every day of the rest of my life thanking God that Cindy Gordon is still here, and that she survived.

"What do you think about that?"

"Excuse me. I didn't hear you. My ears are stopped up." I dig my right hand deep into my pocket, searching for some tissues. I've been trying valiantly to hide this cold I woke up with because I know if anyone notices I'm sick, they'll stop me from coming to visit. I don't know if I can stay away from the hospital for two weeks to rid myself of a common cold. *The doctors can sew someone's vein back to their heart, but they can't cure a damn cold. How can that be?* Surreptitiously, I dab my nostrils and listen to Theresa again as she gives me the names of all the dolls and toys she excavated from Cindy's room and brought to the hospital. Theresa's rambling on and on, not asking for any dialogue, yet she seems to notice if my attention strays.

With the practice of being an only child, I point my gaze directly at Theresa, but in my mind, I am many miles away, thinking about Graham Jackson and what he looked like in the low light of a movie theater. How his laughter sounded, deep and rumbling, infectious. How his cologne enveloped me like an invisible caress. And guilt now wraps itself around my thoughts like the tendrils of morning glory.

Why am I thinking of him? I'm married. Married.

I'm having what Jack would have called "a sappy moment."

Jack.

"What are you thinking of?" Therese's knitting needles stop clacking.

I need to be honest from now on. I can't tell any more lies. "Jack. I was thinking of Jack." *There you go again, Beth. Lying through your teeth.*

"Oh." The knitting needles start again. "Well, I guess you'd think about him every once in a while. But I don't put the two of you together in my mind anymore. Guess it's because you're...well, we're friends." She pauses, but the needles continue, then she grunts. "I think about him all the time, too. Driving that truck. Wonder where he's gone. Do you? Seriously, Beth, tell me the truth."

I nod, desperately wanting to do as Theresa asks and tell her the truth, but I turn to look out the window so she won't see the fear in my eyes.

"I never think about the two of you as man and wife. I don't know the man, but I guess I have a monster in my head. After what he did and all," Theresa continues. "Guess I like you and hate him. That's it. Point blank. Especially since he doesn't even act like a man or anything. A man would come forward and at least apologize for what he's done, not hide like a goddamn ostrich. I don't know how someone like you could be married to someone like that..."

The knitting needles clack furiously, as if she's hiding her anger in her yarn, storing her horrible thoughts by knitting them into the sweater she's creating one row at a time. "I'm sorry. I know you're married to him and all. I just don't understand, I guess, how a person as sweet as you could stay with anyone like him..."

"Neither do I," I reply, and it's the truth. I don't understand any of it. Not one whit.

Two for Tea

7:18 P.M.

Loretta stands outside Beth's apartment in the hallway, dressed in khaki pants, her hands stuffed in the pockets, a cigarette dangling out of the corner of her mouth—a female Humphrey Bogart.

"Come over and have tea with me. The house is too quiet," she says. A demand rather than an invitation. The old Loretta. Not the sniveling, sobbing Loretta who fell apart after Angela died, yet she's changed and softened somehow.

I glance behind me, searching for something to say. I can't join my next-door neighbor for tea, but I'm not fast enough. Loretta's hand comes out of her pocket and latches onto my arm. Before I know it, I'm sitting at the Indelicato kitchen table, feeling out of place. This isn't something I planned to do. I was going to head up to the hospital this afternoon. Theresa had mentioned that now that Cindy was awake, she would have me over for dinner after visiting hours some night soon. ("My mother will sit with Cindy for a while—has been dying to do it, as a matter of fact—and you and I can sit down for a proper meal with the kids. I can show you where we live. And the kids can see me for a little while. They haven't had my cooking for a while.")

The thought of going to the Cherry Street Projects, being in Theresa's building with Theresa's family, and surrounded by other buildings full of other families sharing dinners thrills me because I haven't had dinner with anyone my age for years. I'm also a bit embarrassed to admit I've fantasized about the kids and the families in the Projects for almost three years. *What would raising a daughter or a son be like in that place?* I've watched the games of "Red Rover" that the kids have when the sun is setting late on a July night, and I've longed to help a child roll the three balls necessary to make a perfect snowman during a January storm. I've always wanted to see what the little apartments look like inside. They look like little attached houses—four in a row from the outside. The house where Theresa, Bill, and the kids live is at the end of one of the buildings surrounding the play area. The kitchen door opens into the play yard, where the women hang their wet clothes in the warmer months. And Theresa has a wreath on the front door. I noticed the wreath long before I became friends with Theresa. Long before.

Loretta is brusquely moving around at the stove. She brandishes a teapot like a gun and slaps a cup on the table. No saucer. Mumbles something about having to search for the sugar the other morning. "Angela didn't like it, so she didn't want it on the table. Now I can have my sugar on the table."

I want to tell Loretta that I must go, that I have a dinner to attend, a family to be part of, but Loretta's suddenly talking about Angela's funeral and "that cop who's been so helpful"—Graham Jackson. Without a warning, Graham's face comes to my mind. His smile, that little crooked tooth on the lower right side. His dark eyes crinkle when he laughs. His voice.

I shiver.

I accept the tea from Loretta and sip it, covering my heated cheeks. *Why does this man make me so flustered?*

"I don't know what I would have done without him the other day," Loretta says as she settles into her chair. "Really needed someone to lean on, y'know? And there he was, all dressed up in that spiffy uniform, ready to lend a hand to an old lady. Did you know he comes from a huge family? They've lived in Everett all their lives. His dad worked as a waiter for a hotel in Boston and wore those fancy white gloves. Always told his kids he wanted them to be better than him. Told them they should fight to go to school and that it didn't matter what color their skin was. He said that all kids deserve an education. Imagine that! Someone whose grandparents escaped from the plantation on the Underground Railroad, and he's teaching his kids how to do the best they can."

She smiles and shakes her head. "Graham told me he got a lot from his father's lectures. Wishes his dad was still around to see how successful he's become." Loretta takes a sip of her tea and sighs. "Told me all about his sisters and brothers and how much he loves those nieces and nephews of his. They don't make 'em like that anymore. Angela knew it the minute she met him. She was good at spotting people's true personalities. Never gave her credit for it." She pauses and takes another sip of her tea. "I feel bad for that now."

Picking idly at the red plastic tablecloth, I wait for more. If Loretta's anything like her sister, she'll keep going without being asked. I am not sure I want to know what Angela and Loretta thought about me and Jack, but maybe if I stay quiet, she won't ask any questions about us.

"So, you and me, we're alone now, huh?" Loretta's voice is gruff. She reaches for a cigarette, lights it, and puffs.

I sneak a glimpse of Loretta's face, then look away. There's a pile of dishes in the kitchen sink, unwashed. Angela was the housekeeper in this family. Now, dishes, pots, and pans are piling up. I want to wash them, to straighten up the apartment, but I tuck my hands under my legs and ignore the urge. "Yes, I guess we are."

"How long's it been since Jack's been gone?"

"Since November 8th or 9th. I forget." *What a lie that is. I can never forget that date. And it feels like forever that Jack's been gone.*

"Almost a month now." It's Loretta's turn to gaze off thoughtfully. "Don't think he's coming back, do you?"

A sigh escapes me. I shake my head. *No, I don't think he's coming back, and to tell the truth, it's getting to where I don't care.*

"No reason why we can't have a few meals together then, me and you. Would save us both money. I know you haven't got much coming in, if anything, right? And all I've got is that measly little social security check. Might as well pool our resources, huh?" There's almost a plead in Loretta's scratchy voice.

Loretta's reaching out, needing me, wanting my companionship, and I'm expected to respond. "That would be nice," I answer, immediately wondering how I can *say that. I have nothing to give this woman.* But another emotion steals into me: I feel some comfort in this strange woman's home, the warmth—not only physical but heartfelt—the Indelicato sisters have brought into my life. Something's opening up deep inside, an emotion that's been shut off for a long time.

On impulse, I reach across the table and pat Loretta's hand. "That would be nice."

Loretta smiles, pauses a brief second, and then moves away as if unused to the awkward beginnings of a new friendship herself. She clears her throat. "More tea?"

Nodding, I welcome the moment to collect myself, studying my short, ragged fingernails, caught—as always—by the sight of the wedding band glinting on my finger like a blinking yellow light. Jack wouldn't understand how I feel at this very moment, couldn't appreciate the gratitude and apprehension mixing like oil and water in my thoughts, the exhilarating freedom of sitting and having tea with another woman.

"Why didn't you come to Angela's funeral?" Loretta asks.

"Huh?" I look up at her. Loretta's eyes are red and filled with tears.

"You were here when Angela died. That Thanksgiving dinner was for you, but you didn't attend the funeral. I want to know why."

Because I fear death. Because I've had enough of it. Because I feel like I caused it. "I…I… I don't know. I guess I just…I didn't…."

"Spit it out, girl. There's got to be a reason you would disappear instead of coming to a friend's funeral. Not like your dance card is full. Got nothin' else to do. No job. No husband at home. But you disappear almost every day. Where could you go that was more important than coming to my sister's funeral?"

The cup in my hands has become cold even though Loretta filled it with hot water seconds ago. My throat constricts, and I concentrate on the plastic tablecloth's singular, ragged crack.

Loretta shifts herself heavily in the kitchen chair and leans across the table. "I have to know," she says, her voice slightly less strident. "Angela always wanted to know what was happening in other people's lives, always thought ours was boring, and I never paid attention. But this time, I have to know. I need to know why my sister wasn't important to you, even though you were important to her."

The question is fair. Loretta has a right to ask. She deserves an answer, but there isn't one. "I couldn't. I just couldn't."

"Why? Did you think I was gonna blame you for what happened to Angela? I told you before how much I appreciated what you had done that day and how you helped us. Didja think I would change my mind?" Loretta's voice cracks a little. "What is it about you, Beth? How come you hide like a little mouse with a secret? There's more to this. I know there is. More to the shit with Jack. More to your life. I ain't no shrink, but I'd say you're hiding something."

"No, no, I'm not hiding anything. I wouldn't say I like funerals, is all. I just don't like them...some people are like that, you know. I was sorry, Miss Indelicato. But...I couldn't...I just couldn't...."

The curl of steam from the teapot rises into the range hood above, and I try to think about other things: the programs I watched last night, how I should clean out my bedroom closet, the bills I need to pay, and how I should revisit the pawnbroker. *I have that bracelet of Grandma's and a couple of pieces of China that Mama gave me.*

"Please don't ignore me, Beth. This is important. I need to know."

"Yes, I understand." The room is so quiet that I can hear a door shut somewhere down the hallway. Muffled voices. Footsteps. I want to get up and run away like I did the other day, but something has happened to me that makes me think I must stay, must explain myself, and that if I do, Loretta will not only listen, she'll understand. And I desperately need someone to understand. "I couldn't come, Miss Indelicato. I just couldn't."

"Call me Loretta, honey. And why?"

"I guess it's because I've gone to too many funerals in my life. They kind of...I guess they scare me a little."

"It's not something any of us enjoy. I've been to a few myself. But that's when we need other people."

"I know."

Again, silence.

Memories I've refused to acknowledge for many years flood my brain. The moment at Mama's funeral when Dad turned away, when he whispered to someone else—I don't remember who—that the baby was what Mama wanted more than anything else. She needed that baby. And hearing those words made me grieve far more than finding my mother in that crimson-stained tub. *Mama needed that other baby, the baby that she miscarried, more than she needed me. What's wrong with me?*

"Whatever you're thinking of is pretty awful. I can tell by your face. Say it, Beth. Get it out. Talk about it." Loretta's sizeable, warm hand covers mine. It's tentative. Trembling.

The corners of my mouth are dry. I sip the tea and find it's not as cold as I expected. Instead, it's warm, sweet, and soothing as it rolls down my throat and into my chest, expanding my diaphragm and easing the tightness that has threatened to take my breath away.

"Tell me," Loretta urges again, quieter this time, calmer.

Like the snap of an elastic, one memory rolls off another, and they collide, the impact of which brings me out of my chair with a groan. "My mother..."

Loretta says nothing and keeps her hand on mine.

"My mother...died when I was eleven. I found her. The funeral, well, it was the second one I'd been to. My grandma died a few years before that. I didn't want to go, but they made me. Daddy made me." I fidget a bit, thinking that maybe I'm being disloyal to Daddy by telling on him this way.

The air smelled of mothballs that day, and people I didn't recognize filled the funeral home. Black suits and dresses moved back and forth in front of where I sat, murmuring voices and piles of food that went uneaten. People kept grabbing at me, trying to hug me, saying things I didn't want to hear like, "Your mother's with the angels now, sweetheart." and "You'll see her again someday, don't you fear."

"There were flowers everywhere: white roses, pink carnations, ugly stems of gladioli, wreaths with banners that read 'loved one' and 'cherished wife.'" I kept my gaze on the window beyond Loretta's head rather than looking at her as I spoke. "I tried to stay close to Daddy, holding on to his suit coat, hiding against his side, keeping my damaged cheek turned away from those who'd stare at it, trying not to cry, trying to be brave like he'd told me that morning before we left the house. I did whatever he said, trying to be the girl Mama always wanted me to be. But there was no hiding in that funeral home. I leaned my head under his arm and kept it there throughout the service."

The coffin, gold and mahogany, stood on a pedestal at the other end of the room. And Mama inside, dressed in a long-sleeved white wool dress. The dress Daddy chose specifically because it would cover Mama's wrists. I had wanted to sit next to the coffin all night, told Daddy I needed to stay there, that Mama needed her, but Daddy had screamed at me, told me Mama had sinned, that she needed no protection from anyone on earth, that she would not be with the angels. "She's going straight to hell!" he'd said.

I don't tell Loretta that part.

"What happened to your mother, Beth?" Loretta asks when I'm silent for a while. "How did she die? She must have been awfully young since you weren't even a teenager."

I nod and swallow. "She was only thirty-five."

"Oh, God, how horrible. A life unlived."

Turning my palms up, I lace my fingers in with Loretta's and know I will trust her, have to trust her, and let it all loose. "She killed herself, my mother. She sliced her wrists wide open, and I found her in the tub before my father got home from work. I couldn't wake her up, you know? I put every bandage in the house around her wrists, but it wasn't enough."

"Jesus...."

"It was my fault. I killed her." I don't raise my eyes, don't see Loretta's reaction, nor do I care. The urge to tell the story, the entire story, swallows me like a tidal wave. I have no control anymore.

"Daddy always wanted a boy," I tell her, "but Mama kept trying and trying to get pregnant and couldn't. Finally, she did, and she was happy. I remember the day she lost the baby; Daddy came home and paced back and forth in front of the bathroom...kept telling her it'd be okay. They'd try again. And that night, I heard them talking. I think I overheard them talking a lot, but this is the only time I remember because they were talking about me. Daddy was saying it was Mama's fault that they'd had me to begin with, that she wanted a baby too early, and that's why they thought God had punished them when they had me, the baby with the red stain on her face. Daddy yelled at her that she needed to do better, needed to give him a little boy, a perfect little boy, to carry on his name, that I wasn't good enough. Especially since I was...."

Loretta tightens her grip on my hand but doesn't say anything.

"Especially since I was flawed. That's the word he used: flawed. My birthmark meant God disapproved of me, he said. I'd always brought bad luck to them, he said."

"That bastard." Loretta's voice is growly, low, sinister. "How dare he? God, a beautiful girl like you. How dare he say something so cruel?"

Puzzled, I cock my head and study Loretta momentarily. She has a sympathetic look on her face. I believe she really cares. "But he's right. I have a defect. Mama knew it, too. Daddy loved me anyway. Despite the birthmark."

"I don't believe that." Loretta shakes her head so violently that the loose skin below her chin quivers like a turkey's neck. "No mother could feel their child was anything less than perfect, especially one like you. I don't know you well, Beth Robbins, but I can tell you honestly that I know you're good and pure-hearted, and that mark on your face means nothing. It doesn't cover up the beauty in your eyes, the luster of your hair, or the graceful way you move. Your mother must have seen that, honey. She knew what a special daughter you were."

As much as I yearn to believe Loretta's words, I can't. My eyes burn with unreleased tears. "If she loved me as much as you think, she wouldn't have killed herself. It was my fault that she lost that baby. I killed her."

"No, you didn't! Think back, Beth. Think about growing up and spending time with your mother. Did she act like she didn't love you? Prove to me that she didn't love you!"

Struggling, I try to pull my hands away, but Loretta holds tight. "It's true. She didn't. Dad told me again and again. Over and over. She killed herself because I wasn't good enough, and she couldn't have the baby she wanted. She wanted a boy. A perfect little boy."

"No. Think about it some more, Beth. We always remember the worst, but there must be more. What did she do with you when you were little? Did she take care of you when you were sick? Did she come to school to see your teachers? Did she tell you stories at night? Think, Beth. Think!"

"I don't want to. Please, Loretta. I really don't want to talk about this anymore. I didn't go to Angela's funeral because I'd been to my grandmother's, my mother's, and my father's, and I didn't feel like I could attend anymore. I'm sorry, Loretta...I'm really sorry." I'm crying now—large, sloppy gasps—and I wish I could stop.

"Okay. Let's not talk about Angela right now." Loretta turns away, takes a deep breath, then looks back. "Let's talk about you. No child is unworthy of their parents' love, Beth. If I had a little girl, nothing could make me stop loving her—no defect, as you call it. No deformity. Nothing. I can't believe your mother didn't love you. And I don't think you do either. So, tell me. Tell me what she was like when you were growing up."

A long sigh. I bite into my lip until my mouth tastes like copper. Still, Loretta won't loosen her grip or withdraw her questions.

In the slow seconds that follow, the horrible memory of the funeral recedes like a wave rolling back into the tidal ocean, and the flood of emotions calms and slows to a trickle. Then I see Mama's face (smiling, loving), hear her voice (singing, crooning), and feel the pristine emotion that can only be defined as love.

"She was the most beautiful woman in the world," I begin, "and she could do anything."

Do You Work?

Friday, December 6, 1957

Sleet clouds pile against each other in the early morning sky like slabs of silver and white marble. Impenetrable. Silent. No light refracting through their outer edges.

There are no other people on Broadway and no lights in the supermarket or the drugstore windows. A gloom of sadness stretches across the darkened windows of Cahill's Funeral Home, even though the building is a miniature version of the White House. The apartment building on the corner of Hancock Street sits back from the sidewalks of Broadway, a chain-link fence surrounding a sad lawn area. In direct contrast, Dr. Stoller's house across the street looks down on Broadway like a haughty Brahmin matron, and a stone wall lifts the manicured lawns to eyesight level so that passersby see the green expanse and its lush gardens. In the springtime, bright yellow and red tulips ordered straight from Holland line the walkway to the majestic front door.

I love the house, its white pillars reaching the second floor, and through the floor-to-ceiling windows framing the front door, I can see the secretary's desk in the foyer. I've been to Dr. Stoller's house for Halloween when I was little and have seen the doctor in his office half a dozen times every year. Sometimes, I think about visiting to tell him about my life, to hear his robust laugh, and to get some medication that will make all my pains—imagined and real—go away. Looking up at the second-floor windows now where a faint light beams, I imagine the doctor getting dressed to go to the hospital and deliver a baby or to attend to an accident victim.

What would it be like to live in a house like that, to have an upstairs and a downstairs, a chandelier in the living room, a piano in the corner, and room for a studio where I could paint on actual canvas and use dozens of tubes of paint: amber and citron, indigo and pistachio, cinnamon, raven, plum, goldenrod, cardinal, vermillion, ultramarine? What would it be like to be free to paint the sunshine-yellow flowers that grow in front of the house in the middle of July? What would it be like to take vacations to the beaches of Florida and paint the azure ocean and the periwinkle sky, the palomino beige sands, and the alabaster shells with interiors as pristinely pink as the bottom of a baby's foot?

It's easy to daydream when Everett is quiet, and no one asks me to pay the rent, tells me that I need to cook supper, or reminds me there are clothes to be washed. The city often intrudes on me like Jack did, slowly and quietly, determined to keep me off guard, and I'd give anything to be somewhere else. Maybe New Hampshire or down in Florida, or maybe over there in Paris, where I would wander the streets, paint-covered and ecstatically happy. But then I think about Loretta, Theresa, and Graham...and I don't know, but something keeps me here. *Would Jack be surprised if he came back and I was still here? Still here, but different.*

The streetlights shine brightly, guiding me as I pick my way along the sidewalk, trying to avoid the crusty, dirty remains of the last snowstorm and the puddles of icy water threatening to seep over the tops of my ankle-high boots. I'm going to the Navy Yard, determined to get there before any of the day shift arrives, to stand at the gates and talk to people as they arrive for work. Maybe someone there has seen Jack or knows where the blonde woman lives. I have to know. Either I will face it and move on, or I will be stuck in limbo, like one of those mice who run on wheels and never go anywhere. I have the edgy feeling of tumbling over the cliff as my mother did, but something deep inside is guarding me, protecting me against that loss of control, and it keeps pushing me through every painful moment of the day.

Keeping the thought of squaring off with Jack upfront is the key to maintaining control and getting on with my life, either with or without him. And I have to find out where he is, convince him that he no longer needs to guard our "secret," and tell him that no matter what happens... I am ready to face it.

This has got to end.

I waver off the sidewalk, knowing there is no danger in wandering into the middle of the quiet street, enjoying the temporary pause in time that coats the city like a strangling blanket. Through the heavy quiet, there's a sense that life is more straightforward, that expectations are clearly defined, but that the city and everything beneath the surface rumbles like a hibernating bear, breathing and snoring and ready to rouse, threatening to disrupt our understanding of the universe. Within half an hour or so, there will be no walking down the yellow line in the middle of Broadway. I'll have to stay on the sidewalk again, behave myself, and forget that being alive means you have to take chances and gamble. Every day. Soon, the bus will start its regular trips up and down Broadway, traveling to Everett Station, where everyone gets off to take the El to downtown Boston. Every half hour, then every fifteen minutes, and at the height of the workday, every five. But I still have an hour or two alone. I've learned to guard those hours when I have no one to answer to, and I wonder whether looking for Jack is the wisest thing to do. I should follow the yellow line and ignore the sidewalk. One foot in front of the other. Thoughts of cars and trucks and buses. The uncertainty of my next move weighs heavily on me.

Jack's truck.

Only twenty minutes ago, when I left by the rear door of the apartment building so no one would see me (even though I knew few would be awake at 4:35 A.M.), I saw the space in the apartment parking lot where the truck used to be. When I passed it, a brief, fleeting memory quickly made my eyes fill: Jack couldn't start the truck one day and finally popped the hood to discover that a family of squirrels had gotten in over the weekend and made the engine their new home. They'd filled the whole front end of the truck with pinecones. I could hear him laughing all the way upstairs. That was a good memory of him, but it made my heart pause and my shoulders hunched in pain.

One foot in front of the other.

When I crest the hill after passing the square brick mass of the high school and catch my first glimpse of the night lights in Everett Square, the area's lights appear cradled in the basin like a vast cotton ball. Each building's edges blur, indistinctly melting into the next. The Immaculate

Conception Church's spire disappears into the early morning fog, while The First National Bank's clock creates a dim orange circle in the distance. I squint as if that will help bring everything into focus, but I don't see anything more clearly, except there's now an indistinct form moving warily in the middle of Broadway, about two blocks down the hill.

Someone else is following the yellow line.

As I draw closer, I hear singing. A deep, raspy voice. The voice of someone who has destroyed their throat.

A woman.

A woman dressed in bright colors. Too many colors. Deep-blood red and royal purple. Pastel pink and sun-bright yellow. Layer after layer of skirts and blouses, strange layers of stripes and lacy petticoats, and a wildly flowered hat atop it all. More than one hat.

Still closer, almost creeping now, I know who it is: Connie, the crazy lady. I have seen her many times before and grew up with stories about the woman, how she had once led an everyday life with a husband everyone knew because he delivered the morning eggs and milk. Two handsome sons: big boys with brawny laughs. Connie had been attractive, Daddy once said. He knew her from before the beginning of the war—before she lost her husband in a messy hunting accident, then her younger son to pneumonia, and finally, her oldest son on the beach at D-Day. Connie went over the edge when she received that news, and then she was hospitalized. She's been in and out ever since. And when she's out, everyone in Everett knows. She stands, arms akimbo, in front of huge delivery trucks, screams in the faces of frightened school children, dumps trash cans upside down, and uses both hands to scoop through the trash, pushing handfuls into her dirty mouth. She causes trouble, but she's funny, too. The kids get a big kick out of Crazy Connie's antics. All I feel when I look at her is how much pain she has endured.

Connie doesn't know I'm there, watching her. Everett's old crazy lady is dancing. Singing. She is kicking her heels up as if she's Mrs. Vanderbilt gone to the ball.

Into the morning mist, her voice carries an unclear melody, the hint of a lullaby in the rusted metal sound. Then, the song comes into focus for me.

It has always enticed me to dance: "Don't sit under the apple tree with anyone else but me..."

The strength of the mind. Her memory of that song overcomes the pain.

The colors Crazy Connie wears blur and melt—streaks of bright sunset colors: pumpkin, saffron, rosy red—as she moves her arms and legs, keeping in the rhythm of her discordant tune. She becomes a strange female version of Joseph in his many-colored coat.

The moment is purely magical. Sometimes in everyone's life, you can look back years later and remember every blessed detail: what you wore, how the air smelled, the way the veins ran down the backs of your hands, how it felt for warm blood to flow through your veins, how each swallow of air slipped into your nostrils and down your throat and filled up your stomach cavity so that it pressed against the waistband of your skirt, how it felt to breathe.

This is one of those times.

I move slowly, opening my pocketbook and lifting out the little sketch pad I've been keeping in there for the times I go to the hospital and play with Theresa's kids. I put one blind hand into the bag and hunt for the pencil, keeping the sketch pad under my arm. I never take my eyes off Connie, who blissfully continues her dance with the elements.

"...anyone else but me...anyone else but me...no, no, no..." she sings, her voice wobbling as she dances.

I sketch her, following the lines of the ankle-length scarf that Connie has wrapped around her neck, exaggerating the jagged edges of her grayish-orange hair and the thin, stringy strands that flop over her dried and pinched shoulders. As my pencil flies quickly over the paper, I know the contrast of the vibrant woman in the street and the muted city buildings in the background will make a powerful watercolor. *Maybe the guy at the gallery can sell it. He seems to like the portraits.* Excited, I draw quickly, willing the sky to stay that safe color of morning before the sun rises and reveals all the world's truths. *If only I could keep drawing. If only I could stay in the middle of the street, watching this woman, free of the world and its problems, safe in my dreamlike realm.*

If only I could believe in miracles.

For just one moment. One time in my life. No worries. No memories. No expectations.

The drawing is one of my best, but it's almost ruined when a large black Buick rounds the corner off Hampshire Street and comes close to hitting me. I skitter to the sidewalk, and when I turn around, Connie's gone. The sky is lightening with early morning streaks of purple and slate blue turning lighter blue on the bottom edge of the horizon.

Suppressing a shiver, I'm suddenly struck by the thought that I could be Connie, that I've endured as many deaths of people I've loved, that I've felt on the edge of insanity more than once, that I'd like to disappear into the side streets and become anonymous and slightly dangerous like Crazy Connie: unattached to the rest of the world.

The thought surprises me and brings unexpected memories of Mama and Dad. Someone once told me that when you lose a mother, you'll never have anyone else in your life who will care as much about you and what you do, about whether you have a cold or a pain in your stomach, about whether you will become rich and famous or die poor and unknown. Yet a father cares for his children, too, and sometimes I miss Dad more than I miss the woman who *chose* to leave me. At least Dad didn't go away on purpose.

Is it easier to be disconnected from reality like Connie? Why is it that some people suffer, and others disappear into a madness that takes them away from the pain? Why can't I? It would be so much easier if...

Instantly, I feel guilty for feeling that way. It's a moment of fragility that I've experienced far too often in my life, and I wouldn't say I like that feeling of vulnerability. I'm angry at myself for feeling that way. Mama couldn't help how she felt. She had lost control. That's the one thing I'm positive about: she couldn't stop the darkness.

But Jack could. Why couldn't he stand by me when the police came to the door? Why couldn't we handle the accident together? Instead, he let me lie and teeter on the edge of the abyss into which Connie and many others have already fallen.

Maybe this act of lying I've cultivated is not the easy way out.

Maybe Connie's madness is enviable.

Maybe staying focused on life and what happens daily is the true madness.

I toss my head back, swallow the 'what ifs', and shove the drawing into my pocketbook. I force myself to move to the safety of the sidewalk, the ribbon of cement emerging in the weak morning light. I force myself to face forward and move on.

Forgive Me, Father, For I Have Sinned

6:35 A.M.

The Immaculate Conception Church is not extremely pretty: all red brick and straight-up columns on the front of the building, no gargoyles like some of the other churches in town, no muted stained-glass windows, but a deep and wide entranceway with impressively luxurious steps going into the vestry reminds everyone who enters of the magnificence of Catholicism. The doors are closed at this time of day, and there's no one going in or out of the entranceways as there usually are at other times. I've been here many times with Mama and Daddy and one time long ago with a girlfriend. *What was her name? Joanna? Short, missing one tooth in front, always giggled when she had to leave me sitting in the aisle while she went into that telephone booth of a confessional. Joan. That's it. Joan Rodale.* Jack came here when he first arrived home from Korea. He really found some solace in this church for a while. I haven't been inside for at least a couple of years.

Even though I don't officially belong to any church, I love visiting them. I love their glorious architectural elements (the flying buttresses and arched ceilings), and I also love the sad and pained statues of Jesus and the saints. I admire the Catholic way of presenting the heart as separate from the body. It makes sense to me. I'm sure my mind and heart are linked, but only emotionally. Otherwise, my body is in control. Everyone is that way. Look at men. If they could control their bodies, they wouldn't cheat like Jack.

When I was little, we attended church several times a year, mainly for the Christmas and Easter holidays. We watched the pageants, tried to sing along with the music (though only Mama knew the words to any of the hymns), and repeated our names to whatever priest was on duty. It seemed there was always someone new, Daddy said. But I soon realized it wasn't the new priests and nuns; it was us.

Now, I'm struck by an urge to go into the vestry and enter the main chapel.

It's early yet, and it's cold. I'll go in for a minute or two. I won't bother anyone this early in the morning.

I mount the steps and count three footsteps to cross each stair. Same as when I was a child. The church door has a large round handle in the middle. I pull on it and swing the heavy oak door wide enough to slip inside. Pause a moment to let my eyes adjust to the inside gloom. The door hushes closed, and I can hear nothing but my breathing. It's like entering a living being, like walking into one chamber of a heart.

My heels echo as I head toward the altar. In the middle stands an ivory-colored Jesus on the cross, his eyes heavenward, a dribble of blood along the right side of his face, the crown of thorns on his brow. The painting of 'Jesus in the Garden' that the Methodists on Ferry Street have hung in their small side chapel is prettier. The Jesus in that painting looks peaceful, handsome, and not in agony like this one. At least the chapel is quiet, but any quiet chapel will do when in need.

As I've seen people do in the past, I nod with respect to the altar and cross to the table with its tiers of red glass candleholders. When I was a kid, I didn't understand why Mama wouldn't let me light every one. "It would be prettier, Mama. The church would have more light." Mama would smile and look around to see if anyone was watching, then let me put the match to two candles instead of one. "Just two, Bethie. You're only supposed to light one at a time. It's a sin if you waste them. They're for people who need to remember someone or forget their troubles. You don't have anyone to forget and no troubles to think of, so you better not light any more than two."

Can I light more than two now, Mama? I've got plenty of people to remember and lots of trouble I want to forget.

I sit in the third row, set my pocketbook down, and kneel on the maroon velvet prayer bench. Dropping my forehead against my folded hands, I start, "Forgive me, Father, for I have sinned. I have lied many times in the past couple of weeks and hurt one of your children badly..."

Brick Walls and Thick Mists

7 A.M.

At the Navy Yard in Charlestown, the wind from the Mystic River cuts through the yard, making the workers walk at an angle, hunched into their pea coats, collars turned up, hands stuffed deep into their pockets. Stretching as far as I can see are rows and rows of brick buildings that house the spinning jenny (like the one Jack worked on) and the rope maker machines. To my left, some retired destroyers, like the USS Cassin Young, line up in neat rows—gray metal monsters softened by the colorful flags that flutter from the masts in the chilly breeze. The destroyers are disappearing one by one, though Jack has always said the government will keep them afloat as long as the "Commies are any kind of a threat at all."

A raw ball of anger rises in my chest, making my heart pound, my eyes narrow, and my thoughts as clear and sharp as the pain that Jack has purposely inflicted upon me. And I'm mad at myself. Ashamed.

This has got to stop.

I'm determined to find Jack, to face him, tell him how much I hate what he's done, then I'll turn myself in, tell the officers that I was in the car, that I am as much at fault as my husband. I'll hold my wrists out so they can slap the manacles on and let them lead me to a single, smelly jail cell where I'll sit on the edge of a worn mattress until a judge offers me my punishment, as I should be.

My mind is made up.

Positioning myself near the gate, I question the guys as they hunch by, some with cigars hanging from the corner of their mouths, some wearing navy blue knitted caps pulled down over their ears, some with angry forehead lines that deepen when they glance my way when I ask, "Do you know Jack Robbins? Have you seen him lately? Is he still working?"

Most shake their heads and continue through the chain-link gate to the brick government buildings where they'll design ships, transport government documents from one office to another, or fix engine parts. Several men look at me, smile, then avert their eyes when the wind whips my hair and they see the birthmark on my cheek.

Three men, joking and swinging iron-colored lunch pails, crowd past me. One of them, young and dark-haired, gives me the once-over.

"Hey, missy, do you want to go to the Chelsea Grill for a beer and a bowl of spaghetti?" he says after I ask my questions. His buddies laugh as if the guy's Red Skelton, like the guy's getting paid to say something hilarious.

"Do any of you know Jack Robbins?" I hug my pocketbook close and stand stiff-legged, chin out, as though that will protect me.

The dark-haired guy says, "Sure, I know him. What'll it get me, honey?"

His buddies laugh again. I pretend to ignore them and fight the urge to snap at them. *They shouldn't push me. Not today.* "I'm his wife, and I'm looking for him."

"We all are. He owes me money—and Butch over there, too," the guy replies. "Left you high and dry, too, did he? Maybe I should take over for him, huh?"

The guys laugh again. Some other men coming through the gate slow down and pay attention. I'm the only woman in the group. This was probably a bad idea, more trouble than it's worth, but I can't stop now.

"I just want to know if you can give me an address or a phone number. It's important. I need to get hold of him as soon as possible."

"What's the matta, honey? Ain't I good enough for you? That Jack was a slob. He cheated on you left and right, didn't he, now? I won't do that, little girl. You'd have nothing to worry about with me."

I would swear the guy is drunk if it weren't so early in the morning. I hate that he's telling me what I've always known about Jack, yet I'm surprised that it doesn't bother me and doesn't dig into the sensitive part of me as it would have a couple of weeks ago. For the first time since the accident, I wonder if I am still in love with my husband. *Is this what it feels like to fall out of love?* Could this vacuum, this numbness, be the denial of something else, something more visceral lurking right underneath the surface? Anger, maybe? I'm not sure of anything anymore, but I know I can't go on without seeing Jack, without ending this roller coaster. If it means we need to divorce, so be it. I just need to know.

"He disappeared a while ago. Have any of you seen him? I know he hasn't been to work, but maybe some of you—one of you—has talked to him?" I look past the young guy to his friends, who ignore me and stare at him as if expecting him to pick up what Jack Robbins left behind.

"Nah, he hasn't been around since that accident he was in, since the cops started lookin' for him," the guy says and looks over his shoulder at his friends, who all shake their heads negatively, nudging each other and whispering. "Maybe you ought to call Betty or Cathy or that other broad...what's her name, Joey? Remember that blond he was running with?"

Joey, a short, stocky man wearing a Navy cap plunked squarely on his head, yells out, "Wasn't that Linda Nuvembria?"

A tall man off to my right chimes in, "No, Linda, don't see Jack no more. She's with Charlie Oden now."

They all guffaw as if the man has told a wonderful joke. Several more men in pea coats move to the fringes of the crowd I've attracted. Their posture reveals an air of expectation, and I'm reminded of the time a group of dogs surrounded a bitch in heat and almost ripped her to shreds. There's the same pacing, wide-eyed breathiness, stiff-shouldered anticipation here. The men all wear their maleness cockily as they do their sailor hats: raunchily, at rakish angles, shoved on the back of a head of greased hair. None of them seem willing to protect me. They're just here for the show.

Maybe this wasn't such a good idea after all.

"A cute thing like you doesn't deserve a rotten bastard like Jack. Why don't you give me your number, and I'll show you what a real man is all about." The guy takes another step toward me, close enough to smell last night's beer on his breath and to see the hard negativity in his dirt brown eyes. Lots of guys have that look nowadays. I saw it in Jack's eyes when he came home from Korea. "I can take you out on the town," the guy says. "We can get a pizza and have a good time. Whaddya think?"

"I'm just looking for Jack. That's all I want. I need to find out where my husband is. It's important." I try to smile and move away, but it's too late.

The group closes ranks, and suddenly, there's nowhere else to go. Instinctively, I duck my head and fall into my old habit of seeing everything from beneath my lashes. I have no clue what they're about to do, but I'm terrified.

"Aw, go out with him, girlie," one of the older guys growls.

"Yeah, Roy here won't hurt ya." That comes from somewhere in the back of the group. I don't know who's speaking.

"He ain't coming back, that Jack. We ain't seen him since he left, and those cops came lookin' for him." Another voice. This one is to my right. Repeating what everyone else has already told me.

Voices from all directions. My heart beats faster. *You stupid girl. Why did you come here? What did you think you were going to accomplish? Why do you need to see him, anyway? Is it really going to help? Is it really going to make any difference? No, get strong, you idiot. Buck up! If you don't fight for yourself, who will?*

"Okay, get out of my way, guys," I tell them, sounding more brave than I feel. "Let me go home. You're pushing. Please don't push me. I don't like it when people push me." *Get a grip on yourself, Beth. What the hell is wrong with you?*

Someone grabs my shoulder from behind. Another guy moves in from the right. I swing out my pocketbook and spin around in a circle, hoping to hit as many of them as possible. I stumble. Everyone laughs. Screams of laughter. That kind of laughter, I've heard it before. In a schoolyard. Behind the library. At the playground right after Mama died. *"Look at the poor girl with the big ugly birthmark on her face. Isn't she funny? Isn't she a piece of work?"*

"Stop!" My hands are fisted. My head rears up, teeth bared. "All I want to know is where my husband is. If you guys can't help me, then leave me alone!"

The laughter dies down. A new sound begins. It's a more ominous, rumbling sound, as if I've done something unacceptable by not cooperating with their game.

"Hey, now I know why he left," someone in the back says.

"You don't want her anyway, Ron. She's used goods." The guy in front elbows the one beside him, who started this whole mess. Several men in the group's rear peel away, leaving the pack and moving toward the buildings past the gate.

My face burns. I long to say something, but the men before me have all melted into a blur. I can't tell who's talking. Then the guy they've called Ron reaches out to me with a reddened finger and pokes my cheek. "You can't have offers like this every day, Jack's wife. Sure, you don't want to take me up on it?" He sneers—tobacco stains on his teeth.

"Ah, leave her be. There's the horn," someone else says, and the group breaks up and disintegrates like a bowl of sugar left out in the rain.

Miraculously, two seconds later, I'm alone.

Shaken, I'm about to hurry out of there when another figure in a pea coat moves toward me. I dart to the right, determined not to be caught in anyone else's way, but the man is quicker. He reaches out and grabs the sleeve of my coat. Now I'm furious and sick of being treated like an animal captured in a trap. All of the anger roused by the men and the frustration of not being able to find out anything about Jack come to a head, and I kick out at this new man, astonished when he groans in pain and says my name.

It's only then that I get a good look at him. "Graham?"

"Sheesh, Beth, you don't have to break my leg. I was only trying to help."

"What are you doing here?"

"What are *you* doing here?" He's bent over, rubbing his leg, a mix of curiosity and pain in his eyes as he looks up at me. He's not wearing his hat or uniform, and there are no police cars anywhere nearby.

"I've got to find out where my husband is. I guess...I decided...well, enough is enough. This has got to end. But when I came here, well, those guys..." I gesture feebly behind me, feeling a little silly. All the men have headed into the buildings where they work, and we're alone. He can't possibly know what I'm talking about, and trying to explain it at this point is useless. "Look, I'm sorry about what I've done..."

"Ah, don't worry about it. I'll live."

"I don't mean about that." I gestured toward his leg.

"You meant to kick me? Is that what I get for trying to help you?" He's smiling, kidding me, but his mahogany-colored eyes narrow slightly. "Y'know, we've already been here, my partner and I, and it doesn't seem like anyone knows anything. You could've asked me."

I sigh. "All I want to know is where he is. I've got to talk to him. And after I talk to him, I've got to tell you, Theresa, Loretta, and…" I'm not sure where I'm going with this explanation and why I feel compelled to tell him about it, other than he's the cop who investigated the accident, and he should know the truth.

This has got to end.

It starts to drizzle, and we look up and then at each other. Graham smiles, and I am surprised to reluctantly smile back. I am even more surprised that there's another emotion rising in the pit of my stomach: a warmth, a realization that it's safe to be with this man, that he's not at all like Jack, that he might even protect me against Jack, and that everything might be okay.

But it's not and never will be, and I have no right to feel this way. God, what's wrong with me? This man is not only not my husband, he's a police officer. And a Negro. Am I crazy?

"Let me give you a ride home—again." Graham chuckles. "This is getting to be a habit, huh? I'm heading in for my shift, but I still have half an hour. I might ask some questions around here, but I can do that later. And whatever I find out, I'll tell you. I promise."

"They can't tell you anything." The empty walkway into the Navy Yard and its imposing buildings seem to mock me. *Go ahead*, they seem to say, *tell him.*

"Jack's the only one who knows what happened that day," I say. *Jack and me.*

"And he'll get what's due him, but right now, let's get out of this rain."

Graham's closer now. I can smell his Old Spice aftershave. Then his hand is on my shoulder, and he keeps it there as we walk to his car. His touch is surprising—and surprisingly gentle. His hand is not heavy. It's respectful and kind. Comforting. When he takes it away to let me in the car's passenger side, I want to grab it back and place it around my shoulders again, but the moment's gone.

As he pulls away from the curb, I realize I have no right to expect him or anyone else to comfort me, and the morning becomes suddenly chilly again.

The Saltiness of His Mouth

In front of us, the Mystic River Bridge rises atop cement stanchions that poke high into the breaking fog. The steel and cable arches that lead into the heart of Boston sketch the skies like penciled-in lines, unfinished and never-ending. Massive warships and tankers are docked on the south side of the bridge, and the Constitution, one of the country's oldest ships, nestles against the dock below. In eighth grade, my teacher, Mrs. Pitcher, took the class on a special field trip to see the historic frigate. Mama was supposed to come on that trip, but she had a 'bad day' and told me to go alone, that I'd have more fun with my friends. Much like today, the day had been cold and dreary, and I had stuck close to Mrs. Pitcher. She let me carry some paper and a pencil with me and though she had complimented my quick pencil sketches of the sailors in old-time garb, it wasn't enough. The absence of Mama, her comforting presence, created a gaping hole in the experience.

Now, the bridge hums with cars that I imagine are driven by lawyers and bankers on their way to work on Tremont Street or Beacon Hill. There are other people in the world, other traumatic events in other lives, and I know it, but right now, at this very moment, for me, the only thing that matters in the world is that I have failed. The last of my dignity whispers out of my body and rises into the rumble of Boston as it rouses to meet the work day.

"I'll open the door for you," Graham says from behind my shoulder.

I twist my head to the left. His badge glows, and he winks at me. I step aside, let him open the door, and lower myself in without raising my eyes to his face. If I do, it'll make me feel cherished and warm. And that's scary. Feeling any positive emotion in this moment of deep distress is terrifying. I'm in big trouble, anyway. Why make it worse?

It takes a couple of moments before either of us speaks, and then we both try at the same time.

I nod at him, silently giving him the go-ahead to start, not trusting myself to say anything.

"Those guys didn't have much to tell you about your husband, did they?" A shadow moves along Graham's jaw as if some unseen hand is monitoring what he says and how he says it.

"Nobody seems to know where he is." Looping my hands through my pocketbook strap, I rock back and forth. "I have to talk to him. I can't take this anymore. He hasn't called, and I need to talk to him. We need to set things straight." I'm clipping my words; I don't care that Graham will know the truth in only a matter of seconds.

It's time he knows the truth about me, even though it'll change everything. Look at him looking at me. Why is he doing that? What did I do to make this happen? What the hell is he doing here? Who am I kidding—he's here because of Jack. He's just doing his job, acting like a cop. How suspicious do I look?

"The man has disappeared. No one knows anything." The words are more a question than a statement, and he tests me with a quick glance. "If you'd asked me, I could have told you. I'm not supposed to get close to...certain people, but I think we've become friends."

I will ignore the obvious question in his mind about whether we're friends. I know all too well how people feel about seeing Black men with white women, yet I don't understand why people judge others because of the color of their skin. I saw the news reports about Emmitt Till a couple of years ago and never understood why someone would kill a Negro man for doing the same thing white men do every day: whistle at a woman. And the poor kid was only 14 years old. Not even a man yet! He is certainly not old enough to fight for his country. I can't help but imagine how terrified he was as that angry mob beat him—hitting him over and over again before they threw his unconscious body into the river. Mississippi. I never want to go there. Yes, I know why Graham's nervous about being friends with me.

As for me, it's too scary to talk about *any* relationship right now. Always has been. "How many people have you talked to? Have you called Jack's family? Do any of his cousins know where he is? I don't speak to them anymore." *I'm talking too damn fast. He's got to know there's something wrong. Those eyes of his. He doesn't miss a thing.* "Jack didn't like me to talk to them, but I know he saw them occasionally. Without me."

Graham squirms a little. "I'm not supposed to tell you this, but Frankie and I have done all the investigating the department told us to, but we didn't find out a thing. Then I started snooping a little on my own time, and for the rest of the stuff, well, I... I found out for myself. Things have been busy lately, and since the little girl was okay...well, things like this get shoved aside when you have burglaries and families who are trying to kill each other, drunks who keep causing fights, and crazy people who like to walk in traffic. Every day is an adventure at the Everett Police Department."

He tries to smile, but it becomes a painful look that tells me exactly how busy Everett has become. It's ironic because a while ago, during the war, someone said that the police force was quieter than usual. There wasn't much violence in the barrooms, on the streets, and in homes, once the guys were gone, and the women managed all the aspects of daily family life. No guys home to beat on their wives and kids, no robberies, no bar fights. Leave the women in charge, and things became peaceful. After World War II, the crime level went up again, as if the war had been responsible for actually keeping the homeland a little more tranquil.

Graham's still taking. "...and we just keep our eyes open in case anything happens..." His tone is both apologetic and disgusted, as though he believes they should have done more. "Anyway, I went around alone and talked to all his friends and family. Nobody has seen him. Guess your husband owes some of them money."

I nod. *Typical of Jack to owe everyone money.* He often complained about paying off half the guys at work before he even brought his paycheck home, yet I never knew where he spent it, though I suspected most of it went to the local barrooms.

"He's using this accident as an excuse to avoid everyone," I say. "I should have known better a long time ago. This was the perfect opportunity for him to take off. No one will ever see or hear from him again, and I'm left holding the bag. Everyone's going to think he did me this great favor, but he has destroyed my life. Cuts me down to the smallest pieces. And he knows there's absolutely nothing I can do about it." I cut my eyes to Graham, and he's looking back at me with such compassion that I can't help but totally and completely trust him.

"How can someone be so cruel?" I ask him, though I don't expect an answer.

My eyes are burning, and I'm angry that Jack's reduced me to crying again. Sobbing. One hand is clenched into a fist and rhythmically, softly, beating against the door. "This isn't fair! He almost killed her, and he should be here—he should be taking some responsibility for this, not me!"

Graham pulls the car to the curb. We're in a neighborhood in Chelsea that I don't recognize. Stark elms line the tiny street, their crooked limbs bravely reaching beyond the Victorian tenement houses for the pale streams of winter sunlight. *How bleak it all looks.* My shoulders bow inward to my chest.

"I can't tell you how much my heart aches for you." Graham's hand is back on my shoulder, comforting and warm. "No one should have to be going through this. You've got a big heart, and I understand how you want to protect your husband, but maybe you should leave it be. Maybe you're better off if he doesn't come back." He takes a moment and swallows hard, his Adam's apple sliding up and down. "I enjoy being with you, Beth. It's easy for me to be around you, y'know?"

"Me?" *You can't be serious.* "I'm not much of a conversationalist."

"I don't like chatterboxes. I had enough of that when I was growing up with a bunch of sisters and brothers. Unless you're louder than everyone else, you don't get anyone to listen to you in a big family. I always sat on the sidelines and let everyone else talk, then along comes Beth Robbins, and she listens when I talk. I catch you looking at me sometimes, too. It's nice to have someone listen to *me* for a change."

Slowly, his words sink in. I digest them, roll around in my mind exactly what he means, and it surprises me. Perhaps he's trying to tell me he is no longer acting as a police officer. Maybe he's speaking to me as a man. Maybe what he's saying is that he cares. Pure and simple. Perhaps I'm making too much of this—reading more into it than what he means.

Even as he reaches for me, an intense question in his eyes, and pulls me to him, I'm protesting—but only to myself. Silently. The words "stop" or "don't" never reach my lips because I've been waiting for this. Deep in my heart of hearts, I've been wanting this. Whether right or wrong, I've been drawn to this man and wondered what it would be like if...

This isn't right. You're still married, Beth Robbins. No matter what Jack has done with other women, that doesn't make it right for you to do it with another man. Especially this one. Are you crazy?

His lips meet mine. The subconscious voice fades. I close my eyes, sink into myself and him, swallowing the first touch of his lips against mine, then leaning in for more. It has been easy to allow myself to hate Jack for what he's done, especially since he left me for the blonde woman. Yet here I am doing the same thing. Cheating.

I'm weak. God, I'm so weak. This shouldn't be happening. What the hell am I doing? He smells so good. He's warm. Bigger shoulders than Jack. Softer lips. Can he feel me shivering? How can I be doing this? I'm married...but so was Jack. Does he feel like this with that blonde woman? But it's wrong. Letting him take the blame is wrong, whether or not he's here to defend himself.

On the other hand...

It would serve Jack right if someone finally punished him for all he'd done.

And it would be so easy to reach for the solace that Graham is offering.

God, it feels good to taste the saltiness of his mouth, to feel cradled against his chest. But when the points of his badge prick at my breast, I pull away.

"Shit." He mutters the word under his breath as if he realizes what he's done and instantly regrets it.

I slink toward the window, sucking in a breath and holding it. *Don't say a word.*

A couple of kids cross in front of the car, tossing a football back and forth, their jacket collars turned up like gangsters. They're staring in the car window and talking among themselves as if trying to decide whether they should offer me some help. I can see the shock on their faces and realize with a start that they're judging us. Kids. They are judging me.

"I'm sorry." Graham jerks the car back into traffic.

"It's okay."

"No, it's not. It was totally uncalled for."

"It was as much my fault as it was yours."

"No. I shouldn't have...shit." He hits the steering wheel with the palm of his hand. "I'm really sorry. Really. I have never...it's just that..."

"Stop." I turn to him, reach for his hand, and grasp it as tightly as possible, though I can barely curl my fingers over his large palm. His hand is hard and unyielding. "Please don't apologize. It's the first time in a long time that someone has actually kissed me like they cared. I liked it, and no one will ever know about it, believe me. But there's something I need to tell you."

I smooth my skirt and try to put the words together. Then we drive out of the neighborhood and into an area I recognize. We are back in Everett. It's as if we've passed over an invisible line of demarcation—only a few more minutes with him in the car. No matter where you are in Everett, you never have more than two miles to go before you're out of Everett again. My heart sinks as Graham brakes for a red light.

"Listen, I... I know how you feel about Jack," he says, "and you need to see and talk to him. I understand all of that. You don't need to tell me. I know how angry you've been. I've seen it in your eyes every time we ask you about him, and I don't blame you. He's worthless, and it'd be a whole sight easier if he never showed his mug around here again." Graham's eyes darken, then he touches my cheek, and his features blur perceptibly as if something he sees in my face melts him. He appears vulnerable, as delicate as an early-morning cobweb, the kind that will whisk away, never to return, if you breathe on it.

This has got to stop.

A car horn beeps, startling us both. Graham keeps driving and turns onto Ferry Street. He turns away from me, focusing on traffic. His jaw hardens and becomes resolute. With every moment, we're moving closer to my apartment building, yet farther away from each other. He has taken his hand away from my face, yet my cheek still feels his touch. I frantically fight for the right thing to say; how can I tell him, explain what I've done, and why I've waited so long to tell the truth? How can I explain how angry I was at Jack and at myself, too? How will anyone ever understand how it has felt? How can anyone know how it feels to be ignored my whole life? What it means to live without Jack, the person who understood my confusion when

Mama took her life, as well as the sorrow when Dad followed soon after. I know now that I loved Jack because he was all I had. He was there when no one else was.

I hate being depressed, hate that the trait that killed Mama has shown its ugly face in my own personality. I try to fight it, and now here is yet another reason to battle my demons. It felt incredible to be opened to the world again, to have friends, to go out of the house and talk to people, to be free of Jack's impatience, his ignorance, and his alcoholism. Wonderful to be human. Even if I'm the worst kind of human, at least I've been alive.

Graham drives by Glendale Park. Strips of dirty snow run down the hills where the kids usually ride their sleds. Dark rivulets of mud streak the ball fields. The park is empty now in the drab of winter, but on a good high-blue summer's day, Everett's residents habitually take their dogs for a walk, roll their babies in strollers, and let their toddlers pick buttercups. Old men sit on the park benches installed along the outer rim of the park to chat, play checkers, or cheer as their favorite baseball team takes one of the four diamonds. It's an enormous park for large Italian and Irish families who settled in the town early in Massachusetts' history. It's a city of immigrants, a true splinter of Boston, but with the flavor of a New York borough, complete with residents who speak several languages fluently and encourage their children to do the same.

Though Everett has always been home to me, I've never felt part of the cultural communities that make up Boston's suburbs. I've never felt comfortable with the Irish kids who lived throughout the Glendale Square area, nor do I fit in with the Italians from the Line, one of the toughest neighborhoods in the city. I'm one of those anomalies: the second-generation child of two immigrant families who weren't purely Italian, Irish, or Jewish. There is enough of a mixture of nationalities to be American, but too much of a mix to belong to my own neighborhood. I've always regretted that I don't even have siblings or cousins, relatives that would make me feel like part of a tribe. I think everyone needs that. Graham obviously grew up as part of a large family and has that sense of belonging. It's ironic that he experiences that feeling even though his people have been spurned from just about every kind of neighborhood. How do people who have spent their lives fighting for their rights build a safe spot for themselves? How can he have found that safe place, and I have not?

"Glendale Park," he murmurs, as if he's forgotten I'm there beside him. "My brothers and I came here at night to play ball when I was a kid... the only time we could get a diamond." He drifts off, as drawn into his memories as I am into mine.

Family is supposed to mean a large group of people, not just parents and one child. Sisters, brothers, aunts, uncles, and cousins. It should mean warmth, hugs, fights, and support, not loneliness.

I often come to the park to sit and watch the families pass by, thinking all the while about the day I'd have a family of my own. Sometimes, I asked Jack to go with me, but he never really wanted to, preferring instead to sit in a darkened bar, talking about what he did in Korea or which player the Red Sox would draft that year. He was so far removed from the idea of family that he didn't understand when I kept asking why he refused to contact his siblings, aunts, uncles, and cousins. I wanted to share his family with him, but he considered that kind of contact out-of-bounds.

Graham's the kind of guy who will make sure his family takes a special walk in the park every Sunday after church. He'll teach his sons how to throw a football so that it spins like the Sputnik missile through the air. He'll beam at his little girl's first fumbled attempts to dance. He'll lie and say his wife's dried and burned roast tastes tender and juicy. He's an honorable man, a guy you can trust, someone who'll warm the bed at night. Every night. Someone who'll come home on time for supper. Someone who'll be kind...

"If I didn't think you felt the same way..." Graham startles me out of my thoughts. When I turn to look at him, he speaks to the windshield as if too ashamed to face me. "...I wouldn't have reached for you. I just thought...It just seemed like you, you know, you..." He has moved away a little. His eyes keep flickering to the people on the sidewalk.

I realize that he's talking about us and what we could face. If. Us.

Everett's a small town. He's a cop. Lots of people know him. Though he hasn't mentioned it, I know we can't be seen together. *Why does it seem like everyone's looking at us now? We haven't done anything.* It could mean his job and, of course, my marriage. And even though I'm afraid my marriage is already over anyway, I made an oath to Jack a long time ago, and I also made a promise to myself that I'd live honestly. I intend to keep the one about being true to myself. Perhaps if I do, everything else will fall into place. It doesn't feel right to be lying to the people who've become part of my life.

Then what are you doing, Beth? Make it right.

We don't speak again, and when we reach the apartment building, I spring out of the car before Graham comes to a complete stop at the curb.

"Thanks for the ride, Officer," I say pointedly before I close the Buick's splashy red and white door.

His answer is muffled and unintelligible, and before I reach the apartment lobby, he's pulled away. I watch from inside the hallway as his car disappears into the distance and wonder why I'm always watching someone leave.

A Married Woman

Saturday, December 6, 1957

Cops say that your partner knows you better than anyone else in the world, better than a wife, a lover, or a child. Even better than your own mother. Graham has always believed that's true, but Frank is a little less perceptive than the usual cop. He's more concerned with what's on his plate (literally) than what's going on with any of the cases they're working on. At breakfast, he finishes off half a dozen donuts with three cups of coffee and launches into the day's work, talking a mile a minute and wrapping up routine traffic tickets by the dozens. At break time, he strides down the hallways of the police station, yelling his "hey-how-are-ya-buddy" and "whatcha been up to lately" lines at all the guys in the department. Graham follows along, does his work, joins in the worn-out jokes, and pays attention when someone asks him a question, and though he feels like the world has changed drastically in the past couple of weeks, Frankie notices nothing different.

It's lunchtime before Graham finally addresses the question plaguing him like an ingrown toenail.

"Do you think the captain would get suspicious if I pulled myself off the Robbins' hit-and-run?" he asks Frank. He'd love a cigarette right now. There is nothing better than the powerful pull of a Camel, but he's sworn off for a while. He hates to admit it, but he thinks it's because he saw Beth wrinkle her nose at someone smoking as they walked by on the street the night he took her and Miss Indelicato to the movies.

Frank's mouth falls open a little, and his coal-black eyebrows raise, then he scrunches his shoulders up to his ears and holds out his hands. "Hey, you got *me* suspicious, never mind the captain. What's going on with you, huh? You got something on the side I should know about?"

They're walking toward the patrol car with only two hours left on their shift. Lunch was the special roast beef sandwich and French fries at the Silver Wolf Bar and Grill on Chelsea Parkway, their regular place to eat. Frank loves their chicken cacciatore, and Graham is partial to their pepper steak sandwiches. The late-afternoon servers love spoiling cops, which always means an extra helping of apple pie and ice cream. For Frank, that is reason enough to take an extra fifteen minutes (as long as he has his radio nearby "just in case anything traumatic occurs, know what I mean?"). Fifteen more minutes for Graham to stew.

Now, he stalls. He doesn't want to answer Frank, but he knows Frank will find out about Beth eventually, so maybe this is the best way to tell him. Rolling a toothpick around in his cheek, Graham tries not to look his partner directly in the eye. Frank might sometimes act out of touch, but the guy can usually tell when Graham's lying. Two things could come out of this conversation: Frank will be ecstatic to know that Graham's falling for someone, or the famous Italian temper will flare, and Graham will be on the receiving end. Either way, he's got what Desi Arnaz would say is some 'splainin' to do. He suspects that Frankie's going to let loose with a major lecture after he asks, "What the fuck are you doin'?" And Graham's not so sure he wants to explain how he feels.

"Well, are you gonna talk to me about it or sit there like the cat that ate the canary?" Frank reaches for the patrol car door, juggling the leftover bag and his keys. "Why the hell would you want off that case? Nothing happenin' on it, anyway. I can think of many more exciting things to investigate."

Graham grunts, climbs in his door and settles into the seat. The leather squeaks a little, and Frank burps.

"'Scuse me, but are you going to finish, or are you going to leave me in suspense? Jesus, Jackson, how must I get it out of you? Give you a blow job?"

"You don't need to get so explicit."

The car's engine roars to life, and Frankie leans a little too hard on the gas pedal. Graham hates it when Frank drives. It's like riding a bull. Fits and starts. Bucking and jerking.

"Okay, screw you." Frankie jerks into traffic. "I don't wanna know. Okay? I don't want to know. Tell me nothin', okay? Just don't tell me anything. You can go talk to the captain and tell him whatever you want. I don't wanna know a thing."

They're both quiet. Frank drives down the Revere Beach Boulevard and takes a left by Everett Stadium. The football team is practicing, so they slow down to watch a few runs. Still, neither one of them speaks. Frank burps again, a long and slow one this time.

Graham groans. "You're a pig, you know that, Frankie? God, your mother would slap you if she heard you burp like that without excusing yourself."

"I'm a pig? I'm a pig! What about you, Mr. Clean? You're the one thinking about diddling a married woman." Frank looks toward the passenger seat, catching Graham off guard, then grins. "What do you think? I'm stupid. You think I can't tell you've been thinkin' of that broad? Why else would you want off the case?"

"She's not a broad."

"Sure, sure. She's not a broad. But she's still married, ain't she?"

Graham nods. The thought of it angers him, but there's nothing he can do. Frank is right.

"Listen, I'll see if there's any action on the case. If there isn't, I'll tell the captain we both want off so there won't be anybody thinking anything about you, okay? But I'll tell you, if I so much as catch you wandering within a thousand feet of the Robbins' apartment again, I'll do what her husband would if he finds out. Get me?" He pokes Graham in the shoulder. Hard. "We don't want any racist incidents here now. This is Massachusetts, not Mississippi. Know what I mean?"

For the first time, Graham thinks of Jack Robbins as an adversary. It is possible the man will eventually come home, figure he's safe and sound, and that the cops won't catch him because how long will they hang around for a hit-and-run driver when there are murderers on the loose? He'll let his guard down. And when he does, Graham will be waiting for him.

Arresting Jack Robbins is a lovely thought.

Change the Channel, Please

Sunday, December 7, 1957

Lying on my bed, fully clothed, breathing deeply, I study the indentations in the rose-colored chenille bedspread I bought two months ago. Seems like years ago—another life. The spread already looks a little thin, and the deep red of the wool blanket beneath shows through the worn spots. I've got a bad habit: washing the bed clothing at least once every couple of days, even the spread. Now, the chenille is showing the effects of my obsession with bleach. I idly poke at the tufted ridges, picking the cotton threads, not daring to move anything but a finger or two for fear that I'll bring up another bout of retching over the porcelain toilet bowl.

It's been two hours, but my nausea hasn't settled down. I'm tired and cold, yet I can't bring myself to roll over or slide under the covers. I must have the flu, and I'm struggling to remember what Mama did for a stomach bug.

Wintergreen tea? A peppermint lozenge under the tongue? Sleep. Just sleep.

When I open my eyes again, it's dark, and Bud Collier's voice is the first thing I hear. I've left the TV on and have been half-listening to it. The program is "To Tell the Truth," without seeing the television screen, I can guess the man's identity.

"He's a doll collector," I mumble into the pillow. "How come you can't get it, Miss Kitty Carlisle?"

Rolling off the bed, I slide into my slippers before heading for the bathroom. A cold facecloth over my cheeks and forehead revives me a little, and my stomach rumbles, and hunger pangs for the first time all day. Then it lurches, and I stand still momentarily, wondering if I will retch again. I put the toilet lid down and sit on it, then grab the brush and start the habitual hundred strokes through my hair, forcing myself to count and breathe. *Count and breathe.* The brush feels good on my scalp.

Cracker. Saltine crackers and some weak tea. That's Mama's remedy for the flu.

Shivering, I pause at my bureau and rustle through the drawers for a heavy Irish knit sweater and thick wool socks. Though my legs are still cold, and my nose is running, I can feel my shoulder muscles loosen a little with the sweater's warmth. It's buttoned up to my chin when the water is hot for the tea. I head back to the bedroom to find a quilt and bring it out to the couch to watch the "Loretta Young Show." I'm just about settled when I hear a shuffle outside the front door and a dull thud.

At first, I'm unsure whether someone has knocked or fallen, so I listen. I'm doing more of that these days: listening, moving toward the sound, and not running away.

Please let it not be Mr. Fits. I don't want to deal with him right now. Go away, Fitsie Boy. Leave me alone.

Another dull thump. This time, accompanied by an "ouch."

"Beth, are you there?" It's Loretta's voice. *Not Loretta Young, but Loretta Indelicato.* "I thought you might like some potato soup. I made extra..."

Teacup in hand, I open the door without hesitation. I don't care if Loretta sees me in the big socks and chunky sweater with my hair all a mess and the smell of an afternoon nap still around me. Loretta has food. The woman has brought soup.

Awkward but smiling, Loretta holds out an ironstone bowl, a dinner plate cockeyed atop it. Angela would have held a soup tureen. She would have been wearing an apron, and her cheeks would have been rosy from cooking all day. Loretta looks like she might have opened a can of Campbell's and heated it for three minutes on a low flame. But that's okay.

"Wow, you got the windows open or something? Like an icebox in here." Loretta speaks around the ever-present cigarette in the corner of her mouth. "This'll warm you up." She thrusts the bowl at me again.

Taking the soup, I rock back and forth from one foot to the other, then head to the kitchen. "Um...sit down if you like."

Loretta's already moving toward the couch, glued to the television screen. "Is this that show where Loretta Young wears a different outfit every week?"

"Yes. Sometimes I like what she wears, but sometimes I wonder if she really dresses like that. They say her gowns cost an awful lot of money." I find two bowls and pour an equal amount of soup into each. It smells wonderful. Hot, creamy, wholesome. It's probably a little too creamy for my queasy stomach, but maybe it'll help coat it. Perhaps it'll be just what the doctor ordered.

Hell, it's better than the alternative: tea and Saltines. There is nothing else in the house to eat.

"Thank you for this. I was going to go shopping today, but I'm not feeling well."

I place the bowls on a TV tray, one of the two Jack and I used on weekends when we had dinner in front of the television. He usually lasted about half an hour or three beers (whichever came first) before he'd be in a full snore. Then I could watch anything I liked.

When shows like "Loretta Young" appear, life seems possible again. Here's an elegant woman, classy and classic, far above any housewife on the other shows I like to watch. Yet Loretta Young can be anybody. All she has to do is widen her eyes and change how she speaks, and she's a farm girl. Another change of clothing, and she becomes a murderer. She makes everyone believe.

Loretta's fascinated by the television, so I place the TV tray in front of her and sit on the other end of the couch with the quilt over my legs. Being with this next-door neighbor I barely knew could have been uncomfortable, but it's not. The room even seems a little warmer. Before I pick up the tea again, I grab the back of my head where I've gathered my insane hair into an elastic and undo it, letting its weight fall against my neck to cover the birthmark—as I always do when people are around.

Glancing over with the quick, narrow-eyed sight of a critic, Loretta says, "Your hair looks better up. You got a nice neckline." Then she turns back to the television, her gaze riveted, as though the comment was automatic, a compliment she didn't have to think twice about delivering. Loretta's lackadaisical manner makes me pause.

A nice neckline? Did she mean that? No, just politeness. Maybe her mother taught her to do that. Maybe she got it from Angela. Or maybe, stupid Beth, and *maybe it's true.*

With a smile, I settle back into the couch. Having someone else in the apartment's a little strange, but it's nice. Alone, I have finally learned to tame the nighttime itchiness, sit on my couch and relax, and resist the impulse to tip the stack of *Better Homes* magazines. The pile is so straight and sober that I sometimes even shove one a little to the right to break my obsession for making sure the three or four I own are all perfectly in line. There was a time when I wouldn't have been able to deal with that one magazine being a little out of place. But now…now, when I sit down, I kick off my slippers, letting them pile against each other like drunken lovers. I fold my legs under the quilt and knit my fingers around the teacup, and I don't care if the TV's volume is too loud because I have someone to talk to now.

As Loretta watches her namesake, her summer-green eyes widen, and she leans forward a little on the couch, consumed by the scene on the television, as if she's never seen the program before, as if she's terrified she'll never see it again.

Who would have thought a couple of months ago that we'd be sitting here side by side? A couple of female bookends. A couple of women, single and alone.

For a split second, I am happy, yet I immediately feel guilty. Happiness is not a feeling to which I'm accustomed.

And is it appropriate now? Is happiness even allowable in situations like this? I don't know anymore; whatever this bug is, it's draining my energy, so I don't care.

Sipping the soup, I will my stomach to calm down.

Two hours later, Loretta is still there, perched on the couch, attention still on the television set. Now we're talking during the commercials, and she's making me laugh, sharing her wry look at the world. The nausea has disappeared, but I still don't feel like I could dance a jig.

Loretta spouts off quirky comments about every television program, asks questions, and treats me as if she values my opinions as if I'm the expert.

Me. Ha! The expert on television.

She confesses she's read the *TV Guide* for the past couple of years, poring over the mini synopses of what will happen next on "I Love Lucy" or previews of the new shows for next season. Still, she and Angela never owned a TV, so she didn't watch the shows. She just fantasized about them. She asks me about "Guiding Light," Jack Benny, and Milton Berle. (*Does Edward Morrow always do the news with that hat on? How often do they run Shirley Temple's movies? She especially liked the dancing in* The Little Colonel.)

"Angela always talked about how she wanted a television, but we couldn't afford it." Loretta's cigarette smoke curls make swirly blue clouds in front of the TV. "Two old ladies living all alone. Nuts to even think about it..."

My panther-shaped lamp highlights her profile. Loretta's facial planes are angled and sharp. Not pointed, not witchlike, but firm, like a man's, making her strangely attractive. I want to draw her profile. Her clear eyes, punctuated by arched sketches of eyebrows, narrow into a steely-eyed gaze that reminds me of a woman who's worked hard on a cattle farm all her life. I imagine Loretta, her hand shading her eyes, gazing far into the horizon, spotting the tracks of something exotic like an antelope. Yet, she has never been out of the city and has never had a more exciting adventure than a long train ride to the western part of Massachusetts for a family funeral.

"You're going to have it pretty hard now that Jack's gone," she says, catching me off guard.

"I think I'm going to have to get a job," I reply, though the thought of going for interviews makes my stomach hurt again.

No one's going to pay me to draw.

"Doesn't look like you have a choice. You're not old enough for social security, or I'd tell you to apply for it. It's great not having to worry about the money for the rent or the food, though they give you a pittance," Loretta spits a speck of something out of her mouth and onto her finger, rubbing it quickly against her pants. "And I think there's some law about being able to get help if you're not getting money from your husband. Have you heard from him at all?"

I shake my head. *Why does everyone keep asking that question? Does she want me to feel worse than I already do, or does she suspect?* My stomach gurgles like water going down the drain.

"Do you mind if I ask you something?" Loretta's voice is more severe than usual, but she doesn't take her eyes off the screen.

"No, go ahead."

"Did you and Jack have walloping fights? Angie and I heard a few things over there at our place."

Should I answer this? 'fess up? The fights weren't my fault. I can't be blamed for them. Or can I?

"We had a couple of arguments. Y'know, all married couples have their spats. Making up is the best part." I do my best to grin coquettishly, even though Loretta's not looking, and it feels stupid.

"It always is. The guy I used to be with—you know, during the War— we had spats on a regular basis. I used to like it when we made up. That was the best part." Now it's Loretta's turn to grin like a little girl, but she does it with panache as if the memory is precious, something she's relied upon during the years to get her through rough times. "Angela always told me I would meet someone else, but I never did. Never met someone like him. Can't even say his name anymore, and sometimes I can't even remember what he looked like..."

I glance at the wedding pictures on the wall. I can't imagine not remembering how Jack smiled or how his voice became gravelly when he was tired.

But it's easy to forget the fights.

Sometimes, late at night, when I can't sleep, I think of nothing but the good moments, the times when we laughed and made love, and it hurts to know that he probably doesn't think of me at all, that he never really has. But during the day, I'm stronger, and I remember how he'd push me up against the wall and threaten to kill me. I can see his face, all screwed up and crazy looking, as if he'd totally lost his mind.

I look around the apartment and realize how nice and peaceful it is now. Yet it hurts to have him somewhere out there; probably still with that blonde, and no matter how much I would like to believe he's staying away so that I won't get into trouble, it still hurts that he's not calling to see if I'm okay. *What if they'd taken me to jail? Now, he would never know the difference.*

"Did Angela ever tell you the story about my guy?" Loretta reaches for another cigarette.

"No, she didn't. I didn't know your sister very well until about a couple of weeks before...you know..."

Loretta, with her eyes flickering to the television screen and the Crest commercial, then to a spot on the rug under the coffee table, seems captivated by the stain. This peculiar fascination unsettles me, reminding me of the rawness that follows the loss of a loved one.

"Tell me the story," Beth says now. "Tell me what Angela would have said."

"You really want to know?"

"Yeah."

Loretta's chest fills with air, and she seems momentarily younger. "Angela would have said I was stupid. She would start by telling you how wonderful her marriage was and how I could have had the same life if the war hadn't happened. But she never lauded it over me. Nope, Angela didn't shove it in my face that she had a life and the beginnings of a family. Maybe because she never got what she wanted herself. She lost three kids, y'know. Three miscarriages. She was pretty good about that. Never cried on your shoulder. Yeah, she was strong. Funny, though. She was funny. Do you know what I mean in a 'ha-ha' way and in a cuckoo way?" She glances up at me, hopeful for some agreement. Their bond was unbreakable, a connection transcending words and time.

The moment bursts with life. Suddenly, I'm rapt in Loretta's words, eager to hear about the sisters' bond. I crave stories that transport me from the present. Every fiber of my being is alert. The colors in the living room pulse with energy. The parlor lamp's light Illuminates the crimson rosebush on the Good Housekeeping magazine cover. Loretta's deep brown shoes gleam like polished mahogany. Her usually plain hair takes on a lustrous sheen where it curls over her ears. The gold face of her watch sparkles as if crafted by Tiffany. The room seems to come alive as if it's sharing in the story's magic.

The moment glistens. I'll remember it for the rest of my life. I love the comfort I feel, the warmth in my hands and feet, and the satisfaction of digesting a good meal, the fun of talking to someone who can make me laugh.

We are both alive. We are survivors. And, somehow, we've found each other.

I've been given a gift. Life is a gift. This moment is a gift. I'm filled with a deep sense of gratitude for the opportunity to hear Loretta's story and to be a part of this shared experience. It's a reminder of the preciousness of life and the power of human connection.

"When did you both decide to live together?" Absentmindedly, I pull the afghan off the back of the couch and cover my shoulders. As the night grows longer, the apartment grows colder. The only thing that saves me from freezing completely is that I'm in a middle-floor apartment, and the people downstairs keep their thermostats in the 80s. I've discovered that if I open all the floor grates, their heat will rise into my place, but if a Canadian cold front comes like it's supposed to tonight, I'll have to think about turning up the thermostat, which costs money. For now, I snuggle into the knitted afghan and hope Loretta keeps bringing over soup. And conversation.

"Oh, let me think a minute..." Loretta puffs on the cigarette and stares at the ceiling. "I think I was in my mid-30s when we started living together. Angela had been out on her own for quite a while, but Harry died, and she couldn't make it alone anymore. Yeah, it was more than twenty years ago because Angela kept time by when Harry died, and right before Thanksgiving, she was saying something about him being gone over twenty years. Poor soul. He was a good man. One of the few."

I tap the cigarette ashes in the black and white ceramic ashtray Jack used to use, then straighten up. "She was down and out when he went. She kept saying she was okay and tried to keep her head above water. I'll tell you, we had some whoppers of fights back then. She and I fought moving in together, but it seemed the only sensible thing to do after a while."

"You loved each other, though, I could tell."

"Yeah, so? What sisters don't?" Taking a tug on the cigarette, Loretta smiles wryly. "Some days, there were more fights than I could count, and I'd swear to God I was going to leave her high and dry and go someplace else, but Everett has always been our home. All our family was here: our mother and father, our grandparents—God bless 'em—the rest of the family. All our friends. Everyone we knew growing up. But things changed after the war. This city is a lot different from what it used to be. I never thought I'd see as much traffic as we got on Broadway now. And the farms all disappearing, one by one. You know Vernal Street and Glendale Street used to be nothing but farms?"

I shake my head, amazed. Some chicken and egg farms in Everett still support themselves, but most residential areas are old, and land is at a premium. Everett is just two square miles, and tens of thousands live here. I never really thought of what it would have been like before.

"My guy—the one from the war?—came from one of those farms on Vernal," Loretta continues. "Used to drive their trucks to market before he signed up. This was the first world war, not the one with Hitler and all them guys. Both me and Loretta, we were upset about what was going on. No one knew how big it was and how many people that war would affect. It wasn't very good. Horrible. But those guys, when they got all doodied up in their dough-boy hats and those high button spats...well, it seemed like they were knights, and they should have the King's permission to fight on his behalf, you know? I just fell for that uniform—hook, line, and sinker. That guy was more handsome than Rudy Valentino. I still have that picture of him in the uniform, his hands folded over his lap. He had this wide mouth and these real dark, deep-set eyes, so when he posed for the picture, it seemed he was looking right at me. Gave me the chills, it did." Loretta smiles. It's a wonderful memory, the guy she was nuts about.

"What did you and Angela look like, then?" I ask, enjoying the conversation's sharing and 'girlfriend' feel. "My mama was beautiful before she married Dad. I loved how she dressed, that short haircut and dresses with fringes and cigarettes in long-handled holders. I thought she was the most gorgeous woman in the neighborhood, yet there she was in the kitchen, cooking my supper later every night. My mother, the glamor queen. After she died, I remember my father used to hold her picture up and dance with it as if she was there. He'd sing to her, call her his 'precious moonflower.'"

"She sounds pretty, Beth. Angela was, too, when she was young. Pretty spiffy, but me?" She laughs, a jagged, almost hysterical sound. "I didn't want none of that. Just wanted to be comfortable. I finally got permission to wear what I wanted when Kate Hepburn stepped up to the plate with her men's pants and her big white shirt with that cardigan slung over her shoulders. Ain't no way I was giving up comfort for no man. So, I didn't. I wore what I wanted, went where I wanted, and didn't get married like everyone else. Living with my sister is much easier than giving up my freedom for a guy. At least, Angela, she *knew* something about me...." Loretta pales, and then her eyes redden.

Again, I sense that the discussion is painful. It's hard to respond acceptably. Now I know how everyone felt around me after Mama died.

"Never thought she'd go before I would. Now, there's no one there. It's strange."

Loretta sniffles and blinks hard, as though her grief embarrassed her.

"I know. It's tough..."

Blinking more quickly, Loretta turns her head away. "You don't have a sister. How could you know?"

"I had a mother. And a father. And now I have a husband who's disappeared. It hurts just as much as if he was dead. Sometimes you feel like it will never end, but it gets better." *Does it really? Does it ever get better? Yes, when you can talk to someone.* My shoulders tighten. Strangely, things are falling apart, yet I have more friends now than I have in my whole life. This makes little sense.

The couch sighs as Loretta gets up and walks to the living room window. "I'm sorry. I didn't mean to come over and make you miserable. Just wanted a little company, I guess."

"It's okay."

"Thought maybe you were as lonely as I am."

"I am."

"You don't mind me coming over?" She turns from the window and looks slightly surprised. Then she folds her large hands over each other.

"No, I don't."

For the first time since Beth has met her, Loretta appears fragile. She rubs her hands together a few times, then sniffs and reaches into her pocket. She comes out with a cigarette and lights it.

"You're going to think I'm mean for saying this, but I've got something I've wanted to tell you." Loretta inhales deeply.

"What?"

"Maybe you're better off without him. Your husband, I mean. I heard you fight. Me and Angela both heard you. We thought he was going to kill you sometimes. Angela always wanted to call the cops, but I stopped her. Maybe she was right. If we had, maybe he would have left a long time ago."

On the television, Loretta Young is saying goodnight. Gracious Loretta Young. She is so different from the other Loretta in front of me. Loretta Indelicato is reliable, maybe. Gruff, surely. But never gracious or lovely or well-spoken. Not even a little attractive. Yet I want this Loretta, who's in the same room as me, to stay here and talk and share her life and stories about her family. I want her to continue bringing over warm food and companionship. I realize this relationship would never have happened without Jack's truck.

"Maybe I am better off without him." I rub the heels of my hands against my eye sockets and swallow back the lump in my throat.

A spiral of smoke rises from Loretta's cigarette and dissipates into the living room curtains. "How did you end up with a guy like that? You're a nice girl, and he seems like such a...well...he's a chump. Look at what he did to you. An awful accident like that, and he takes off like a hoodlum into the night with another babe. How can you sit there and be Miss Prim-and-Proper? Why aren't you madder at him?"

"It's not his fault." *Tell her. It's time someone knew.*

"Bull crap, it's not his fault. Well, then, whose is it?"

"Mine."

"What?"

"I was driving the truck."

"What?"

"I said I was driving the truck. I was the one who hit Cindy. Not Jack." *There, it's out. Why haven't the cops come to the door? I'm confessing. Someone should arrest me.*

"Quit trying to cover for him."

"I'm not. He's been covering for me. I think that's why he left. This way, the cops think it's all him. They don't know I was there when it happened."

Loretta's mouth has fallen open. I see two crooked teeth in the bottom row. Nicotine stains. The mottled red of Loretta's fat tongue.

"He told me not to say anything because I can't drive. I'm not supposed to. Don't have a license. Jack knew and said he'd take care of it, but he hasn't. And I've got to tell someone, Loretta. I've got to let someone know, but no one gives me a chance. I've been trying and trying, but no one will let me talk about it...." Now I'm crying like a fool. "It happened so fast. I didn't know how to stop. Couldn't stop...he wasn't supposed to be driving...."

Then Loretta's sitting beside me, hand on my knee, and soft and soothing woman sounds issuing from her throat. There are no words, just sounds, and I need those sounds. I lean into her and let the tears flow.

When the sobbing slows, Loretta pulls away, which doesn't surprise me. People rarely deal with sadness very well. I can remember kids in school hanging off to the side in the schoolyard, whispering behind their hands. No one ever said, "I'm sorry for your loss, Beth. So sad to hear about your mother, Beth." No one ever called and said, "Come out with us, Beth. Let's go have a good time." No one ever told me the first time I cried after getting married that Jack Robbins was no good and that the only reason he wanted me was because no one else wanted *him.*

That bothered me, but crying alone became another refuge over the years. It was a habit during my marriage to Jack. He became predictable. If I cried, he would leave me alone. That's how much he hated it.

Is that why I stayed with you, Jack? Because I didn't want to be with someone I loved so much? Too much. Because I didn't want to lose someone I cared about again? That makes sense, because one more loss would have killed me.

"Now tell me about it," Loretta commands in that no-nonsense voice she used to use with Angela. "And tell me about losing your mother, about what happened to your father, about how you felt. Tell me everything,"

I don't even hesitate. It makes sense to start at the beginning. "After my mother died, my father started fading away. And so did I. Sometimes, we'd be together for days and not even speak to each other. After he died, I became a ghost."

"That happened to Angela when our parents died, too. She took it real hard," Loretta says, then a commercial on the television momentarily catching her attention.

Please don't make me stop now. I've waited too long to talk about this.

"When Jack came home from Korea, he thought he could bring me back to the land of the living, but he pushed me into purgatory. Yes, that's where I've been: purgatory. And now...it's strange." I pull my knees up, circle my arms around them, and look around the apartment. Everything feels like it belongs to someone else except the picture of Mama and Daddy's wedding day.

"It took a near murder to make me feel alive again," I say. Now that the story is coming, I know I will tell it for the rest of her life to anyone who'll listen, punished by telling the tale the way the man was in that old English poem. *What was it? Miss Brown taught it to us in ninth grade: The Ancient Mariner or something like that.*

"I feel like people are starting to see me. Y'know, to understand me? Like I'm beginning to be Beth again. The before-Beth. The one who had a mother, not Beth, the poor orphan. If I keep drawing, maybe someday I can color myself in. Is that strange?"

I sniffle, thinking how unpredictable people are and that Mama had taught me when I was a child how to be a friend, but I never got the chance to have one—a real friend.

Why did I forget that?

"I know. I used to feel that way, too. I miss my mother." Loretta groans a little and shifts to sit on the other hip. "Mothers make us who we are, but we let ourselves be the women we want to be. People determine who we are by our families and who we marry. That's why no one can figure me out. I didn't marry anyone. But enough about me. Tell me about Jack. There must've been a reason you stayed with him."

I shrug. "Jack used to drink. He'd drink *every* night."

"Yeah, I know."

"That night, the bartender called me..."

Reliving the accident is more complicated than I ever imagined it would be. It takes two hours for me to pace out the accident, answer Loretta's questions, then make more tea and answer more questions. Loretta vacillates between being compassionate for me and angry at Jack. When I reach the part where Cindy's body flew into the air, and I panicked, tried to stop and felt Jack's feet hit mine, pressing gas...I fall apart. Sobbing so hard, my head bounces on Loretta's shoulder, even though she's holding me as tightly as she can. She says all the right things—*It wasn't your fault. You didn't know how to drive. You shouldn't have gone to get him. It was his fault, the accident. Not yours.*—and eventually, my sobs subside.

"You know, something like this happened to me once," Loretta says matter-of-factly. "I was fooling around; Angela and I were throwing rocks. I hit this bird, which fell out of the air and kerplunk onto the sidewalk. It was Mrs. Flaherty's parakeet. She loved that damn bird. Well, my mother hears from Mrs. Flaherty later that day. Has she seen the bird? My mother says, no, she hasn't, but Angela and I were standing there, and I guess Mrs. Flaherty had talked to someone else who had seen us throwing rocks, and she was calling to see whether either of us would confess. My mother gives us one of her looks, and Angela stands there and takes the blame." Loretta shakes her head from side to side. "I never felt right after that. I avoided Mrs. Flaherty like the plague, but I couldn't admit to it or confess. Never told my mother about it. It was too difficult."

"It's not the same," I say. "Parakeets and children."

"Of course not." Loretta catches herself and lights another cigarette. "Go on. What happened next?"

I continue the story, knowing Loretta is listening, though she keeps staring at the television and putting distance between us. She reaches a heavy hand over as if to comfort me. Then she pulls away abruptly. I don't blame her. After all, what I've done is unforgivable.

We're talking about a child who almost died and a wife who hasn't been able to tell the truth and who's letting her husband take the blame...I'm guilty of more than a hit-and-run accident.

"I've deceived everyone who's reached out to me, everyone who's taken an interest, everyone who's cared..." I finish quietly.

"I can't believe you're saying that, Beth Robbins. After what he's done to you? Shoot! He left you holding the bag. It was his fault! You weren't supposed to be driving. Wouldn't have been if he wasn't dead-ass drunk. Then, when you had the accident—and I'm stressing it was an *accident*—he didn't even let you stop. He pressed that big ol' foot against yours and made you speed by. And you are feeling guilty? It was him who didn't stop. He's the one who told you he'd take care of everything, and then he leaves like a thief in the night. I can't believe you're letting this continue. He's gone. It's time to move on. Take care of this mess before it gets any worse."

We sit side-by-side on the couch without speaking as the Star-Spangled Banner plays and the television station shuts down for the evening. Both of us are drained of energy.

"You know something, I've seen it all," Loretta says at five past midnight. "I've lived through two world wars. I've even seen a satellite get shot into space. But the most important thing I know is that people must tell each other the truth. They have to share. You need to tell Theresa."

"I know," I answer. "I know that all too well, and I will."

Strange Sense of Calm

Monday, December 8

I'm sitting by the window overlooking Broadway, drawing, trying to stay quiet, thinking about how things have come together. I know I need to talk to Theresa, and I will, but I don't want to think about it right now. I just want to draw. The *scritch-scritch-scritch* of the pencil is the only sound in the apartment. I've turned off the television for the first time in a few days, and the absence of voices has awakened the quietness inside my brain, and the simple questions like, 'Should I add crimson here or will maroon be better?' or 'the curve of that lock of hair needs to be softer, but how can I draw that?' It's not the first time since the accident that I've felt comfortable with the silence, and I'm not afraid that my brain will start running away with scenes that I don't want to replay, as it has so many times before.

On the table behind me is a stack of sketches of Crazy Connie dancing down Broadway, at least fifteen of them, all depicting various parts of her moving body: a foot encased in a snow boot, pointing elegantly like a dancer; a side view of her face, her mouth open, eyes half closed, gazing enigmatically toward the heavens; her Joseph's dream coat- color clothes waving against the bleak gray backdrop of city buildings. Beside that stack is another one of gigantic steel-colored ships resting in the slips at the Navy Yard, casting their monstrous shadows on the Mystic River, and sketches of the men working on those floating cities, the faces of the guys I talked to the day I went to the boatyard to find Jack. I drew the genuine anger in their eyes and the cynicism in the cut of their lips. Stories that they told without saying a word. Their lives. Their days on the battlefields in Europe or Korea. I connected with them more on the page than when we met face to face. And besides that pile of drawings, still another stack: sketches of the people who'd lately become part of my life: Loretta, Angela, Graham, Officer Frank, Theresa, Cindy.

I'm not sure which ones I will bring to the Chelsea gallery, and it's OK that I haven't decided yet. Right now, all I need to do is to relish this moment, the feeling of the air I breathe traveling through my nose and into my body, the dampness of the window sweating with winter moisture, the texture of the paper beneath my palm, and the power of the charcoal pencil in my hand.

Life. I need to relish life.

As the pencil moves like it has a life of its own, the pieces of Broadway arise from the paper: brick buildings, storefronts, Buicks and Fords, trucks, and people on the sidewalk. It's the first time I've drawn the city, and working with perspective is a struggle. I bite my lip. I have to use the eraser several times, but then the drawing comes together, and the lines become straighter and cleaner. Half an hour later, I finally am satisfied enough to put the pencil down and smile.

It's no Rembrandt, but it'll do.

I hold the drawing in my hands and know I'm smiling stupidly, which feels odd because I'm not necessarily a "smiley" person. Despite what's gone on the past month and the fact that I've been depressed about it, I feel content when I sit down to draw or paint. I smile. I sometimes wonder if all the prominent artists—Van Gogh, Rembrandt, Renoir, Da Vinci—found the same kind of peace when I'm drawing. I think some of them did not. It was probably just the opposite. I've heard that some artists suffer from melancholia. I can't help but wonder why creative people (who are much more talented than I am) tend to commit suicide.

Suicide.

I sigh and look down from the window again. I don't want to think of Mama right now. I want to continue to feel that openness in my chest, not the pain that remembering her brings.

With the pencil to the paper again, I force myself back into that strange sense of calm. For long moments, all I hear is the scratch of charcoal against the rough drawing pad.

I now know what artists mean when discussing being passionate about their work. To me, the time I spend trying to make a person's face come alive on paper or finding precisely the right stroke that will show the fold of a skirt or the angle a person's mouth makes when they smile is time that I forget everything else. Nothing else matters when I sit with my sketch pad. Nothing hurts. Nothing disturbs me. I am absorbed. I am truly me. There is no one sitting in my head telling me what to do. No one judging what I'm saying or how I'm tilting my head or pursing my lips. It's freedom. It's love. It's the most profound sense of myself and life. It's passion.

Sometimes when I draw my mind goes in a thousand different directions. There are others when it's so quiet that I wonder whether I'm thinking at all. And sometimes (like now), I think about thinking. I suppose some people would think that's a definition of insanity, but I realize this is happiness. Short-lived, perhaps, but happiness for at least a few moments.

My pencil lines become darker and harsher as thoughts of Jack take away my calm. I remove my hand away from the drawing.

I don't want him intruding on my life anymore.

Threatening Noises

Tuesday, December 9

Graham listens to his mother's washing machine, waiting impatiently for it to stop so he can take his wet clothes out and hang them on the line before the weather changes. It's his day off, and he's spending time at his mother's doing his laundry before heading to Frankie's for a spaghetti and meatballs dinner. In the living room, his mother is sitting in the armchair, a bag of darning in her lap, her head drooping on her chest. Her snores, as loud as a man's, echo throughout the rest of the house. Everyone else in the family is at work or at school, which is fine with Graham, since he would rather not have to answer for the furrows in his brow. He's spent the whole day wondering how he will handle the situation with Beth Robbins. He's in trouble. He's feeling things for her that he shouldn't. And he wants to tell her, even though he knows it's probably not going to come to anything.

The washing machine chug-chug-chugs, a hypnotizing rhythm that lures him in. He leans his head back against the chair and lets his mind wander. *What would it be like to spend time with Beth Robbins?* He considers the nasty side comments and stares he often gets from the guys he works with and knows they would be even more emphatic if the men knew he was in love with a white woman. One of "theirs." Frankie might not care, though he'd have one of those serious, 'you gotta listen to me because I'm older than you' discussions with Graham, a kind of Dutch uncle lecture, the talk that you give to someone who doesn't seem to know any better, but you love them anyway. In most states, especially in the South, it's illegal for a Negro man to have a relationship with a white woman, but the North is different.

Graham shifts his head and looks out the window at the bare maple trees in his mother's backyard. Across the yard, the Levine's kitchen windows are steamy as Ruth Levine, the brood's matriarch, a woman as strong and tiny as his own mother, cooks the evening meal. One floor above the Levines, the D'Angelo family grows larger by the year. They have at least seven kids, the last time Graham counted, and the families in these buildings all share gossip on the doorstep during the summer months. They can count on each other for casseroles when someone dies or is sick, yet when it comes time for celebrations like weddings, the faces in the church all hail from the same clan. Deep down, families still don't want their kids mixing with the other races, though there's no law against interracial relationships. Mrs. Levine wants her girls to marry nice Jewish boys. Mr. D'Angelo would beat his daughters with his yardstick if he found out they had dated any of Graham's brothers. And Graham's mom would frown and grumble if he brought Beth Robbins home.

Yes, it wouldn't be easy to be in love with Beth. No matter how strong his emotions are, it's been a long time since he's ever wondered what kind of life he could have with any woman. He knows it's probably crazy to imagine a life with anyone, especially with his life on the force, but he's insane to think of a life with a white woman who's still married.

He suddenly realizes the washing machine has stopped, and his mother's phone is ringing in the living room. He hears her drowsy voice answering, and then she says, "Wait a minute," and calls his name.

"I'm here, Momma," he answers, figuring she wants him to talk to one of his siblings, and he strolls into the living room.

She holds the phone to him, her eyes wide and alert. "It's Senator Kennedy," she whispers, as though saying it aloud will be disrespectful.

"Kennedy?"

She nods. He takes the phone, and she folds her hands on her lap like she's in church.

"This is Graham."

The undeniable Harvard accent purrs through the phone, and wasting no time, Jack Kennedy says that he needs some extra security at Caroline's christening. Would Graham be so kind as to give up a couple of weekend hours to help? "You'd be paid, of course...." Kennedy's last word comes out sounding like 'cawss.'

"I'd have to check the schedule at the station."

"By all means, Graham. I want Bostonians there, you understand. The christening's in New York. St. Patrick's. Archbishop Cushing's going to officiate. Lee, Jackie's sister, and my brother Bobby will be the godparents; we expect an upscale group of people. Real class. There've been some...well, to be perfectly honest, some threats lately, so I think my people should be around. Y'know, Bostonians. That's why I thought of you. You up for it?"

"Absolutely, sir. Just tell me when I need to be there."

They spend a few moments talking about hotel details and meeting places. As Graham jots the information on a paper pad, his mother hovers in the background, dancing in her chair, then fluttering nearby as if she can't wait for him to get off the phone to share the details. And when he does, her face is alight as though she's just been invited to the queen's ball.

When he leaves with his basket of still-warm laundry, he knows she will pick up the phone and call her friends and family. She can't wait to brag on her boy.

Get It Out of the Lot

"Kennedy wants both of us," Graham tells Frankie as they store their civilian clothes in their lockers at the station. "He's going to pay for our airfare to New York City. No uniforms, just private clothes. We're there for support more than anything else."

"Will he pay us?"

"Of course. Double our hourly rate."

Frankie slams his locker shut. "I'm in. Nothing like a couple of extra bucks at this time of the year, right?"

"Yeah, right, of course." Graham follows Frank down the hallway, thinking he's grateful not to have a couple of kids to pay for right now. He can barely pay his rent and occasionally gives his mother a couple of bucks.

They're almost out of the station when a voice calls them back. The captain's door is open, and he's on the phone when they stick their heads in.

"What's up, Cap?" Frankie asks, twirling his hat around with one finger. He's always all smiles when he talks to Captain Morrison, as though that will get him a raise.

"That blue truck. Get it out of the impound lot. I don't have any more room, and it's been there for a month. You can take it back to..." He pushes some papers around on his desk. "Elizabeth Robbins is listed as the owner. You know where she lives, right?"

Frankie shoots Graham a questioning look. "The guy hasn't been brought in yet, Cap. You sure you want to give the truck back?"

"The guy doesn't own it. Elizabeth Robbins does. We got what we need from it, right?" Captain reshuffles the papers. "Blood sample matches the victim. All personal items were removed and accounted for, right?"

Both Graham and Frank nod.

"Then get it out of my lot. Keys are in it. Make sure you collect the fees that are due. Hundred and seventy-three fifty. By the way, you two will cover for Donnelly and Darcey today. They got traffic duty for that doctor's funeral. See Jameson at the desk." The captain adjusts his glasses and tucks his double chin back into his chest, dismissing them.

"Got it, Cap. We'll take care of everything." Frank salutes, though it isn't necessary.

On the way down the hall, he turns to Graham and says, "Why don't you get the truck and return it? I'll meet you outside the Robbins apartment on Broadway in about half an hour. That's enough time, right?"

Graham nods, knowing that if he says anything right now, he'll give away how unreasonably excited he is to complete a task he'd rather hand off to anyone else. Any chance to see Beth Robbins is a good one.

Less than half an hour later, he pulls into the parking lot behind Beth's apartment building and shuts the truck off. The damn thing wouldn't start, so he got one of the mechanics to give the battery a jump, which took the better part of twenty minutes—and his hands were still frozen from waiting for the truck to warm up. He's not surprised the Robbins guy hasn't bothered to come out of hiding to get his vehicle. It isn't worth it.

Struggling to keep his balance on the icy pavement, Graham rounds the building and sees the patrol car already waiting in front of the building; Frankie is inside and probably nice and warm. The window rolls down, and Frank yells, "Where the hell have you been? I've been waiting forever."

"It's not forever. Don't exaggerate."

"Well, hurry up. We got work to do. There's a break-in at the Butterworth Flower Shop. Give the woman her keys, make her sign off, and let's get going."

"Yeah, yeah, alright." Graham enters the lobby, shaking the ice off his shoes and blowing into his cupped hands. He rings Beth's doorbell and waits for the buzz that releases the lock to let him into the hallway. Before he knocks on the door, it opens, and Beth stands there, smiling.

"Hello...I saw the patrol car, so I knew it was you." She's breathless and flushed, her bluebell eyes sparkling even more than usual, as if she's happy to see him. "Come in, come in." She opens the door wide, and then her eyes shift to the papers he holds.

"I can't stay but a moment," he says, regretting that Frank is outside because he wants far more than a moment with her, wants to invent a reason to stay for the afternoon, to sit beside her on the couch, perhaps share a cup of tea and some conversation, see her continue to smile at him the way she is right now.

"The station has released your truck from the impound lot; all you need to do is sign these papers. I've left it in your parking lot." He hands her the release and a pen, his fingers touching hers for the briefest of seconds.

"What? The truck? But I can't drive it. It's no good to me." Despite her protest, she takes the paper anyway, her smile now gone.

"It's yours. The title is in your name. Maybe you can sell it?"

"Sell it? If Jack ever found out…"

"He can't do anything since you own it. You can do with it what you want."

"I don't think…Graham, what if…"

"Let's talk about this," Graham steps forward and puts his hand on hers. "I can't now, but we can discuss this later. I can help you."

She nods, and he can tell she's unsure, but he can do nothing right now with Frankie waiting outside.

"I must go to work now, but I can call you later if your phone works."

"The truck. I don't need it. I don't know, Graham, I don't know."

"Later." He squeezes her hand. "I'll help you. But now, you should sign this, and I need to go. Think about this. Selling the truck would give you some cash. It's yours."

Her hand shakes as she signs the release form and hands it back to him, her lips pressed into a thin line, as though having the truck back is the last thing she wants. When she closes the door, he sighs deeply and wonders if there's anything else he can do to find Jack Robbins and jail him for what he's done. He wonders if there's anything he can do to make sure Jack Robbins never comes near Beth again.

It's Been A Month, Jack

Wednesday, December 10, 1957

There's a lacy ice rim around the kitchen window when I finish my morning tea, place the cup in the sink, and shrug into my woolen cardigan. If it's this cold inside, it's got to be positively frigid on the street.

Maybe one more day staying home wouldn't hurt. Theresa won't notice if I'm not there. Her family is with her. Besides, she knows what the weather has been like, and I don't have any other way to get to the hospital besides walking.

I dig into my pocketbook. Did I drop the keys there? No need for an excuse to go back to Loretta's place.

No excuses, Beth. This is it, sweetheart. The jig's up. Go.

Loretta and I have had some serious conversations over the past few days. Loretta's gotten her fill of television, and I've gotten my fill of Campbell's soup. We've kept each other company and reminded each other to eat and stay warm. There have been Scrabble games and late-night stories about friends and family. Loretta even brought out a couple of picture albums the other night, and I dug around in my mother's hope chest for the scrapbook Mama had kept of my early days in school. We know more about each other now than I do about some of the kids I grew up with in the old neighborhood. A lot more, as a matter of fact.

Then Loretta saw my drawings.

"What are these? Pretty. Oooh, look at this sunset. I saw a sunset like that once up in New Hampshire. My cousin Eddie had a place named after a guy in Randolph, Rudolph, or some town like that. The place was elegant. All in the woods and private, like a private estate. That side of the family was a little better off. I think Cousin Eddie's father was a Capone kind of guy."

She picked up the stack and flipped through some of them. They're from what I call my 'sunrise/sunset' period. I spent a couple of months going to the banks of the Mystic River day after day, morning and evening, when I first learned how to use watercolors. One of my art teachers once told me that artists go through a period when all they can create are beginnings and endings, sunrises, and sunsets. The paintings are not very good, and I know better than to embarrass myself by taking them to the gallery in Chelsea. But Loretta doesn't know art and is obviously in love with the amateurish drawings.

"I've always wanted to study art seriously," I said, taking Loretta's stack of paintings and placing them back in the hope chest.

"Looks to me like you're already an artist."

"No, not yet. Still just learning."

Now I stand at the doorway, mentally counting the change in the bottom of my handbag and wondering if there's enough there for another tablet of drawing paper. *What does it matter? After tonight, I will not be here, anyway.*

Perhaps it's fitting that it's bitterly cold outside. Maybe it's proper that I be punished as much as possible today. The weather beats against me, and soon, so will everyone in my life. The door squeals as if it's physically in pain when I open it. I almost apologize, then think, *I'm nuts, I'm really losing it. Who am I apologizing to? And for what? If Mr. Fits saw me now, he'd call the funny wagon. Yeah, go ahead, Beth Robbins, apologize to the damn door.*

"If only I could drive that damn truck, I wouldn't be romping around in 10-below weather like the idiot I am," I mumble as I push my way outside. Though the truck is in the parking lot, I won't drive it. I'll never get in it again. No matter what.

The brilliant winter sun forces me to shade my eyes. In weather like this, you need to keep moving. Even with the extra ponderous layer of wool undies and the heavy socks weighing heavy inside my boots, I feel my body temperature drop what feels like an instant 50 degrees. I'll be amazed if I make it to the hospital without losing the tip of my nose. Every noise—the snapping of the maple branches, the crunch of a truck as it comes to a halt at the end of Chestnut Street, the rattle of the frozen telephone wires— seems exaggerated, louder than usual, more dramatic. Almost unreal. A more persistent snap forces my attention skyward. I half expect to see a large branch hurtling down from the sky, but it's only a stalagmite of ice falling from the rooftop. When I was a kid, I would have retrieved the three-foot-long dagger and spent a couple of minutes sucking it as greedily as though it were a Popsicle. Out of the corner of my eye, the sun bounces off something metallic like a mirror. Instinctively, I turn and can't believe what I'm seeing. I blink.

"Jack!"

"Hi, Beth." He's standing beside the red Cadillac, a little startled as if he didn't expect to meet me on the street in front of our apartment, but he recovers his shock and saunters toward me as if it's 95 degrees and we're in Miami Beach. His navy-blue pea coat is half open, a lit cigarette cupped in his hand and a smart-ass grin on his face. The white sweater and sky-blue shirt underneath his jacket are new, and the shirt's newly ironed. A woman's touch. "How you doing'? You okay?"

"Of course not. Did you really expect I'd be all right?" The retort comes easily, sharply, surprising me. In the past, a remark like that would land me on the floor, looking up at him with a handprint on my cheek. Now, I gaze past him into the car, but he's alone.

If he has the car, he's still with that woman.

"Well, I didn't think you'd be doing a jig, but—"

"You haven't called. Where've you been?" My shoulders tense, and I hunch up around my ears. I'm shaking from head to foot. Every single inch of my body trembles. "I didn't know where you were."

"I told you I was going to lie low for a while. That was the only way we could do it, 'member? Everything's cooled off now, right? The cops aren't calling you anymore, right?"

"It's been a month, almost." A hot wave ripples through my chest. Seeing him standing here calmly reminds me that he's pulled the wool over my eyes. Before. I need to remember *he* was the one who made us flee the scene. *He* was drunk. *He* deserted me. The accident was his fault. It was his foot that pressed mine on the gas.

"Yeah, I figured that would be enough." Jack takes a drag on the cigarette, and he's close enough for me to notice his ring finger is bare.

Bastard.

He sees my glance and rubs his thumb along the palm pad where the ring would have rested. His eyes stare unblinkingly into mine. He is daring me! He smiles a little as though I'm a silly child, then takes another puff and blows it into the sky, but it rests above his head like a puffy, sallow cloud.

Who is this man? Who's he pretending to be? This isn't him. This isn't the drunk idiot who barely made it through dinner every night. This man is brighter, sharper, and more dangerous. I don't know him. I probably never have.

I pull my collar up around my throat. "It's freezing out here," I say. But I don't want to invite him into the apartment. Used to be his apartment. Ours. But it's mine now. My home. It feels extraordinary to be standing in the middle of the apartment house parking lot in front of the man I'm still married to. I want nothing more than to pick up my leaden feet and propel myself as far away as possible from Jack and that bloody red car, but I can't even open my mouth, let alone run.

"You don't happen to have the keys to the truck on you, do you? I should really start 'er up and let 'er run for a while. Where is she? Ol' Betsy needs to feel the oil in her valves a little. Juice her up." Jack snorts. His sarcastic laugh. The kind he always makes when he thinks he's been funny, but no one else sees the joke. "You probably haven't even turned her over while I've been gone, have you? You got her parked somewhere safe?"

"No. I'm not supposed to drive, Jack, remember? I don't have a license. Besides, the truck is still in the impound lot." *Not quite true.* I speak each word clearly and slowly, hoping he'll get the point, praying he'll take the hint. Scared yet defiant, I hold my ground. Suddenly, it's much warmer than a few moments ago. Even as I dig into my pocketbook for the truck keys, I feel my face redden with anger. I had switched them to another keychain, taking them off my house ring long ago.

One night, in the middle of a bad dream, I got out of bed and forced the heavy ignition key and door key off the circular metal holder that bears my initials, convinced that if I continued to carry them, they would symbolize my guilt. If I tossed the keys, it would have lightened the load in my purse and mind, but I still carry them—probably because I knew deep down that, eventually, I'd have to hand them back to Jack.

I reach the keys out to him now, but he doesn't take them. Instead, he extends his arms to me like some benevolent god, as though he expects me to walk into them, no questions asked. "Miss me, honey?"

You bastard! In a lightning streak of emotions, the same surge of fury that I felt the night I threw the bottle at the wall, that inexplicable loosening of all bonds of control, the spilling over of emotions that made me feel dangerous. I could kill him now, and I wouldn't regret it.

"No, Jack. I didn't miss you. And you know why? Because even though no one would tell me and even though you didn't call me, I knew you were with that blonde bimbo. You did the cruelest thing anyone could ever do, Jack. You left me trying to cover for you and myself. You left an accident where a child almost died, and you made me lie about the worst thing I ever did in my whole life. And you knew I'd suffer. You knew I'd be the most miserable I've ever been in my whole life, and I think you enjoyed the thought. You've probably been snickering with your little girlfriend about stupid ol' Bethie, haven't you? You'd do anything to get rid of me so you could be with her. Even if it meant going to jail."

I pause for a breath. "You've asked me to live half a life, Jack. I don't want to do that. No. No more."

"Ah, here we go again..." His voice rises and echoes off the building's walls. "Feel sorry for me, poor Beth always says. Right? Cut me some friggin' slack!" He comes toward me, his hands squeezing into fists. "C'mon, Bethie," his voice low, wheedling. "You forgive me, don't cha?"

Arms akimbo, I shrug off his advance and am rewarded by the baffled look on his face. I've never had the guts to stand up to Jack before. This is a side of me he doesn't know.

"She's just a friend, Bethie." Jack steps back and throws his hands up in the air. "Where the hell was I supposed to go after that night? To my sister's? She'd be calling you or the cops within the first five minutes. You know what a busybody she is. Or to one of the guys from work? They wouldn't be able to keep their goddamn mouths shut."

He's doing an excellent job of acting. His voice sounds convincing, but his eyes narrow, as if warning me not to question his motives. "Shit, I did this all for you, Beth, and this is the thanks I get? This is how you say 'thank you for saving my ass, Jack'?" He grabs my face and squeezes my cheeks together so hard I can taste blood on the inside of my mouth, then draws my head closer to his so all I can see are his bared teeth and his cruel eyes. "You're fortunate I love you enough to have done this for you," he hisses.

With all my strength, I pull away and slap his hand. "If this is love, Jack, I don't want any part of it." I stare right back at him, narrowing my own eyes. "If you're going to hit me, go ahead. Go ahead. You'll be surprised, Jack. You're going to get it. I'm going to make sure I hurt you as much as you hurt me." My legs are quaking as though I'm standing in the middle of an earthquake fault.

"Bethie, Bethie, Bethie...you're a sad, sad mental case. Here, I take the chance of a lifetime to cover for you, and you're standing here telling me I was wrong? I don't believe you."

"You'd better. That little girl almost died, Jack."

He arches his eyebrows. "I know that. Why do you think I stayed away, stupid?"

"You stayed away because you didn't want to be with me."

"Now that's not true. I told you that night that I'd—"

"That you'd be back and take care of me, but you didn't come back. You were out there having a good time with your new girlfriend—."

"Yeah, Beth. That's right." His lip curls and a lock of dark hair falls over his eye. He shoves it back. "She's a helluva lot cuter than you are. Less of a bitch, too. And she doesn't want to hide behind me like you always do. Jesus, what's wrong with you? Why can't you admit I did a good thing for you? Take responsibility for this one, Beth. Don't try to hide from this like you hide from everything else." He spits on the street as if I'm the most disgusting thing he's ever met.

In front of someone else, I'd feel guilty, less of a human being because of what I'd done and how I'd lied about it. But he's looking at me as if I don't already feel that way, as if I'm too dumb to realize what I've done. What we've done.

When I took our wedding vows, for better or worse, I believed husbands cared for their wives. No matter what. I guess that's why Jack always confused me. I never knew how he was going to react. He was always unpredictable, doing precisely the opposite of what Dad would do. (I do not know why I kept thinking Jack would be as upright and honest as my father, my only male role model, especially since Jack didn't have Dad's patience.) Nor was he kind. Instead, Jack could make me feel horrible if I had a great day, if the sun shone on my face, or if the drawing I'd done that afternoon gave me a little smidgeon of pleasure. He should have been supportive. He should have made me feel good. But, no, as soon as he slumped through the door every night, he'd find a way to stun me with an offhanded insult or he'd goad me into tears.

But not anymore.

"We hit her—the little girl. Cindy," I say. "I might have been behind the wheel, but you're just as guilty. If you hadn't gotten drunk, I wouldn't have had to go to that bar after you. And if you'd been able to drive, I wouldn't have been behind the wheel, but you wouldn't...stop...drinking." I shake my head back and forth. "You wouldn't listen to the bartender, and you wouldn't listen to me. You don't listen to anyone. Ever. Then you have the nerve to ride off right under my nose with that blonde...that blonde...bitch! And now I will pay for this for the rest of my life. They think you did it, Jack. There's no reason for me to say otherwise."

Jack steps back as if I've just slapped him.

There is a momentary pause, and he recovers and lunges into my face. "Are you absolutely nuts? No, don't answer that. I know the answer. You're fuckin' crazy! Don't take a genius to figure that out. You're a goddamn crackpot! You can't deal with the truth, so you'll lay it on me, right? You're going to lay all this shit in my lap. Well, let me tell you, little lady, there ain't no way you're getting away with this. You'd better straighten up right now or...."

"Or what, Jack? What're you going to do to me?" My voice storms over his like a banshee. "Are you going to make sure I get mine? Huh? What can you do to me that's worse than what I'm going through?"

There must be people in their apartment windows. Loretta can't see this side of the building, but others can. Others can hear us arguing. Judging us, whispering behind their hands. But this time, I don't care. I don't allow myself to imagine what people are saying. Don't sneak a sidelong glance to see who's watching. This time, I will not hide.

"I want this to stop, Jack. I'm going to tell them. Even if it means we go to jail, I must tell them." A clean, smooth sense of clarity creeps over me. It permeates me as wholly as a dye, coloring each thought and building a palette of brilliance that I have only seen in the work of Grand Masters. I note the coarseness of the skin on his cheek, the day's growth of beard etching his chin, and the jagged line between his eyebrows that I always traced lightly with my finger when he was asleep. And I can smell the beer. He's been drinking already, which doesn't surprise me.

Beyond the building, the groan of a bus going past the end of the street, the sound of someone talking in the distance. I long to blend into that sound, to be anywhere but where I stand now, yet there is no more running away. The realization that I'm an adult, facing adult fears, keeps me anchored where I stand and brings back a remembered emotion: the feeling when my father let go of the bicycle seat when he first taught me how to ride and how I flew down the street on the reconditioned two-wheeler that he'd rescued from the trash. How it felt to keep pedaling, keep moving, not to look back and to trust in myself, to be swept away by the feeling of independence, a feeling that was a mixture of fear and exhilaration. *I'll never be able to share this with you, Jack. You aren't a part of my life anymore. Perhaps you never were.*

And then Dad is there, behind me, urging me on, telling me not to stop, to keep going, and laughing, his faith in me complete and robust. *You can do anything, Beth. Look at you! You're riding a bike, sweetie. Keep pedaling! Don't stop, or you'll fall off! Go ahead, honey, you're fine. Keep it up, and you'll keep going. If you need to stop, press backward on the brake, swing your leg over, and jump off. It's nice and easy.* Daddy's voice melts back into the past, but the bike's momentum carries me into the present.

"Things haven't been right with us for a long time, Jack. Why don't we call it quits?" It's one of those moments when I feel outside of myself. Strong.

The irony of my comment strikes me at the same instant that Jack's eyes widen. He had already called it quits the night he left. His face registers a quick span of emotions, then the familiar rush of red up his neck, and his mouth hardens like granite. "You're the one who was driving the goddamn truck!" he screams in my face, his nose physically touching mine. "What the fuck is wrong with you?" His voice echoes, and there is no reason to answer the rhetorical question.

I don't back down from him. I stand still. Suddenly, I know I've pushed him too far, and I'm scared.

"I asked you a frigging question!" He yanks me close.

"I will not answer you, Jack, and you'd better take your hands off me." *I'm not blinking. I'm not moving. I'm not going to be afraid. Nothing he can do will hurt me.* "I have a question for you, Jack. Answer me this: What did I do to you that made you want to hurt me like this?"

"What the hell are you talking about? I covered for you. I went away so no one would find out what you did."

"You went away because you wanted to leave me. I wasn't drunk. You were. You just wanted to leave. You've wanted to for a long time. I know that. The accident was just a convenient excuse for you to go. Don't you think I know about all those nights you spent with that blonde woman? Where do you think I was while you were out with her? Do you think I was having a party or something? Do you remember me having any friends? No, I never did, Jack. You never wanted me to have friends, so I cut myself off from the rest of the world, and I stayed home and waited for you. Every night. And when you came home and threw up all over the couch, I was the one who cleaned it." I take a deep breath, remembering the twelve towels I'd had to use that night, washing them out in icy water in the kitchen sink, using up two bars of Ivory soap, trying to clean the stench out of them. The smell. The godawful smell from what he'd thrown up on me.

It's me pushing forward now and Jack stepping back. Shocked.

"Don't you think I know about the phone calls you've been getting since August?" My voice quivers despite myself. "Do you think I'm so stupid that I can't sense another woman on you? Can't smell her? You used me—and then you left me, knowing I wouldn't say anything to anyone else because I was so scared."

Why does this feel so good when I know nothing has ever been this bad for me? Why is my head clear for the first time since I was ten years old? How can it be that seeing him doesn't move me anymore?

"This couldn't have worked better for you than if you'd planned it. I think you were secretly happy when we hit Cindy. No matter how drunk you were."

"Oh, now you even know the kid's name, huh? Well, I'll tell you something, Bethie." His lip curls further upwards, and he points a dirty fingernail at me. "I've been keeping track of what's going on. I already know the kids are all right, and I know the cops backed off, too. And see? Here's where I'm doing you a favor. Here's where you're getting off easy. I know the police ain't lookin' for me anymore, so I come back to get the truck and help you out a little, give you a little money..."

His voice goes a little sing-songy, as it usually does when he's had enough and about to flip out. This is where I need to watch it. Duck, if necessary.

"But I don't know why I keep doing this 'cause you don't seem to fuckin' appreciate it!" He yells the last couple of words for emphasis.

A window shade in the apartment snaps upward like a shot. Both of us jump.

"This is YOUR FAULT," he screams now. The volume is all the way up. "You hit the kid, not me! I don't know where the hell you get off putting this all in my lap. You were driving the truck!"

"But it was your foot on top of mine on the pedal, Jack Robbins. I was the one trying to reach the brake. I wanted to stop. I didn't want to go over the speed limit through the Projects. You did! You pushed your foot on mine and that little girl...Cindy...I wanted to go back and see if she was okay. I wanted to take responsibility for the accident. I wanted to apologize to someone. But no. You wanted to leave. I never understood that until now. You don't have a bone of compassion in your whole body. How many times did I beg you that night, Jack? How long did I cry and plead with you to take me back there so I could find that family? You kept telling me how much trouble I'd get into, how the cops would arrest me and take me away, but I didn't care about that. No. No."

The hairs on the back of my neck are on end. My breathing is shallow. "You left me to handle this on my own. You. Bastard."

A window on the third floor opens. Jack's eyes flicker upward, then menacingly back at me. "You've got to shut up."

"But you got me," I continue. No fear now. "You scared me into believing that you'd leave me. They put me in jail, and I couldn't stand that. But I would have taken whatever punishment they wanted to give me. I would have done it...for you. Or at least that's what I thought."

I wipe the back of my hand against my mouth.

Jack folds his fists as if he's going to swat me.

I take a step to the side. "I'm not finished yet, Jack."

Jack's hand flies out and grazes my face. I'm good at ducking his punches. He doesn't connect because I've had a lot of practice.

I laugh and watch him glance up again at the open windows. "Why don't you take a picture, huh?" he yells at the woman on the third floor. The woman says something about calling the cops, but I have no fear of that now.

"You weren't as drunk as I thought you were that night, Jack. You saw your golden moment, and you took it. Have you planned your getaway, huh? It didn't dawn on me until now that you knew the instant I hit little Cindy that you had me right where you wanted me. You might've been drunk, but somehow, it registered that this was the way you could get out of the marriage. You left me holding the bag, thinking you'd get away scot-free, without a care. No bills. No responsibilities. You and that...that whore girlfriend of yours."

"All right. All right. That's enough," Jack is gritting his teeth now and circling me like a wolf circles a sheep.

I square my shoulders and meet his eyes. But he's puzzled. What has worked in the past—his clenched fists, the way he gets right up to my face, the harsh voice—does not work now for him.

"It's time for me to live like a human being again, Jack." My voice is surprisingly calm, yet forceful. Quiet. Strong. "It's time for me to be Beth again. I don't need to shut out the rest of the world like you wanted me to. I can have friends. I can do things. I can draw like I always wanted to."

My last comment gives him pause. Then he snickers as if I'm one of the sad cases, a person who gets sent to Danvers, to the crazy hospital. "Right. Everything is hunky-dory for you now, huh? You think so, huh? You're going to frigging jail, woman! The only friends you're going to have are baby killers and thieves. Just your style."

Don't look at me like that. I'm not crazy.

He's still laughing derisively. "Y'know, I thought you'd be happy to see me. But now I wonder why I even bothered. You've gotten really weird. Even more weird than before." Jack shifts to the other foot, and the red Caddy is in my line of sight again.

"I have changed. I've gotten smarter."

"No such luck."

The words sting. I duck my head, then realize this is what I've always done, never quite facing my problems. I force myself to look up, look into his eyes, and see myself reflected in his complicated glance. It's not an easy thing to do. It means facing my own darkest demons, realizing that he's right, that I'm the one who's guilty here, and that he's really done me a favor.

"Why did you come back?" I ask. "I was doing fine without you. I was going to take care of everything. I have friends now."

"Who? The crazy ladies down the hall? And I suppose you've been going to the ball like Cinderella, huh? Let's face it, Bethie, you need me."

"No, I don't. I just need me. The real me."

"The *real* you? What the hell does that mean? I swear you're getting nuttier and nuttier. Just like your mother."

Another slap across the face. *There you go again, Jack. Reaching down into my gut and pulling up that soft, heated mass of pain. Reaching down into the blood and heart of me and squeezing for all you're worth, making sure I see the worst parts of me. I hate you for that. God, I hate you.*

I reel from the slap and the burn it has left behind, but I refuse to touch my face to salve the skin. Instead, I face him squarely, as I have done several times during this conversation. No more. No more.

"My mother wasn't nutty. Leave my mother out of this!"

"Your mother slit her own goddamn wrists," Jack says, as if revealing a juicy piece of gossip designed to destroy me. "If that ain't nutty, I don't know what is."

"Stop it, Jack."

"No, why should I? I ain't done nothin' wrong. All I did was stick up for you."

"You have never stood up for me. You've punished me in more ways than I can count. You've beaten me, called me names, told me I was ugly, and never once made me feel like you appreciated me. You made me wipe up your slop, cook your food, swallow your insults, and keep me thinking I was lucky. The only reason you stayed with me was because...because...why did you stay, Jack?"

"Because I was supposed to!"

A couple more windows have opened. Heads poking from behind curtains. Jack grips my arm. He's cutting off the blood to my fingers. *Maybe someone will call the cops.*

"Fuck you! Fuck them!" He spins, still holding me, yanking me along with him, and gives the world the finger.

I'm horrified that our fight has suddenly become so public. "Let go of my arm." I try to pull away.

"Hey! Why don't you take a picture?" he yells at the windows, where people are now openly watching us. "Huh? Take a picture!"

When Jack's jacket opens, the heat from his body lifts and the potent smell of old beer rises from him. The odor turns my stomach.

In the distance, the whine of a siren comes closer.

He cocks his head at me, staggers. "If it weren't for me, you'd be in jail! You'd be rotting behind bars. I know how long they looked for me. They asked questions at the Naval Yard. They called all my friends and family, but no one knew where I was." He says this with a sly smile, as if pleased he hid himself so well as if this were a game.

"Not even you knew where I was, huh?" He squeezes my biceps hard. "I did you the biggest favor of your life, and this is the frigging thanks I get? You've never appreciated me. I worked for you for years and gave up going out with the guys. It is so convenient for you to forget how I paid the bills.

And now you're playing with crayons again? You're drawing again and thinking you're going to be an artist? Some Van Gogh or something? Where the hell do you think you are? Fantasy Land? You need to come back to Earth. God knows I've tried to make our marriage work, but you're never gonna grow up."

"Let go of my arm, Jack. You're hurting me. Is this why you came back? Huh? Do you need someone to beat up on? Does your new girlfriend fight back?"

"What's that got to do with anything?"

"That's why you stayed with me, isn't it? Because I always let you have your way. Because I never fought back when you decided you'd like to use me as a punching bag for a while."

"That's enough! Just listen to me, Missy. I'll tell you what people think about you. You're someone they pity. They look at you and say, 'Look at the ugly bitch with the blotch on her face.' Then they look at me and feel sorry because I married you. I don't need anyone feeling sorry for me. It's you. They need to feel sorry for you. "

"No!" The vehemence in my voice strengthens me and empowers me. "I don't need to listen to you anymore! It's over. I'm done with you. You need to leave me alone. Go back to your bimbo."

The slap is lightning quick and connects with my cheekbone so hard I can hear it crack. My head jerks to the side. I groan, and the heat of his hand on my skin reminds me that no matter how far away he's been during this past month, he continues to hurt me and continues to inflict pain.

But this time, I'm not taking it anymore.

Without thinking, I slap him back, and seeing the shock in his eyes is gratifying. I have no idea where that came from. "Don't ever hit me again, Jack! You'll never touch me again for as long as I live."

The siren is louder now. In the apartment building windows, there's a flash of a blue light. *It's the cavalry. They've come to take him away, just in time.* A door slams, and voices call out. *Graham. Frank. Loretta. Oh, God.*

"What in the hell is going on down here?" Loretta struts out the back door of the apartment building without a jacket. Not even a sweater. She holds a lit cigarette in her right hand, and the left points at Jack. "Get your hands off her, you bastard! What the hell do you think you're doing?" Her straight gray hair is sticking out around her ears. She stands with her legs spread apart, arms akimbo, taking up space like a grown-up.

"It's okay, Loretta. Jack was just leaving." I don't take my eyes off his face.

Slowly, he releases my arm. The siren gets closer. Blue lights fill the parking lot—two patrol cars. Someone has called the cops. I look at Loretta, who's watching Graham, Frank, and two other cops get out of the vehicles. Someone else made the call. Loretta's too surprised.

I turn around to check Jack's face, but he's gone.

He ran, and in a hurry, he dropped the Caddy keys on the ground to my right. Behind me, voices murmur. Yelling. Feet pounding into the distance. Frank yells, "You take that side of the building. I'll take the street."

They're chasing Jack.

I recognize Graham's deep, rumbling voice as he speaks to someone. Loretta is saying something about a 'ruckus down here' and wanting to 'investigate the situation.' No one notices when I bend down and scoop up the keys. They all think they've found their criminal. He ran off. They need to recoup and find him.

I move towards the red Caddy. Instinctively. No one notices. *No one ever notices me. Why should it be any different now?*

I'm in the car in a heartbeat and immediately inhale the smell of a woman's perfume before I twist the key in the ignition, press lightly on the gas, and push the clutch all the way in, the same way I've seen Jack do thousands of times. I'm halfway down the street, about to negotiate the passage between the two police cars, parked at a ninety-degree angle to one another when Graham's eyes meet mine. His mouth drops open. He races to the driver's side window.

"What are you doing, Beth? We're about to arrest your husband here. You can't be in this car. We need to talk to you." He has his hand on the window and sprints to keep up with me. He nervously glances at the ground passing beneath him. "Beth, you can't drive. You don't have a license. Don't force me to come after you. I don't want to have to..."

I don't slow down. I don't really know how. And I don't want to. I yell out the window as I leave the parking lot: "I have to go, Graham! I can't stay here right now. Believe me, you'll understand later. Please. Try to understand."

Full Circle

2:35 P.M.

Thankfully, there are no other cars on Chestnut Street, so I take the left out of the driveway and negotiate the hill's upward slope of the hill without problems. Gripping the wheel tightly and suppressing a hysterical giggle, I glance around the car's interior, amazed that I'm inside the blonde's car. What would the woman think if she knew Jack came to visit me in this car? And that I stole it?

I pinnacle the hill when I realize I will have to stop at the light on Ferry Street and that I don't know whether to brake and shift to keep the car from stalling. I slide across Cherry Street. *God, how the hell am I going to find out how to shift gears while passing the very spot where the accident occurred? Whatever possessed me to do this?*

How odd it is that I'm continuing the journey as I started it, but in Jack's girlfriend's car instead of that damn truck. I feel like I'm going back to the very beginning, to the argument with Jack, the feel of his foot pressing on mine, that godawful thud, and the sight of Cindy's body flying through the air and my heart pausing mid-beat and the sound of Jack's voice urging me to keep on going. I need to make everything right. To heal. I need to come full circle.

The Cadillac glides past Theresa's apartment in the projects. I quickly glance over my left shoulder and see the yellow curtains at her front windows. Holding my breath and praying that my heart stays within its chest cavity, I try to ignore the patch of kids playing near the big brick house on the corner of Cherry and Woodlawn Streets. I shift back into first gear. The Cadillac grinds and rumbles a little, begrudgingly gripping the road and rounding the corner.

How did I get here? Where the hell did this courage come from? Is it just stupidity? And precisely what the hell am I going to do now? What will I say to Theresa: 'Gee, I'm sorry I hit your kid, but she's okay now, so let's just be friends and forget all about it'?

For God's sake, no. Not that. But what?

My knee quivers from the tension of reaching for the gas and brake pedals. Jack set this seat way back for those long legs of his.

Where will he go now that he's really on the run? Will he keep living with that woman? Will the cops never find out who she is? He'll probably be happy, laughing about his crazy wife in prison, and I'll be...I'll be...

Flashes of the tentative, new-friendship moments with Angela and Loretta and Theresa and Graham fly through my mind: the sly grin Loretta gave me the first time I scored triple points in Scrabble, the first time Angela brought over a spicy-smelling cacciatore, the blue-flowered polished cotton tablecloth Loretta refused to remove from the kitchen table, the "girl secrets" with Theresa late at night in Cindy's hospital room after spending the day coloring with the kids, the night at the movies with Graham, his profile in the dark theater, the white of his eyes, the curl of his eyelashes, the shadow of down along his eyebrows.

In only a month, I finally discovered what it's like to have friends. I hadn't known this feeling in my twenty-five years. I might have told you a week ago that I would never have friends, but now...it's a first, and it doesn't seem fair that it's come about like this.

I'm at the hospital now, forced to find a parking space, then to—amazingly—try to maneuver this boat of a car into it. Bucking. Stalling. False starts. Finally, I decide that's enough and leave the Caddy at a forty-five-degree angle, its bumper brushing the cement guard. Somehow, it seems appropriate that I leave this car at the curb. Purposefully, I leave the keys in the ignition, and the car door unlocked before I walk away and don't look back.

In the hospital, I fly down the hallway like a ghost, heading for the room where Theresa spends all her days and most of her nights. Cindy's probably sleeping, the kids are probably still at school, and the nurses are probably taking temperatures, checking monitors, and smiling at Cindy, the miracle child.

I'm almost there. It's almost over.

I unbutton my coat as I pass the nurses' station, which is white-curtained and quiet. It is hot in here. I pull off my hat and gloves and hold them both in my hand as I stand, slightly out of breath, at the door to Cindy's room.

The room looks nothing like it did a month ago. The beeping machines are gone, brightly colored get-well cards decorate the walls, a large Kewpie doll stands in one corner, a pile of stuffed animals leans against the wall, and an extra coverlet lays neatly folded at the foot of the bed. Cindy no longer reclines, and the bed has a minuscule bump. Now, she sits up, smiles, and animatedly talks to Theresa head-to-head. Cindy's silver-blonde bangs are slightly askew, as if she's had them trimmed recently. I vaguely remember Theresa saying the kids' hair hadn't been cut in a while and that they were looking "shaggy." It's tough to tell if Theresa needs a haircut because she always wears rollers, a pink peony kerchief tied over them. It's not a look I admire, but how could you not love that beaming face? Theresa's enamored with her children. It would have killed her if Cindy had died.

Theresa glances up with a broad smile when she catches my eye. "Well, take a gander at you. Is it storming out there? You're all blown and flushed."

"Oh, well, I...I didn't walk. Something happened."

Rising from her perch on the bed's side rails, she comes closer. "What's up?" She peers directly into my eyes, lifts the back of her hand to my forehead, and tests the heat of my brow. "Are you feeling okay?"

"Yeah, I'm okay." I'm flustered. Uncomfortable. Queasy. "I have something to tell you."

"You look...hmmm...something's wrong."

"No—" *Stop, Theresa. Let me get two words in.*

"Sick to your stomach?"

Well, yes, a little. I nod.

With a snap of her fingers, Theresa snorts, throws her head back to the ceiling, and her arms out to the sides as if the world's mysteries have suddenly become transparently clear. "I know what you've got to tell me. When was the last time you had your...you know, your monthly?"

"My..."

"Period. Your friend. You know..."

The hitch in my throat cuts off my air. *What the hell? Is she right? Could I be?*

"You're pregnant, Beth. Can't you tell?" Theresa smiles. We've often talked about how much I want children. "Jesus, all I have to do is look at you. The swollen breasts, the puffiness around the eyes, the flush on your cheeks—"

"No, that's not possible..." But even as I protest, I know Theresa is right. It's been a month, but Jack and I were intimate before then. *Christ. Now what?*

"If there's one thing I know, it's what a woman's body does when it's pregnant." Theresa nods definitively and folds her arms across her chest. She's wearing a white man's shirt under a wool jumper. Her fur-lined boots are kicked off in the corner, and she pads around in a pair of holey, woolen, red knee socks.

Cindy sits in the middle of the hospital bed, covered with crayons and free-floating pages ripped from several coloring books. She blissfully does not pay any attention to me or her mother, fascinated by the purple crayon she holds in her hand. Her eyes close slightly, drowsily.

"So, how long has it been?"

"What do you mean?"

"What's wrong? You're not happy you're pregnant, are you?"

"I think I'll wait for a doctor to tell me whether I am." I shrug my coat off then think I can make a quicker exit if I keep it on.

"There's something else up, huh?" Theresa straightens out a pile of Golden Books on the right side of the bed.

"Yes, actually there is..."

"Don't tell me that having his child will be a mixed blessing for you. That's nothing surprising." Slapping another book onto the pile, she shoves the books against the wall with a thud.

"I don't even know whether you're right that I'm pregnant, so I haven't even thought about that. I've had some other stuff, uh, on my mind."

"Like what?"

"Like what I did to Cindy."

Theresa stops straightening the toys near the books. Sits back on her heels. "What do you mean, exactly?"

An invisible hand squeezes my windpipe succinctly, as if I flattened a straw between my fingers. "I was driving the truck. It wasn't Jack. It was me." The room goes a little hazy, but I hold on.

Theresa is worrying her bottom lip with her teeth.

"I had to go get him at the bar. He was drunk, always got like that. This time, he was too drunk to drive. One thing led to another, and then I was behind the truck's steering wheel. It was raining, and Jack screamed at me like a crazy man. I was scared stiff. It started raining hard when we were going through the Projects. The window wipers weren't keeping the windows clear. Jack yelled at me, pushing his feet against mine, telling me to go faster, and then Cindy was in front of the car..."

I can't breathe, but Theresa's staring at me. I have to continue. I've come this far, and I can't stop now.

"And I couldn't find the brake. It wasn't there. I repeatedly slammed my foot, but the brake wasn't there. I couldn't find it. Then Jack was yelling at me that I was a foolish woman. 'Damn it, Beth, he said. You have to go. Get out of here.' Then, the truck was flying, and we were out of the projects. We were on Ferry Street, and we couldn't slow down, and Jack was screaming, and I was crying, and I really didn't know how to stop, Theresa, and ever since then, I haven't been able to sleep, and I couldn't have lived this past month if you didn't let me come up here and see her..."

I hiccough and swallow as hard as I can.

"Theresa, you don't know how awful I feel. There are just so many excuses, and I have run plumb dry. I have to tell the truth. I need to take the punishment for what I've done. I have to...I need to tell you I'm sorry. I'll understand if you hate me. I'd hate me too if I were you. No matter what they do to me—jail or fines or pulling out my teeth one by one—nothing will ever be enough punishment for what I've done to you and your family and...to Cindy. I will never forgive myself for not telling you. And the cops. I should've kicked at Jack...I should've hit him...but I didn't know how...I didn't know how to drive or how to stop. Have the instincts, y'know? I just don't. I don't. Know what to do in circumstances like that. I didn't know what to do."

Silence.

I fumble in my bag for tissues. "I know how you must feel, as her mother and all."

"You can't possibly know." Theresa rises from the floor, fists at her side, her voice low. "You're not a mother yet. You can't possibly know what it felt like to hear your daughter was pronounced dead on arrival at this hospital. There's no way on God's green earth that you can imagine what it was like that first twenty-four hours when we did not know whether this kid right here would make it." Her slightly crooked top teeth grind against her square lower teeth.

"You're right." The salty pain of tears and my throat tightly closing makes it impossible to continue. I shake my head. *There's no chance that I can make this go away, Theresa. There's no other way for us to deal with this. It's got to be this way. It's got to be painful.*

"You almost killed her." In the small hospital room, the hiss in Theresa's voice is evil. Hateful.

"I expect you to hate me, Theresa. I know this is unforgivable." *Why didn't I bring any Kleenex?* I lift my blouse sleeve to my nose and wipe. I don't know what else to say. "I'm so sorry. Will you please find it...some way of forgiving me...in your hearts? Will you—"

A flat fingernail points to my face, less than an inch from my eyes. It's a clean nail, heartily pink. The hand is chapped and red—a working hand. "Don't ask me to forgive you," Theresa growls. "How DARE you ask me to forgive you? How can you do that? How can you be around me almost daily for the past month and act like nothing's wrong? Huh? How can you tell me you're sorry when you were the one I trusted? You were the one I felt bad for! And I thought you were my friend when you were here, playing with my kids, talking to me in the middle of the night, and listening to what the doctors said."

She takes a breath, and her cheeks flush. "How can one human being do that? Are you sick or something? Do you have any feelings? Was this all one big joke to you? Something you could watch on TV, like one of those damn soap operas you're so stuck on?"

"It was an accident, Theresa." That's a truth I have believed for a long time. It's always been an accident. Everything that happens is accidental. All those knee scrapings and burned fingers were accidents. The times when Mama forgot to come to pick me up from school were accidents. The suicide. Dad's death. Jack's leaving. Everything was accidental. Nothing was planned. That's life.

"Maybe that moment was an accident. The very minute you hit Cindy with the truck was an accident, but the rest of it, Beth..." Theresa's finger is trembling. "...the rest of it wasn't an accident at all. The rest of it was your choice." She jabs the finger to my chest as she says the last word.

I'm ready for this. I expected this anger. I need to continue. Roll over and play dead.

"Yes, and it's my choice to tell you the truth now," I say. "I had to tell you because I can't live with myself anymore."

"No wonder." Like someone chewing, Theresa works her lower jaw. Nothing more comes out of her mouth. She groans and turns her back on me.

It's easier now. Not having to look at Theresa's face allows me to continue. "I'll understand if you never forgive me, Theresa. Believe me, I will. But I want you to know something. I want you to know something I didn't realize until today until Jack came home and...."

"Jack came home?"

"Yes, and after the cops came...."

"What cops?"

"The same ones who questioned me after the accident..."

"The same ones? You mean they knew about Jack coming home?"

Stumped, I pause. *Did Graham know Jack was there? Or did he get a call from the neighbors?* "I don't know."

"If the cops were there, why didn't they arrest him?"

"They might have. I left—"

"What in the hell are you talking about? You're not making any sense."

I shake my head and wave my hand, trying to get her attention and explain. "Listen, what happened today doesn't make any difference. I was coming here to tell you the truth and apologize." I concentrate and try to find the right words. "I'm trying to say that I've learned far more about human beings in the last month than I ever knew in my entire life. I'm unsure why or how, but this accident changed me."

"You know, I don't give a rat's ass how you've changed! I care about this kid right here, and thanks to you, she's gone through hell...and she's not quite finished. A couple of days ago, the doctors and nurses gave Cindy a party because she'd gone to the bathroom alone. A small miracle. That she's still going through hell is painfully obvious. Look at her! She looks more like a toddler than a first-grader. And it's because of you, Beth!"

I know that. I lean my forehead against the cool glass of the door's window. *Where is the chair that used to be in this corner? I need some place to sit down. God, I want to puke. This coat is too damn heavy. This place is too damn hot.*

In the bed, Cindy sits up straight, attracted for the first time by the knot of adults near the doorway. "Mommy?"

A mother to the marrow of her bones, Theresa pauses, finger in midair. Her eyes shift to the right and back toward her daughter.

I seize the moment, summon my courage again, and step forward. "Theresa, listen to me. You've got to believe me when I say I've tried over and over to tell you or Graham or someone—anyone who'll listen. I've been dying with this. I've hated myself for every moment. Believe me. If Cindy...if she hadn't made it, I couldn't have lived with myself. I can't even look at myself in the mirror every day. I didn't know what to do."

Ashen, eyes on Cindy, Theresa sits sideways on the bed. She heaves a long, shaky sigh.

"In this past month, I've learned a lot of hard lessons," I continue. "I never thought I'd go through anything more painful than losing both parents, but the day I saw Cindy lying there in the middle of the street, I lost myself. There are a lot of things that a person can go through in life, Theresa.

There are a lot of things you can endure, and somehow you live on, but I can't live with the guilt of hitting Cindy. I want you to know that."

Please look at me. Please tell me that you hate me, that there is nothing else I can say, that you never want to see me again. Or tell me I'm forgiven. But don't sit there silently.

"You've taught me a lot, you and Bill. You've shown me it's possible to have a full and loving family. What you have is something pretty valuable. And even if you never speak to me again, I consider myself lucky to have been part of your family, even for a little while."

One of the Irish nurses comes to the door. "Is everything all right, Ma'am?"

Theresa's head shakes a little. She's crying, but she motions the nurse away. The prim-faced brunette gives me a dour look, but leaves with a whisper of starched cotton.

"Ever since I was sixteen, I've wanted a baby," I say. "You know that, Theresa. We've talked about it. I wanted a baby so bad that I married Jack to get pregnant. But that didn't happen. We tried and tried and tried, and then he started thinking he wasn't a man anymore. And I knew I wasn't good enough for him. Both of us felt like we weren't good enough, so Jack started drinking, and I acted less and less like a wife. He came home later and later, and when he was home, he wasn't conscious for long. I found myself in the schoolyard a lot. I saw your kids and the other kids who lived in the projects. I started daydreaming about having kids like that myself."

A little boy, maybe a little boy with a Roy Rogers cowboy hat. A little girl her daddy would call a princess. A house with three bedrooms, an oak tree in the backyard, a lilac bush that would bloom in May.

I place my hand on my flat belly. I'm still amazed to think it might have finally happened. "To think I'm pregnant now is somehow...I don't know the word...it's...it's..."

"Ironic," Theresa pronounces the word flatly.

"Ironic. Yes. It's like I've been blessed and damned," I whisper.

"What are you going to do now?" Theresa's voice is riddled with tears.

"Well, I have to tell the cops."

Theresa slides her arm around Cindy, quiet now and comfortable within the circle of her mother's body. "Yes, you do, and I can't forgive you for this, Beth. You lied to me. Pretended you were something you weren't."

"I know, Theresa. And God, I'm sorry. I'm so sorry." I've always thought I would start sobbing when I could finally release the confession, but there's nothing. Nothing. All my emotions are already spent. "I just didn't know what to do. I had no way of fixing what I'd done, and even though I kept trying to tell people, I didn't have the strength to make them listen. It seemed easier just to let Jack take the blame. I didn't know what else to do."

"Do you know now?" Theresa's voice is worn out. "Do you know what to do now? Will you know what to do for the rest of your life?"

I scrunch up the tissue in my pocket and bring it to my eyes. "Yes. I'm going to the cops. I'm going to let them know it was me. Not Jack. I'm going to confess."

"You won't forget?"

"How could I? I will have to live with this for the rest of my life. I'm going to tell this story to everyone I ever meet..."

"I won't say I'll ever forgive you," Theresa says, wiping at her cheek, "but I know it must have been an accident. I know you well enough to believe that...and right now, I want you out of my sight. Go have that baby and never come near me again. You hear? I never want to see you again. If it wasn't because you're pregnant, I'd want you in jail forever, but... go. Get out of here. Now."

My fingers spread, and I'm overrun by an urge to touch her hand, but Theresa turns away enough to let me know she's done.

I deserve this.

The hallway noises somehow come back into focus. I'm not even aware that I tuned out all the hospital sounds: the rustle of the nurses as they wheeled the medicine cart from room to room, the droning voice asking Doctor Stoller to pick up on line 53, the cry of another child down the hall. As I move out of the room, I smell the disinfectant in the air, feel the heat from a ceiling vent against my forehead, and swallow the pain in the depths of my throat. I can barely see the white walls and gray marble floor before me.

I wish I could draw this hallway. That water faucet. The sign on that door. The orderly behind the Army green desk. This corner has its nicks and cracks in the molding.

Then I'm at the doorway. It's snowing—enormous white flakes like Ivory Snow detergent. I pause.

I tilt my head back and open my mouth, letting the snow trickle down my throat.

Companionship and Occasional Conversation

Thursday, December 11, 1957

It's late in the afternoon. Time crawls during the dusk hours for Loretta, so she tries to fill it, and every day, she struggles with how to do that. She has a pot of beef stew on the stove, and though the smell of the simmering meat fills the apartment with a mouth-watering warmth, all she can think is that she'll be sitting at the kitchen table alone to eat it. She'll eat the stew for the next couple of nights, freeze the rest in one of her Pyrex bowls, and defrost it on some winter night when she needs a warm soup to thaw her old bones. Angela used to say that making beef stew was like cutting firewood: you warmed up cutting the beef into cubes and skinned the carrots, you warmed up again as the stew simmered for an hour on top of the stove, and you warmed up a third time when you ate a bowl. "And if you're lucky, it'll warm you again a month later when you take it out of the freezer to eat the leftovers."

Angela. Loretta never thought she'd miss her sister as much as she does. The apartment is far too empty without her bustling about, the useless gossip she'd share after a visit to the mailboxes downstairs, the stupid conversations about what kinds of potatoes tasted best, the memories they shared (though they never agreed on what happened).

Maybe she should take some stew to Beth. If the two of them shared more meals, it would be better than having a sister. She would still have the companionship and occasional conversation, but it wouldn't be constant, and if she wanted to go home and read the newspaper, she could. Besides, what Beth had to talk about was more interesting, and the best part was that Beth had a television set. Yes, she will take some stew to Beth.

She rustles through the silverware drawer, finds the soup ladle, and spoons the stew into a large bowl. Her mouth waters as she watches the carrots, potatoes, onions, turnips, and beef spill into the bowl. She tops the bowl with a dish and then looks for her keys. With keys and a bowl in hand, she's about to leave when she has a last-minute inspiration. She returns to the kitchen counter to cut some Italian bread into large chunks, wraps them in a clean dish towel, and then heads out again.

In the hallway, she can hear Beth's television. Lucy yells at Desi. Loretta knocks and smiles.

What's In Their Hearts

6 P.M.

"If you just sign it, we can pass it along to the captain and monitor the situation. I know you're nervous about the guy, but this is all we can do right now." Frankie pats Graham on the shoulder. He holds the report about Jack Robbins' visit to his wife and the eyewitness accounts of how he threatened her. They've already argued whether to include information about Beth taking off in the red Cadillac, mainly since the police found it abandoned, parked at the bottom of Reed Avenue near the hospital. Graham doesn't want it mentioned, and though Frankie doesn't care, he reminds Graham that leaving information off an official report can open a big can of "man-eating worms."

"Let me get some more info before we go off half-cocked on this one," Graham says to Frankie as they walk down the hallway. "I just don't trust this guy, and even though Mrs. Robbins shouldn't have taken the car, you and I both know she's terrified. Not thinking straight."

Frankie casts a sidelong glance at Graham. "If she's guilty, she's guilty, man. Don't go making excuses for her."

Something is wrong with this, but they have bigger fish to fry. Last night, a guy was shot by the graveyards near Revere, and the lieutenant assigned them to assist the detectives with some leg work. It's their chance to prove to the captain that they're not just beat patrol cops. Graham knows all Frankie can think about is the raise they'll get if they can manage a promotion, so he lets it go.

They drop the report off in the captain's office, then head for the locker room, change, and chat about nothing on their way out to their cars. It's cold and dark. They waste no time saying goodnight and getting into their respective vehicles.

Graham hunches down behind the wheel of the Buick, wondering how long it will take to heat up. He forgot his gloves this morning, and the bitter cold makes him pull his hands inside his sleeves until the car's heat comes on and the frost melts off the windshield. He turns on the wipers and sits for a few more moments. Frankie has already left the parking lot and is heading home to his family. It's ravioli tonight, he had told Graham before they left the precinct house. Graham doesn't know what he's going to eat. He's on his own at his apartment. Maybe he'll take out one of those frozen dinners. A beer would taste good, too.

On the way home, he purposely rides by Beth's apartment on Broadway and peers up at her windows. The lights are on. He imagines what she's doing, whether she's talking to someone, watching television, or eating dinner. He thinks about what it would be like to do that with her, eat supper across the table from her, what it would be like to crawl into bed next to her at the end of the night, to lie on the pillows whispering to each other, to share their days, smell her hair, feel her heartbeat against his chest. Then, he shoves the thoughts out of his mind as brutally as possible.

He can't think about that.

He can't.

Pressing the gas pedal, he leaves Beth's apartment in his rearview mirror and drives to his mother's house to pick up the mail she had called him about that morning. The Christmas lights adorned her front door every year since he was in fifth grade are lit and welcoming when he pulls up. He wonders whether his brother James helped her with them. She's getting too old to get up on the ladder by herself.

The house is warm and smells like fresh bread when he opens the door. The sounds of clanging silverware and his family's voices come from the kitchen. Those sounds instantly soothe him no matter what happens during his day. He smiles as he removes his jacket and hat and hangs them in the hallway closet. Nothing like home, especially when his loud and loving family is there for dinner. They remind him he's normal. Just a man. Not a pariah, not a cop in a uniform, not a Negro. Just a man.

His mother greets him at the kitchen door. "Thought I heard you come in, son. You're just in time for some pot roast and potatoes and carrots. Pull up a chair." She hugs him tight, smelling like onions and dish soap, then bustles about, rearranging her grown children at the table until everyone fits. Throughout the meal, she doesn't sit down, satisfied; instead, she refills bowls of vegetables and ensures everyone has enough gravy. When everyone is finished, she makes herself a plate and argues a little when her daughters insist on doing the dishes and cleaning the stove, but only a little. There aren't many times when the whole family is home except on holidays, and her ear-to-ear smile says volumes about how happy she is to feed them all in her cramped kitchen.

Graham and his younger brothers move to the parlor to watch the evening news. From the kitchen, the sound of giggles and snapping towels tells Graham the girls are having too much fun washing the dishes. Graham sinks into what used to be his father's armchair and wishes he had a cigarette for the first time in a while. Eyes drooping, he half-listens to the surrounding conversations, bits and pieces of teasing, his siblings sharing news of their day, their jobs. He drifts off.

When he awakes, the house is quiet, and he instantly jerks to an upright position, wondering what time it is. Next to him, his mother sits quietly in the other chair, her clacking knitting needles the only sound in the house. Someone has shut the television off.

"You okay, son?" she asks, leaning over to put a hand on his arm. "You groaned a little in your sleep, but I didn't want to disturb you."

"I'm fine, I'm fine. What time is it?"

"Around 8. Maybe a little later."

"I need to go home."

"Just set a minute. No rush."

He rubs his fists against his eyes, and images of Beth come into his mind for no reason. He wonders what she's doing and wants to see her. "I'm screwed up," he says aloud.

"S'cuse me?" Momma leans in again.

"I'm screwed up. Or maybe it's not me; maybe it's the rest of the world."

"Ain't that the truth," Momma snickers. "But why are you thinking about that now? You have one of your dreams or somethin'?"

"No. Just have something on my mind."

"What, son? You know you can always talk to your mother. I'm here for you. I always have been. Always will be."

He shrugs his shoulders and pulls away a little. Momma's not prejudiced, never has been, but she's like most of the old folk he knows. They have always been aware of how lucky they are to live in New England rather than down South, but they still act as though expressing their opinion or "getting out of place," as Momma calls it, would get them lynched. If she knew how he was feeling about a white woman, she might not understand.

"C'mon, Graham. Tell me what's on your mind."

"I don't know...I sometimes think about people and how cruel they can be. I wonder how people can hate people they don't even know. Why can't it be different? Color of their skin shouldn't be an issue. It should be what's in their hearts that matters."

Momma shifts in her chair and sighs deeply. This isn't the first time they've had this kind of conversation. He's talked about this since the first time someone teased him in grammar school, and he came home with a bloody lip. Even then, she was telling him how to be more even-keeled and how to deal with conflict without fighting, and he learned what she taught him. That's what kept him safe during the war, and that's been his greatest strength as a police officer.

"You're my most philosophical child," Momma says quietly. "And you know, that's what always gets you hurt. You must remember, son, that if you wear your heart on your sleeve, people will know where to stick their knives. Don't do that. Just keep smilin'. Keep them off balance."

He laughs. "You've said that a million times, but I still can't do it."

"Maybe by the time I get to a million and a thousand, you'll learn it."

"I just don't understand how people can tell you how to love and who to hate. It just makes little sense. It's not like that in Paris. People didn't look at me for the color of my skin there. They wanted to know who I was."

"I don't know about Paris. I know Boston. And here, well, it's different. But it's not as bad as other places. My cousins down south have it a lot worse. They told me how people were angry as a wet hen after President Eisenhower passed the Civil Rights Act and were scared to send their kids to school. Hoo-ee!" She throws her hands up in the air. "Your daddy and I did the best thing by staying put right here in Everett. It's not perfect—no Paris—but it's home, and we haven't had any big problems, knock on wood." She knocks on the arm of her chair.

He takes a deep breath. "What would you think if I fell in love with a white girl?"

Her sharp, dark eyes bore into him. "You trying to tell me something?"

"No. I'm just curious. How would you feel?"

She clicks her tongue against her teeth, a habit that has always warned her children that she's not happy with whatever they do. "It's not so much how I'd feel, son. It's what you and that girl must abide by in the world. You know as well as I do people don't like races mixing. If you're seriously falling for someone who's white, you'd best make sure your love is more vital than any hate you might come up against."

With a groan, she gets out of her chair and wipes her hands on the apron still wrapped around her waist. Reaching over, she cups his chin in her hand and bends down to kiss his cheek. "That's enough talk for tonight, son. Go home. And if you think you're fallin' for some white woman, think about it hard. Then, when you're done thinkin', think again. Love is powerful, Graham Jackson, but some people's hate is a bit stronger."

More Reds and Black and White

Friday, December 12

The art on Mr. Shingler's gallery walls has changed since I was last there. I study it carefully while he finishes his phone call, paying close attention to the lines of perspective on a painting of the Mystic River (and trying not to eavesdrop). The midnight blues and specks of silver in the outlines of the buildings and the artist's concentration on the arch of boat hulls the artist speaks to me. It's been a long time since I've been in Boston at night, but the painting brings me back to summer nights when I was a child, when Daddy would take me to see the boats coming into the harbor. We'd sit on the pier, speaking in whispers as if talking in regular voices would disturb the waves in the water and search the horizon for sails. Long moments of silence would go by, but it didn't matter because he was with me, and the world was safe. I get that sense now from this painting and know that's what I want to do for people who look at my art, though my paintings of the Mystic are nowhere near as good as this one. When art can evoke emotions, it's done its work. I touch the gilt frame, and it's like holding Dad's hand once again.

"He does nothing but scenes in Boston," Mr. Shingler startles me. He's behind me, his long fingers gesturing toward the painting. His nails are perfectly pink and more manicured than my own. "The tourists love his work. I've sold a lot of them to the hotels downtown, too. But I'm sure you're not here to buy, right, Mrs. Robbins? You've brought me more of your own work, no?"

Wordlessly, I give him the package of drawings and paintings I wrapped last night in a brown paper bag and tied with twine.

"I sold one of your portraits the other day," he tells me as he unwraps the package. "We got twenty-five dollars for it. I'm afraid I have done little else these past couple of weeks, but I have some of your work being framed, and as soon as it is done, I'll devote that corner over there to your work. Okay, little one?"

It's more than okay. It's a dream come true. But I don't say that. I just nod and smile as I wander the gallery, leaving him alone with what I've brought. The package contains more drawings than I've given him before, and they're all new: several portraits of Theresa's kids, more sketches of still lifes from my apartment, and others that I imagined, four watercolors of Mystic River scenes, and three of Crazy Connie dancing down Broadway. Those are my favorites, and this time, I actually kept one for myself and hung it with thumbtacks on my bedroom wall. I purposely used pastels when painting her: her Joseph's coat of many colors, her body moving the way a ballerina would. It's almost like artistic poetry. Someday, when I'm richer, I'll get it framed. I kept several others, too, but those sketches are ones I won't share with anyone. They're all sketches of Graham's hands. I've been drawing his hands from memory for the past couple of weeks, and I'm keeping them for two reasons. First, I know they might be hard to sell, and second, I get far too much pleasure from those drawings. I don't want to share them with anyone else.

I steal a glance at Mr. Shingler. He hasn't said a word since he opened the package, and part of me is terrified that he won't like any of the artwork I've brought him this time. My heart pounds. *It would be fair play if I didn't sell anything, but I need money if I have to hire a lawyer.*

"Amazing," he says finally. He slowly puts the drawings down on the table. Smoothing the last one along the edges, never taking his eyes off them.

"Amazing?"

"No training, yet your work keeps improving. You have the eye, Mrs. Robbins. You definitely have the eye." His voice is low and soft. "Look at how your art has changed. You're using bright pumpkins and scarlets; the lines are volatile, alive, and even the sketches are more vibrant." He flips through the pages, then stops at one as if he hadn't seen it before. "Oh, but no, this one, this isn't your style." He points to the sketch of Broadway I'd completed sitting in my window. "Nothing here. No movement. No color. No people. No, I can't take that one."

"I was practicing perspective," I say.

"Well, we all need practice, but the practice work needs to be filed away. Tossed, sometimes." He laughs, cocks his head, and taps his finger against his chin, thinking. "What you need is a formal class. Why don't you register for art school?" Finally, he looks at me, a wide smile stretching his thin lips.

I shake my head frantically. *No art school for me. Not now.*

"Listen, if I can gather enough of your work, I'll do a show for you. Then we'll find you a benefactor who'll help you out. Maybe put you through school."

Am I really hearing this?

He keeps talking excitedly, chattering about the future, my work, and all the things that can come of this.

I'm numb.

When he finally gives me my check for the painting he sold and ushers me out the door, my feet don't touch the ground all the way to the bus stop.

Fifty-five dollars! I can go to the bank tomorrow and put it in a new savings account—my own.

Dumping the Caddy

That night, Loretta comes over right before the evening news. She brings some lasagna, and I share the loaf of bread I'd bought on the way home from Chelsea. I tell her about the gallery, and she listens intently, then says. "We need to celebrate. I've got some Mogen David. Let me bring it over." then shuffles out before I can say anything and comes back moments later with a bottle of wine so dusty I could write my name on it. But it tastes good, and I'm happy about the celebration.

Like an old married couple, we watch television silently for a few hours. During the commercial, Loretta yawns and asks, "What happened with Theresa?"

I don't want to answer. The question kind of ruins the day. I pretend not to hear her when the program comes back on, but she's not having any of it.

"Hey." She reaches over and shakes my shoulder. "What happened with Theresa?"

I sigh and wonder why I ever bothered trusting Loretta. I have known from the start that she's persistently nosy. I know she won't ever let me slide by. She's going to push until she gets an answer. My stomach twists uncomfortably, and I shift my legs to give it some release. *Do I have to answer her?* I sneak a sidelong glance at her and have to giggle. Her eyebrows arch as high as they'll go, and she's looking down her nose at me with a sneer that says I will not get away without a story.

"Okay, okay, okay." In a rush of words, I tell her the story of going to the hospital in the blood-red Cadillac, blurting out the way I finally revealed to Theresa what really happened the day of the accident. Without a word about how horrible I felt throughout it all, I finish by telling Loretta how I dumped the Caddy on the way home from the hospital. But I don't tell her I'm pregnant. I'm sure now, but I can't tell anyone.

"You really think the cops—or Jack—will not find it? Good lord, a red Cadillac in the middle of the Chelsea junkyards? It's going to stick out like a sore thumb. They probably already found it, for God's sake. What were you thinking?"

"But I parked it between two abandoned buildings by the thread factory. Then I put some garbage cans in front of it. No one will notice if it snows in the next few days."

Loretta laughs cynically, the sound like a low-pitched dog bark. "Sometimes I wonder if you are as naïve as you seem or whether you just wish things were the way you want them to be." She twists around to face me squarely. "If it weren't for Graham, you'd probably be in the hoosegow right now, rather than sitting here watching television."

She's right. I slump back against the couch cushions, pulling my cardigan closer around me. *What if Jack finds the car before the cops do? Would Graham tell me if the cops already did? He doesn't have to.* I haven't wanted to entertain that thought, but I must. I must. I know now that I don't like the life I had before. I don't want him in this apartment. Don't want him touching me. Don't want my heart to beat out of my chest when I hear his steps in the hallway.

"You're right," I tell Loretta. "And I will pay for this for the rest of my life."

Now it's Loretta's turn to sigh. "It shouldn't be you paying for this. It should be Jack. That asshole."

I can't help but gasp. "If Angela were still around, you wouldn't be using foul language like this."

"If Angela were around, she wouldn't have any patience with what's going on. She would've told Jack off long ago. She might've been timid, but she was the first to speak up when she saw something that wasn't right. That woman wasn't afraid of nothin'." Loretta pushes back a wave of gray hair from her face, gathers it in a little makeshift bun at the back of her neck, then rubs her fist against her nose and sniffs. "I think about her a lot, what she'd do, what she'd say, and I know that when we argued, I was wrong most of the time." She sniffs again. "I miss her."

I reach over and pat her heavily veined hand, which she didn't use to wipe her nose. She doesn't respond, which doesn't surprise me. Loretta lets no one get under her skin.

"Y'know, if the cops found the car, they probably wouldn't even let you know. Jack might not have even reported it stolen," she continues as if we never talked about Angela.

"They know I took it. They were right there."

"But how would they know unless he tells them he doesn't have it back? They don't have the time to run after cars if they don't even know about them. Don't you think? They've got other things to do."

"Yeah, like making sure that people who hit little girls and take off are arrested…" The comment slips out of my mouth before I even think about it, and I cringe as I realize what I've said.

Loretta scrunches up her eyes. "Maybe because Theresa has told no one about your visit. Maybe she needs to make the complaint like Jack about the car."

She looks so sure of herself that I pause for a moment. "No. That can't be right. If that were true, the cops wouldn't have shown up at my house when it first happened."

"Oh, you're right. Well, whatever the case, unless something happens within the next couple of days, I think it's all on Jack."

"It might be on him, but he's never going to be bothered about it like I am. He lost nothing but a little sleep over worrying about his truck. Everything else has been on me. He doesn't even know what Cindy looks like."

"And he probably never will. He's not you, Beth. He doesn't have your sensibilities and never will. You can't expect him to understand something that you feel deep in your soul."

"Maybe no man ever will."

"I wouldn't say that. No, I definitely wouldn't say that."

White Gauze at St. Patrick's

Saturday, December 13, 1957

The weather in New York is unusually warm on December 13th. Every other detail officer on the street has told Graham that usually they'd be "freezing our asses off" doing a detail outside St. Patrick's in the middle of December. Instead, it's like springtime. He stands outside the enormous doors leading into the cathedral, wearing plain clothes and sunglasses, though there's no need for them. From where he stands, he can see Rockefeller Center, where everyone ice skates (though there's no one there today), and he wonders whether Beth Robbins knows how to ice skate. In his mind's eye, he sees her chestnut hair flying, a laugh coming from her lips, her arms spread wide as she tries to balance on one leg, wobbly on the ice skates but enjoying herself, smiling at him and gliding directly toward him as if he's the only other person on earth.

"What're ya smilin' at, boyo?" One of the uniformed cops, red-cheeked and watery-eyed, comes up next to him. He's got an Irish accent, as it seems half the New York police force does. Most of them also have a substantial prejudice against anyone with brown skin, like Graham's. Instinctively, he steps away a little and feels his shoulders stiffen.

"Just thinking. It's a nice day."

"Yeah, the Kennedys couldn't have planned it better. More money than God himself, they got. Can even buy the weather in December!" He laughs, smacks his hands together, and moves across the broad stairs.

Everyone knew Jack Kennedy was getting ready for a big move. *Time* magazine even hinted that he would run for president. Kennedy was a prominent voice in the Senate who wanted racial justice, so it made sense that he would put his money where his mouth was—and Graham was happy to be on the bandwagon. Jack Kennedy made him proud to be from

Massachusetts, and he knew Jack meant what he said whenever he backed a policy or an idea. He had a vision, Graham told his mother, and she agreed. When he had told her about the trip to New York, she giggled like a teenager and begged him to bring home photos of the Kennedys and their new baby girl. Nothing could convince her that he would be nowhere near the actual christening. He might not even see Jack at all.

"Just try," she insisted. "No one'll believe me if I tell them what my boy's doing, honey. You got to try."

Ultimately, it was easier to say he would than to explain where his duty post might be. She'd be disappointed when he came home, but he planned to buy some New York newspapers before he left. They'd run the story and photos, which might be enough for her friends. Maybe he could get someone to take a shot of him in front of the cathedral. Maybe that Irish cop that just spoke to him. Graham fingered the Brownie camera he had stuck in his pocket before he left his hotel room this morning. Maybe he'd even show Beth the photos. He hadn't told her where he was going before he left. He didn't even know how she felt about the Kennedys, whether she cared about politics, or even if she cared about whether he was in New York. But he wanted to know. If there was one thing he'd realized on the trip up here, he wanted to know a lot more about Beth, and he wasn't happy about being this far away from her.

One guy in his detail signals that Graham needs to move down a few steps and that the Kennedy family will come out the door any minute now. Two dark sedans pull up to the sidewalk, and a fan of officers surrounds the cars. A blue line of men rises up the stairs to the door. Graham and the other private security detail officers form a circle, ready to envelop Jack and his family as soon as they move through the giant oak doors of St. Patrick's. The family and friends who attended the christening file down the stairs, laughing and talking as they move into the winter sunlight. Several faces seem familiar, but he concentrates on listening for the Kennedy brogue. As soon as he hears Jack's laugh, he swivels toward the sound, catching the eye of the Irish cop, who instantly spreads both arms and allows the Kennedy detail to take over and form a personal barrier around the senator and his family.

Behind Graham, Jacqueline Kennedy softly thanks one of the priests and excuses herself as she bumps into his shoulder. Gazing back, he sees the white gauze of the baby's gown and a tiny white satin bootie. The group swoops down the stairs and into the waiting cars in one smooth movement. Less than a few moments later, the others leave him on the sidewalk as they gather in a tight knot, chatting and lighting up cigarettes. Everyone smiles as though they have just christened their own child.

"That Jackie, she's a real bonnie lass," the Irish cop says. "Don't see many like her these days, no, sir." He puffs his cigarette and holds the pack to Graham, who shakes his head. "You know them personally now, do ya?"

A little embarrassed, Graham nods. The cop nudges him on the arm. "Thought there was something special about you, boyo. We don't see too many cops like you on the beat. But with that Jack Kennedy, now. He's gonna change all that. Sure enough."

They smile at each other conspiratorially, and Graham feels comfortable enough to ask the burly cop to take his photo. When he gets it developed, it doesn't surprise him that you can barely see his face against the brilliance of the spirals of St. Patrick's in the background, but it's obvious he's smiling—a big, toothy grin.

In the Parking Lot

Monday, December 14, 1957

I'm in no mood to get out of bed and would rather snuggle into the pillows (I use both now that Jack's gone and feel very decadent doing so—*love that word: decadent. Jack would laugh if I used it, but now I can say whatever I want to*) and close my eyes against the sun already streaming through my window. Morning sickness comes in waves, and it's usually better if I arise slowly.

My dreams last night took me to a place where I was happy and things were good. I can't tell anyone this, but I was with Graham. *That's definitely a secret I'm going to keep to myself. No one would understand. Not even Loretta.* I don't remember the details, only the feeling. And it was a good one. Too good. I lean back against the pillows, savoring it for a moment longer. It makes every square inch of my body feel alive. Womanly. I run my hands down my sides, over my full breasts and my hipbones, and breathe in slowly with a slight smile. Yes, I feel good. I open my eyes reluctantly. It's morning. I need to get up.

The sunlight is sneaking through the Venetian blinds. I envision drawing the patterns of light crossing the arms of the ladies' chair in the room's corner, making stripes against the brocade flowers. It's a small scene, a story at that moment when the light patterns change, but it's the still life I have in this apartment, and one of the art books I looked at in the library a long time ago said that artists need to "mine those tiny moments and make them artistic."

With a groan, I swing my legs out of bed, reaching for the slippers since I know the floor will be cold. I shuffle to the living room, grab my sketch pad, and sprint back to the bed, cuddling under the covers, my blue chenille bathrobe over my shoulders, as I draw for the better part of an hour in my little world. When I'm done, there are three separate sketches: one of the light patterns on the chair, one of the rumpled bed with an imagined cat nestled into the folds of the blanket, and a third of a dark male figure standing in the shadows by the chair, the faintest of lights illuminating his shoulders. Mr. Shingler will like that one. That one's my best, I think, looking at the clock. 10:45.

I flip through the half dozen dresses in my closet, trying to find one that will be warm enough for the day and comfortable. It might be my imagination, but I think my waist is thickening. It's supposed to be cold, and I have some errands to do, so I choose the brown wool. I'll be ready to walk to the store with nylons underneath and a pair of warm socks under my boots. I lay them all on the chair and run the water in the tub.

I do my best thinking in the bath. There's something about the swirling hot water, the steam rising from it, the silence of the bathroom. Something that makes my brain kick into gear. Something in that steamy bathroom always makes me think things through. By the time I got out to towel off, I'd decided I'd worried enough about what Jack would do and had too many nights being afraid of what would happen. He has already forgotten about me and our marriage and is probably making plans to divorce me. I need to get ready for that possibility. I need to accept the fact that my marriage is over. Done.

Shrugging into my dress, I shiver a little, anticipating the icy winter wind that will slice through my skirt and up my legs, and I realize I could wear pants the way Loretta does. Those Katharine Hepburn wide-leg pants. They must be ten times warmer than a dress. But Jack never liked them. He was fond of my legs and demanded that I wear dresses. That's another change I can make. I can be warm now.

I feel my lips curl upward with the thought.

As I approach Loretta's apartment a few moments later, my heels clack like gunshots against the hall floor. I've gotten into the habit of asking whether she needs anything when I go to the store because she doesn't get out as much as I do. She won't admit it, but she's still grieving about Angela, and she sinks into it some days by simply sitting in her living room chair reading books from the library. I'm not sure she'd eat at all if we didn't eat together occasionally. I think she'd forget to feed herself, pure and simple.

Loretta's head, wrapped in a bright blue and red scarf Aunt Jemima-style, pokes out the doorway. She smiles when she sees it's me and beckons me in. Though it's lunchtime, she's still in her red plaid bathrobe. Under it, I can see the edges of a pair of blue men's pajamas. I wonder whether she bought them or whether they're her dead husband's. Whatever the case, it's weird that she's wearing men's clothes. But then again, Loretta's an original. Probably Kate Hepburn wears men's pajamas, too.

"I need a few things," Loretta says. "Made out a list last night, as a matter of fact." She rummages on the kitchen counter, then finds a torn envelope covered with her large, loopy handwriting. "Here. Can you read this?" She thrusts it into my hands.

I read it to her: "Bag of russet potatoes, a stick of lard, half a dozen eggs, five pounds of sugar...what's this?"

"Hmmm...can't tell. Lemme get my glasses." She shuffles into the living room. When she returns, her black-rimmed spectacles perch on her slightly hooked nose like a drunken crow.

"Lemme see. Okay, that's pistachios. Had a yen for them last night. Don't know whether McKinnon's will have them, but if they do, get me a quarter pound."

She shoves a ten-dollar bill in my hand as I leave, commenting off-handedly that she needs to get dressed by the time I return.

Out of the corner of my eye, I see Mr. Fits coming from the other end of the hall, so instead of taking the stairs to Broadway and the busy sidewalk, I duck down the back staircase to the parking lot to avoid him. It's not that I owe him any money. It's just that he's smoking that stinky cigar that always makes me sick. Besides, he's not a nice man.

My first thought as I step out the door is that it's not as cold as I thought, and that's a relief.

Then I hear a truck door and see movement beside the old blue Ford in the corner of the parking lot.

Jack.

He crosses the parking lot quickly and grabs my arm. "What the hell do you think you were doing taking the Caddy the other day, you stupid bitch? And now you're going to steal the truck, too?" He's wearing a pea coat and a knitted cap drawn low on his forehead, a Camel hangs from his lip. His eyes smoke with hatred for me. I realize in a heartbeat that he probably always looked that way.

His fingers dig into my forearm like a lobster claw. I can't pull away. He's too damn strong.

"You're hurting me, Jack. I'm sorry I took the Cadillac, but you'll get it back, right?" I'm looking around, trying to figure out if I yelled, would anyone hear me?

"Doesn't matter whether I get it back." He's breathing into my face, and I can smell the booze. Could he possibly be drinking first thing in the morning? It's not even lunchtime. "Point is you took somethin' didn't belong to you. Right?"

My throat tightens, and so do his fingers. The pain shoots up to my shoulder. I fight back the tears burning behind my eyelids and blink ferociously. "Jack, you're hurting me. Listen, let's talk, huh?"

"Why are those cops lookin' for me? Did you lie to them? Did you tell them I was driving the truck? I bet you did. Bet you never once admitted you were behind the wheel."

"I'm going to tell them, but the cops, they're not around right now. I have to wait for them—"

His hand smashes the side of my face before I can blink. The coppery taste of blood fills my mouth. I stumble. His iron claw digs further into my arm as he pulls me to stand in front of him, nose to nose.

"Should've left you a long time ago, you stupid bitch. You've been nothin' but a pain in my ass ever since I got home. All you do is whine and cry about me not bein' there, but you know why I'm not? Cause of you! Look at you." He pushes me away at arm's length. Scrutinizes my face with a scrunched-up lip as if I disgust him. "No makeup. No lipstick. No bother to be pretty. Shirley now knows how to look like a woman. She knows what to do for a man. You? You're nothin' but a meek little mouse too scared to speak half the time. You don't stick up for your man. You don't cook good.

You don't fuck like a wife's supposed to. You don't do nothin' but whine and cry!"

He's yelling now and not making any sense. I shush him as if it will make a difference, but he doesn't hear me. Keeps raving. I realize Shirley's the blonde woman, but I don't care what her name is. A few weeks ago, it would have mattered, but it doesn't now. In the split second of that thought, I realize how amazed I am by that.

I must be smiling a little because his eyes narrow, his fist clenches, and I know I'm going to get it. The hard part of his palm slams against my jawbone when that realization goes through my mind. A stomach-felt groan fills the air, and I know it's mine. The lights dim as the sound reverberates into the distance. I'm crying. Begging. Threatening if he does it again, I'm going to scream, yet I know I have no power against his strength.

I struggle to free myself, and I have no idea what I'm saying or doing, but I sense—somehow, I know—that there's someone behind me.

"You fucking bastard." A woman's voice. Hard and low. It's Loretta. "You goddamn, fucking bastard. Don't you have anything better to do than to beat up women?"

Jack's hand slips from my throat. There's an immediate sense of relief, like that pain you've had for weeks suddenly disappears—a piece of heaven. I float for a brief second.

"And who the fuck do you think you are?" Jack says to Loretta.

I want to look at the two of them and say something, but I can't move. I'm on the ground now. It's cold. I push my hand beneath me and struggle to get up. My fingers come away crusted with ice crystals and a mixture of sand and salt. All I can think of is that I need to wipe them off.

"I'm at least *human*," Loretta hisses at Jack. She's on one side of me. Jack's on the other. Facing off over my body.

Jack's growling laugh slices through the air. At any second, he can reach across and grab Loretta by the throat as he did me. I try to warn her, but I haven't got a voice. In the distance, I can hear sirens, and I realize we will have a full-blown circus here in less than a couple of minutes.

From the corner of my eye, there's a flash. I don't know what it is, but it's bright.

"Do you really think you'll get away with this?" Loretta's saying to Jack.

"Who's gonna stop me? You? You're nothing but an old bitch without any steam. You haven't been off the goddamn couch for years. What the hell are you gonna do to me? Go back in the house, old woman. Jesus Christ, you're just in the fuckin' way." He reaches over with one beefy hand and swats at her. Loretta ducks.

"I called the cops, you know." She maneuvers to the right, blocking my view of whatever's mirroring the light.

"Yeah, so I hear the sirens. So what? This is my wife. I ain't done nothin' wrong."

"You have a right to beat her?"

"She deserves it."

"No woman deserves to be treated the way you treat her."

I struggle to lift myself up and feel something hot and sticky between my legs. Jack's face distorts like he's reflected by one of those carnival mirrors..

"Jack, stop. Please. Stop."

He lifts his foot. I can see the stitching on the sole of his shoe. He brings it down across my cheek. It stings as though the bits of sand are miniature razor blades.

"Goddamnit, STOP!" Loretta yells.

Jack's hand grabs her arm. She yelps, twists, and then somehow comes straight up and launches her foot into his groin. He stumbles. I roll out of the way. He falls to one knee beside me, swearing all the time, punching me over and over, his fists hitting my stomach, my back, my cheek. Everywhere hurts. I can't move.

A blue light flashes through the parking lot, and I realize what's been mirroring the sunlight. It's the truck. Jack's truck.

There's a crunch as it strikes Jack in the back and pushes him to the ground. Pins him. Another crunch, a thud, and Jack's face is against the ice, right next to mine.

I stare into his eyes as they go lifeless. A heavy stream of hot liquid runs down my legs.

Behind me, I hear my name. It's Graham.

"It's over," Loretta says flatly from behind me. "It's over."

I know she's right. It's over. My world goes black.

One Woman Show

September 28, 1958

Mr. Shingler buzzes around the gallery like a cockatiel, and his tail feathers are on fire. "I think we're ready, I think we're ready, I think we're ready," he chirps.

I laugh, and as I do, I realize that every time I laugh, it amazes me. My heart feels open and warm, like it has never been alive. Just for the heck of it, I laugh again.

This is my day. My first solo art show. I can hardly believe it. All around me, on every wall, are works I've created in the past year. Some of them—the ones I worked on right after Jack died—are dark, but through the months, my style has changed, and I'm no longer producing gray paintings of forests and great horned owls but of misty sunrises over the Mystic and blurred portraits of children and women.

Last week, Mr. Shingler gave me my greatest compliment ever: "You don't need to go to art school, my dear," he said, patting my hand. "You just needed to unleash that raw talent hiding inside you."

Getting to this place has taken a lot, but it finally feels good. I no longer have nightmares of the accident, of Jack's lifeless body, of the sirens screaming as the ambulance took me to the hospital, of the moment I realized I had lost the only child I had ever carried. I had many conversations with Loretta, Graham, and Theresa during the first few months.

Yes, Theresa. She showed up at the hospital as soon as she heard and told me she had forgiven me, assured me she knew that what had happened to Cindy was just an accident and that I had suffered enough because of it. And she made a point of going to the cops to tell them not to press charges against me. That took some work on her and Graham's, but it worked. I was "pardoned," if that's the right word. It was a tough time, and I went into a deep depression, pushing everyone away, even Graham. I haven't seen him in about six months, but that's okay. Though I think of him daily, I know I wouldn't be where I am now without his help when I needed it the most.

There's a snapping sound, and Mr. Shingler motions to me as he moves to the gallery door. "Come, come, come. Your public awaits!" He opens the door with a flourish, and the first people drift in.

An hour later, I'm sure the bottom half of my face will fall off from smiling so much, but I can't stop. This is beyond my wildest dreams. At least half of my paintings sport sold stickers. Everyone I've ever known seems to have shown up, as well as all of Mr. Shingler's customers, and I'm feeling like I don't have to count on my tips from my part-time waitressing job anymore. I'll be able to pay my bills and put some in savings after today's sales. *Amazing. Do they realize this doesn't feel like work to me? How can I get paid for this?*

Theresa's across the room, sitting beside Loretta, who's earnestly discussing the doll she's carrying with Cindy. Mr. Shingler is taking yet another deposit on one of the paintings—a twilight scene of an old house, lit from the inside, large oaks in front—from someone I don't recognize. The crowd is thinning, the day is winding down, and I'm ready to kick off my heels, heat a TV dinner, and watch Ed Sullivan. Loretta will come over and watch with me. She still doesn't have a TV, and I've concluded that her coming to watch mine has become a habit. That's okay. I enjoy her.

I'm shaking Dr. Stoller and his wife's hands when I catch the unmistakable blue of a police officer's uniform moving through the room. *Graham. He came, after all.* I thank the Stollers for coming, hoping I'm not being rude, and usher them toward the door, but I'd much rather talk to Graham.

He saunters toward me, hat in hand, his dark eyes shining. "Boy, this is some show! These are all yours, huh?"

I nod, feeling a bit like a schoolgirl, and I know I'm blushing.

"Wow. These are great. I'm impressed." Though he's talking about my paintings, he's looking straight into my eyes. "You look really...wow. Your eyes—do you know they're as blue as the sky? That always amazes me—but they're sparkling. You look...I don't know how to put it. Happy, I guess. Great."

He does, too, but how can you say that to a guy?

I reach for his arm and squeeze his bicep. "Thanks, Officer." I laugh, and so does he.

We stroll around the gallery like old friends, arm in arm. I tell him the story of each painting, and he seems sincerely interested. I realize I'm talking quickly and excitedly, but it doesn't matter. It feels good. I have missed him.

When all the paintings are sporting sale tags, and there's no one left in the gallery but Mr. Shingler and Loretta, they both glance at me and nod, as if permitting me to do whatever I wish. Graham catches the unspoken signal and leans toward me.

"I'm taking a new job," he says quietly. "I'm leaving the force."

"Oh?"

"Senator Kennedy offered me a job with his security detail." He ducks his head, as if embarrassed at how proud he is.

"Wow. That's great, Graham."

"Yes, he just called today. I know it's weird, but you were the first person I wanted to tell. Maybe we can celebrate together? Go out to dinner?"

"I'd like that. I'd really like that."

As we leave, I turn and wave at Loretta and Mr. Shingler. They both send bright smiles in my direction. I glance at Graham, who's already looking at me, and feel his hand slip behind my back. It's comforting. I lift my face and smile at him. His eyes hold a question that he doesn't have to voice. Then he's closing his eyes, and I'm closing mine, and the kiss is just as warm and soft as I thought it would be. And my heart jumps. His hand is firm against my back, his smile is broad, and he says softly, "Beth Robbins, I've been waiting a long time to do that."

"You know, Graham Jackson, I have, too, and I think we don't have to wait anymore."

Graham threads his fingers through mine and raises them between us. He kisses my knuckles, and with his mouth still against my hand whispers, "Are you ready to take this on?" He touches his chin to our interwoven fingers.

Burnt Sienna and Titanium White. Mix them together. Endless combinations.

Over Graham's shoulder, the sunset has deepened to a dark purple, and the lights on the bridge reflect on the Mystic River below. So many colors. This world changes with every millisecond. New colors invented every single day.

"I'm ready."

-end-

About the Author

A prolific writer and author, Dawn Reno Langley has earned both an MFA and a Ph.D. Along with writing, Dawn is certified to teach yoga and loves offering yoga and writing workshops. She enjoys traveling, experiencing everything from washing and feeding elephants in Thailand to having a candle-lit dinner in a Tuscany vineyard. She owns a white VW Beetle, named Janis, one of the last ones made, and collects bumper stickers from bookstores when on book tours. Izzy, her emotional support animal, is a 13-year-old black and white Schichon who resides with her in North Carolina.

MAXY AWARDS
FINALIST
ANALYZING
THE PRESCOTTS
DAWN RENO LANGLEY

Note from Dawn Reno Langley

Word-of-mouth is crucial for any author to succeed. If you enjoyed *The Mystic*, please leave a review online—anywhere you are able. Even if it's just a sentence or two. It would make all the difference and would be very much appreciated.

Thanks!
Dawn Reno Langley

We hope you enjoyed reading this title from:

www.blackrosewriting.com

Subscribe to our mailing list – *The Rosevine* – and receive **FREE** books, daily deals, and stay current with news about upcoming releases and our hottest authors.
Scan the QR code below to sign up.

Already a subscriber? Please accept a sincere thank you for being a fan of Black Rose Writing authors.

View other Black Rose Writing titles at www.blackrosewriting.com/books and use promo code **PRINT** to receive a **20% discount** when purchasing.